The Firing Line

by

Robert W. Chambers

Double 9
BOOKS

The Firing Line
by Robert W. Chambers

Copyright © 2024

All Rights reserved.

ISBN: 978-93-61424-75-5

Published by

DOUBLE 9 BOOKS
2/13-B, Ansari Road
Daryaganj, New Delhi – 110002
info@double9books.com
www.double9books.com
Tel. 011-40042856

This book is under public domain

ABOUT THE AUTHOR

Robert William Chambers was an American artist and writer who was born May 26, 1865, and died December 16, 1933. He is best known for his 1895 collection of short stories called The King in Yellow. Born in Brooklyn, New York, Chambers was the son of William P. Chambers (1827–1911), a business and bankruptcy lawyer, and Caroline Smith Boughton. When his mom was twelve, William P. was an intern with her famous business lawyer father, Joseph Boughton. This is how his parents met. In the end, they joined forces to start the law firm of Chambers and Boughton. It did well even after Joseph's death in 1861. The great-grandfather of Robert Chambers was a sailor in the British Royal Navy named William Chambers. He married Amelia Saunders (1765–1822), who was the great-granddaughter of Tobias Saunders of Westerly, Rhode Island. First, they moved from Westerly to Greenfield, Massachusetts. Then they moved to Galway, New York, where they had their son, also named William Chambers (1798–1874). The second William finished from Union College when he was 18. He then went to a college in Boston to study medicine. While he was still in school, he married Eliza P. Allen (1793–1880), who was a direct daughter of Roger Williams, who founded Providence, Rhode Island. They were some of the first people to live in Broadalbin, New York. Walt Boughton Chambers was his brother and a builder.

CONTENTS

CHAPTER I
A SKIRMISH

As the wind veered and grew cooler a ribbon of haze appeared above the Gulf-stream.

Young Hamil, resting on his oars, gazed absently into the creeping mist. Under it the ocean sparkled with subdued brilliancy; through it, shoreward, green palms and palmettos turned silvery; and, as the fog spread, the sea-pier, the vast white hotel, bathing-house, cottage, pavilion, faded to phantoms tinted with rose and pearl.

Leaning there on his oars, he could still make out the distant sands flecked with the colours of sunshades and bathing-skirts; the breeze dried his hair and limbs, but his swimming-shirt and trunks still dripped salt water.

Inshore a dory of the beach guard drifted along the outer line of breakers beyond which the more adventurous bathers were diving from an anchored raft. Still farther out moving dots indicated the progress of hardier swimmers; one in particular, a girl capped with a brilliant red kerchief, seemed to be already nearer to Hamil than to the shore.

It was all very new and interesting to him—the shore with its spectral palms and giant caravansary, the misty, opalescent sea where a white steam-yacht lay anchored north of him—the *Ariani*—from which he had come, and on board of which the others were still doubtless asleep—Portlaw, Malcourt, and Wayward. And at thought of the others he yawned and moistened his lips, still feverish from last night's unwisdom; and leaning forward on his oars, sat brooding, cradled by the flowing motion of the sea.

The wind was still drawing into the north; he felt it, never strong, but always a little cooler, in his hair and on his wet swimming-shirt. The flat cloud along the Gulf-stream spread thickly coastward, and after a little while the ghosts of things terrestrial disappeared.

All around him, now, blankness—save for the gray silhouette of the *Ariani*. A colourless canopy surrounded him, centred by a tiny pool of ocean. Overhead through the vanishing blue, hundreds of wild duck were stringing out to sea; under his tent of fog the tarnished silver of the water formed a floor smoothly unquiet.

Sounds from the land, hitherto unheard, now came strangely distinct; the cries of bathers, laughter, the muffled shock of the surf, doubled and redoubled along the sands; the barking of a dog at the water's edge. Clear and near sounded the ship's bell on the *Ariani*; a moment's rattle of block and tackle, a dull call, answered; and silence. Through which, without a sound, swept a great bird with scarce a beat of its spread wings; and behind it, another, and, at exact intervals another and another in impressive processional, sailing majestically through the fog; white pelicans winging inland to the lagoons.

A few minutes later the wind, which had become fitful, suddenly grew warm. All around him now the mist was dissolving into a thin golden rain; the land-breeze freshened, blowing through distant jasmine thickets and orange groves, and a soft fragrance stole out over the sea.

As the sun broke through in misty splendour, the young man, brooding on his oars, closed his eyes; and at the same instant his boat careened violently, almost capsizing as a slender wet shape clambered aboard and dropped into the bows. As the boat heeled under the shock Hamil had instinctively flung his whole weight against the starboard gunwale. Now he recovered his oars and his balance at the same time, and, as he swung half around, his unceremonious visitor struggled to sit upright, still fighting for breath.

"I beg your pardon," she managed to say; "may I rest here? I am—" She stopped short; a flash of sudden recognition came into her eyes—flickered, and faded. It was evident to him that, for a moment, she thought she had met him before.

"Of course you may stay here," he said, inclined to laugh.

She settled down, stretching slightly backward as though to give her lungs fuller play. In a little while her breathing grew more regular; her eyes closed for a moment, then opened thoughtfully, skyward.

Hamil's curious and half-amused gaze rested on her as he resumed the oars. But when he turned his back and headed the boat shoreward a quick protest checked him, and oars at rest, he turned again, looking inquiringly at her over his shoulder.

"I am only rowing you back to the beach," he said.

"Don't row me in; I am perfectly able to swim back."

"No doubt," he returned drily, "but haven't you played tag with Death sufficiently for one day?"

"Death?" She dismissed the grotesque suggestion with a shrug, then straightened up, breathing freely and deeply. "It is an easy swim," she remarked, occupied with her wet hair under the knotted scarlet; "the fog confused me; that was all."

"And how long could you have kept afloat if the fog had not lifted?" he inquired with gentle sarcasm. To which, adroitly adjusting hair and kerchief, she made no answer. So he added: "There is supposed to be a difference between mature courage and the fool-hardiness of the unfledged—"

"What?"

The quick close-clipped question cutting his own words silenced him. And, as he made no reply, she continued to twist the red kerchief around her hair, and to knot it securely, her doubtful glance returning once or twice to his amused face.

When all had been made fast and secure she rested one arm on the gunwale and dropped the other across her knees, relaxing in every muscle a moment before departure. And, somehow, to Hamil, the unconscious grace of the attitude suggested the "Resting Hermes"—that sculptured concentration of suspended motion.

"You had better not go just yet," he said, pointing seaward.

She also had been watching the same thing that he was now looking at, a thin haze which again became apparent over the Gulf-stream.

"Do you think it will thicken?" she asked.

"I don't know; you had a close call last time—"

"There was no danger."

"I think there was danger enough; you were apparently headed straight out to sea—"

"I heard a ship's bell and swam toward it, and when the fog lifted I found you."

"Why didn't you swim toward the shore? You could hear the surf—and a dog barking."

"I"—she turned pink with annoyance—"I suppose I was a trifle tired— if you insist. I realised that I had lost my bearings; that was all. Then I heard a ship's bell.... Then the mist lifted and I saw you—but I've explained all that before. *Look* at that exasperating fog!"

Vexation silenced her; she sat restless for a few seconds, then:

"What do you think I had better do?"

"I think you had better try to endure me for a few minutes longer. I'm safer than the fog."

But his amusement left her unresponsive, plainly occupied with her own ideas.

Again the tent of vapour stretched its magic folds above the boat and around it; again the shoreward shapes faded to phantoms and disappeared.

He spoke again once or twice, but her brief replies did not encourage him. At first, he concluded that her inattention and indifference must be due to self-consciousness; then, slightly annoyed, he decided they were not. And, very gradually, he began to realise that the unconventional, always so attractive to the casual young man, did not interest her at all, even enough to be aware of it or of him.

This cool unconsciousness of self, of him, of a situation which to any wholesome masculine mind contained the germs of humour, romance, and all sorts of amusing possibilities, began to be a little irksome to him. And still her aloofness amused him, too.

"Do you know of any decorous reason why we should not talk to each other occasionally during this fog?" he asked.

She turned her head, considered him inattentively, then turned it away again.

"No," she said indifferently; "what did you desire to say?"

Resting on his oars, the unrequited smile still forlornly edging his lips, he looked at his visitor, who was staring into the fog, lost in her own reflections; and never a glimmer in her eyes, never a quiver of lid or lash betrayed any consciousness of his gaze or even of his presence. And he continued to inspect her with increasing annoyance.

The smooth skin, the vivid lips slightly upcurled, the straight delicate nose, the cheeks so smoothly rounded where the dark thick lashes swept their bloom as she looked downward at the water—all this was abstractly beautiful; very lovely, too, the full column of the neck, and the rounded arms guiltless of sunburn or tan.

So unusually white were both neck and arms that Hamil ventured to speak of it, politely, asking her if this was not her first swim that season.

Voice and question roused her from abstraction; she turned toward him, then glanced down at her unstained skin.

"My first swim?" she repeated; "oh, you mean my arms? No, I never burn; they change very little." Straightening up she sat looking across the boat at him without visible interest at first, then doubtfully, as though in an effort to say something polite.

"I am really very grateful to you for letting me sit here. Please don't feel obliged to amuse me during this annoying fog."

"Thank you; you *are* rather difficult to talk to. But I don't mind trying at judicious intervals," he said, laughing.

She considered him askance. "If you wish to row in, do so. I did not mean to keep you here at sea—"

"Oh, I belong out here; I'm from the *Ariani* yonder; you heard her bell in the fog. We came from Nassau last night.... Have you ever been to Nassau?"

The girl nodded listlessly and glanced at the white yacht, now becoming visible through the thinning mist. Somewhere above in the viewless void an aura grew and spread into a blinding glory; and all around, once more, the fog turned into floating golden vapour shot with rain.

The girl placed both hands on the gunwales as though preparing to rise.

"Not yet!" said Hamil sharply.

"I beg your pardon?"—looking up surprised, still poised lightly on both palms as though checked at the instant of rising into swift aërial flight—so light, so buoyant she appeared.

"Don't go overboard," he repeated.

"Why not?"

"Because I'm going to row you in."

"I wish to swim; I prefer it."

"I am only going to take you to the float—"

"But I don't care to have you. I am perfectly able to swim in—"

"I know you are," he said, swinging clear around in his seat to face her, "but I put it in the form of a request; will you be kind enough to let me row you part way to the float? This fog is not ended."

She opened her lips to protest; indeed, for a moment it looked as if she were going overboard without further argument; then perhaps some belated idea of civility due him for the hospitality of his boat restrained her.

"You understand, of course, that I am quite able to swim in," she said.

"Yes; may I now row you part way? The fog is closing in again."

She yielded with a pretty indifference, none the less charming because there was no flattery in it for him. He now sat facing her, pushing his oars through the water; and she stole a curious glance at his features—slightly sullen for the moment—noticing his well-set, well-shaped head and good shoulders.

That fugitive glance confirmed the impression of recognition in her mind. He was what she had expected in breeding and physique—the type usually to be met with where the world can afford to take its leisure.

As he was not looking at her she ventured to continue her inspection, leaning back, and dropping her bare arm alongside, to trail her fingers through the sunlit water.

"Have we not rowed far enough?" she asked presently. "This fog is apparently going to last forever."

"Like your silence," he said gaily.

Raising her eyes in displeasure she met his own frankly amused.

"Shall I tell you," he asked, "exactly why I insisted on rowing you in? I'm afraid"—he glanced at her with the quick smile breaking again on his lips—"I'm afraid you don't care whether I tell you or not. Do you?"

"If you ask me—I really don't," she said. "And, by the way, do you know that if you turned around properly and faced the stern you could make better progress with your oars?"

"By 'better' do you mean *quicker* progress?" he asked, so naïvely that she concluded he was a trifle stupid. The best-looking ones were usually stupid.

"Yes, of course," she said, impatient. "It's all very well to push a punt across a mill-pond that way, but it's not treating the Atlantic with very much respect."

"*You* were not particularly respectful toward the Atlantic Ocean when you started to swim across it."

But again the echo of amusement in his voice found no response in her unsmiling silence.

He thought to himself: "Is she a prude, or merely stupid! The pity of it!—with her eyes of a thinking goddess!—and no ideas behind them! What she understands is the commonplace. Let us offer her the obvious."

And, aloud, fatuously: "This is a rarely beautiful scene—"

"What?" crisply.

And feeling mildly wicked he continued:

—"Soft skies, a sea of Ionian azure; one might almost expect to see a triareme heading up yonder out of the south, festooned with the golden fleece. This is just the sort of a scene for a triareme; don't you think so?"

Her reply was the slightest possible nod.

He looked at her meanly amused:

"It's really very classical," he said, "like the voyage of Ulysses; I, Ulysses, you the water nymph Calypso, drifting in that golden ship of Romance—"

"Calypso was a *land* nymph," she observed, absently, "if accuracy interests you as much as your monologue."

Checked and surprised, he began to laugh at his own discomfiture; and she, elbow on the gunwale, small hand cupping her chin, watched him with an expressionless directness that very soon extinguished his amusement and left him awkward in the silence.

"I've tried my very best to be civil and agreeable," he said after a moment. "Is it really such an effort for you to talk to a man?"

"Not if I am interested," she said quietly.

He felt that his ears were growing red; she noticed it, too, and added: "I do not mean to be *too* rude; and I am quite sure you do not either."

"Of course not," he said; "only I couldn't help seeing the humour of romance in our ocean encounter. I think anybody would—except you—"

"What?"

The crisp, quick question which, with her, usually seemed like an exclamation, always startled him into temporary silence; then he began more carefully:

"There was one chance in a million of your finding my boat in the fog. If you hadn't found it—" He shook his head. "And so I wish you might recognise in our encounter something amusing, humourous"—he looked cautiously at her—"even mildly romantic—ah—enough to—to—"

"To what?"

"Why—to say—to do something characteristically—ah—"

"What?"

"—Human!" he ventured—quite prepared to see her rise wrathfully and go overboard.

Instead she remained motionless, those clear, disconcerting eyes fixed steadily on him. Once or twice he thought that her upper lip quivered; that some delicate demon of laughter was trying to look out at him under the lashes; but not a lid twitched; the vivid lips rested gravely upon each other. After a silence she said:

"What is it, *human*, that you expect me to do? Flirt with you?"

"Good Lord, no!" he said, stampeded.

She was now paying him the compliment of her full attention; he felt the dubious flattery, although it slightly scared him.

"Why is it," she asked, "that a man is eternally occupied in thinking about the effect he produces on woman—whether or not he knows her—that seems to make no difference at all? Why is it?"

He turned redder; she sat curled up, nursing both ankles, and contemplating him with impersonal and searching curiosity.

"Tell me," she said; "is there any earthly reason why you and I should be interested in each other—enough, I mean, to make any effort toward civility beyond the bounds of ordinary convention?"

He did not answer.

"Because," she added, "if there is not, any such effort on your part borders rather closely on the offensive. And I am quite sure you do not intend that."

He was indignant now, but utterly incapable of retort.

"Is there anything romantic in it because a chance swimmer rests a few moments in somebody's boat?" she asked. "Is that chance swimmer superhuman or inhuman or ultra-human because she is not consciously, and simperingly, preoccupied with the fact that there happens to be a man in her vicinity?"

"Good heavens!" he broke out, "do you think I'm that sort of noodle—"

"But I *don't* think about you at all," she interrupted; "there is not a thought that I have which concerns you as an individual. My homily is delivered in the abstract. Can't you—in the abstract—understand *that*?—even if you are a bit doubtful concerning the seven deadly conventions?"

He rested on his oars, tingling all over with wrath and surprise.

"And now," she said quietly, "I think it time to go. The sun is almost shining, you see, and the beauty of the scene is too obvious for even you to miss."

"May I express an opinion before you depart?"

"If it is not a very long or very dissenting opinion."

"Then it's this: two normal and wholesome people—man and a woman, can *not* meet, either conventionally or unconventionally, without expressing some atom of interest in one another as individuals. I say two—perfectly—normal—people—"

"But it has just happened!" she insisted, preparing to rise.

"No, it has not happened."

"Really. You speak for yourself of course—"

"Yes, I do. I *am* interested; I'd be stupid if I were not. Besides, I understand conventions as well as you do—"

"You don't observe them—"

"I don't worship them!"

She said coolly: "Women should be ritualists. It is safer."

"It is not necessary in this case. I haven't the slightest hope of making this incident a foundation for another; I haven't the least idea that I shall ever see you again. But for me to pretend an imbecile indifference to you or to the situation would be a more absurd example of self-consciousness than even you have charged me with."

Wrath and surprise in her turn widened her eyes; he held up his hand: "One moment; I have not finished. May I go on?"

And, as she said nothing, he resumed: "During the few minutes we have been accidentally thrown together, I have not seen a quiver of human humour in you. *There* is the self-consciousness—the absorbed preoccupation with appearances."

"What is there humourous in the situation?" she demanded, very pink.

"Good Lord! What is there humourous in any situation if you don't make it so?"

"I am not a humourist," she said.

She sat in the bows, one closed hand propping her chin; and sometimes her clear eyes, harboring lightning, wandered toward him, sometimes toward the shore.

"Suppose you continue to row," she said at last. "I'm doing you the honour of thinking about what you've said."

He resumed the oars, still sitting facing her, and pushed the boat slowly forward; and, as they continued their progress in silence, her brooding glance wavered, at intervals, between him and the coast.

"Haven't you *any* normal human curiosity concerning me?" he asked so boyishly that, for a second, again from her eyes, two gay little demons seemed to peer out and laugh at him.

But her lips were expressionless, and she only said: "I have no curiosity. Is that criminally abnormal?"

"Yes; if it is true. Is it?"

"I suppose it is too unflattering a truth for you to believe." She checked herself, looked up at him, hesitated. "It is *not* absolutely true. It was at first. I am normally interested now. If you knew more about me you would very easily understand my lack of interest in people I pass; the habit of not permitting myself to be interested—the necessity of it. The art of indifference is far more easily acquired than the art of forgetting."

"But surely," he said, "it can cost you no effort to forget me."

"No, of course not." She looked at him, unsmiling: "It was the acquired habit of indifference in me which you mistook for—I think you mistook it for stupidity. Many do. Did you?"

But the guilty amusement on his face answered her; she watched him silently for a while.

"You are quite right in one way," she said; "an unconventional encounter like this has no significance—not enough to dignify it with any effort toward indifference. But until I began to reprove man in the abstract, I really had not very much interest in you as an individual."

And, as he said nothing: "I might better have been in the beginning what you call 'human'—found the situation mildly amusing—and it *is*—though you don't know it! But"—she hesitated—"the acquired instinct operated automatically. I wish I had been more—human; I can be." She raised her eyes; and in them glimmered her first smile, faint, yet so charming a revelation that the surprise of it held him motionless at his oars.

"Have I paid the tribute you claim?" she asked. "If I have, may I not go overboard at my convenience?"

He did not answer. She laid both arms along the gunwales once more, balancing herself to rise.

"We are near enough now," she said, "and the fog is quite gone. May I thank you and depart without further arousing you to psychological philosophy?"

"If you must," he said; "but I'd rather row you in."

"If I must? Do you expect to paddle me around Cape Horn?" And she rose and stepped lightly onto the bow, maintaining her balance without effort while the boat pitched, fearless, confident, swaying there between sky and sea.

"Good-bye," she said, gravely nodding at him.

"Good-bye, Calypso!"

She joined her finger tips above her head, preliminary to a plunge. Then she looked down at him over her shoulder.

"I *told* you that Calypso was a *land* nymph."

"I can't help it; fabled Calypso you must remain to me."

"Oh; am I to remain—anything—to you—for the next five minutes?"

"Do you think I could forget you?"

"I don't think so—for five minutes. Your satisfied vanity will retain me for so long—until it becomes hungry again. And—but read the history of Ulysses—carefully. However, it *was* nice of you—not to name yourself and expect a response from me. I'm afraid—I'm afraid it is going to take me almost five minutes to forget you—I mean your boat of course. Good-bye!"

Before he could speak again she went overboard, rose swimming with effortless grace. After a dozen strokes or so she turned on one side, glancing back at him. Later, almost among the breakers, she raised one arm in airy signal, but whether to him or to somebody on the raft he did not know.

For five minutes—the allotted five—he lay on his oars watching the sands. At moments he fancied he could still distinguish her, but the distance was great, and there were many scarlet head-dresses among the bathers ashore and afloat.

And after a while he settled back on his oars, cast a last glance astern, and pulled for the *Ariani*, aboard of which Portlaw was already bellowing at him through an enormous megaphone.

Malcourt, who looked much younger than he really was, appeared on the after deck, strolling about with a telescope tucked up under one arm, both hands in his trousers pockets; and, as Hamil pulled under the stern, he leaned over the rail: "Hello, Hamil! Any trade with the natives in prospect? How far will a pint of beads go with the lady aborigines?"

"Better ask at the Beach Club," replied Hamil, laughing; "I say, Malcourt, I've had a corking swim out yonder—"

"Go in deep?" inquired Malcourt guilelessly.

"Deep? It's forty fathoms off the reef."

"I didn't mean the water," murmured Malcourt.

CHAPTER II
A LANDING

The *Ariani* was to sail that evening, her destination being Miami and the West Coast where Portlaw desired to do some tarpon fishing and Wayward had railroad interests. Malcourt, always in a receptive attitude, was quite ready to go anywhere when invited. Otherwise he preferred a remunerative attention to business.

Hamil, however, though with the gay company aboard, was not of them; he had business at Palm Beach; his luggage had already been sent ashore; and now, prepared to follow, he stood a little apart from the others on the moonlit deck, making his adieus to the master of the *Ariani*.

"It's been perfectly stunning—this cruise," he said. "It was kind of you, Wayward; I don't know how to tell you how kind—but your boat's a corker and you are another—"

"Do you like this sort of thing?" asked Wayward grimly.

"Like it? It's only a part of your ordinary lives—yours and Portlaw's; so you are not quite fitted to understand. But, Wayward, I've been in heavy harness. You have been doing this sort of heavenly thing—how many years?"

"Too many. Tell me; you've really made good this last year, haven't you, Garry?"

Hamil nodded. "I had to."

He laid his hand on the older man's arm. "Why do you know," he said, "when they gave me that first commission for the little park at Hampton Hills—thanks to you—I hadn't five dollars in all the world."

Wayward stood looking at him through his spectacles, absently pulling at his moustache, which was already partly gray.

"Garry," he said in his deep, pleasant voice that was however never very clear, "Portlaw tells me that you are to do his place. Then there are the new parks in Richmond Borough, and this enormous commission down here among the snakes and jungles. Well—God bless you. You're twenty-five and busy. I'm forty-five and"—he looked drearily into the younger man's eyes—"burnt out," he said with his mirthless laugh—"and still drenching the embers with the same stuff that set 'em ablaze.... Good-bye, Garry. Your boat's alongside. My compliments to your aunt."

At the gangway the younger man bade adieu to Malcourt and Portlaw, laughing as the latter indignantly requested to know why Hamil wasted his time attending to business.

Malcourt drew him aside:

"So you're going to rig up a big park and snake preserve for Neville Cardross?"

"I'm going to try, Louis. You know the family, I believe, don't you?"

Malcourt gazed placidly at him. "Very well indeed," he replied deliberately. "They're a, good, domestic, mother-pin-a-rose-on-me sort of family.... I'm a sort of distant cousin—run of the house and privilege of kissing the girls—not now, but once. I'm going to stay there when we get back from Miami."

"You didn't tell me that?" observed Hamil, surprised.

"No," said Malcourt carelessly, "I didn't know it myself. Just made up my mind to do it. Saves hotel expenses. Well—your cockle-shell is waiting. Give my regards to the family—particularly to Shiela." He looked curiously at Hamil; "particularly to Shiela," he repeated; but Hamil missed the expression of his eyes in the dusk.

"Are you really going to throw us over like this?" demanded Portlaw as the young men turned back together across the deck.

"Got to do it," said Hamil cheerfully, offering his hand in adieu.

"Don't plead necessity," insisted Portlaw. "You've just landed old man Cardross, and you've got the Richmond parks, and you're going to sting me for more than I'm worth. Why on earth do you cut and run this way?"

"No man in his proper senses really knows why he does anything. Seriously, Portlaw, my party is ended—"

"Destiny gave Ulysses a proud party that lasted ten years; wasn't it ten, Malcourt?" demanded Portlaw. "Stay with us, son; you've nine years and eleven months of being a naughty boy coming to you—including a few Circes and grand slams—"

"He's met his Circe," cut in Malcourt, leaning languidly over the rail; "she's wearing a scarlet handkerchief this season—"

Portlaw, laughing fatly, nodded. "Louis discovered your Circe through the glasses climbing into your boat—"

"What a busy little beast you are, Malcourt," observed Hamil, annoyed, glancing down at the small boat alongside.

"'Beast' is good! You mean the mere sight of her transformed Louis into the classic shote," added Portlaw, laughing louder as Hamil, still smiling through his annoyance, went over the side. And a moment later the gig shot away into the star-set darkness.

From the bridge Wayward wearily watched it through his night glasses; Malcourt, slim and graceful, sat on the rail and looked out into the Southern dusk, an unlighted cigarette between his lips.

"That kills our four at Bridge," grumbled Portlaw, leaning heavily beside him. "We'll have to play Klondike and Preference now, or call in the ship's cat.... Hello, is that you, Jim?" as Wayward came aft, limping a trifle as he did at certain times.

"That girl had a good figure—through the glasses. I couldn't make out her face; it was probably the limit; combinations are rare," mused Malcourt. "And then—the fog came! It was like one of those low-down classical tricks of Jupiter when caught philandering."

Portlaw laughed till his bulky body shook. "The Olympian fog was wasted," he said; "John Garret Hamil 3d still preserves his nursery illusions."

"He's lucky," remarked Wayward, staring into the gloom.

"But not fortunate," added Malcourt; "there's a difference between luck and fortune. Read the French classics."

Wayward growled; Malcourt, who always took a malicious amusement in stirring him up, grinned at him sideways.

"No man is fit for decent society until he's lost all his illusions," he said, "particularly concerning women."

"Some of us have been fools enough to lose our illusions," retorted Wayward sharply, "but you never had any, Malcourt; and that's no compliment from me to you."

Portlaw chuckled. "We never lose illusions; we mislay 'em," he suggested; "and then we are pretty careful to mislay only that particular illusion which inconveniences us." He jerked his heavy head in Malcourt's direction. "Nobody clings more frantically to illusions than your unbaked cynic; Louis, you're not nearly such a devil of a fellow as you imagine you are."

Malcourt smiled easily and looked out over the waves.

"Cynicism is old-fashioned," he said; "dogma is up to date. Credo! I believe in a personal devil, virtuous maidens in bowers, and rosewood furniture. As for illusions I cherish as many as you do!" He turned with subtle impudence to Wayward. "And the world is littered with the shattered fragments."

"It's littered with pups, too," observed Wayward, turning on his heel. And he walked away, limping, his white mess jacket a pale spot in the gloom.

Malcourt looked after him; an edge of teeth glimmering beneath his full upper lip.

"It might be more logical if he'd cut out his alcohol before he starts in as a gouty marine missionary," he observed. "Last night he sat there looking like a superannuated cavalry colonel in spectacles, neuritis twitching his entire left side, unable to light his own cigar; and there he sat and rambled on and on about innate purity and American womanhood."

He turned abruptly as a steward stepped up bearing a decanter and tray of glasses.

Portlaw helped himself, grumbling under his breath that he meant to cut out this sort of thing and set Wayward an example.

Malcourt lifted his glass gaily:

"Our wives and sweethearts; may they never meet!"

They set back their empty glasses; Portlaw started to move away, still muttering about the folly of self-indulgence; but the other detained him.

"Wayward took it out of me in 'Preference' this morning while Garry was out courting. I'd better liquidate to-night, hadn't I, Billy?"

"Certainly," said Portlaw.

The other shook his head. "I'll get it all back at Miami, of course. In the mean time—if you don't mind letting me have enough to square things—"

Portlaw hesitated, balancing his bulk uneasily first on one foot, then the other.

"I don't mind; no; only—"

"Only what?" asked Malcourt. "I told you I couldn't afford to play cards on this trip, but you insisted."

"Certainly, certainly! I expected to consider you as—as—"

"I'm your general manager and I'm ready at all times to earn my salary. If you think it best to take me away from the estate for a junketing trip and make me play cards you can do it of course; but if you think I'm here to throw my money overboard I'm going back to-morrow!"

"Nonsense," said Portlaw; "you're not going back. There's nothing doing in winter up there that requires your personal attention—"

"It's a bad winter for the deer—I ought to be there now—"

"Well, can't Blake and O'Connor attend to that?"

"Yes, I suppose they can. But I'm not going to waste the winter and my salary in the semi-tropics just because you want me to—"

"O Lord!" said Portlaw, "what are you kicking about? Have I ever—"

"You force me to be plain-spoken; you never seem to understand that if you insist on my playing the wealthy do-nothing that you've got to keep me going. And I tell you frankly, Billy, I'm tired of it."

"Oh, don't flatten your ears and show your teeth," protested Portlaw amiably. "I only supposed you had enough—with such a salary—to give yourself a little rope on a trip like this, considering you've nobody but yourself to look out for, and that *I* do that and pay you heavily for the privilege"—his voice had become a mumble—"and all you do is to take vacations in New York or sit on a horse and watch an army of men plant trout and pheasants, and cut out ripe timber—O hell!"

"*What* did you say?"

Portlaw became good-humouredly matter of fact: "I *said* 'hell,' Louis—which meant, 'what's the use of squabbling.' It also means that you are going to have what you require as a matter of course; so come on down to my state-room and let us figure it up before Jim Wayward begins to turn restless and limp toward the card-room."

As they turned and strolled forward, Malcourt nudged him:

"Look at the fireworks over Lake Worth," he said; "probably Palm Beach's welcome to her new and beardless prophet."

"It's one of their cheap Venetian fêtes," muttered Portlaw. "I know 'em; they're rather amusing. If we weren't sailing in an hour we'd go. No doubt Hamil's in it already; probably Cardross put him next to a bunch of dreams and he's right in it at this very moment."

"With the girl in the red handkerchief," added Malcourt. "I wish we had time."

"I believe I've seen that girl somewhere," mused Portlaw.

"Perhaps you have; there are all kinds at Palm Beach, even yours, and," he added with his easy impudence, "I expect to preserve my notions concerning every one of them. Ho! Look at that sheaf of sky-rockets, Billy! Zip! Whir-r! Bang! Great is Diana of the Ephesians!—bless her heart!"

"Going up like Garret Hamil's illusions," said Portlaw, sentimentally. "I wonder if he sees 'em and considers the moral they are writing across the stars. O slush! Life is like a stomach; if you fill it too full it hurts you. What about *that* epigram, Louis? What about it?"

The other's dark, graceful head was turned toward the fiery fête on shore, and his busy thoughts were with that lithe, dripping figure he had seen through the sea-glasses, climbing into a distant boat. For the figure reminded him of a girl he had known very well when the world was younger; and the memory was not wholly agreeable.

CHAPTER III
AN ADVANCE

Hamil stood under the cocoanut palms at the lake's edge and watched the lagoon where thousands of coloured lanterns moved on crafts, invisible except when revealed in the glare of the rushing rockets.

Lamps glittered everywhere; electric lights were doubly festooned along the sea wall, drooping creeper-like from palm to palmetto, from flowering hibiscus to sprawling banyan, from dainty china-berry to grotesque screw-pine tree, shedding strange witch-lights over masses of blossoms, tropical and semi-tropical. Through which the fine-spun spray of fountains drifted, and the great mousy dusk-moths darted through the bars of light with the glimmering bullet-flight of summer meteors.

And everywhere hung the scent of orange bloom and the more subtle perfume of white and yellow jasmine floated through the trees from gardens or distant hammocks, combining in one intoxicating aroma, spiced always with the savour of the sea.

Hamil was aware of considerable noise, more or less musical, afloat and ashore; a pretentious orchestra played third-rate music under the hotel colonnade; melody arose from the lantern-lit lake, with clamourous mandolins and young voices singing; and over all hung the confused murmur of unseen throngs, harmonious, capricious; laughter, voice answering voice, and the distant shouts as brilliantly festooned boats hailed and were hailed across the water.

Hamil passed on to the left through crowded gardens, pressing his way slowly where all around him lantern-lit faces appeared from the dusk and vanished again into it; where the rustle of summer gowns sweeping the shaven lawns of Bermuda grass sounded like a breeze in the leaves.

Sometimes out of the dusk all tremulous with tinted light the rainbow ray of a jewel flashed in his eyes—or sometimes he caught the glint of eyes above the jewel—a passing view of a fair face, a moment's encountering glance, and, maybe, a smile just as the shadows falling turned the garden's brightness to a mystery peopled with phantoms.

Out along the shell road he sauntered, Whitehall rising from tropic gardens on his right, on his left endless gardens again, and white villas stretching away into the starlight; on, under the leaning coco-palms along quays and low walls of coquina where the lagoon lay under the silvery southern planets.

After a little he discovered that he had left the bulk of the throng behind, though in front of him and behind, the road was still dotted with white-clad groups strolling or resting on the sea-wall.

Far out on the lake the elfin pageant continued, but now he could scarcely hear the music; the far cries and the hiss of the rockets came softly as the whizzing of velvet-winged moths around orange blossoms.

The January night was magnificent; he could scarcely comprehend that this languid world of sea and palm, of heavy odour and slow breezes, was his own land still. Under the spell the Occident vanished; it was the Orient—all this dreamy mirage, these dim white walls, this spice-haunted dusk, the water inlaid with stars, the fairy foliage, the dew drumming in the stillness like the sound of goblin tattooing.

Never before had he seen this enchanted Southern land which had always been as much a part of his mother-land as Northern hill and Western plain—as much his as the roaring dissonance of Broadway, or the icy silence of the tundras, or the vast tranquil seas of corn rippling mile on mile under the harvest moon of Illinois.

He halted, unquiet in the strangeness of it all, restless under its exotic beauty, conscious of the languor stealing over him—the premonition of a physical relaxation that he had never before known—that he instinctively mistrusted.

People in groups passed and repassed along the lagoon wall where, already curiously tired, he had halted beside an old bronze cannon—some ancient Spanish piece, if he could judge by the arms and arabesques covering the breech, dimly visible in the rays of a Chinese lantern.

Beyond was a private dock where two rakish power-boats lay, receiving their cargo of young men and girls—all very animated and gay under the gaudy electric lanterns strung fore and aft rainbow fashion.

He seated himself on the cannon, lingering until both boats cleared for the carnival, rushing out into the darkness like streaks of multi-coloured flame; then his lassitude increasing, he rose and sauntered toward the hotel which loomed like a white mountain afire above the dark masses of tropic trees. And again the press of the throng hemmed him in among the palms and fountains and hedges of crimson hibiscus; again the dusk grew gay with voices and the singing overtone of violins; again the suffocating scent of blossoms, too sweet and penetrating for the unacclimated, filtered through and through him, till his breath came unevenly, and the thick odours stirred in him strange senses of expectation, quickening with his pulses to a sudden prophecy.

And at the same instant he saw the girl of whom he had been thinking.

She was on the edge of a group of half a dozen or more men in evening dress, and women in filmy white—already close to him—so near that the frail stuff of her skirt brushed him, and the subtle, fresh aroma of her seemed to touch his cheek like a breath as she passed.

"Calypso," he whispered, scarcely conscious that he spoke aloud.

A swift turn of her head, eyes that looked blankly into his, and she had passed.

A sudden realisation of his bad manners left his ears tingling. What on earth had prompted him to speak? What momentary relaxation had permitted him an affront to a young girl whose attitude toward him that morning had been so admirable?

Chagrined, he turned back to seek some circling path through the dense crowd ahead; and was aware, in the darkness, of a shadowy figure entering the jasmine arbour. And though his eyes were still confused by the lantern light he knew her again in the dusk.

As they passed she said under her breath: "That was ill-bred. I am disappointed."

He wheeled in his tracks; she turned to confront him for an instant.

"I'm just a plain beast," he said. "You won't forgive me of course."

"You had no right to say what you did. You said 'Calypso'—and I ought not to have heard you.... But I did.... Tell me; if I am too generous to suspect you of intentional impertinence, you are now too chastened to suspect that I came back to give you this chance. That is quite true, isn't it?"

"Of course. You *are* generous and—it's simply fine of you to overlook it."

"I don't know whether I intend to overlook it; I was surprised and disappointed; but I *did* desire to give you another chance. And I was so afraid you'd be rude enough to take it that—I spoke first. That was logical. Oh, I know what I'm doing—and it's particularly common of me—being who I am—"

She paused, meeting his gaze deliberately.

"You don't know who I am. Do you?"

"No," he said. "I don't deserve to. But I'll be miserable until I do."

After a moment: "And you are not going to ask me—because, once, I said that it was nice of you not to?"

The hint of mockery in her voice edged his lips with a smile, but he shook his head. "No, I won't ask you that," he said. "I've been beastly enough for one day."

"Don't you care to know?"

"Of course I care to know."

"Yet, exercising all your marvellous masculine self-control, you nobly refuse to ask?"

"I'm afraid to," he said, laughing; "I'm horribly afraid of you."

She considered him with clear, unsmiling eyes.

"Coward!" she said calmly.

He nodded his head, laughing still. "I know it; I almost lost you by saying 'Calypso' a moment ago and I'm taking no more risks."

"Am I to infer that you expect to recover me after this?"

And, as he made no answer: "You dare not admit that you hope to see me again. You *are* horribly afraid of me—even if I have defied convention and your opinions and have graciously overlooked your impertinence. In spite of all this you are still afraid of me. Are you?"

"Yes," he said; "as much as I naturally ought to be."

"*That* is nice of you. There's only one kind of a girl of whom men are really afraid.... And now I don't exactly know what to do about you—being, myself, as guilty and horrid as you have been."

She regarded him contemplatively, her hands joined behind her back.

"Exactly what to do about you I don't know," she repeated, leisurely inspecting him. "Shall I tell you something? I am not afraid to; I am not a bit cowardly about it either. Shall I?"

"If you dare," he said, smiling and uncertain.

"Very well, then; I rather like you, Mr. Hamil."

"You *are* a trump!" he blurted out, reddening with surprise.

"Are you astonished that I know you?"

"I don't see how you found out—"

"Found out! What perfectly revolting vanity! Do you suppose that the moment I left you I rushed home and began to make happy and incoherent inquiries? Mr. Hamil, you disappoint me every time you speak—and also every time you don't."

"I seem to be doomed."

"You are. You can't help it. Tell me—as inoffensively as possible—are you here to begin your work?"

"M-my work?"

"Yes, on the Cardross estate—"

"You have heard of that!" he exclaimed, surprised.

"Y-es—" negligently. "Petty gossip circulates here. A cracker at West Palm Beach built a new chicken coop, and we all heard of it. Tell me, do you still desire to see me again?"

"I do—to pay a revengeful debt or two."

"Oh! I have offended you? Pay me now, if you please, and let us end this indiscretion."

"You will let me see you again, won't you?"

"Why? Mr. Hamil."

"Because I—I *must*!"

"Oh! You are becoming emphatic. So I am going.... And I've half a mind to take you back and present you to my family.... Only it wouldn't do for *me*; any other girl perhaps might dare—under the circumstances; but *I* can't—and that's all I'll tell you."

Hamil, standing straight and tall, straw hat tucked under one arm, bent toward her with the formality and engaging deference natural to him.

"You have been very merciful to me; only a girl of your caste could afford to. Will you forgive my speaking to you as I did?—when I said 'Calypso!' I have no excuse; I don't know why I did. I'm even sorrier for myself than for you."

"I *was* hurt.... Then I supposed that you did not mean it. Besides"—she looked up with her rare smile—"I knew you, Mr. Hamil, in the boat this morning. I haven't really been very dreadful."

"You knew even *then*?"

"Yes, I did. The Palm Beach News published your picture a week ago; and I read all about the very remarkable landscape architect who was coming to turn the Cardross jungle into a most wonderful Paradise."

"You knew me all that time?"

"All of it, Mr. Hamil."

"From the moment you climbed into my boat?"

"Practically. Of course I did not look at you very closely at first.... Does that annoy you? It seems to ... or something does, for even in the dusk I can see your ever-ready blush—"

"I don't know why you pretend to think me such a fool," he protested, laughing; "you seemed to take that for granted from the very first."

"Why not? You persistently talked to me when you didn't know me—you're doing it now for that matter!—and you began by telling me that I was fool-hardy, not really courageous in the decent sense of the word, and that I was a self-conscious stick and a horribly inhuman and unnatural object generally—and all because I wouldn't flirt with you—"

His quick laughter interrupted her. She ventured to laugh a little too—a very little; and that was the charm of her to him—the clear-eyed, delicate gravity not lightly transformed. But when her laughter came, it came as such a surprisingly lovely revelation that it left him charmed and silent.

"I wonder," she said, "if you can be amusing—except when you don't mean to be."

"If you'll give me a chance to try—"

"Perhaps. I was hardly fair to you in that boat."

"If you knew me in the boat this morning, why did you not say so?"

"Could I admit that I knew you without first pretending I didn't? Hasn't every woman a Heaven-given right to travel in a circle as the shortest distance between two points?"

"Certainly; only—"

She shook her head slowly. "There's no use in my telling you who I am, now, considering that I can't very well escape exposure in the near future. That might verge on effrontery—and it's horrid enough to be here with you—in spite of several thousand people tramping about within elbow touch.... Which reminds me that my own party is probably hunting for me.... Such a crowd, you know, and so easy to become separated. What do you suppose they'd think if they suspected the truth?... And the worst of it is that I cannot afford to do a thing of this sort.... You don't understand; but you may some day—partly. And then perhaps you'll think this matter all over and come to a totally different conclusion concerning my overlooking your recent rudeness and—and my consenting to speak to you."

"You don't believe for one moment that I could mistake it—"

"It depends upon what sort of a man you really are.... I don't know. I give you the benefit of all doubts."

She stood silent, looking him candidly in the eyes, then with a gesture and the slightest shrug, she turned away toward the white road outside. He was at her elbow in two steps.

"Oh, yes—the irony of formality."

She nodded. "Good night, then, Mr. Hamil. If circumstances permitted it would have been delightful—this putting off the cloak of convention and donning motley for a little unconventional misbehaviour with you.... But as it is, it worries me—slightly—as much as the episode and your opinion are worth."

"I am wondering," he said, "why this little tincture of bitterness flavours what you say to me?"

"Because I've misbehaved; and so have you. Anyway, now that it's done, there's scarcely anything I could do to make the situation more flagrant or less flippant—"

"You don't really think—"

"Certainly. After all is said and done, we *don't* know each other; here we are, shamelessly sauntering side by side under the jasmine, Paul-and-Virginia-like, exchanging subtleties blindfolded. You are you; I am I; formally, millions of miles apart—temporarily and informally close together, paralleling each other's course through life for the span of half an hour—here under the Southern stars.... O Ulysses, truly that island was inhabited by one, Calypso; but your thrall is to be briefer than your prototype's. See, now; here is the road; and I release you to that not impossible she—"

"There is none—"

"There will be. You are very young. Good-bye."

"The confusing part of it to me," he said, smiling, "is to *see* you so—so physically youthful with even a hint of almost childish immaturity!—and then to *hear* you as you *are*—witty, experienced, nicely cynical, maturely sure of yourself and—"

"You think me experienced?"

"Yes."

"Sure of myself?"

"Of course; with your cool, amused poise, your absolute self-possession—and the half-disdainful sword-play of your wit—at my expense—"

She halted beside the sea-wall, adorably mocking in her exaggerated gravity.

"At your expense?" she repeated. "Why not? You have cost me something."

"You said—"

"I know what I said: I said that we might become friends. But even so, you have already cost me something. Tell me"—he began to listen for this little trick of speech—"how many men do you know who would not misunderstand what I have done this evening? And—do *you* understand it, Mr. Hamil?"

"I think—"

"If you do you are cleverer than I," she said almost listlessly, moving on again under the royal palms.

"Do you mean that—"

"Yes; that I myself don't entirely understand it. Here, under this Southern sun, we of the North are in danger of acquiring a sort of insouciant directness almost primitive. There comes, after a while, a certain mental as well as physical luxury in relaxation of rule and precept, permitting us a simplicity which sometimes, I think, becomes something less harmless. There *is* luxury in letting go of that live wire which keeps us all keyed to one conventional monotone in the North. I let go—for a moment—to-night. *You* let go when you said 'Calypso.' You couldn't have said it in New York; I couldn't have heard you, there.... Alas, Ulysses, I should not have heard you anywhere. But I did; and I answered.... Say good night to me, now; won't you? We have not been very wicked, I think."

She offered her hand; smooth and cool it lay for a second in his.

"I can't let you return alone," he ventured.

"If you please, how am I to explain you to—the others?"

And as he said nothing:

"If I were—different—I'd simply tell them the truth. I could afford to. Besides we'll all know you before very long. Then we'll see—oh, yes, both of us—whether we have been foolishly wise to become companions in our indiscretion, or—otherwise.... And don't worry about my home-arrival. That's my lawn—there where that enormous rubber-banyan tree straddles across the stars.... Is it not quaint—the tangle of shrubbery all over jasmine?—and those are royal poincianas, if you please—and there's a great garden beyond and most delectable orange groves where you and I and the family and Alonzo will wander and eat pine-oranges and king-oranges and mandarins and—oh, well! Are you going to call on Mr. Cardross to-morrow?"

"Yes," he said, "I'll have to see Mr. Cardross at once. And after that, what am I to do to meet you?"

"I will consider the matter," she said; and bending slightly toward him: "Am I to be disappointed in you? I don't know, and you can't tell me." Then, impulsively: "Be generous to me. You are right; I am not very old, yet. Be nice to me in your thoughts. I have never before done such a thing as this: I never could again. It is not very dreadful—is it? Will you think nicely of me?"

He said gaily: "Now you speak as you look, not like a world-worn woman of thirty wearing the soft, fresh mask of nineteen."

"You have not answered me," she said quietly.

"Answered you, Calypso?"

"Yes; I ask you to be very gentle and fastidious with me in your thoughts; not even to call me Calypso—in your thoughts."

"What you ask I had given you the first moment we met."

"Then you *may* call me Calypso—in your thoughts."

"Calypso," he pleaded, "won't you tell me where to find you?"

"Yes; in the house of—Mr. Cardross. This is his house."

She turned and stepped onto the lawn. A mass of scarlet hibiscus hid her, then she reappeared, a pale shape in the dusk of the oleander-bordered path.

He listened; the perfume of the oleanders enveloped him; high under the stars the fronds of a royal palm hung motionless. Then, through the stillness, very far away, he heard the southern ocean murmuring in its slumber under a million stars.

CHAPTER IV
RECONNAISSANCE

Hamil awoke early: long before breakfast he was shaved, dressed, and hungry; but in the hotel late rising appeared to be fashionable, and through the bewildering maze of halls and corridors nobody was yet astir except a few children and their maids.

So he sauntered about the acres of floor space from rotunda to music room, from desk to sun parlour, through the endless carpeted tunnel leading to the station, and back again, taking his bearings in this wilderness of runways so profusely embowered with palms and furniture.

In one wide corridor, lined like a street with shops, clerks were rearranging show windows; and Hamil strolled from the jewellers to the brilliant but dubious display of an Armenian rug dealer; from a New York milliner's exhibition, where one or two blond, sleepy-eyed young women moved languidly about, to an exasperating show of shells, curiosities, and local photographs which quenched further curiosity.

However, beyond the shops, at the distant end of an Axminster vista flanked by cabbage-palms and masterpieces from Grand Rapids, he saw sunshine and the green tops of trees; and he made toward the oasis, coming out along a white colonnade overlooking the hotel gardens.

It was early enough for any ambitious bird to sing, but there were few song-birds in the gardens—a palm warbler or two, and a pair of subdued mocking-birds not inclined to be tuneful. Everywhere, however, purple and bronze grackle appeared, flying or walking busily over the lawns, sunlight striking the rainbow hackle on their necks, and their pale-yellow or bright-orange eyes staring boldly at the gardeners who dawdled about the flowery labyrinths with watering-can and jointed hose. And from every shrub and tree came the mildly unpleasant calling of the grackle, and the blackbirds along the lagoon answered with their own unmusical "Co-ca-*chee*!—Co-ca-chee-e!"

Somehow, to Hamil, the sunshine seemed to reveal more petty defects in this semi-tropical landscape than he could have divined the night before under the unblemished magic of the stars. For the grass was not real grass, but only that sparse, bunchy, sun-crisped substitute from Bermuda; here and there wind-battered palmetto fronds hung burnt and bronzed; and the vast hotel, which through the darkness he had seen piled up above the trees in cliff-like beauty against the stars, was actually remarkable only for its size and lack of architectural interest.

He began to wonder whether the inhabitants of its thousand rooms, aware of the pitiless clarity of this semi-tropical morning sunlight, shunned it lest it reveal unsuspected defects in those pretty lantern-lit faces of which he had had glimpses in the gardens' enchanted dusk the night before. However, the sunshine seemed to render the little children only the lovelier, and he sat on the railing, his back against a pillar, watching them racing about with their nurses, until the breakfast hour at last came around and found him at table, no longer hungry.

A stream of old ladies and gentlemen continued toddling into the breakfast rooms where an acre or two of tables, like a profuse crop of mushrooms, disturbed the monotony of the hotel interior with a monotony still more pronounced. However, there was hazy sunshine in the place and a glimpse of blessed green outside, and the leisurely negroes brought him fruit which was almost as good as the New York winter markets afforded, and his breakfast amused him mildly.

The people, too, amused him—so many dozens of old ladies and gentlemen, all so remarkably alike in a common absence of distinguishing traits—a sort of homogeneous, expressionless similarity which was rather amazing as they doubtless had gathered there from all sections of the Republic.

But the children were delightful, and all over the vast room he could distinguish their fresh little faces like tufts of flowers set in a waste of dusty stubble, and amid the culinary clatter their clear, gay little voices broke through cheerfully at moments, grateful as the morning chatter of sparrows in early spring.

When Hamil left his table he halted to ask an imposing head-waiter whether Miss Palliser might be expected to breakfast, and was informed that she breakfasted and lunched in her rooms and dined always in the café.

So he stopped at the desk and sent up his card.

A number of young people evidently equipped for the golf links now pervaded hall and corridor; others, elaborately veiled for motoring, stopped at the desk for letters on their way into the outer sunshine.

A row of rather silent but important-looking gentlemen, morning cigars afire, gradually formed ranks in arm-chairs under the colonnade;

people passing and repassing began to greet each other with more vivacity; veranda and foyer became almost animated as the crowd increased. And now a demure bride or two emerged in all the radiance of perfect love and raiment, squired by *him*, braving the searching sunshine with confidence in her beauty, her plumage, and a kindly planet; and, in pitiful contrast, here and there some waxen-faced invalid, wheeled by a trained nurse, in cap and cuffs, through sunless halls into the clear sea air, to lie motionless, with leaden lids scarcely parted, in the glory of a perfect day.

A gentleman, rotund of abdomen, wearing a stubby red moustache, screwed a cigar firmly into the off corner of his mouth and, after looking aggressively at Hamil for fully half a minute, said:

"Southern Pacific sold off at the close."

"Indeed," said Hamil.

"It's like picking daisies," said the gentleman impressively. And, after a pause, during which he continued to survey the younger man: "What name?" he inquired, as though Hamil had been persistently attempting to inform him.

Hamil told him good-naturedly.

"Pleased to meet you, Mr. Hamil. My name is Rawley—probably the name is familiar to you?—Ambrose Rawley"—he coughed—"by profession a botanist."

Hamil smiled, recognising in the name the most outrageously expensive of New York florists who had made a fortune in cut flowers.

"Have a drink?" persisted Mr. Rawley. "No? Too early for you? Well, let's get a couple of niggers and wheel-chairs."

But Hamil declined with the easy good-humour which characterised him; and a few moments later, learning at the office that his aunt would receive him, followed his negro guide through endless carpeted labyrinths and was ushered by a maid into a sunny reception-room.

"Garry!—you dear boy!" exclaimed his amazingly youthful aunt, holding out both arms to him from the door of her bedroom, partly ajar. "No—don't come near me; I'm not even in complete negligée yet, but I will be in one minute when Titine fastens me up and makes the most of my scanty locks—" She looked out at him with a laugh and gave her head a little jerk forward, and her splendid chestnut hair came tumbling down in the sunshine.

"You're prettier than ever," said her nephew; "they'll take us for bride and groom as usual. I say, Constance, I suppose they've followed you down here."

"Who, Garry," —very innocently.

"The faithful three, Colonel Vetchen, Cuyp, and old—I mean the gracefully mature Courtlandt Classon. Are they here?"

"I believe so, dear," admitted his aunt demurely. "And, Garry, so is Virginia Suydam."

"Really," he said, suddenly subdued as his aunt who was forty and looked twenty-five came forward in her pretty chamber-gown, and placed two firm white arms around him and kissed him squarely and with vigour.

"You dear!" she said; "you certainly are the best-looking boy in all Florida. When did you come? Is Jim Wayward's yacht here still? And why didn't he come to see me?"

"The *Ariani* sailed for Miami last night after I landed. I left my card, but the office people rang and rang and could get no answer—"

"I was in bed! How stupid of me! I retired early because Virginia and I had been dissipating shamefully all the week and my aged bones required a rest.... And now tell me all about this new commission of yours. I have met the Cardross family; everybody at Palm Beach is talking about the magnificent park Mr. Cardross is planning; and your picture has appeared in the local paper, and I've told everybody you're quite wonderful, and everybody now is informing everybody else that you're quite wonderful!"

His very gay aunt lay back in her great soft chair, pushing with both fair hands the masses of chestnut hair from her forehead, and smiling at him out of her golden brown eyes—the jolliest, frankest of eyes—the sort even women trust instinctively at first glimpse.

So he sat there and told her all about his commission and how this man, Neville Cardross, whom he had never even seen, had written to him and asked him to make the most splendid park in America around the Cardross villa, and had invited him to be his guest during his stay in Florida.

"They evidently are nice people from the way Mr. Cardross writes," he said. "You say you know them, Constance?"

"I've met them several times—the way you meet people here. They have a villa—rather imposing in an exotic fashion. Why, yes, Garry, they *are* nice; dreadfully wealthy, tremendously popular. Mrs. Carrick, the married daughter, is very agreeable; her mother is amiable and dreadfully stout. Then there's a boy of your age—Gray Cardross—a well-mannered youth who drives motors, and whom Mr. Classon calls a 'speed-mad cub.' Then there is Cecile Cardross—a débutante of last winter, and then—" Miss Palliser hesitated, crossed one knee over the other, and sat gently swinging her slippered foot and looking at her nephew.

"Does that conclude the list of the Cardross family?" he asked.

"N-no. There remains the beauty of the family, Shiela." She continued to survey him with smiling intentness, and went on slowly:

"Shiela Cardross; *the* girl here. People are quite mad about her, I assure you. My dear, every man at Palm Beach tags after her; rows of callow youths sit and gaze at her very footprints in the sand when she crosses the beach; she turns masculine heads to the verge of permanent dislocation. No guilty man escapes; even Courtlandt Classon is meditating treachery to me, and Mr. Cuyp has long been wavering and Gussie Vetchen too! the wretch!... We poor women try hard to like her—but, Garry, *is* it human to love such a girl?"

"It's divine, Constance, so you'll like her."

"Oh, yes; thank you. Well, I do; I don't know her well, but I'm inclined to like her—in a way.... There's something else, though." She considered her handsome nephew steadily. "You are to be a guest there while this work of yours is in hand?"

"Yes—I believe so."

"Then, dear, without the slightest unworthy impulse or the faintest trace of malice, I wish to put you on your guard. It's horrid, but I must."

"On my guard!" he repeated.

"So he sat there and told her all about his commission."

"Yes—forearm you, Garry. Shiela Cardross is a rather bewildering beauty. She is French convent-bred, clever and cultivated and extremely talented. Besides that she has every fashionable grace and accomplishment at the ends of her pretty fingers—and she has a way with her—a way of looking at you—which is pure murder to the average man. And beside that she is very simple and sweet to everybody. As an assassin of hearts she's equipped to slay yours, Garry."

"Well?" he inquired, laughing. And added: "Let her slay. Why not?"

"This, dear. And you who know me will acquit me of any ignoble motive if I say that she is not your social equal, Garry."

"What! I thought you said—"

"Yes—about the others. But it is not the same with Shiela Cardross. I—it seems cruel to say it—but it is for your sake—to effectually forestall any possible accident—that I am going to tell you that this very lovely girl, Shiela, is an adopted child, not a daughter. That exceedingly horrid old gossip, Mrs. Van Dieman, told me that the girl was a foundling taken by Mr. and Mrs. Cardross from the Staten Island asylum. And I'm afraid Mrs. Van Dieman knows what she's talking about because she founded and still supports the asylum."

Hamil looked gravely across at his aunt. "The poor little girl," he said slowly. "Lord, but that's tough! and tougher still to have Mrs. Van Dieman taking the trouble to spread the news. Can't you shut her up?"

"It *is* tough, Garret. I suppose they all are dreadfully sensitive about it. I begged Mrs. Van Dieman to keep her own counsel. But she won't. And you know, dear, that it would make no difference to me in my relations with the girl—except that"—she hesitated, smiling—"she is *not* good enough for you, Garry, and so, if you catch the prevailing contagion, and fall a victim, you have been inoculated now and will have the malady lightly."

"My frivolous and fascinating aunt," he said, "have you ever known me to catch any prevailing—"

"O Garret! You know you have!—dozens of times—"

"I've been civilly attentive to several girls—"

"I wish to goodness you'd marry Virginia Suydam; but you won't."

"Virginia!" he repeated, astonished.

"Yes, I do; I wish you were safely and suitably married. I'm worried, Garry; you are becoming too good-looking not to get into some horrid complication—as poor Jim Wayward did; and now he's done for, finished! Oh, I wish I didn't feel so responsible for you. And I *wish* you weren't going to the Cardrosses' to live for months!"

He leaned forward, laughing, and took his aunt's slim hands between his own sunburned fists. "You cunning little thing," he said, "if you talk that way I'll marry you off to one of the faithful three; you and Virginia too. Lord, do you think I'm down here to cut capers when I've enough hard work ahead to drive a dozen men crazy for a year? As for your beautiful Miss Cardross—why I saw a girl in a boat—not long ago—who really was a beauty. I mean to find her, some day; and that *is* something for you to worry about!"

"Garry! *Tell* me!"

But he rose, still laughing, and saluted Miss Palliser's hands.

"If you and Virginia have nothing better on I'll dine with you at eight. Yes? No?"

"Of course. Where are you going now?"

"To report to Mr. Cardross—and brave beauty in its bower," he added mischievously. "I'll doubtless be bowled over first shot and come around for a dinner and a blessing at eight this evening."

"Don't joke about it," she said as they rose together and stood for a moment at the window looking down into the flowering gardens.

"Is it not a jolly scene?" she added—"the fountain against the green, and the flowers and the sunshine everywhere, and all those light summer gowns outdoors in January, and—" She checked herself and laid her hand on his arm; "Garry, do you see that girl in the wheel-chair!—the one just turning into the gardens!"

He had already seen her. Suddenly his heart stood still in dread of what his aunt was about to say. He knew already somehow that she was going to say it, yet when she spoke the tiny shock came just the same.

"That," said his aunt, "is Shiela Cardross. Is she not too lovely for words?"

"Yes," he said, "she is very beautiful."

For a while they stood together there at the window, then he said good-bye in a rather subdued manner which made his aunt laugh that jolly, clear laugh which never appealed to him in vain.

"You're not mortally stricken already at your first view of her, are you?" she asked.

"Not mortally," he said.

"Then fall a victim and recover quickly. And *don't* let me sit here too long without seeing you; will you?"

She went to the door with him, one arm linked in his, brown eyes bright with her pride and confidence in him—in this tall, wholesome, clean-built boy, already on the verge of distinction in his rather unusual profession. And she saw in him all the strength and engaging good looks of his dead father, and all the clear and lovable sincerity of his mother—her only sister—now also dead.

"You *will* come to see me sometimes—won't you, Garry?" she repeated wistfully.

"Of course I will. Give my love to Virginia and my amused regards to the faithful three."

And so they parted, he to saunter down into the cool gardens on his way to call on Mr. Cardross; she to pace the floor, excited by his arrival, her heart beating with happiness, pride, solicitude for the young fellow who was like brother and son to her—this handsome, affectionate, generous boy who had steadily from the very first declined to accept one penny of her comfortable little fortune lest she be deprived of the least luxury or convenience, and who had doggedly educated and prepared himself, and contrived to live within the scanty means he had inherited.

And now at last the boy saw success ahead, and Miss Palliser was happy, dreaming brilliant dreams for him, conjuring vague splendours for the future—success unbounded, honours, the esteem of all good men; this, for her boy. And—if it must be—love, in its season—with the inevitable separation and a slow dissolution of an intimacy which had held for her all she desired in life—his companionship, his happiness, his fortune; this also she dreamed for his sake. Yes—knowing she could not always keep him, and that it must come inexorably, she dreamed of love for him—and marriage.

And, as she stood now by the sunny window, idly intent on her vision, without warning the face of Shiela Cardross glimmered through the dream, growing clearer, distinct in every curve and tint of its exquisite perfection; and she stared at the mental vision, evoking it with all the imagination of her inner consciousness, unquiet yet curious, striving to look into the phantom's eyes—clear, direct eyes which she remembered; and a thrill of foreboding touched her, lest the boy she loved might find in the sweetness of these clear eyes a peril not lightly overcome.

"She is so unusually beautiful," said Miss Palliser aloud, unconscious that she had spoken. And she added, wondering, "God knows what blood is in her veins to form a body so divine."

CHAPTER V
A FLANK MOVEMENT

Young Hamil, moving thoughtfully along through the gardens, caught a glimpse of a group under the palms which halted him for an instant, then brought him forward, hat off, hand cordially outstretched.

"Awf'lly glad to see you, Virginia; this is very jolly; hello, Cuyp! How are you, Colonel Vetchen—oh! how do you do, Mr. Classon!" as the latter came trotting down the path, twirling a limber walking-stick.

"How-dee-do! How-dee-do!" piped Courtlandt Classon, with a rickety abandon almost paternal; and, replying literally, Hamil admitted his excellent physical condition.

Virginia Suydam, reclining in her basket chair, very picturesque in a broad hat, smiled at him out of her peculiar bluish-green eyes, while Courtlandt Classon fussed and fussed and patted his shoulder; an old beau who had toddled about Manhattan in the days when the town was gay below Bleecker Street, when brownstone was for the rich alone, when the family horses wore their tails long and a proud Ethiope held the reins, when Saratoga was the goal of fashion, and old General Jan Van-der-Duynck pronounced his own name "Wonnerdink," with profane accompaniment.

They were all most affable—Van Tassel Cuyp with the automatic nervous snicker that deepened the furrows from nostril to mouth, a tall stoop-shouldered man of scant forty with the high colour, long, nervous nose, and dull eye of Dutch descent; and Colonel Augustus Magnelius Pietrus Vetchen, scion of an illustrious line whose ancestors had been colonial governors and judges before the British flag floated from the New Amsterdam fort. His daughter was the celebrated beauty, Mrs. Tom O'Hara. She had married O'Hara and so many incredible millions that people insisted that was why Colonel Vetchen's eyebrows expressed the acute slant of perpetual astonishment.

So they were all cordial, for was he not related to the late General Garret Suydam and, therefore, distantly to them all? And these men who took themselves and their lineage so seriously, took Hamil seriously; and he often attempted to appreciate it seriously, but his sense of humour was too strong. They were all good people, kindly and harmless snobs; and when he had made his adieux under the shadow of the white portico, he lingered a moment to observe the obsolete gallantry with which Mr. Classon and Colonel Vetchen wafted Virginia up the steps.

Cuyp lingered to venture a heavy pleasantry or two which distorted his long nose into a series of white-ridged wrinkles, then he ambled away and disappeared within the abode of that divinity who shapes our ends, the manicure; and Hamil turned once more toward the gardens.

The hour was still early; of course too unconventional to leave cards on the Cardross family, even too early for a business visit; but he thought he would stroll past the villa, the white walls of which he had dimly seen the evening before. Besides his Calypso was there. Alas! for Calypso. Yet his heart tuned up a trifle as he thought of seeing her so soon again.

And so, a somewhat pensive but wholly attractive and self-confident young opportunist in white flannels, he sauntered through the hotel gardens and out along the dazzling shell-road.

No need for him to make inquiries of passing negroes; no need to ask where the House of Cardross might be found; for although he had seen it only by starlight, and the white sunshine now transformed everything under its unfamiliar glare, he remembered his way, étape by étape, from the foliated iron grille of Whitehall to the ancient cannon bedded in rusting trunnions; and from that mass of Spanish bronze, southward under the tall palms, past hedges of vermilion hibiscus and perfumed oleander, past villa after villa embowered in purple, white, and crimson flowering vines, and far away inland along the snowy road until, at the turn, a gigantic banyan tree sprawled across the sky and the lilac-odour of china-berry in bloom stole subtly through the aromatic confusion, pure, sweet, refreshing in all its exquisite integrity.

"Calypso's own fragrance," he thought to himself—remembering the intimate perfume of her hair and gown as she passed so near to him in the lantern light when he had spoken without discretion.

And suddenly the reminiscent humour faded from his eyes and mouth as he remembered what his aunt had said of this young girl; and, halting in his tracks, he recalled what she herself had said; that the harmless liberties another girl might venture to take with informality, armoured in an assurance above common convention, she could not venture. And now he knew why.... She had expected him to learn that she was an adopted daughter; in the light of his new knowledge he understood that. No doubt it was generally known. But the child had not expected him to know more than that; and, her own knowledge of the hopeless truth, plainly enough, was the key to that note of bitterness which he had detected at times, and even spoken of—that curious maturity forced by unhappy self-knowledge, that apathetic indifference stirred at moments to a quick sensitive alertness almost resembling self-defence. She was aware of her own story; that was certain. And the acid of that knowledge was etching the designs of character upon a physical adolescence unprepared for such biting reaction.

He was sorry he knew it, feeling ashamed of his own guiltless invasion of the girl's privacy.

The only reparation possible was to forget it. Like an honourable card-player who inadvertently sees his opponent's cards, he must play his hand exactly as he would have in the beginning. And that, he believed, would be perfectly simple.

Reassured he looked across the lawns toward the Cardross villa, a big house of coquina cement, very beautiful in its pseudo-Spanish architecture, red-tiled roofs, cool patias, arcades, and courts; the formality of terrace, wall, and fountain charmingly disguised under a riot of bloom and foliage.

The house stood farther away than he had imagined, for here the public road ended abruptly in a winding hammock-trail, and to the east the private drive of marl ran between high gates of wrought iron swung wide between carved coquina pillars.

And the house itself was very much larger than he had imagined; the starlight had illuminated only a small portion of its white façade, tricking him; for this was almost a palace—one of those fine vigorously designed mansions, so imposing in simplicity, nicknamed by smug humility—a "cottage," or "villa."

"By jingo, it's noble!" he exclaimed, the exotic dignity of the house dawning on him by degrees as he moved forward and the southern ocean sprang into view, turquoise and amethyst inlaid streak on streak to the still horizon.

"What a chance!" he repeated under his breath; "what a chance for the noblest park ever softened into formality! And the untouched forests beyond!—and the lagoons!—and the dunes to the east—and the sea! Lord, Lord," he whispered with unconscious reverence, "what an Eden!"

One of the white-haired, black-skinned children of men—though the point is locally disputed—looked up from the grass where he squatted gathering ripe fruit under a sapodilla tree; and to an inquiry:

"Yaas-suh, yaas-suh; Mistuh Cahdhoss in de pomelo g'ove, suh, feedin' mud-cat to de wile-puss."

"Doing *what*?"

"Feedin' mud-fish to de wile-cat, de wile lynx-cat, suh." The aged negro rose, hat doffed, juicy traces of forbidden sapodillas on his face which he naïvely removed with the back of the blackest and most grotesquely wrinkled hand Hamil had ever seen.

"Yaas-suh; 'scusin' de 'gator, wile-cat love de mud-fish mostest; yaas, suh. Ole torm-cat he fish de crick lak he was no 'count Seminole trash—"

"One moment, uncle," interrupted Hamil, smiling; "is that the pomelo grove? And is that gentleman yonder Mr. Cardross?"

"Yaas-suh."

He stood silent a moment thoughtfully watching the distant figure through the vista of green leaves, white blossoms, and great clusters of fruit hanging like globes of palest gold in the sun.

"I think," he said absently, "that I'll step over and speak to Mr. Cardross.... Thank you, uncle.... What kind of fruit is that you're gathering?"

"Sappydilla, suh."

Hamil laughed; he had heard that a darky would barter 'possum, ham-bone, and soul immortal for a ripe sapodilla; he had also once, much farther northward, seen the distressing spectacle of Savannah negroes loading a freight car with watermelons; and it struck him now that it was equally rash to commission this aged uncle on any such business as the gathering of sapodillas for family consumption.

The rolling, moist, and guileless eye of the old man whose slightly pained expression made it plain that he divined exactly what Hamil had been thinking, set the young man laughing outright.

"Don't worry, uncle," he said; "they're not my sapodillas"; and he walked toward the pomelo grove, the old man, a picture of outraged innocence, looking after him, thoughtlessly biting into an enormous and juicy specimen of the forbidden fruit as he looked.

There was a high fence of woven wire around the grove; through scented vistas, spotted with sunshine, fruit and blossoms hung together amid tender foliage of glossy green; palms and palmettos stood with broad drooping fronds here and there among the citrus trees, and the brown woody litter which covered the ground was all starred with fallen flowers.

The gate was open, and as Hamil stepped in he met a well-built, active man in white flannels coming out; and both halted abruptly.

"I am looking for Mr. Cardross," said the younger man.

"I am Mr. Cardross."

Hamil nodded. "I mean that I am looking for Mr. Cardross, senior—"

"I am Mr. Cardross, senior."

Hamil gazed at this active gentleman who could scarcely be the father of married children; and yet, as he looked, the crisp, thick hair, the clear sun-bronzed skin which had misled him might after all belong to that type of young-old men less common in America than in England. And Hamil also realised that his hair was silvered, not blond, and that neither the hands nor the eyes of this man were the hands and eyes of youth.

"I am Garret Hamil," he said.

"I recognise you perfectly. I supposed you older—until my daughter showed me your picture in the *News* two weeks ago!"

"I supposed *you* older—until this minute."

"I *am*!"

Looking squarely into each other's faces they laughed and shook hands.

"When did you come, Mr. Hamil?"

"Last night from Nassau."

"Where are you stopping?"

Hamil told him.

"Your rooms are ready here. It's very good of you to come to see me at once—"

"It's very good of you to want me—"

"Want you, man alive! Of course I want you! I'm all on edge over this landscape scheme; I've done nothing since we arrived from the North but ride over and over the place—and I've not half covered it yet. That's the way we'll begin work, isn't it? Knock about together and get a general idea of the country; isn't that the best way?"

"Yes, certainly—"

"I thought so. The way to learn a country is to ride over it, fish over it, shoot over it, sail around it, camp in it—that's my notion of thoroughly understanding a region. If you're going to improve it you've got to care something about it—begin to like it—find pleasure in it, understand it. Isn't that true, Mr. Hamil?"

"Yes—in a measure—"

"Of course it's true," repeated Cardross with his quick engaging laugh; "if a man doesn't care for a thing he's not fitted to alter or modify it. I've often thought that those old French landscape men must have dearly loved the country they made so beautiful—loved it intelligently—for they left so much wild beauty edging the formality of their creations. Do you happen to remember the Chasse at Versailles? And that's what I want here! You don't mind my instructing you in your own profession, do you?"

They both laughed again, apparently qualified to understand one another.

Cardross said: "I'm glad you're young; I'm glad you've come. This is going to be the pleasantest winter of my life. There isn't anything I'd rather do than just this kind of thing—if you'll let me tag after you and talk about it. You don't mind, do you?"

"No, I don't," said Hamil sincerely.

"We'll probably have rows," suggested Cardross; "I may want vistas and terraces and fountains where they ought not to be."

"Oh, no, you won't," replied Hamil, laughing; "you'll understand things when I give reasons."

"That's what I want—reasons. If anybody would only give me reasons!—but nobody does. Listen; will you come up to the house with me and meet my family? And then you'll lunch with them—I've a business luncheon at the club—unfortunately—but I'll come back. Meanwhile there'll be somebody to show you about, or you can run out to the Inlet in one of the motor-boats if you like, or do anything you like that may amuse you; the main thing is for you to be amused, to find this place agreeable, to like this kind of country, to like us. *Then* you can do good work, Mr. Hamil."

A grinning negro shuffled up and closed the gate as they left the grove together and started across the lawn. Cardross, cordial in his quick, vigorous manner, strolled with his hands in his coat pockets, planting each white-shod foot firmly as he walked, frequently turning head and shoulders squarely toward his companion when speaking.

He must have been over fifty; he did not appear forty; still, on closer and more detailed inspection Hamil understood how much his alert, well-made figure had to do with the first impression of youth. Yet his expression had nothing in it of that shadow which falls with years—nothing to show to the world that he had once taken the world by the throat and wrung a fortune out of it—nothing of the hard gravity or the underlying sadness of almost ruthless success, and the responsibility for it.

Yet, from the first, Hamil had been aware of all that was behind this unstudied frankness, this friendly vigour. There was a man, there—every inch a man, but exactly of what sort the younger man had not yet decided.

A faded and very stout lady, gowned with elaborate simplicity, yet somehow suggesting well-bred untidiness, rolled toward them, propelled in a wheeled-chair by a black servant.

"Dear," said Mr. Cardross, "this is Mr. Hamil." And Mrs. Cardross offered him her chubby hand and said a little more than he expected. Then, to her husband, languidly:

"They're playing tennis, Neville. If Mr. Hamil would care to play there are tennis-shoes belonging to Gray and Acton."

"Thank you, Mrs. Cardross," said Hamil, "but, as a matter of fact, I am not yet acclimated."

"You feel a little sleepy?" drawled Mrs. Cardross, maternally solicitous; "everybody does for the first few days." And to her husband: "Jessie and Cecile are playing; Shiela must be somewhere about—You will lunch with us, Mr. Hamil? There's to be a tennis luncheon under the oaks—we'd really like to have you if you can stay."

Hamil accepted as simply as the invitation was given; Mrs. Cardross exchanged a few words with her husband in that perfectly natural drawl which at first might have been mistaken for languid affectation; then she smiled at Hamil and turned around in her basket chair, parasol tilted, and the black boy began slowly pedalling her away across the lawn.

"We'll step over to the tennis-courts," said Cardross, replacing the straw hat which he had removed to salute his wife; "they're having a sort of scratch-tournament I believe—my daughters and some other young people. I think you'll find the courts rather pretty."

The grounds were certainly quaint; spaces for four white marl courts had been cleared, hewn out of the solid jungle which walled them in with a noble living growth of live oak, cedar, magnolia, and palmetto. And on these courts a very gay company of young people in white were playing or applauding the players while the snowy balls flew across the nets and the resonant blows of the bats rang out.

And first Mr. Cardross presented Hamil to his handsome married daughter, Mrs. Acton Carrick, a jolly, freckled, young matron who showed her teeth when she smiled and shook hands like her father; and then he was made known to the youngest daughter, Cecile Cardross, small, plump, and sun-tanned, with ruddy hair and mischief in every feature.

There was, also, a willowy Miss Staines and a blond Miss Anan, and a very young Mr. Anan—a brother—and a grave and gaunt Mr. Gatewood and a stout Mr. Ellison, and a number of others less easy to remember.

"This wholesale introduction business is always perplexing," observed Cardross; "but they'll all remember you, and after a time you'll begin to distinguish them from the shrubbery. No"—as Mrs. Carrick asked Hamil if he cared to play—"he would rather look on this time, Jessie. Go ahead; we are not interrupting you; where is Shiela—"

And Hamil, chancing to turn, saw her, tennis-bat tucked under one bare arm, emerging from the jungle path; and at the same instant she caught sight of him. Both little chalked shoes stood stockstill—for a second only—then she came forward, leisurely, continuing to eat the ripe guava with which she had been occupied.

Cardross, advancing, said: "This is Mr. Hamil, dearest; and," to the young man: "My daughter Shiela."

She nodded politely.

"Now I've got to go, Shiela," continued Cardross. "Hamil, you'll amuse yourself, won't you, until I return after luncheon? Shiela, Mr. Hamil doesn't care to play tennis; so if you'll find out what he does care to do—" He saluted the young people gaily and started across the lawn where a very black boy with a chair stood ready to convey him to the village and across the railroad tracks to that demure little flower-embowered cottage the interior of which presents such an amazing contrast to the exterior.

CHAPTER VI
ARMISTICE

The young girl beside him had finished her guava, and now, idly swinging her tennis-bat, stood watching the games in the sunken courts below.

"Please don't consider me a burden," he said. "I would be very glad to sit here and watch you play."

"I have been playing, thank you."

"But you won't let me interfere with anything that—"

"No, Mr. Hamil, I won't let you interfere—with anything."

She stood swinging her bat, apparently preoccupied with her own thoughts—like a very grave goddess, he thought, glancing at her askance—a very young goddess, immersed in celestial reverie far beyond mortal comprehension.

"Do you like guavas?" she inquired. And, closing her own question: "But you had better not until you are acclimated. Do you feel *very* sleepy, Mr. Hamil?"

"No, I don't," he said.

"Oh! You ought to conform to tradition. There's a particularly alluring hammock on the veranda."

"To get rid of me is it necessary to make me take a nap?" he protested.

"So you refuse to go to sleep?"

"I certainly do."

She sighed and tucked the tennis-bat under her left arm. "Come," she said, moving forward, "my father will ask me what I have done to amuse you, and I had better hunt up something to tell him about. You'll want to see the groves of course—"

"Yes, but I'm not going to drag you about with me—"

"Come," she repeated; and as he stood his ground obstinately: "Please?"—with a rising inflection hinting at command.

"Why on earth don't you play tennis and let me sit and watch you?" he asked, joining and keeping step with her.

"Why do you ask a woman for reasons, Mr. Hamil?"

"It's too bad to spoil your morning—"

"I know it; so in revenge I'm going to spoil yours. Our trip is called 'Seeing Florida,' so you must listen to your guide very attentively. This is a pomelo grove—thank you," to the negro who opened the gate—"here you see blossoms and ripe fruit together on the same tree. A few palmettos have been planted here for various agricultural reasons. This is a camphor bush"—touching it with her bat—"the leaves when crushed in the palm exhale a delightful fragr—"

"Calypso!"

She turned toward him with coldest composure. "*That* never happened, Mr. Hamil."

"No," he said, "it never did."

A slight colour remained in his face; hers was cool enough.

"Did you think it happened?" she asked. He shook his head. "No," he repeated seriously, "I know that it never happened."

She said: "If you are quite sure it never happened, there is no harm in pretending it did.... What was it you called me?"

"I could never remember, Miss Cardross—unless you tell me."

"Then I'll tell you—if you are quite sure you don't remember. You called me 'Calypso.'"

And looking up he surprised the rare laughter in her eyes.

"You are rather nice after all," she said, "or is it only that I have you under such rigid discipline? But it was very bad taste in you to recall so crudely what never occurred—until I gave you the liberty to do it. Don't you think so?"

"Yes, I do," he said. "I've made two exhibitions of myself since I knew you—"

"*One*, Mr. Hamil. Please recollect that I am scarcely supposed to know how many exhibitions of yourself you may have made before we were formally presented."

She stood still under a tree which drooped like a leaf-tufted umbrella, and she said, swinging her racket: "You will always have me at a disadvantage. Do you know it?"

"That is utterly impossible!"

"Is it? Do you mean it?"

"I do with all my heart—"

"Thank you; but do you mean it with all your logical intelligence, too?"

"Yes, of course I do."

She stood, head partly averted, one hand caressing the smooth, pale-yellow fruit which hung in heavy clusters around her. And all around her, too, the delicate white blossoms poured out fragrance, and the giant swallow-tail butterflies in gold and black fluttered and floated among the blossoms or clung to them as though stupefied by their heavy sweetness.

"I wish we had begun—differently," she mused.

"I don't wish it."

She said, turning on him almost fiercely: "You persisted in talking to me in the boat; you contrived to make yourself interesting without being offensive—I don't know how you managed it! And then—last night—I was not myself.... And then—*that* happened!"

"Could anything more innocent have happened?"

"Something far more dignified could have happened when I heard you say 'Calypso.'" She shrugged her shoulders. "It's done; we've misbehaved; and you will have to be dreadfully careful. You will, won't you? And yet I shall certainly hate you heartily if you make any difference between me and other women. Oh, dear!—Oh, dear! The whole situation is just unimportant enough to be irritating. Mr. Hamil, I don't think I care for you very much."

And as he looked at her with a troubled smile, she added:

"You must not take that declaration *too* literally. Can you forget—various things?" "I don't want to, Miss Cardross. Listen: nobody could be more sweet, more simple, more natural than the girl I spoke to—I dreamed that I talked with—last night. I don't want to forget that night, or that girl. Must I?"

"Are you, in your inmost thoughts, fastidious in thinking of that girl? Is there any reservation, any hesitation?"

He said, meeting her eyes: "She is easily the nicest girl I ever met—the very nicest. Do you think that I might have her for a friend?"

"Do you mean this girl, Calypso?"

"Yes."

"Then I think that she will return to you the exact measure of friendship that you offer her.... Because, Mr. Hamil, she is after all not very old in years, and a little sensitive and impressionable."

He thought to himself: "She is a rather curious mixture of impulse and reason; of shyness and audacity; of composure and timidity; of courage and cowardice and experience. But there is in her no treachery; nothing mentally unwholesome."

They stood silent a moment smiling at each other rather seriously; then her smooth hand slid from his, and she drew a light breath.

"What a relief!" she said.

"What?"

"To know you are the kind of man I knew you were. That sounds rather Irish, doesn't it?..." And under her breath—"perhaps it is. God knows!" Her face grew very grave for a moment, then, as she turned and looked at him, the shadow fell.

"Do you know—it was absurd of course—but I could scarcely sleep last night for sheer dread of your coming to-day. And yet I knew what sort of a man you must be; and this morning"—she shook her head—"I couldn't endure any breakfast, and I usually endure lots; so I took a spin down the lake in my chair. When I saw you just now I was trying to brace up on a guava. Listen to me: I am hungry!"

"You poor little thing—"

"Sympathy satisfies sentiment but appetite prefers oranges. Shall we eat oranges together and become friendly and messy? Are you even *that* kind of a man? Oh, then if you really are, there's a mixed grove just beyond."

So together, shoulder to shoulder, keeping step, they passed through the new grove with its enormous pendent bunches of grape-fruit, and into a second grove where limes and mandarins hung among clusters of lemons and oranges; where kum-quat bushes stood stiffly, studded with egg-shaped, orange-tinted fruit; where tangerines, grape-fruit, and king-oranges grew upon the same tree, and the deep scarlet of ripe Japanese persimmons and the huge tattered fronds of banana trees formed a riotous background.

"This tree!" she indicated briefly, reaching up; and her hand was white even among the milky orange bloom—he noticed that as he bent down a laden bough for her.

"Pine-oranges," she said, "the most delicious of all. I'll pick and you hold the branch. And please get me a few tangerines—those blood-tangerines up there.... Thank you; and two Japanese persimmons—and two more for yourself.... Have you a knife? Very well; now, break a fan from that saw-palmetto and sweep a place for me on the ground—that way. And now please look very carefully to see if there are any spiders. No spiders? No scorpions? No wood-ticks? Are you sure?"

"There *may* be a bandersnatch," he said doubtfully, dusting the ground with his palmetto fan.

She laughed and seated herself on the ground, drew down her short white tennis-skirt as far as it would go over her slim ankles, looked up at him confidently, holding out her hand for his knife.

"We are going to be delightfully messy in a moment," she said; "let me show you how they prepare an orange in Florida. This is for you—you must take it.... And this is for me. The rind is all gone, you see. Now, Ulysses. This is the magic moment!"

And without further ceremony her little teeth met in the dripping golden pulp; and in another moment Hamil was imitating her.

They appeared to be sufficiently hungry; the brilliant rind, crinkling, fell away in golden corkscrews from orange after orange, and still they ate on, chattering away together between oranges.

"Isn't this primitive luxury, Mr. Hamil? We ought to wear our bathing-clothes.... Don't dare take my largest king-orange! Yes—you may have it;—I won't take it.... Are you being amused? My father said that you were to be amused. What in the world are you staring at?"

"That!" said Hamil, eyes widening. "What on earth—"

"Oh, that's nothing—that is our watchman. We have to employ somebody to watch our groves, you know, or all the negroes in Florida would be banqueting here. So we have that watchman yonder—"

"But it's a *bird*!" insisted Hamil, "a big gray, long-legged, five-foot bird with a scarlet head!"

"Of course," said the girl serenely; "it's a crane. His name is Alonzo; he's four feet high; and he's horridly savage. If you came in here without father or me or some of the workmen who know him, Alonzo would begin to dance at you, flapping his wings, every plume erect; and if you didn't run he'd attack you. That big, dagger-like bill of his is an atrocious weapon."

The crane resembled a round-shouldered, thin-legged old gentleman with his hands tucked under his coat-tails; and as he came up, tiptoeing and peering slyly at Hamil out of two bright evil-looking eyes, the girl raised her arm and threw a kum-quat at him so accurately that the bird veered off with a huge hop of grieved astonishment.

"Alonzo! Go away this instant!" she commanded. And to Hamil: "He's disgustingly treacherous; he'll sidle up behind you if he can. Give me that palmetto fan."

But the bird saw her rise, and hastily retreated to the farther edge of the grove, where presently they saw him pretending to hunt snails and lizards as innocently as though premeditated human assassination was farthest from his thoughts.

There was a fountain with a coquina basin in the grove; and here they washed the orange juice from their hands and dried them on their handkerchiefs.

"Would you like to see Tommy Tiger?" she asked. "I'm taming him."

"Very much," he said politely.

"Well, he's in there somewhere," pointing to a section of bushy jungle edging the grove and around which was a high heavy fence of closely woven buffalo wire. "Here, Tommy, Tommy, Tommy!" she called, in her fresh young voice that, at times, broke deliciously in a childish grace-note.

At first Hamil could see nothing in the tangle of brier and saw-palmetto, but after a while he became aware of a wild-cat, tufted ears flattenend, standing in the shadow of a striped bush and looking at him out of the greenest eyes he had ever beheld.

"Pretty Tom," said the girl caressingly. "Tommy, come and let Shiela scratch his ears."

And the lynx, disdainfully shifting its blank green gaze from Hamil, hoisted an absurd stub of a tail and began rubbing its lavishly whiskered jowl against the bush. Nearer and nearer sidled the lithe grayish animal, cautiously the girl advanced, until the cat was rubbing cheek and flank against the woven-wire fence. Then, with infinite precaution, she extended her hand, touched the flat fierce head, and slowly began to rub it.

"Don't!" said Hamil, stepping forward; and at the sound of his voice and step the cat whirled and struck, and the girl sprang back, white to the lips.

For a moment she said nothing, then looked up at Hamil beside her, as pale as she.

"I am not hurt," she said, "only startled."

"I should not have spoken," he faltered. "What an ass I am!"

"It is all right; I ought to have cautioned you about moving or speaking. I thought you understood—but please don't look that way, Mr. Hamil. It was not your fault and I am not hurt. Which teaches me a lesson, I hope. What is the moral?—don't attempt to caress the impossible?—or something similarly senseless," she added gaily. And turning on the crouching lynx: "Bad Tommy! Wicked, treacherous, *bad*—no! *Poor* old Tom! You are quite right. I'd do the same if I were trapped and anybody tried to patronize me. I know how you feel—yes, I do, Tommy Tiger. And I'll tell old Jonas to give you lots and lots of delicious mud-fish for your dinner to-night—yes, I will, my friend. Also some lavender to roll on.... Mr. Hamil, you are still unusually colourless. Were you really afraid?"

"Horribly."

"Oh, the wire is too strong for him to break out," she observed coolly.

"I was not afraid of that," he retorted, reddening.

She turned toward him, smilingly remorseful.

"I know it! I say such things—I don't know why. You will learn how to take them, won't you?"

They walked on, passing through grove after grove, Alonzo tiptoeing after them, and when, as a matter of precaution from time to time, Shiela looked back, the bird pretended not to see them until they passed the last gate and locked it. Then the great crane, half flying, half running, charged at the closed gate, dancing and bounding about; and long after they were out of sight Alonzo's discordant metallic shrieks rang out in baffled fury from among the trees.

They had come into a wide smooth roadway flanked by walks shaded by quadruple rows of palms. Oleander and hibiscus hedges ran on either side as far as the eye could see, and long brilliant flower-beds stretched away into gorgeous perspective.

"This is stunning," he said, staring about him.

"It is our road to the ocean, about two miles long," she explained. "My father designed it; do you really like it?"

"Yes, I do," he said sincerely; "and I scarcely understand why Mr. Cardross has called me into consultation if this is the way he can do things."

"That is generous of you. Father will be very proud and happy when I tell him."

They were leaning over the rail of a stone bridge together; the clear stream below wound through thickets of mangrove, bamboo, and flowering vines all a-flutter with butterflies; a school of fish stemmed the current with winnowing fins; myriads of brown and gold dragon-flies darted overhead.

"It's fairyland—the only proper setting for you after all," he said.

Resting one elbow on the stone parapet, her cheek in the hollow of her hand, she watched the smile brightening in his face, but responded only faintly to it.

"Some day," she said, "when we have blown the froth and sparkle from our scarcely tasted cup of acquaintance, you will talk to me of serious things sometimes—will you not?"

"Why—yes," he said, surprised.

"I mean—as you would to a man. You will find me capable of understanding you. You once said to me, in a boat, that no two normal people of opposite sex can meet without experiencing more or less wholesome interest in one another. Didn't you say that? Very well, then; I now admit my normal interest in you—untinged by sentiment. Don't disappoint me."

He said whimsically: "I'm not intellectual; I don't know very much about anything except my profession."

"Then talk to me about it. Goodness! Don't I deserve it? Is a girl to violate precept and instinct on an ill-considered impulse only to find the man in the case was not worth it? And how do you know what else I violated—merely to be kind. I must have been mad to do it!"

He flushed up so vividly that she winced, then added quickly: "I didn't mean that, Mr. Hamil; I knew you were worth it when I did it."

"The worst of it is that I am not," he said. "I'm like everybody who has been through college and chooses a profession for love of it. I do know something about that profession; outside of it, the least I can say for myself is that I care about everything that goes on in this very jolly world. Curiosity has led me about by the nose. The result is a series of acquired smatterings."

She regarded him intently with that clear gaze he found so refreshing—a direct, fearless scrutiny which straightened her eyebrows to a fascinating level and always made him think of a pagan marble, with delicately chiselled, upcurled lips, and white brow youthfully grave.

"Did you study abroad?"

"Yes—not long enough."

She seemed rather astonished at this. Amused, he rested both elbows on the parapet, looking at her from between the strong, lean hands that framed his face.

"It was droll—the way I managed to scurry like a jack-rabbit through school and college on nothing a year. I was obliged to hurry post-graduate courses and Europe and such agreeable things. Otherwise I would probably be more interesting to you—"

"You are sufficiently interesting," she said, flushing up at his wilful misinterpretation.

And, as he laughed easily:

"The horrid thing about it is that you *are* interesting and you know it. All I asked of you was to be seriously interesting to me—occasionally; and instead you are rude—"

"Rude!"

"Yes, you are!—pretending that I was disappointed in you because you hadn't dawdled around Europe for years in the wake of an education. You are, apparently, just about the average sort of man one meets—yet I kicked over several conventions for the sake of exchanging a few premature words with you, knowing all the while I was to meet you later. It certainly was not for your beaux yeux; I am not sentimental!" she added fiercely. "And it was not because you are a celebrity—you are not one yet, you know. Something in you certainly appealed to something reckless in me; yet I did not really feel very sinful when I let you speak to me; and, even in the boat, I admit frankly that I enjoyed every word that we spoke—though I didn't appear to, did I?"

"No, you didn't," he said.

She smiled, watching him, chin on hand.

"I wonder how you'll like this place," she mused. "It's gay—in a way. There are things to do every moment if you let people rob you of your time—dances, carnivals, races, gambling, suppers. There's the Fortnightly Club, and various charities too, and dinners and teas and all sorts of things to do outdoors on land and on water. Are you fond of shooting?"

"Very. I *can* do that pretty well."

"So can I. We'll go with my father and Gray. Gray is my brother; you'll meet him at luncheon. What time is it?"

He looked at his watch. "Eleven—a little after."

"We're missing the bathing. Everybody splashes about the pool or the ocean at this hour. Then everybody sits on the veranda of *The Breakers* and drinks things and gossips until luncheon. Rather intellectual, isn't it?"

"Sufficiently," he replied lazily.

She leaned over the parapet, standing on the tips of her white shoes and looked down at the school of fish. Presently she pointed to a snake swimming against the current.

"A moccasin?" he asked.

"No, only a water snake. They call everything moccasins down here, but real moccasins are not very common."

"And rattlesnakes?"

"Scarcer still. You hear stories, but—" She shrugged her shoulders. "Of course when we are quail shooting it's well to look where you step, but there are more snakes in the latitude of Saint Augustine than there are here. When father and I are shooting we never think anything about them. I'm more afraid of those horrid wood-ticks. Listen; shall we go camping?"

"But I have work on hand," he said dejectedly.

"That is part of your work. Father said so. Anyway I know he means to camp with you somewhere in the hammock, and if Gray goes I go too."

"Calypso," he said, "do you know what I've been hearing about you? I've heard that you are the most assiduously run-after girl at Palm Beach. And if you are, what on earth will the legions of the adoring say when you take to the jungle?"

"Who said that about me?" she asked, smiling adorably.

"Is it true?"

"I am—liked. Who said it?"

"You don't mean to say," he continued perversely, "that I have monopolised the reigning beauty of Palm Beach for an entire morning."

"Yes, you have and it is high time you understood it. *Who* said this to *you*?"

"Well—I gathered the fact—"

"Who?"

"My aunt—Miss Palliser."

"Do you know," said Shiela Cardross slowly, "that Miss Palliser has been exceedingly nice to me? But her friend, Miss Suydam, is not very civil."

"I'm awfully sorry," he said.

"I could tell you that it mattered nothing," she said, looking straight at him; "and that would be an untruth. I know that many people disregard such things—many are indifferent to the opinion of others, or say they are. I never have been; I want everybody to like me—even people I have not the slightest interest in—people I do not even know—I want them all to like me. For I must tell you, Mr. Hamil, that when anybody dislikes me, and I know it, I am just as unhappy about it as though I cared for them."

"It's absurd for anybody not to like you!" he said.

"Well, do you know it really is absurd—if they only knew how willing I am to like everybody.... I was inclined to like Miss Suydam."

Hamil remained silent.

The girl added: "One does not absolutely disregard the displeasure of such people."

"They didn't some years ago when there were no shops on Fifth Avenue and gentlemen wore side-whiskers," said Hamil, smiling.

Shiela Cardross shrugged. "I'm sorry; I was inclined to like her. She misses more than I do because we are a jolly and amusing family. It's curious how much energy is wasted disliking people. Who is Miss Suydam?"

"She's a sort of a relative. I have always known her. I'm sorry she was rude. She is sometimes."

They said no more about her or about his aunt; and presently they moved on again, luncheon being imminent.

"You will like my sister, Mrs. Carrick," said Shiela tranquilly. "You know her husband, Acton, don't you? He's at Miami fishing."

"Oh, yes; I've met him at the club. He's very agreeable."

"He *is* jolly. And Jessie—Mrs. Carrick—is the best fun in the world. And you are sure to like my little sister Cecile; every man adores her, and you'll do it, too—yes, I mean sentimentally—until she laughs you out of it."

"Like yourself, Calypso, I'm not inclined to sentiment," he said.

"You can't help it with Cecile. Wait! Then there are others to lunch with us—Marjorie Staines—very popular with men, and Stephanie Anan—you studied with her uncle, Winslow Anan, didn't you?"

"Yes, indeed!" he exclaimed warmly, "but how did you—"

"Oh, I knew it; I know lots about you, you see.... Then there is Phil Gatewood—a perfectly splendid fellow, and Alex Anan—a dear boy, ready to adore any girl who looks sideways at him.... I don't remember who else is to lunch with us, except my brother Gray. Look, Mr. Hamil! They've actually sat down to luncheon without waiting for us! What horrid incivility! Could your watch have been wrong?—or have we been too deeply absorbed?"

"I can speak for one of us," he said, as they came out upon the lawn in full view of the table which was spread under the most beautiful live-oaks he had ever seen.

Everybody was very friendly. Gray Cardross, a nice-looking boy who wore spectacles, collected butterflies, and did not look like a "speed-mad cub," took Hamil to the house, whither Shiela had already retired for an ante-prandial toilet; but there is no dust in that part of the world, and his preparations were quickly made.

"Awfully glad you came," repeated young Cardross with all the excessive cordiality of the young and unspoiled. "Father has been checking off the days on the calendar since your letter saying you were coming by way of Nassau. The Governor is dying to begin operations on that jungle yonder. When we camp I'm going—and probably Shiela is—she began clamoring to go two weeks ago. We all had an idea that you were a rather feeble old gentleman—like Mr. Anan—until Shiela brought us the picture they published of you in the paper two weeks ago; and she said immediately that if you were young enough to camp she was old enough to go too. She's a good shot, Mr. Hamil, and she won't interfere with your professional duties—"

"I should think not!" said Hamil cordially; "but—as for my camping— there's really almost nothing left for me to do except to familiarise myself with the character of your wilderness. Your father tells me he has the surveys and contour maps all ready. As a matter of fact I really could begin the office work at once—"

"For Heaven's sake don't do that! and don't say it!" exclaimed the young fellow in dismay. "Father and Shiela and I are counting on this trip. There's a butterfly or two I want to get at Ruffle Lake. Don't you think it extremely necessary that you go over the entire territory?—become thoroughly saturated with the atmosphere and—"

"Malaria?" suggested Hamil, laughing. "Of course, seriously, it will be simply fine. And perhaps it is the best thing to do for a while. Please don't mistake me; I *want* to do it; I—I've never before had a vacation like this. It's like a trip into paradise from the sordid horror of Broadway. Only," he added slowly as they left the house and started toward the luncheon party under the live-oaks, "I should like to have your father know that I am ready to give him every moment of my time."

"That's what he wants—and so do I," said young Cardross.... "Hello! Here's Shiela back before us! I'd like to sit near enough to talk to you, but Shiela is between us. I'll tell you after luncheon what we propose to do on this trip."

A white servant seated Hamil on Mrs. Cardross's right; and for a while that languid but friendly lady drawled amiable trivialities to him, propounding the tritest questions with an air of pleased profundity, replying to his observations with harmlessly complacent platitudes—a good woman, every inch of her—one who had never known an unkindly act or word in the circle of her own family—one who had always been accustomed to honor, deference, and affection—of whom nothing more had ever been demanded than the affections of a good wife and a good mother.

Being very, very stout, and elaborately upholstered, a shady hammock couch suited her best; and as she was eternally dieting and was too stout to sit comfortably, she never remained very long at table.

Gray escorted her houseward in the midst of the festivities. She nodded a gracious apology to all, entered her wheel-chair, and was rolled heavily away for her daily siesta.

Everybody appeared to be friendly to him, even cordial. Mrs. Acton Carrick talked to him in her pretty, decisive, animated manner, a feminine reflection of her father's characteristic energy and frankness.

Her younger sister, Cecile, possessed a drawl like her mother's. Petite, distractingly pretty, Hamil recognised immediately her attraction—experienced it, amused himself by yielding to it as he exchanged conventionally preliminary observations with her across the table.

Men, on first acquaintance, were usually very easily captivated, for she had not only all the general attraction of being young, feminine, and unusually ornamental, but she also possessed numberless individualities like a rapid fire of incarnations, which since she was sixteen had kept many a young man, good and true, madly guessing which was the real Cecile. And yet all the various and assorted Ceciles seemed equally desirable, susceptible, and eternally on the verge of being rounded up and captured; that was the worst of it; and no young man she had ever known had wholly relinquished hope. For even in the graceful act of side-stepping the smitten, the girl's eyes and lips seemed unconsciously to unite in a gay little unspoken promise—"This serial story is to be continued in our next—perhaps."

As for the other people at the table Hamil began to distinguish one from another by degrees; the fair-haired Anans, sister and brother, who spoke of their celebrated uncle, Winslow Anan, and his predictions concerning Hamil as his legitimate successor; Marjorie Staines, willowy, active, fresh as a stem of white jasmine, and inconsequent as a very restless bird; Philip Gatewood, grave, thin, prematurely saddened by the responsibility of a vast inheritance, consumed by a desire for an artistic career, looking at the world with his owlish eyes through the prismatic colors of a set palette.

There were others there whom as yet he had been unable to differentiate; smiling, well-mannered, affable people who chattered with more or less intimacy among themselves as though accustomed to meeting one another year after year in this winter rendezvous. And everywhere he felt the easy, informal friendliness and goodwill of these young people.

"Are you being amused?" asked Shiela beside him. "My father's orders, you know," she added demurely.

They stood up as Mrs. Carrick rose and left the table followed by the others; and he looked at Shiela expecting her to imitate her sister's example. As she did not, he waited beside her, his cigarette unlighted.

Presently she bent over the table, extended her arm, and lifted a small burning lamp of silver toward him; and, thanking her, he lighted his cigarette.

"Siesta?" she asked.

"No; I feel fairly normal."

"That's abnormal in Florida. But if you really don't feel sleepy—if you really don't—we'll get the *Gracilis*—our fastest motor-boat—and run down to the Beach Club and get father. Shall we—just you and I?"

"And the engineer?"

"I'll run the *Gracilis* if you will steer," she said quietly.

"I'll do whichever you wish, Calypso, steer or run things."

She looked up with that quick smile which seemed to transfigure her into something a little more than mortal.

"Why in the world have I ever been afraid of you?" she said. "Will you come? I think our galley is in commission.... Once I told you that Calypso was a land-nymph. But—time changes us all, you know—and as nobody reads the classics any longer nobody will perceive the anachronism."

"Except ourselves."

"Except ourselves, Ulysses; and we'll forgive each other." She took a step out from the shadow of the oaks' foliage into the white sunlight and turned, looking back at him.

And he followed, as did his heroic namesake in the golden noon of the age of fable.

As they came in sight of the sea he halted.

"That's curious!" he exclaimed; "there is the *Ariani* again!"

"The yacht you came on?"

"Yes. I wonder if there's been an accident. She cleared for Miami last night."

They stood looking at the white steamer for a moment.

"I hope everything's all right with the *Ariani*" he murmured; then turned to the girl beside him.

"By the way I have a message for you from a man on board; I forgot to deliver it."

"A message for *me*?"

"From a very ornamental young man who desired to be particularly remembered to Shiela Cardross until he could pay his respects in person. Can you guess?"

For a moment she looked at him with a tremor of curiosity and amusement edging her lips.

"Louis Malcourt," he said, smiling; and turned again to the sea.

A sudden, still, inward fright seized her; the curious soundless crash of her own senses followed—as though all within had given way.

She had known many, many such moments; one was upon her now, the clutching terror of it seeming to stiffen the very soul within her.

"I hope all's well with the *Ariani*" he repeated under his breath, staring at the sea.

Miss Cardross said nothing.

CHAPTER VII
A CHANGE OF BASE

February, the gayest winter month on the East Coast, found the winter resorts already overcrowded. Relays and consignments of fashion arrived and departed on every train; the permanent winter colony, composed of those who owned or rented villas and those who remained for the three months at either of the great hotels, had started the season vigorously. Dances, dinners, lawn fêtes, entertainments for local churches and charities left little time for anything except the routine of the bathing-hour, the noon gathering at "The Breakers," and tea during the concert.

Every day beach, pier, and swimming-pool were thronged; every day the white motor-cars rushed southward to Miami, and the swift power-boats sped northward to the Inlet; and the house-boat rendezvous rang with the gay laughter of pretty women, and the restaurant of the Beach Club flashed with their jewels.

Dozens of villas had begun their series of house-parties; attractive girls held court everywhere—under coco-palm and hibiscus, along the beach, on the snowy decks of yachts; agreeable girls fished from the pier, pervaded bazaars for charity, sauntered, bare of elbow and throat, across the sandy links; adorable girls appeared everywhere, on veranda, in canoes, in wheel-chairs, in the surf and out of it—everywhere youth and beauty decorated the sun-drenched landscape. And Hamil thought that he had never before beheld so many ornamental women together in any one place except in his native city; certainly, nowhere had he ever encountered such a heterogeneous mixture of all the shades, nuances, tints, hues, and grades which enter into the warp and weft of the American social fabric; and he noticed some colours that do not enter into that fabric at all.

East, West, North, and South sent types of those worthy citizens who upheld local social structures; the brilliant migrants were there also—samples of the gay, wealthy, over-accented floating population of great cities—the rich and homeless and restless—those who lived and had their social being in the gorgeous and expensive hotels; who had neither firesides nor taxes nor fixed social obligations to worry them, nor any of the trying civic or routine duties devolving upon permanent inhabitants—the jewelled throngers of the horse-shows and motor-shows, and theatres, and night restaurants—the people, in fact, who make ocean-liners, high prices, and the metropolis possible, and the name of their country blinked at abroad. For it is not your native New Yorker who supports the continual fête from the Bronx to the sea and carries it over-seas for a Parisian summer.

Then, too, the truly good were there—the sturdy, respectable, and sometimes dowdy good; also the intellectuals—for ten expensive days at a time—for it is a deplorable fact that the unworthy frivolous monopolise all the money in the world! And there, too, were excursionists from East and West and North and South, tired, leaden-eyed, uncomfortable, eating luncheons on private lawns, trooping to see some trained alligators in a muddy pool, resting by roadsides and dunes in the apathy of repletion, the sucked orange suspended to follow with narrowing eyes the progress of some imported hat or gown.

And the bad were there; not the very, very bad perhaps; but the doubtful; over-jewelled, over-tinted of lip and brow and cheek, with shoes too shapely and waists too small and hair too bright and wavy, and—but dusty alpaca and false front cannot do absolute justice to a pearl collar and a gown of lace; and tired, toil-dimmed eyes may make mistakes, especially as it is already a tradition that America goes to Palm Beach to cut up shindies, or watch others do it.

So they were all there, the irreproachable, the amusing, the inevitable, the intellectual, the good, and the bad, the onduléd, and the scant of hair.

And, belonging to one or more of these divisions, Portlaw, Wayward, and Malcourt were there—had been there, now, for several weeks, the latter as a guest at the Cardross villa. For the demon of caprice had seized on Wayward, and half-way to Miami he had turned back for no reason under the sun apparently—though Constance Palliser had been very glad to see him after so many years.

The month had made a new man of Hamil. For one thing he had become more or less acclimated; he no longer desired to sleep several times a day, he could now assimilate guavas without disaster, and walk about without acquiring headaches or deluging himself in perspiration. For another he was enchanted with his work and with Shiela Cardross, and with the entire Cardross family.

The month had been a busy one for him. When he was not in the saddle with Neville Cardross the work in the new office and draughting-room required his close attention. Already affairs were moving briskly; he had leased a cottage for his office work; draughtsmen had arrived and were fully occupied, half a dozen contractors appeared on the spot, also a forester and assistants, and a surveyor and staff. And the energetic Mr. Cardross, also, was enjoying every minute of his life.

Hamil's plan for the great main park with its terraces, miles of shell and marl drives, its lakes, bridges, arbours, pools, shelters, canals, fully satisfied Cardross. Hamil's engineers were still occupied with the drainage problem, but a happy solution was now in sight. Woodcutters had already begun work on the great central forest avenue stretching straight away for four miles between green jungles topped by giant oaks, magnolias, and palmettos; lesser drives and chair trails were being planned, blazed, and traced out; sample coquina concrete blocks had been delivered, and a rickety narrow-gauge railroad was now being installed with spidery branches reaching out through the monotonous flat woods and creeping around the boundaries where a nine-foot game-proof fence of woven buffalo wire was being erected on cypress posts by hundreds of negroes. Around this went a telephone and telegraph wire connected with the house and the gamekeeper's lodges.

Beyond the vast park lay an unbroken wilderness. This had already been surveyed and there remained nothing to do except to pierce it with a wide main trail and erect a few patrol camps of palmetto logs within convenient reach of the duck-haunted lagoons.

And now toward the end of the month, as contractor after contractor arrived with gangs of negroes and were swallowed up in the distant woodlands, the interest in the Cardross household became acute. From the front entrance of the house guests and family could see the great avenue which was being cleared through the forest—could see the vista growing hour by hour as the huge trees swayed, bent, and came crashing earthward. Far away the noise of the felling sounded, softened by distance; snowy jets of steam puffed up above the trees, the panting of a toy locomotive came on the breeze, the mean, crescendo whine of a saw-mill.

"It's the only way to do things," said Cardross again and again; "make up your mind quickly that you want to do them, then do them quickly. I have no patience with a man who'll dawdle about a bit of property for years and finally start to improve it with a pot of geraniums after he's too old to enjoy anything except gruel. When I plant a tree I don't plant a sapling; I get a machine and four horses and a dozen men and I put in a full-grown tree so that I can sit under it next day if I wish to and not spend thirty years waiting for it to grow. Isn't that the way to do things, Hamil?"

Hamil said yes. It was certainly the way to accomplish things—the modern millionaire's way; but the majority of people had to do a little waiting before they could enjoy their vine and fig-tree.

Cardross sat down beside his wife, who was reading in a hammock chair, and gazed at the new vista through a pair of field-glasses.

"Gad, Hamil!" he said with considerable feeling, "I hate to see a noble tree go down; it's like murder to me. But it's the only thing to do, isn't it? The French understand the value of magnificent distances. What a glorious vista that will make, four miles straight away walled in by deathless green, and the blue lagoon sparkling at the end of the perspective! I love it, I tell you. I love it!"

"It will be very fine," said Hamil. His voice sounded a trifle tired. He had ridden many miles since sunrise. There was marl on his riding-breeches.

Cardross continued to examine the work in progress through his binoculars. Presently he said:

"You've been overdoing it, haven't you, Hamil? My wife says so."

"Overdoing it?" repeated the young man, not understanding. "Overdoing what?"

"I mean you've a touch of malaria; you've been working a little too hard."

"He has indeed," drawled Mrs. Cardross, laying aside her novel; and, placidly ignoring Hamil's protests: "Neville, you drag him about through those dreadful swamps before he is acclimated, and you keep him up half the night talking plans and making sketches. He is too young to work like that."

Hamil turned red; but it was impossible to resent or mistake the kindly solicitude of this very large and leisurely lady whose steadily increasing motherly interest in him had at times tried his dignity in that very lively family.

That he was already a successful young man with a metropolitan reputation made little or no impression upon her. He was young, alone, and she liked him better and better every day until that liking arrived at the point where his physical welfare began to preoccupy her. So she sent maids to his room with nourishing broths at odd and unexpected moments, and she presented him with so many boxes of quinine that their disposal became a problem until Shiela took them off his hands and replaced them in her mother's medicine chest, whence, in due time, they returned again as gifts to Hamil.

"Dear Mrs. Cardross," he said, taking a vacant chair beside her hammock, "I really am perfectly well and perfectly acclimated, and I enjoy every moment of the day whether here as your guest or in the saddle with your husband or in the office over the plans—"

"But you are always at work!" she drawled; "we never see you."

"But that's why I am here," he insisted, smiling.

"Neville," she interrupted calmly; "no boy of his age ought to kill himself. Listen to me; when Neville and I were married we had very little, and he began by laying his plans to work every moment. But we had an understanding," she added blandly; "I explained that I did not intend to grow old with a wreck of a man. Now you may see the result of our understanding," nodding toward her amazingly youthful husband.

"Beautiful, isn't it?" observed Cardross, still looking through his field-glasses. "There's a baby-show next week and I'll enter if you like, my dear."

Mrs. Cardross smiled and took Hamil's hand flat between her fair, pudgy palms.

"We want you here," she said kindly, "*not* because it is a matter of convenience, but because we like you. Be a little more amiable, Mr. Hamil; you never give us a moment during the day or after dinner. You haven't been to a dance yet; you never go to the beach, you never motor or sail or golf. Don't you like my children?"

"Like them! I adore them," he said, laughing, "but how can—"

"I'm going to take him camping," observed Cardross, interrupting. "I want some duck-shooting; don't you, Hamil?"

"Of course I do, but—"

"Then we start this week for the woods—"

"I won't let you," interposed his wife; "you'll talk that boy to death with your plans and surveys!"

"No, I'll promise to talk shooting every moment, and do a little of it, too. What do you say, Hamil? Gray will go with us. Are you game?"

"I'd love to, but I promised Malcourt that—"

"Oh, nonsense! Louis can wait for you to go North and lay out Mr. Portlaw's park. I've the first call on you; I've got you for the winter here—"

"But Portlaw says—"

"Oh, bother Mr. Portlaw! We'll take him along, too, if he can tear himself away from the Beach Club long enough to try less dangerous game."

Since Malcourt's arrival he and Portlaw had joyously waded into whatever gaiety offered, neck-deep; Portlaw had attached himself to the

Club with all the deliberation of a born gourmet and a hopeless gambler; Malcourt roamed society and its suburbs, drifting from set to set and from coterie to coterie, always an opportunist, catholic in his tastes, tolerant of anything where pretty women were inclined to be amiable. And they often were so inclined.

For his own curiosity he even asked to be presented to the redoubtable Mrs. Van Dieman, and he returned at intervals to that austere conservatory of current gossip and colonial tradition partly because it was policy, socially, partly because, curiously enough, the somewhat transparent charms of Virginia Suydam, whom he usually met there, interested him—enough to make him remember a provocative glance from her slow eyes—very slow, deeply lidded eyes, washed with the tint of the sea when it is less blue than green. And the curious side of it was that Malcourt and Virginia had met before, and he had completely forgotten. It was difficult to tell whether she had.

He usually remembered women who looked at him like that, tucking them away in his mental list to be investigated later. He had quite a little list in his mental archives of women, wedded and otherwise, who interested him agreeably or otherwise. Neither Mrs. Carrick nor Cecile was on that list. Shiela Cardross was—and had been for two years.

Hamil, sitting on the terrace beside Mrs. Cardross, became very busy with his note-book as soon as that languid lady resumed her book.

"If you're going to import wild boar from Germany," he said to Cardross, "you'll have to fence in some ten miles square—a hundred square miles!—or they'll take to the Everglades."

"I'm going to," returned that gentleman calmly. "I wish you'd ask McKenna to figure it out. I'll supply the cypress of course."

Hamil leaned forward, a little thrilled with the colossal scheme. He never could become quite accustomed to the vast scale on which Cardross undertook things.

"That will make a corking preserve," he said. "What do you suppose is in there now?"

"Some bears and deer, a few lynx, perhaps one or two panthers. The boar will hold their own—if they can stand the summer—and I'm sure they can. The alligators, no doubt, will get some of their young when they breed. I shall start with a hundred couple when you're ready for them. What are you going to do this afternoon?"

"Office work," replied Hamil, rising and looking at his marl-stained puttees and spurs. Then he straightened up and smiled at Mrs. Cardross, who was gently shaking her head, saying:

"The young people are at the bathing-beach; I wish you'd take a chair and go down there—to please me, Mr. Hamil."

"Come, Hamil," added Cardross airily, "take a few days off—on yourself. You've one thing yet to learn: it's only the unsuccessful who are too busy to play."

"But what I'm doing is play," remonstrated the young man good-humouredly. "Well—I'll go to the beach, then." He looked at the steam-jets above the forest, fumbled with his note-book, caught the eye of Mrs. Cardross, put away the book, and took his leave laughingly.

"We go duck-shooting to-morrow," called out Cardross after him.

Hamil halted in the doorway to protest, but the elder man waved him away; and he went to his room to change riding-clothes for flannels and sponge the reek of horse and leather from his person.

The beach was all ablaze with the brilliant colours of sunshades, hats, and bathing-skirts. Hamil lost no time in getting into his swimming-suit; and, as he emerged, tall, cleanly built, his compact figure deeply tanned where exposed, Portlaw, waddling briskly toward the ocean, greeted him with the traditional: "Come on! it's fine!" and informed him furthermore that "everybody" was there.

CHAPTER VIII
MANOEUVERING

Everybody seemed to be there, either splashing about in the Atlantic or playing ball on the beach or congregated along the sands observant of the jolly, riotous scene sparkling under the magnificence of a cloudless sky.

Hamil nodded to a few people as he sauntered toward the surf; he stopped and spoke to his aunt and Colonel Vetchen, who informed him that Virginia and Cuyp were somewhere together chastely embracing the ocean; he nodded to old Classon who was toddling along the wet sands in a costume which revealed considerable stomach; he saw Malcourt, knee-deep, hovering around Shiela, yet missing nothing of what went on around him, particularly wherever the swing of a bathing-skirt caught his quick, handsome eyes.

Then Cecile stretched out an inviting hand to him from the water and he caught it, and together they hurled themselves head first into the surf, swimming side by side out to the raft.

"It's nice to see you again," said the girl. "Are you going to be agreeable now and go about with us? There's a luncheon at two—your fair friend Virginia Suydam has asked us, much to our surprise—but after that I'm quite free if you've anything to propose."

She looked up at him, pink and fresh as a wet rose, balanced there on the edge of the rocking raft.

"Anything to propose?" he repeated; "I don't know; there's scarcely anything I wouldn't propose to you. So you're going to Virginia's luncheon?"

"*I* am; Shiela won't." She frowned. "It's just as it was two years ago when Louis Malcourt tagged after her every second. It's stupid, but we can't count on them any more."

"Does—does Malcourt—"

"Tag after Shiela? Haven't you seen it? You've been too busy to notice. I wish you wouldn't work every minute. There was the jolliest sort of a dance at the O'Haras' last night—while you were fast asleep. I know you were because old Jonas told mother you had fallen asleep in your chair with your head among a pile of blue-prints. On my way to the dance I wanted to go in and tie one of Shiela's cunning little lace morning caps under your chin, but Jessie wouldn't go with me. They're perfectly sweet and madly fashionable—these little Louis XVI caps. I'll show you one some day."

For a few moments the girl rattled on capriciously, swinging her stockinged legs in the smooth green swells that rose above her knees along the raft's edge; and he sat silent beside her, half-listening, half-preoccupied, his eyes instinctively searching the water's edge beyond.

"I—hadn't noticed that Louis Malcourt was so devoted to your sister," he said.

Cecile looked up quickly, but detected only amiable indifference in the young fellow's face.

"They're-always together; *elle s'affiche à la fin!*" she said impatiently. "Shiela was only eighteen before; she's twenty now, and old enough to know whether she wants to marry a man like that or not."

Hamil glanced around at her incredulously. "Marry Malcourt?"

But Cecile went on headlong in the wake of her own ideas.

"He's a sort of a relative; we've always known him. He and Gray used to go camping in Maine and he often spent months in our house. But for two years now, he's been comparatively busy—he's Mr. Portlaw's manager, you know, and we've seen nothing of him—which was quite agreeable to me."

Hamil rose, unquiet. "I thought *you* were rather impressed by Shiela," continued the girl. "I really did think so, Mr. Hamil."

"Your sister predicted that I'd lose my heart and senses to *you*" said Hamil, laughing and reseating himself beside her.

"Have you?"

"Of course I have. Who could help it?"

The girl considered him smilingly.

"You're the nicest of men," she said. "If you hadn't been so busy I'm certain we'd have had a desperate affair. But—as it is—and it makes me perfectly furious—I have only the most ridiculously commonplace and comfortable affection for you—the sort which prompts mother to send you quinine and talcum powder—"

Balanced there side by side they fell to laughing.

"Sentiment? Yes," she said; "but oh! it's the kind that offers witch-hazel and hot-water bottles to the best beloved! Mr. Hamil, why can't we flirt comfortably like sensibly frivolous people!"

"I wish we could, Cecile."

"I wish so, too, Garret. No, that's too formal—Garry! There, that ends our chances!"

"You're the jolliest family I ever knew," he said. "You can scarcely understand how pleasant it has been for me to camp on the edges of your fireside and feel the home-warmth a little—now and then—"

"Why do you remain so aloof then?"

"I don't mean to. But my heart is in this business of your father's—the more deeply in because of his kindness—and your mother's—and for all your sakes. You know I can scarcely realise it—I've been with you only a month, and yet you've done so much for me—received me so simply, so cordially—that the friendship seems to be of years instead of hours."

"That is the trouble," sighed Cecile; "you and I never had a chance to be frivolous; I'm no more self-conscious with you than I am with Gray. Tell me, why was Virginia Suydam so horrid to us at first?"

Hamil reddened. "You mustn't ask me to criticise my own kin," he said.

"No," she said, "you couldn't do that.... And Miss Suydam has been more civil recently. It's a mean, low, and suspicious thing to say, but I suppose it's because—but I don't think I'll say it after all."

"It's nicer not to," said Hamil. They both knew perfectly well that Virginia's advances were anything but disinterested. For, alas! even the men of her own entourage were now gravitating toward the Cardross family; Van Tassel Cuyp was continually wrinkling his nose and fixing his dead-blue eyes in that direction; little Colonel Vetchen circled busily round and round that centre of attraction, even Courtlandt Classon evinced an inclination to toddle that way. Besides Louis Malcourt had arrived; and Virginia had never quite forgotten Malcourt who had made one at a house party in the Adirondacks some years since, although even when he again encountered her, Malcourt had retained no memory of the slim, pallid girl who had for a week been his fellow-guest at Portlaw's huge camp on Luckless Lake.

"Virginia Suydam is rather an isolated girl," said Hamil thoughtfully. "She lives alone; and it is not very gay for a woman alone in the world; not the happiest sort of life.... Virginia has always been very friendly to me—always. I hope you will find her amusing."

"I'm going to her luncheon," said Cecile calmly. "It's quite too absurd for her to feel any more doubt about us socially than we feel about her. That is why I am going. Shall we swim?"

He rose; she clasped his offered hand and sprang to her feet, ready for the water again. But at that instant Malcourt's dark, handsome head appeared on the crest of a surge close by, and the next moment that young gentleman scrambled aboard the raft, breathing heavily.

"Hello, Cecile!" he gasped; "Hello, Hamil! Shiela thought it must be you, but I was sceptical. Whew! That isn't much of a swim; I must be out of condition—"

"Late hours, cards, and highballs," observed Cecile scornfully. "You're horridly smooth and fat, Louis."

Malcourt turned to Hamil.

"Glad to see you've emerged from your shell at last. The rumour is that you're working too hard."

"There's no similar rumour concerning you," observed Cecile, who had never made any pretence of liking Malcourt. "Please swim out to sea, if you've nothing more interesting to tell us. I've just managed to decoy Mr. Hamil here and I'd like to converse with him in peace."

Malcourt, arms folded, balanced himself easily on the raft's pitching edge and glanced at her with that amiably bored expression characteristic of him when rebuffed by a woman. On such occasions his eyes resembled the half-closed orbs of a teased but patient cat; and Cecile had once told him so.

"There's a pretty rumour afloat concerning your last night's performance at the Beach Club," said the girl disdainfully. "A boy like you, making himself conspicuous by his gambling!"

Malcourt winced, but as the girl had apparently heard nothing to his discredit except about his gambling, he ventured an intelligent sidelong glance at Hamil.

The latter looked at him inquiringly; Malcourt laughed.

"You haven't been to the Beach Club yet, have you, Hamil? I'll get you a card if you like."

Cecile, furious, turned her back and went head first into the sea.

"Come on," said Hamil briefly, and followed her. Malcourt took to the water leisurely, going out of his way to jeer at and splash Portlaw, who was labouring like a grampus inshore; then he circled within observation distance of several pretty girls, displayed his qualities as a swimmer for their benefit, and finally struck out shoreward.

When he emerged from the surf he looked about for Shiela. She was already half-way to the beach, walking with Cecile and Hamil toward the pavilion; and, starting across the shallows to overtake her, he suddenly came face to face with Virginia Suydam.

She was moving hip-deep out through the seething tide, slim, graceful, a slight flush tinting the usual delicate pallor of her cheeks. Gussie Vetchen bobbed nimbly about in the vicinity, very busy trying to look at everybody and keep his balance at the same time. Miss Palliser was talking to Cuyp.

As Malcourt waded past, he and Miss Suydam exchanged a pleasantly formal greeting; and, for the second time, something in her casual gaze—the steadiness of her pretty green-tinted eyes, perhaps—perhaps their singular colour—interested him.

"You did not ask *me* to your luncheon," he said gaily, as he passed her through the foam.

"No, only petticoats, Mr. Malcourt. I am sorry that your—fiancée isn't coming."

He halted, perfectly aware of the deliberate and insolent indiscretion of her reply. Every line of her supple figure accented the listless, disdainful intention. As he remained motionless she turned, bent gracefully and laid her palms flat on the surface of the water, then looked idly over her shoulder at him.

He waded back close to her, she watching him advance without apparent interest—but watching him nevertheless.

"Have you heard that anybody and myself are supposed to be engaged?" he asked.

"No," she replied coolly; "have you?"

A dark flush mantled his face and he choked.

For a moment they stood so; her brows were raised a trifle.

"Well?" she asked at last. "Have I made you *very* angry, Mr. Malcourt?" She waded out a step or two toward the surf, facing it. The rollers breaking just beyond made her foothold precarious; twice she nearly lost her balance; the third time he caught her hand to steady her and held it as they faced the surges, swaying together.

She did not look again at him. They stood for a while unsteadily, her hand in his grasp.

"Why on earth did you say such a thing to me?" he asked.

"I don't—know," she said simply; "I really don't, Mr. Malcourt."

And it was true; for their slight acquaintance warranted neither badinage nor effrontery; and she did not understand the sudden impulse toward provocation, unless it might be her contempt for Shiela Cardross. And that was the doing of Mrs. Van Dieman.

"I'm sorry," she said, looking up at him, and after a moment, down at their clasped hands. "Are we going to swim out, Mr. Malcourt?—or shall we continue to pose as newly married for the benefit of the East Coast?"

"We'll sit in the sands," he said. "We'll probably find a lot of things to say to each other." But he dropped her fingers—gently.

"Unless you care to join your—care to join Miss Cardross."

Even while she spoke she remained calmly amazed at the commonness of her own speech, the astonishing surface streak of unsuspected vulgarity which she was naïvely exhibiting to this man.

Vetchen came noisily splashing up to join them, but he found neither of them very attentive to him as they walked slowly to the beach and up to the dry, hot sand.

Virginia curled up in the sand; Malcourt extended himself full length at her feet, clasped fingers supporting his head, smooth, sun-browned legs crossed behind him; and he looked like a handsome and rather sulky boy lying there, kicking up his heels insouciantly or stretching luxuriously in the sun.

Vetchen, who had followed, began an interminable story on the usual theme of his daughter, Mrs. Tom O'Hara, illustrating her beauty, her importance, and the incidental importance of himself; and it was with profound surprise and deep offence that he discovered that neither Malcourt nor Miss Suydam were listening. Indeed, in brief undertones, they had been carrying on a guarded conversation of their own all the while; and presently little Vetchen took his leave with a hauteur quite lost on those who had so unconsciously affronted him.

"Of course it is very civil of you to say you remember me," Virginia was saying, "but I am perfectly aware you do not."

Malcourt insisted that he recalled their meeting at Portlaw's Adirondack camp on Luckless Lake two years before, cudgelling his brains at the same time to recollect seeing Virginia there and striving to remember some corroborative incident. But all he could really recall was a young and unhappily married woman to whom he had made violent love—and it was even an effort for him to remember her name.

"How desperately you try!" observed Virginia, leisurely constructing a little rampart of sand between them. "Listen to me, Mr. Malcourt"—she raised her eyes, and again the hint of provocation in them preoccupied him—"I remembered you, and I have sometimes hoped we might meet again. Is that amends for the very bad taste I displayed in speaking of your engagement before it has been announced?"

"I am not engaged—to be married," he said deliberately.

She looked at him steadily, and he sustained the strain of the gaze in his own untroubled fashion.

"You are not engaged?"

"No."

She straightened up, resting her weight on one bare arm, then leisurely laid her length on the burning sands and, face framed between her fingers, considered him in silence.

In her attitude, in her very conversation with this man there was, for her, a certain sense of abandonment; a mental renouncing of all that had hitherto characterised her in her relations with an always formal world; as though that were necessary to meet him on his own level.

Never before had she encountered the temptation, the opportunity, or the person where the impulse to discard convention, conviction, training, had so irresistibly presented itself. Nor could she understand it now; yet she was aware, instinctively, that she was on the verge of the temptation and the opportunity; that there existed a subtle something in this man, in herself, that tempted to conventional relaxation. In all her repressed, regulated, and self-suppressed career, all that had ever been in her of latent daring, of feminine audacity, of caprice, of perverse provocation, stirred in her now, quickening with the slightest acceleration of her pulses.

Apparently a man of her own caste, yet she had never been so obscurely stirred by a man of her own caste—had never instinctively divined in other men the streak which this man, from the first interchange of words, had brought out in her.

Aware of his attraction, hazily convinced that she had no confidence in him, the curious temptation persisted and grew; and she felt very young and very guilty like a small child consenting to parley with another child whose society has been forbidden. And it seemed to her that somehow she had already demeaned herself by the tentative toward a common understanding with an intellect and principles of a grade inferior to her own.

"That was a very pretty woman you were so devoted to in the Adirondacks," she said.

He recalled the incident with a pleasant frankness which left her unconvinced.

Suddenly it came over her that she had had enough of him—more than was good for her, and she sat up straight, primly retying her neckerchief.

"To-morrow?" he was saying, too civilly; but on her way to the pavilion she could not remember what she had replied, or how she had rid herself of him.

Inside the pavilion she saw Hamil and Shiela Cardross, already dressed, watching the lively occupants of the swimming-pool; and she exchanged a handshake with the former and a formal nod with the latter.

"Garret, your aunt is worrying because somebody told her that there are snakes in the district where you are at work. Come in some evening and reassure her." And to Shiela: "So sorry you cannot come to my luncheon, Miss Cardross.—You *are* Miss Cardross, aren't you? I've been told otherwise."

Hamil looked up, pale and astounded; but Shiela answered, undisturbed:

"My sister Cecile is the younger; yes, I am Miss Cardross."

And Hamil realised there had been two ways of interpreting Virginia's question, and he reddened, suddenly appalled at his own knowledge and at his hasty and gross conclusions.

If Shiela noticed the quick changes in his face she did not appear to, nor the curious glance that Virginia cast at him.

"*So* sorry," said Miss Suydam again, "for if you are going to be so much engaged to-day you will no doubt also miss the tea for that pretty Mrs. Ascott."

"No," said Shiela, "I wouldn't think of missing that." And carelessly to Hamil: "As you and I have nothing on hand to-day, I'll take you over to meet Mrs. Ascott if you like."

Which was a notice to Virginia that Miss Cardross had declined her luncheon from deliberate disinclination.

Hamil, vaguely conscious that all was not as agreeable as the surface of things indicated, said cordially that he'd be very glad to go anywhere with Shiela to meet anybody, adding to Virginia that he'd heard of Mrs. Ascott but could not remember when or where.

"Probably you've heard of her often enough from Louis Malcourt," said Virginia. "He and I were just recalling his frenzied devotion to her in the

Adirondacks; that," she added smilingly to Shiela, "was before Mrs. Ascott got her divorce from her miserable little French count and resumed her own name. She was the most engaging creature when Mr. Malcourt and I met her two years ago."

Shiela, who had been listening with head partly averted and grave eyes following the antics of the divers in the pool, turned slowly and encountered Virginia's smile with a straight, cold gaze of utter distrust.

Nothing was said for a moment; then Virginia spoke smilingly again to Hamil concerning his aunt's uneasiness, turned toward Shiela, exchanged formal adieux with her, and walked on toward her dressing-room and shower. Hamil and Miss Cardross turned the other way.

When Shiela was seated in her double wheel-chair with Hamil beside her, she looked up through her veil unsmiling into his serious face.

"Did you notice anything particularly impertinent in Miss Suydam's question?" she asked quietly.

"What question?"

"When she asked me whether I was Miss Cardross."

The slow colour again burned his bronzed skin. He made no reply, nor did she await any after a silent consideration of his troubled face.

"Where did you hear about me?" she asked.

She had partly turned in her seat, resting both gloved hands on the crook of her folded sunshade, and leaning a little toward him.

"Don't ask me," he said; "whatever I heard I heard unwillingly—"

"You *have* heard?"

He did not answer.

The remainder of the journey was passed in silence. On the road they met Mrs. Cardross and Jessie Carrick driving to a luncheon; later, Gray passed in his motor with his father.

"I have an idea that you and I are to lunch alone," said Hamil as they reached the house; and so it turned out, for Malcourt was going off with Portlaw somewhere and Cecile was dressing for Virginia's luncheon.

"Did you care to go with me to the Ascott-O'Hara function?" asked Shiela, pausing on the terrace. Her voice was listless, her face devoid of animation.

"I don't care where I go if I may go with you," he said, with a new accent of intention in his voice which did not escape her.

She went slowly up the stairs untying her long veil as she mounted. Cecile in a bewildering hat and gown emerged upon the terrace before Shiela reappeared, and found Hamil perched upon the coquina balustrade, poring over a pocketful of blue-prints; and she said very sweetly: "Good-bye, my elder brother. Will you promise to take the best of care of our little sister Shiela while I'm away?"

"The very best," he said, sliding feet foremost to the terrace. "Heavens, Cecile, you certainly are bewitching in those clothes!"

"It is what they were built for, brother," she said serenely. "Good-bye; we won't shake hands on account of my gloves.... Do be nice to Shiela. She isn't very gay these days—I don't know why. I believe she has rather missed you."

Hamil tucked her into her chair, the darky pedalled off; then the young man returned to the terrace where presently a table for two was brought and luncheon announced as Shiela Cardross appeared.

Hamil displayed the healthy and undiscriminating appetite of a man who is too busy mentally and physically to notice what he eats and drinks; Shiela touched nothing except fruit. She lighted his cigarette for him before the coffee, and took one herself, turning it thoughtfully over and over between her delicately shaped fingers; but at a glance of inquiry from him:

"No, I don't," she said; "it burns my tongue. Besides I may some day require it as a novelty to distract me—so I'll wait."

She rose a moment later, and stood, distrait, looking out across the sunlit world. He at her elbow, head bent, idly watched the smoke curling upward from his cigarette.

Presently, as though moved by a common impulse, they turned together, slowly traversed the terrace and the long pergola all crimson and white with bougainvillia and jasmine, and entered the jungle road beyond the courts where carved seats of coquina glimmered at intervals along the avenue of oaks and palmettos and where stone-edged pools reflected the golden green dusk of the semi-tropical foliage above.

On the edge of one of these basins the girl seated herself; without her hat and gloves and in a gown which exposed throat and neck she always looked younger and more slender to him, the delicate modelling of the neck and its whiteness was accentuated by the silky growth of the brown hair which close to the nape and brow was softly blond like a child's.

The frail, amber-tinted little dragon-flies of the South came hovering over the lotus bloom that edged the basin; long, narrow-shaped butterflies whose velvet-black wings were barred with brilliant stripes of canary yellow fluttered across the forest aisle; now and then a giant papilio sailed high under the arched foliage on tiger-striped wings of chrome and black, or a superb butterfly in pearl white and malachite green came flitting about the sparkle-berry bloom.

The girl nodded toward it. "That is a scarce butterfly here," she said. "Gray would be excited. I wish we had his net here."

"It is the *Victorina*, isn't it?" he asked, watching the handsome, nervous-winged creature which did not seem inclined to settle on the white flowers.

"Yes, the *Victorina steneles*. Are you interested?"

"The generation I grew up with collected," he said. "I remember my cabinet, and some of the names. But I never saw any fellows of this sort in the North."

"Your memory is good?"

"Yes," he said, "for what I care about"—he looked up at her—"for those I care about my memory is good, I never forget kindness—nor confidence given—nor a fault forgiven."

She bent forward, elbows on knees, chin propped on both linked hands.

"Do you understand now," she said, "why I could not afford the informality of our first meeting? What you have heard about me explains why I can scarcely afford to discard convention, does it not, Mr. Hamil?"

She went on, her white fingers now framing her face and softly indenting the flushed skin:

"I don't know who has talked to you, or what you have heard; but I knew by your expression—there at the swimming-pool—that you had heard enough to embarrass you and—and hurt me very, very keenly."

"Calypso!" he broke out impulsively; but she shook her head. "Let *me* tell you if it must be told, Mr. Hamil.... Father and mother are dreadfully sensitive; I have only known about it for two years; two years ago they told me—had to tell me.... Well—it still seems hazy and incredible.... I was educated in a French convent—if you know what that means. All my life I have been guarded—sheltered from knowledge of evil; I am still unprepared to comprehend—... And I am still very ignorant; I know that.... So you see how it was with me; a girl awakened to such self-knowledge cannot grasp it entirely—cannot wholly convince herself except at moments—at night. Sometimes—when a crisis threatens—and one has lain awake long in the dark—"

She gathered her knees in her arms and stared at the patch of sunlight that lay across the hem of her gown, leaving her feet shod in gold.

"I don't know how much difference it really makes to the world. I suppose I shall learn—if people are to discuss me. How much difference does it make, Mr. Hamil?"

"It makes none to me—"

"The world extends beyond your pleasant comradeship," she said. "How does the world regard a woman of no origin—whose very name is a charity—"

"Shiela!"

"W-what?" she said, trying to smile; and then slowly laid her head in her hands, covering her face.

She had given way, very silently, for as he bent close to her he felt the tearful aroma of her uneven breath—the feverish flush on cheek and hand, the almost imperceptible tremor of her slender body—rather close to him now.

When she had regained her composure, and her voice was under command, she straightened up, face averted.

"You are quite perfect, Mr. Hamil; you have not hurt me with one misguided and well-intended word. That is exactly as it should be between us—must always be."

"Of course," he said slowly.

She nodded, still looking away from him. "Let us each enjoy our own griefs unmolested. You have yours?"

"No, Shiela, I haven't any griefs."

"Come to me when you have; I shall not humiliate you with words to shame your intelligence and my own. If you suffer you suffer; but it is well to be near a friend—not *too* near, Mr. Hamil."

"Not too near," he repeated.

"No; that is unendurable. The counter-irritant to grief is sanity, not emotion. When a woman is a little frightened the presence of the unafraid is what steadies her."

She looked over her shoulder into the water, reached down, broke off a blossom of wild hyacinth, and, turning, drew it through the button-hole of his coat.

"You certainly are very sweet to me," she said quietly. And, laughing a little: "The entire family adores you with pills—and I've now decorated you with the lovely curse of our Southern rivers. But—there are no such things as weeds; a weed is only a miracle in the wrong place.... Well—shall we walk and moralise or remain here and make cat-cradle conversation?... You are looking at me very solemnly."

"I was thinking—"

"What?"

"That, perhaps, I never before knew a girl as well as I know you."

"Not even Miss Suydam?"

"Lord, no! I never dreamed of knowing her—I mean her real self. You understand, she and I have always taken each other for granted—never with any genuine intimacy."

"Oh! And—this—ours—is genuine intimacy?"

"Is it not?"

For a moment her teeth worried the bright velvet of her lip, then meeting his gaze:

"I mean to be—honest—with you," she said with a tremor in her voice; but her regard wavered under his. "I mean to be," she repeated so low he scarcely heard her. Then with a sudden animation a little strained: "When this winter has become a memory let it be a happy one for you and me. And by the same token you and I had better think about dressing. You don't mind, do you, if I take you to meet Mrs. Ascott?—she was Countess de Caldelis; it's taken her years to secure her divorce."

Hamil remembered the little dough-faced, shrimp-limbed count when he first came over with the object of permitting somebody to support him indefinitely so that later, in France, he could in turn support his mistresses in the style to which they earnestly desired to become accustomed.

And now the American girl who had been a countess was back, a little wiser, a little harder, and more cynical, with some of the bloom rubbed off, yet much of her superficial beauty remaining.

"Alida Ascott," murmured Shiela. "Jessie was a bridesmaid. Poor little girl!—I'm glad she's free. There were no children," she said, looking up at Hamil; "in that case a decent girl is justified! Don't you think so?"

"Yes, I do," he said, smiling; "I'm not one of those who believe that such separations threaten us with social disintegration."

"Nor I. Almost every normal woman desires to live decently. She has a right to. All young girls are ignorant. If they begin with a dreadful but innocent mistake does the safety of society require of them the horror of lifelong degradation? Then the safety of such a society is not worth the sacrifice. That is my opinion."

"That settles a long-vexed problem," he said, laughing at her earnestness.

But she looked at him, unsmiling, while he spoke, hands clasped in her lap, the fingers twisting and tightening till the rose-tinted nails whitened.

Men have only a vague idea of women's ignorance; how naturally they are inclined to respond to a man; how the dominating egotism of a man and his confident professions and his demands confuse them; how deeply his appeals for his own happiness stir them to pity.... They have heard of love—and they do not know. If they ever dream of it it is not what they have imagined when a man suddenly comes crashing through the barriers of friendship and stuns them with an incoherent recital of his own desires. And yet, in spite of the shock, it is with them instinctive to be kind. No woman can endure an appeal unmoved; except for them there would be no beggars; their charity is not a creed: it is the essence of them, the beginning of all things for them—and the end.

The bantering smile had died out in Hamil's face; he sat very still, interested, disturbed, and then wondering when his eyes caught the restless manoeuvres of the little hands, constantly in motion, interlacing, eloquent of the tension of self-suppression.

He thought: "It is a cowardly thing for an egotist with an egotist's early and lively knowledge of the world and of himself to come clamouring to a girl for charity. It *is* true that almost any man can make a young girl think she loves him if he is selfish enough to do it. Is her ignorance a fault? All her training deprecates any acquisition of worldly knowledge: it is not for her: her value is in her ignorance. Then when she naturally makes some revolting mistake and attempts to escape to decency and freedom once more there is a hue and a cry from good folk and clergy. Divorce? It is a good thing—as the last resort. And a woman need feel no responsibility for the sort of society that would deprive a woman of the last refuge she has!"

He raised his eyes, curiously, in time to intercept hers.

"So—you did not know me after all, it seems," she said with a faint smile. "You never suspected in me a *Vierge Rouge*, militant, champion of her downtrodden sex, haranguing whomsoever would pay her the fee of his attention. Did you?"

And as he made no reply: "Your inference is that I have had some unhappy love affair—some perilously close escape from—unhappy matrimony." She shrugged. "As though a girl could plead only a cause which concerned herself.... Tell me what you are thinking?"

She had risen, and he stood up before her, fascinated.

"Tell me!" she insisted; "I shall not let you go until you do!"

"I was thinking about you."

"Please don't!... Are you doing it yet?" closely confronting him, hands behind her.

"Yes, I am," he said, unable to keep his eyes from her, all her beauty and youth and freshness troubling him, closing in upon him like subtle fragrance in the golden forest dusk.

"Are you still thinking about me?"

"Yes."

The rare sweet laughter edged her lips, for an instant; then something in his eyes checked her. Colour and laughter died out, leaving a pale confused smile; and the straight gaze wavered, grew less direct, yet lost not a shade of his expression which also had changed.

Neither spoke; and after a moment they turned away, walking not very near together toward the house.

The sunshine and the open somehow brought relief and the delicate constraint between them relaxed as they sauntered slowly into the house where Shiela presently went away to dress for the Ascott function, and Hamil sat down on the veranda for a while, then retired to undertake the embellishment of his own person.

CHAPTER IX
THE INVASION

They went together in a double chair, spinning noiselessly over the shell road which wound through oleander and hibiscus hedges. Great orange and sulphur-tinted butterflies kept pace with them as they travelled swiftly southward; the long, slim shadows of palms gridironed the sunny road, for the sun was in the west, and already a bird here and there had ventured on a note or two as prelude to the evening song, and over the ocean wild ducks were rising in clouds, swinging and drifting and settling again as though in short rehearsal for their sunset flight.

"Your hostess is Mrs. Tom O'Hara," said the girl; "when you have enough of it look at me and I'll understand. And if you try to hide in a corner with some soulful girl I'll look at you—if it bores me too much. So don't sit still with an infatuated smile, as Cecile does, when she sees that I wish to make my adieux."

"I'm so likely to," he said, "when escape means that I'll have you to myself again."

There was a trifle more significance in the unconsidered speech than he had intended. The girl looked absently straight in front of her; he sat motionless, uncomfortable at his own words, but too wise to attempt to modify them by more words.

Other chairs passed them now along the road—there were nods of recognition, gay salutes, an intimate word or two as the light-wheeled vehicles flashed past; and in a moment more the tall coquina gate posts and iron grille of Mrs. Tom O'Hara's villa, Tsana Lahni, glimmered under an avenue of superb royal palms.

The avenue was crowded with the slender-wheeled basket-bodied chairs gay with the plumage of pretty women; the scene on the lawns beyond was charming where an orange and white pavilion was pitched against the intense green of the foliage, and the pelouse was all dotted and streaked with vivid colours of sunshades and gowns.

"Ulysses among the sirens," she whispered as they made their way toward their hostess, exchanging recognition with people everywhere in the throngs. "Here they are—all of them—and there's Miss Suydam,—too unconscious of us. How hath the House of Hamil fallen!—"

"If you talk that way I won't leave you for one second while we're here!" he said under his breath.

"Nonsense; it only hurts me, not my pride. And half a cup of unforbidden tea will drown the memory of that insolence—"

She bent forward with smiling composure to shake hands with Mrs. Tom O'Hara, a tall, olive-tinted, black-haired beauty; presented Hamil to his hostess, and left him planted, to exchange impulsive amenities with little Mrs. Ascott.

Mrs. Tom O'Hara, a delicate living Gainsborough in black and white, was probably the handsomest woman in the South. She dressed with that perfection of simplicity which only a few can afford; she wore only a single jewel at a time, but the gem was always matchless.

Warm-hearted, generous, and restless, she loved the character of Lady Bountiful; and, naïvely convinced of her own unassailable supremacy, played very picturesquely the rôle of graciousness and patronage to the tenants of her great estates and of her social and intellectual world alike. Hence, although she went where many of her less fashionable guests might not have been asked to go, she herself paid self-confident homage to intellect as she understood it, and in her own house her entourage was as mixed as her notions of a "salon" permitted.

She was gracious to Hamil on account of his aunt, his profession, and himself. Also her instinct was to be nice to everybody. As hostess she had but a moment to accord him, but during that moment she contrived to speak reassuringly of the Suydam genealogy, the art of landscape architecture, and impart a little special knowledge from her inexhaustible reserve, informing him that the name of her villa, Tsa-na Lah-ni, was Seminole, and meant "Yellow Butterfly." And then she passed him sweetly along into a crush of bright-eyed young things who attempted to pour tea into him and be agreeable in various artless ways; and presently he found himself in a back-water where fashion and intellect were conscientiously doing their best to mix. But the mixture was a thin solution—thinner than Swizzles and Caravan, and the experience of the very young girl beside him who talked herself out in thirty seconds from pure nervousness and remained eternally grateful to him for giving her a kindly opportunity to escape to cover among the feather-brained and frivolous.

Then, close to him, a girl spoke of the "purple perfume of petunias," and a man used the phrases, "body politic," and "the gaiety of nations."

So he knew he was among the elect, redundant, and truly precious. A chinless young man turned to him and said:

"There is nobody to-day who writes as Bernard Haw writes."

"Does anybody want to?" asked Hamil pleasantly.

"You mean that this is an age of trumpery romance?" demanded a heavy gentleman in dull disdain. "William Dean has erased all romance from modern life with one smear of his honest thumb!"

"The honest thumb that persistently and patiently rubs the scales from sapphire and golden wings in order to be certain that the vination of the Ornithoptera is still underneath, is not the digit of inspiration," suggested Hamil.

The disciple turned a dull brick-colour; but he betrayed neither his master nor himself.

"What, in God's name," he asked heavily, "is an ornithoptera?"

A very thin author, who had been listening and twisting himself into a number of shapes, thrust his neck forward into the arena and considered Hamil with the pale grimace of challenge.

"Henry Haynes?" he inquired—"your appreciation in one phrase, Mr. Hamil."

"In a Henry Haynes phrase?" asked Hamil good-humouredly.

"The same old calumny?" said the thin author, writhing almost off his chair.

"I'm afraid so; and the remedy a daily dose of verbifuge—until he gets back to the suffocated fount of inspiration. I am very sorry if I seem to differ from everybody, but everybody seems to differ from me, so I can't help it."

A Swami, unctuous and fat, and furious at the lack of feminine attention, said something suavely outrageous about modern women. He was immediately surrounded by several mature examples who adored to be safely smitten by the gelatinous and esoteric.

A little flabby, featureless, but very fashionable portrait painter muttered to Hamil: "Orient and Occident! the molluskular and the muscular. Mr. Hamil, do you realise *what* the Occident is?"

"Geographically?" inquired Hamil wearily.

"No, symbolically. It is that!" explained the painter, doubling his meagre biceps and punching at the infinite, with a flattened thumb. "That," he repeated, "is America. Do you comprehend?"

The wan young girl who had spoken of the purple perfume of petunias said that *she* understood. It may be that she did; she reviewed literature for the *Tribune*.

Harried and restless, Hamil looked for Shiela and saw Portlaw, very hot and uncomfortable in his best raiment, shooting his cuffs and looking dully about for some avenue of escape; and Hamil, exasperated with purple perfumes and thumbs, meanly snared him and left him to confront a rather ample and demonstrative young girl who believed that all human thought was precious—even sinful thought—of which she knew as much as a newly hatched caterpillar. However, Portlaw was able to enlighten her if he cared to.

Again and again Hamil, wandering in circles, looked across the wilderness of women's hats at Shiela Cardross, but a dozen men surrounded her, and among them he noticed the graceful figure of Malcourt directly in front of her, blocking any signal he might have given.

Somebody was saying something about Mrs. Ascott. He recollected that he hadn't met her; so he found somebody to present him.

"And *you* are the man?" exclaimed Mrs. Ascott softly, considering him with her head on one side. "Shiela Cardross wrote to me in New York about you, but I've wanted to inspect you for my own information."

"Are you doing it now?" he asked, amused.

"It's done! Do you imagine you are complex? I've heard various tales about you from three sources, to-day; from an old friend, Louis Malcourt—from another, Virginia Suydam—and steadily during the last month—including to-day—from Shiela Cardross. But I couldn't find a true verdict until the accused appeared personally before me. Tell me, Mr. Hamil, do you plead guilty to being as amiable as the somewhat contradictory evidence indicates?"

"Parole me in custody of this court and let me convince your Honor," said Hamil, looking into the captivatingly cool and humourous face upturned to his.

Mrs. Ascott was small, and finely moulded; something of the miniature grande dame in porcelain. The poise of her head, the lifted chin, every detail in the polished and delicately tinted surface reflected cool experience of the world and of men. Yet the eyes were young, and there was no hardness in them, and the mouth seemed curiously unfashioned for worldly badinage—a very wistful, full-lipped mouth that must have been disciplined in some sad school to lose its cheerfulness in repose.

"I am wondering," she said, "why Mr. Portlaw does not come and talk to me. We are neighbors in the country, you know; I live at Pride's Fall. I don't think it's particularly civil of him to avoid me."

"I can't imagine anybody, including Portlaw, avoiding you," he said.

"We were such good friends—I don't know—he behaved very badly to me last autumn."

They chatted together for a moment or two in the same inconsequential vein, then, other people being presented, she nodded an amiable dismissal; and, as he stepped aside, held out her hand.

"There are a lot of things I'd like to ask you some day; one is about a park for me at Pride's Fall—oh, the tiniest sort of a park, only it should be quite formal in all its miniature details. Will you let Shiela bring you for a little conference? *Soon?*"

He promised and took his leave, elated at the chances of a new commission, hunting through the constantly arriving and departing throngs for Shiela. And presently he encountered his aunt.

"You certainly do neglect me," she said with her engaging and care-free laugh. "Where have you been for a week?"

"In the flat-woods. And, by the way, don't worry about any snakes. Virginia said you were anxious."

"Nonsense," said his aunt, amused, "Virginia is trying to plague you! I said nothing about snakes to her."

"Didn't you say there were snakes in my district?"

"No. I *did* say there were *girls* in your district, but it didn't worry me."

His face was so serious that the smile died out on her own.

"Why, Garret," she said, "surely you are not offended, are you?"

"Not with you—Virginia has apparently taken her cue from that unspeakable Mrs. Van Dieman, and is acting like the deuce toward Shiela Cardross. Couldn't you find an opportunity to discourage that sort of behaviour? It's astonishingly underbred."

His aunt's eyelids flickered as she regarded him.

"Come to see me to-night and explain a little more fully what Virginia has done, dear. Colonel Vetchen is hunting for me and I'm going to let him find me now. Why don't you come back with us if you are not looking for anybody in particular."

"I'm looking for Shiela Cardross," he said.

"Oh, she's over there on the terrace holding her fascinating court—with Louis Malcourt at her heels as usual."

"I didn't know that Malcourt was usually at her heels," he said almost irritably. It was the second time he had heard that comment, and he found it unaccountably distasteful.

His aunt looked up, smiling.

"Can't we dine together, Garry?"

"Yes."

"Thank you, dear"—faintly ironical. "So now if you'll go I'll reveal myself to Gussie Vetchen. Stand aside, my condescending friend."

He said, smiling: "You're the prettiest revelation here. I'll be at the hotel at eight."

And with that they parted just as the happy little Vetchen, catching sight of them, came bustling up with all the fuss and demonstration of a long-lost terrier.

A few minutes later Hamil found Shiela Cardross surrounded by her inevitable entourage—a jolly, animated circle hemming her in with Malcourt at her left and Van Tassel Cuyp on her right; and he halted on the circle's edge to look and listen, glancing askance at Malcourt with a curiosity unaccustomed.

That young man with his well-made graceful figure, his dark hair and vivid tints, had never particularly impressed Hamil. He had accepted him at his face value, lacking the interest to appraise him; and the acquaintance had always been as casual and agreeable as mutual good-humour permitted. But now Malcourt, as a type, attracted his attention; and for a moment he contrasted this rather florid example with the specimens of young men around him. Then he looked at Shiela Cardross. Her delicately noble head was bent a trifle as she listened with the others to Malcourt's fluent humour; and it remained so, though at moments she lifted her eyes in that straight, questioning gaze which left the brows level.

And now she was replying to Malcourt; and Hamil watched her and listened to her with newer interest, noting the poise, the subtle reserve under the gayest provocation of badinage—the melody of her rare laughter, the unaffected sweetness of her voice, and its satisfying sincerity—satisfying as the clear regard from her lifted eyes.

Small wonder men were attracted; Hamil could understand what drew them—the instinctive recognition of a fibre finer and a metal purer than was often found under the surface of such loveliness.

And now, as he watched her, the merriment broke out again around her, and she laughed, lifting her face to his in all its youthfully bewildering beauty, and saw him standing near her for the first time.

Without apparent reason a dull colour rose to his face; and, as though answering fire with fire, her fainter signal in response tinted lip and cheek.

It was scarcely the signal agreed upon for their departure; and for a moment longer, amid the laughing tumult, she sat looking at him as though confused. Malcourt bent forward saying something to her, but she rose while he was speaking, as though she had not heard him; and Hamil walked through the circle to where she stood. A number of very young men looked around at him with hostile eyes; Malcourt's brows lifted a trifle; then he shot an ironical glance at Shiela and, as the circle about her disintegrated, sauntered up, bland, debonair, to accept his congé.

His bow, a shade exaggerated, and the narrowed mockery of his eyes escaped her; and even what he said made no impression as she stood, brightly inattentive, looking across the little throng at Hamil. And Malcourt's smile became flickering and uncertain when she left the terrace with Hamil, moving very slowly side by side across the lawn.

"Such lots of pretty women," commented Shiela. "Have you been passably amused?"

"Passably," he replied in a slightly sullen tone.

"Oh, only passably? I rather hoped that unawakened heart of yours might be aroused to-day."

"It has been."

"*Not* Mrs. Ascott!" she exclaimed, halting.

"Not Mrs. Ascott."

"Mrs. Tom O'Hara! Is it? Every man promptly goes to smash when Mrs. Tom looks sideways."

"O Lord!" he said with a shrug.

"That is not nice of you, Mr. Hamil. If it is not with her you have fallen in love there is a more civil way of denying it."

"Did you take what I said seriously?" he asked—"about falling in love?"

"Were you not serious?"

"I could be if you were," he said in a tone which slightly startled her. She looked up at him questioningly; he said:

"I've had a stupid time without you. The little I've seen of you has spoiled other women for me. And I've just found it out. Do you mind my saying so?"

"Are you not a little over-emphatic in your loyalty to me? I like it, but not at the expense of others, please."

They moved on together, slowly and in step. His head was bent, face sullen and uncomfortably flushed. Again she felt the curiously unaccountable glow in her own cheeks responding in pink fire once more; and annoyed and confused she halted and looked up at him with that frank confidence characteristic of her.

"Something has gone wrong," she said. "Tell me."

"I will. I'm telling myself now." She laughed, stole a glance at him, then her face fell.

"I certainly don't know what you mean, and I'm not very sure that you know."

She was right; he did not yet know. Strange, swift pulses were beating in temple and throat; strange tumults and confusion were threatening his common sense, paralyzing will-power. A slow, resistless intoxication had enveloped him, through which instinctively persisted one warning ray of reason. In the light of that single ray he strove to think clearly. They walked to the pavilion together, he silent, sombre-eyed, taking a mechanical leave of his hostess, fulfilling conventions while scarcely aware of the routine or of the people around him; she composed, sweet, conventionally faultless— and a trifle pale as they turned away together across the lawn.

When they took their places side by side in the chair she was saying something perfunctory concerning the fête and Mrs. Ascott. And as he offered no comment: "Don't you think her very charming and sincere.... Are you listening to me, Mr. Hamil?"

"Yes," he said. "Everybody was very jolly. Yes, indeed."

"And—the girl who adores the purple perfume of petunias?" she asked mischievously. "I think that same purple perfume has made you drowsy, my uncivil friend."

He turned. "Oh, you heard *that*?"

"Yes; I thought it best to keep a sisterly eye on you."

He forced a smile.

"You were very much amused, I suppose—to see me sitting bras-dessus-bras-dessous with the high-browed and precious."

"Not amused; no. I was worried; you appeared to be so hopelessly captivated by her of the purple perfumery. Still, knowing you to be a man normally innocent of sentiment, I hoped for Mrs. Ascott and the best."

"Did I once tell you that there was no sentiment in me, Calypso? I believe I did."

"You certainly did, brother," she replied with cheerful satisfaction.

"Well, I—"

"—And," she interrupted calmly, "I believed you. I am particularly happy now in believing you." A pause—and she glanced at him. "In fact, speaking seriously, it is the nicest thing about you—the most attractive to me, I think." She looked sideways at him, "Because, there is no more sentiment in me than there is in you.... Which is, of course, very agreeable—to us both."

He said nothing more; the chair sped on homeward. Above them the sky was salmon-colour; patches of late sunlight burned red on the tree trunks; over the lagoon against the slowly kindling west clouds of wild-fowl whirled, swung, and spread out into endless lengthening streaks like drifting bands of smoke.

From time to time the girl cast a furtive glance toward him; but he was looking straight ahead with a darkly set face; and an ache, dull, scarcely perceptible, grew in her heart as they flew on along the glimmering road.

"Of what are you thinking, brother?" she asked persuasively.

"Of something I am going to do; as soon as I reach home; I mean *your* home."

"I wish it were yours, too," she said, smiling frankly; "you are such a safe, sound, satisfactory substitute for another brother." ... And as he made no response: "What is this thing which you are going to do when you reach home?"

"I am going to ask your mother a question."

Unquiet she turned toward him, but his face was doggedly set forward as the chair circled through the gates and swept up to the terrace.

He sprang out; and as he aided her to descend she felt his hand trembling under hers. A blind thrill of premonition halted her; then she bit her lip, turned, and mounted the steps with him. At the door he stood aside for her to pass; but again she paused and turned to Hamil, irresolute, confused, not even daring to analyse what sheer instinct was clamouring; what intuition was reading even now in his face, what her ears divined in his unsteady voice uttering some commonplace to thank her for the day spent with him.

"What is it that you are going to say to my mother?" she asked again.

And at the same instant she knew from his eyes—gazing into them in dread and dismay.

"Don't!" she said breathlessly; "I cannot let—" The mounting wave of colour swept her: "Don't go to her!—don't ask such a—a thing. I am—"

She faltered, looking up at him with terrified eyes, and laid one hand on his arm.

The frightened wordless appeal stunned him as they stood there, confronting one another. Suddenly hope came surging up within her; her hand fell from his arm; she lifted her eyes in flushed silence—only to find hopeless confirmation of all she dreaded in his set and colourless face.

"Mr. Hamil," she said tremulously, "I never dreamed—"

"No, you didn't. I did. It is all right, Shiela."

"Oh—I—I never, never dreamed of it!"—shocked and pitifully incredulous still.

"I know you didn't. Don't worry." His voice was very gentle, but he was not looking at her.

"Is it my—fault, Mr. Hamil?"

"Your fault?" he repeated, surprised. "What have *you* done?"

"I—don't know."

He stood gazing absently out into the flaming west; and, speaking as though unaware: "From the first—I realise it now—even from the first moment when you sprang into my life out of the fog and the sea—Shiela! Shiela!—I—"

"Don't!" she whispered, "don't say it." She swayed back against the wall; her hand covered her eyes an instant—and dropped helpless, hopeless.

They faced each other.

"Believe that I am—sorry," she whispered. "Will you believe it? I did not know; I did not dream of it."

His face changed as though something within him was being darkly aroused.

"After all," he said, "no man ever lived who could kill hope."

"There is no hope to kill—"

"No chance, Shiela?"

"There has never been any chance—" She was trembling; he took both her hands. They were ice cold.

He straightened up, squaring his shoulders. "This won't do," he said. "I'm not going to distress you—frighten you again." The smile he forced was certainly a credit to him.

"Shiela, you'd love me if you could, wouldn't you?"

"Y-yes," with a shiver.

"Then it's all right and you mustn't worry.... Can't we get back to the old footing again?"

"N-no; it's gone."

"Then we'll find even firmer ground."

"Yes—firmer ground, Mr. Hamil."

He released her chilled hands, swung around, and took a thoughtful step or two.

"Firmer, safer ground," he repeated. "Once you said to me, 'Let us each enjoy our own griefs unmolested.'" He laughed. "Didn't you say that—years ago?"

"Yes."

"And I replied—years ago—that I had no griefs to enjoy. Didn't I? Well, then, if this is grief, Shiela, I wouldn't exchange it for another man's happiness. So, if you please, I'll follow your advice and enjoy it in my own fashion.... Shiela, you don't smile very often, but I wish you would now."

But the ghost of a smile left her pallor unchanged. She moved toward the stairs, wearily, stopped and turned.

"It cannot end this way," she said; "I want you to know how—to know—to know that I—am—sensible of w-what honour you have done me. Wait! I—I can't let you think that I—do not—care, Mr. Hamil. Believe that I do!—oh, deeply. And forgive me—" She stretched out one hand. He took it, holding it between both of his for a moment, lightly.

"Is all clear between us, Calypso dear?"

"It will be—when I have courage to tell you."

"Then all's well with the world—if it's still under-foot—or somewhere in the vicinity. I'll find it again; you'll be good enough to point it out to me, Shiela.... I've an engagement to improve a few square miles of it.... That's what I need—plenty of work—don't I, Shiela?"

The clear mellow horn of a motor sounded from the twilit lawn; the others were arriving. He dropped her hand; she gathered her filmy skirts and swiftly mounted the great stairs, leaving him to greet her father and Gray on the terrace.

"Hello, Hamil!" called out Cardross, senior, from the lawn, "are you game for a crack at the ducks to-morrow? My men report Ruffle Lake full of coots and blue-bills, and there'll be bigger duck in the West Lagoons."

"I'm going too," said Gray, "also Shiela if she wants to—and four guides and that Seminole, Little Tiger."

Hamil glanced restlessly at the forest where his work lay. And he needed it now. But he said pleasantly, "I'll go if you say so."

"Of course I say so," exclaimed Cardross heartily. "Gray, does Louis Malcourt still wish to go?"

"He spoke of it last week."

"Well, if he hasn't changed his rather volatile mind telephone for Adams, We'll require a guide apiece. And he can have that buckskin horse; and tell him to pick out his own gun." And to Hamil, cordially: "Shiela and Louis and Gray will probably wander about together and you and I will do the real shooting. But Shiela is a shot—if she chooses. Gray would rather capture a scarce jungle butterfly. Hello, here's Louis now! Are you glad we're going at last?"

"Very," replied Hamil as Malcourt strolled up and airily signified his intention of making one of the party. But as soon as he learned that they might remain away three days or more he laughingly demurred.

The four men lingered for a few minutes in the hall discussing guns, dogs, and guides; then Hamil mounted the stairs, and Malcourt went with him, talking all the while in that easy, fluent, amusing manner which, if he chose, could be as agreeably graceful as every attitude and movement of his lithe body. His voice, too, had that engagingly caressing quality characteristic of him when in good-humour; he really had little to say to Hamil, but being on such excellent terms with himself he said a great deal about nothing in particular; and as he persistently lingered by Hamil's door the latter invited him in.

There Malcourt lit a cigarette, seated lazily astride a chair, arms folded across the back, aimlessly humourous in recounting his adventures at the Ascott function, while Hamil stood with his back to the darkening window, twisting his unlighted cigarette into minute shreds and waiting for him to go.

"Rather jolly to meet Miss Suydam again," observed Malcourt. "We were great friends at Portlaw's camp together two years ago. I believe that you and Miss Suydam are cousins after a fashion."

"After a fashion, I believe."

"She's tremendously attractive, Hamil."

"What? Oh, yes, very."

"Evidently no sentiment lost between you," laughed the other.

"No, of course not; no sentiment."

Malcourt said carelessly: "I'm riding with Miss Suydam to-morrow. That's one reason I'm not going on this duck-hunt."

Hamil nodded.

"Another reason," he continued, intent on the glowing end of his cigarette, "is that I'm rather fortunate at the Club just now—and I don't care to disturb any run of luck that seems inclined to drift my way. Would you give your luck the double cross?"

"I suppose not," said Hamil vaguely—"if I ever had any."

"That's the way I feel. And it's all kinds of luck that's chasing me. *All* kinds, Hamil. One kind, for example, wears hair that matches my cuff-links. Odd, isn't it?" he added, examining the golden links with a smile.

Hamil nodded inattentively.

"I am about seven thousand dollars ahead on the other sort of luck," observed Malcourt. "If it holds to-night I'll inaugurate a killing that will astonish the brothers B. yonder. By the way, now that you have your club ticket why don't you use it?—one way or another."

"Perhaps," replied Hamil listlessly.

A few minutes later Malcourt, becoming bored, genially took his leave; and Hamil turned on an electric jet and began to undo his collar and tie.

He was in no hurry; at times he suspended operations to pace aimlessly to and fro; and after a while, half undressed, he dropped into an arm-chair, clinched hands supporting his temples.

Presently he said aloud to himself: "It's absolutely impossible. It can't happen this way. How can it?"

His heavy pulse answered the question; a tense strain, irksome as an ache, dragged steadily at something within him which resisted; dulling reason and thought.

For a long time he sat there inert, listening for the sound of her voice which echoed at moments through the stunned silence within him. And at last he stumbled to his feet like a stricken man on the firing line, stupefied that the thing had happened to *him*; and stood unsteadily, looking around. Then he went heavily about his dressing.

Later, when he was ready to leave his room, he heard Malcourt walking through the corridor outside—a leisurely and lightly stepping Malcourt, whistling a lively air. And, when Malcourt had passed came Cecile rustling from the western corridor, gay, quick-stepping, her enchanting laughter passing through the corridor like a fresh breeze as she joined Mrs. Carrick on the stairs. Then silence; and he opened his door. And Shiela Cardross, passing noiselessly, turned at the sound.

His face must have been easy to read for her own promptly lost its colour, and with an involuntary recoil she stepped back against the wall, staring at him in pallid silence.

"What is the matter?" he asked, scarcely recognising his own voice. And striving to shake off the unreality of it all with a laugh: "You look like some pretty ghost from dreamland—with your white gown and arms and face. Shall we descend into the waking world together?"

They stood for a moment motionless, looking straight at one another; then the smile died out on his face, but he still strove to speak lightly, using effort, like a man with a dream dark upon him: "I am waiting for your pretty ghostship."

Her lips moved in reply; no sound came from them.

"Are you afraid of me?" he said.

"Yes."

"Of *me*, Shiela?"

"Of us both. You don't know—you don't know!"

"Know what, Shiela?"

"What I am—what I have done. And I've got to tell you." Her mouth quivered suddenly, and she faced him fighting for self-control. "I've got to tell you. Things cannot be left in this way between us. I thought they could, but they can't."

He crossed the corridor, slowly; she straightened up at his approach, white, rigid, breathless.

"What is it that has frightened you?" he said.

"What you—said—to me."

"That I love you?"

"Yes; that."

"Why should it frighten you?"

"Must I tell you?"

"If it will help you."

"I am past help. But it will end you're caring for me. And from making me—care—for you. I must do it; this cannot go on—"

"Shiela!"

She faced him, white as death, looking at him blindly.

"I am trying to think of you—because you love me—"

Fright chilled her blood, killing pulse and colour. "I am trying to be kind—because I care for you—and we must end this before it ends us.... Listen to my miserable, pitiful, little secret, Mr. Hamil. I—I have—I am not—free."

"Not *free*!"

"I was married two years ago—when I was eighteen years old. Three people in the world know it: you, I, and—the man I married."

"Married!" he repeated, stupefied.

She looked at him steadily a moment.

"I think your love has been done to death, Mr. Hamil. My own danger was greater than you knew; but it was for your sake—because you loved me. Good night."

Stunned, he saw her pass him and descend the stairs, stood for a space alone, then scarce knowing what he did he went down into the great living-room to take his leave of the family gathered there before dinner had been announced. They all seemed to be there; he was indifferently conscious of hearing his own words like a man who listens to an unfamiliar voice in a distant room.

The rapid soundless night ride to the hotel seemed unreal; the lights in the café, the noise and movement, the pretty face of his aunt with the pink reflection from the candle shades on her cheeks—all seemed as unconvincing as himself and this thing that he could not grasp—could not understand—could not realise had befallen him—and her.

If Miss Palliser was sensible of any change in him or his voice or manner she did not betray it. Wayward came over to speak to them, limping very slightly, tall, straight, ruddy, the gray silvering his temples and edging his moustache.

And after a while Hamil found himself sitting silent, a partly burnt cigar between his fingers, watching Wayward and his youthful aunt in half-intimate, half-formal badinage, elbow to elbow on the cloth. For they had known one another a long time, and through many phases of Fate and Destiny.

"That little Cardross girl is playing the devil with the callow hereabout," Wayward said; "Malcourt, house-broken, runs to heel with the rest. And when I see her I feel like joining the pack. Only—I was never broken, you know—"

"She is a real beauty," said Miss Palliser warmly; "I don't see why you don't enlist, James."

"I may at that. Garry, are you also involved?"

Hamil said, "Yes—yes, of course," and smiled meaninglessly at Wayward.

For a fraction of a second his aunt hesitated, then said: "Garry is naturally among the devoted—when he's not dog-tired from a day in the cypress-swamps. Have you been out to see the work, James? Oh, you should go; everybody goes; it's one of the things to do here. And I'm very proud when I hear people say, 'There's that brilliant young fellow, Hamil,' or, in a tone which expresses profound respect, 'Hamil designed it, you know'; and I smile and think, 'That's my boy Garry!' James, it is a very comfortable sensation for an old lady to experience." And she looked at Wayward out of her lovely golden eyes, sweet as a maid of twenty.

Wayward smiled, then absently bent his gaze on his wine-glass, lying back in his chair. Through his spectacles his eyes seemed very intent on the frail crystal stem of his glass.

"What are you going to do for the rest of the winter?" she asked, watching him.

"What I am doing," he replied with smiling bitterness. "The *Ariani* is yonder when I can't stand the shore.... What else is there for me to do—until I snuff out!"

"Build that house you were going to build—when we were rather younger, Jim."

"I did; and it fell," he said quietly; but, as though she had not heard. "—Build that house," she repeated, "and line it with books—the kind of books that were written and read before the machine-made sort supplanted them. One picture to a room—do you remember, Jim?—or two if you find it better; the kind men painted before Rembrandt died.... Do you remember your plan?—the plans you drew for me to look at in our front parlour—when New York houses had parlours? You were twenty and I fourteen.... Garry, yonder, was not.... And the rugs, you recollect?—one or two in a room, Shiraz, Ispahan—nothing as obvious as Sehna and Saraband—nothing but Moresque and pure Persian—and one agedly perfect gem of Asia Minor, and one Tekke, so old and flawless that only the pigeon-blood fire remained under the violet bloom.... Do you remember?"

Wayward's shoulders straightened with a jerk. For twenty years he had not remembered these things; and she had not only remembered but was now reciting the strange, quaint, resurrected words in their forgotten sequence; the words he had uttered as he—or what he had once been—sat in the old-time parlour in the mellow half light of faded brocades and rosewood, repeating to a child the programme of his future. Lofty aim and high ideal, the cultivated endeavour of good citizenship, loyalty to aspiration, courage, self-respect, and the noble living of life; they had also spoken of these things together—there in the golden gloom of the old-time parlour when she was fourteen and he master of his fate and twenty.

But there came into his life a brilliant woman who stayed a year and left his name a mockery: Malcourt's only sister, now Lady Tressilvain, doubtfully conspicuous with her loutish British husband, among those continentals where titles serve rather to obscure than enlighten inquiry.

The wretched affair dragged its full offensive length through the international press; leaving him with his divorce signed and a future endurable only when his senses had been sufficiently drugged. In sober intervals he now had neuritis and a limp to distract his mind; also his former brother-in-law with professions of esteem and respect and a tendency to borrow. And drunk or sober he had the *Ariani*. But the house that Youth had built in the tinted obscurity of an old New York parlour—no, he didn't have that; and even memory of it were wellnigh gone had not Constance Palliser spoken from the shadows of the past.

He lifted his glass unsteadily and replaced it. Then slowly he raised his head and looked full at Constance Palliser.

"It's too late," he said; "but I wish I had known that you remembered."

"Would you have built it, Jim?"

He looked at her again, then shook his head: "For whom am I to build, Constance?"

She leaned forward, glancing at the unconscious Hamil, then dropped her voice: "Build it for the Boy that Was, Jim."

"A headstone would be fitter—and less expensive."

"I am not asking you to build in memory of the dead. The Boy who Was is only asleep. If you could let him wake, suddenly, in that house—"

A clear flush of surprise stained his skin to the hair. It had been many years since a woman had hinted at any belief in him.

"Don't you know that I couldn't endure the four walls of a house, Constance?"

"You have not tried this house."

"Men—such men as I—cannot go back to the House of Youth."

"Try, Jim."

His hand was shaking as he lifted it to adjust his spectacles; and impulsively she laid her hand on his twitching arm:

"Jim, build it!—and see what happens."

"I cannot."

"Build it. You will not be alone and sad in it if you remember the boy and the child in the parlour. They—they will be good company—if you wish."

He rested his elbows on the table, head bent between his sea-burned hands.

"If I could only, only do something," she whispered. "The boy has merely been asleep, Jim. I have always known it. But it has taken many years for me to bring myself to this moment."

"Do you think a man can come back through such wreckage and mire— do you think he wants to come back? What do you know about it?—with your white skin and bright hair—and that child's mouth of yours—What do you know about it?"

"Once you were the oracle, Jim. May I not have my turn?"

"Yes—but what in God's name do you care?"

"Will you build?"

He looked at her dumbly, hopelessly; then his arm twitched and he relieved the wrist from the weight of his head, sitting upright, his eyes still bent on her.

"Because—in that old parlour—the child expected it of the boy," she said. "And expects it yet."

Hamil, who, chair pushed back, had been listlessly watching the orchestra, roused himself and turned to his aunt and Wayward.

"You want to go, Garry?" said Constance calmly. "I'll walk a little with James before I compose my aged bones to slumber.... Good night, dear. Will you come again soon?"

He said he would and took his leave of them in the long corridor, traversing it without noticing which direction he took until, awaking from abstraction, he found himself at the head of a flight of steps and saw the portico of the railroad station below him and the signal lamps, green and red and white, burning between the glistening rails.

Without much caring where he went, but not desiring to retrace his steps over half a mile or so of carpet, he went out into the open air and along the picket fence toward the lake front.

As he came to the track crossing he glanced across at the Beach Club where lights sparkled discreetly amid a tropical thicket and flowers lay in pale carpets under the stars.

Portlaw had sent him a member's card; he took it out now and scanned it with faint curiosity. His name was written on the round-cornered brown card signed by a "vice-president" and a "secretary," under the engraved notice: "To be shown when requested."

But when he ascended the winding walk among the palms and orange blossoms, this "suicide's tag," as Malcourt called it, was not demanded of him at the door.

The restaurant seemed to be gay and rather noisy, the women vivacious, sometimes beautiful, and often respectable. A reek of cigarette smoke, wine, and orange blossoms hung about the corridors; the tiny glittering rotunda with its gaming-tables in a circle was thronged.

He watched them lose and win and lose again. Under the soft tumult of voices the cool tones of the house attachés sounded monotonously, the ball rattled, the wheels spun. But curiosity had already died out within him; gain, loss, chance, Fate—and the tense white concentration of the man beside him no longer interested him; nor did a sweet-faced young girl in the corridor who looked a second too long at him; nor the handsome over-flushed youth who was with her and who cried out in loud recognition: "Gad, Hamil; why didn't you tell me you were coming? There's somebody here who wants to meet you, but Portlaw's got her—somewhere. You'll take supper with us anyway! We'll find you a fair impenitent."

Hamil stared at him coolly. He was on no such terms with Malcourt, drunk or sober. But everybody was Malcourt's friend just then, and he went on recklessly:

"You've got to stay; hasn't he, Dolly?—Oh, I forgot—Miss Wilming, Mr. Hamil, who's doing the new park, you know. All kinds of genius buzzes in his head—roulette wheels buzz in mine. Hamil, you remember Miss Wilming in the 'Motor Girl.' She was one of the acetylenes. Come on; we'll all light up later. Make him come, Dolly."

Hamil turned to speak to her. She seemed to be, at a casual glance, the sort of young girl who usually has a mother somewhere within ear-shot. Upon inspection, however, her bright hair was a little too perfectly rippled, and her mouth a trifle fuller and redder than a normal circulation might account for. But there remained in the eyes something as yet unquenched. And looking at her, he felt a sense of impatience and regret that the delicate youth of her should be wasted in the flare and shadow of the lesser world—burning to a spectre here on the crumbling edge of things—here with Malcourt leering at her through the disordered brilliancy of that false dawn which heralds only night.

They spoke together, smilingly formal. He had quietly turned his back on Malcourt.

She hoped he would remain and join them; and her as yet unspoiled voice clashed with her tinted lips and hair.

He was sorry—politely so—thanking her with the natural and unconscious gentleness so agreeable to all women. And as in his manner there was not the slightest hint of that half-amused, half-cynical freedom characteristic of the worldly wise whom she was now accustoming herself to meet, she looked up at him with a faint flush of appreciation.

Malcourt all the while was pulling Hamil by the elbow and talking on at random almost boisterously, checking himself at intervals to exchange familiar greetings with new-comers passing the crowded corridor. His face was puffy and red; so were his lips; and there seemed to be a shiny quality to hair and skin prophetic of future coarsening toward a type, individuals of which swarmed like sleek flies around the gaming-tables beyond.

As Hamil glanced from the young girl to Malcourt, who was still noisily importuning him, a sudden contempt for the man arose within him. So unreasoningly abrupt was the sensation of absolute distrust and dislike that it cut his leave-taking to a curt word of refusal, and he turned on his heel.

"What's the matter with you? Aren't you coming with us?" asked Malcourt, reddening.

"No," said Hamil. "Good-bye, Miss Wilming. Thank you for asking me."

She held out her hand, uncertainly; he took it with a manner so gentle and considerate that she ventured, hesitatingly, something about seeing him again. To which he replied, pleasantly conventional, and started toward the door.

"See here, Hamil," said Malcourt sharply, "is there any reason for your sudden and deliberate rudeness to me?"

"Is there any reason for your sudden and deliberate familiarity with me?" retorted Hamil in a low voice. "You're drunk!"

Malcourt's visage crimsoned: "O hell!" he said, "if your morals are as lofty as your mincing manners—"

Hamil stared him into silence, hesitated, then passed in front of him and out of the door.

Vicious with irritation, Malcourt laid his hand on the girl's arm: "Take it from me, Dolly, that's the sort of citizen who'll sneak around to call on your sort Saturday evenings."

She flushed painfully, but said nothing. "As for me," added Malcourt, "I don't think I've quite finished with this nice young man."

But Dolly Wilming stood silent, head bent, slender fingers worrying her lips, which seemed inclined to quiver.

CHAPTER X
TERRA INCOGNITA

The camp-wagon and led horses left before daylight with two of the Cracker guides, Bulow and Carter; but it was an hour after sunrise when Cardross, senior, Gray, Shiela, Hamil, and the head guide, Eudo Stent, rode out of the *patio* into the dewy beauty of a February morning.

The lagoon was pink; so was the white town on its western shore; in the east, ocean and sky were one vast rosy-rayed glory. Few birds sang.

Through the intense stillness of early morning the little cavalcade made a startling clatter on the shell highway; but the rattle of hoofs was soon deadened in the sand of a broad country road curving south through dune and hammock along the lake shore.

Dew still dropped in great splashes from pine and palm; dew powdered the sparkle-berry bushes and lay like a tiny lake of quicksilver in the hollow of every broad palmetto frond; and all around them earth and grass and shrub exhaled the scented freshness of a dew-washed world.

On the still surface of the lake, tinted with palest rose and primrose, the wild ducks floated, darkly silhouetted against the water or, hoping for crumbs, paddled shoreward, inquiringly peering up at the riders with little eyes of brightest gold.

"Blue-bills," said Cardross to Hamil; "nobody shoots them on the lake; they're as tame as barnyard waterfowl. Yet, the instant these same ducks leave this lagoon where they know they're protected they become as wild and wary and as difficult to get a shot at as any other wild-fowl."

Shiela, riding ahead with Gray, tossed bits of bread into the water; and the little blue-bill ducks came swimming in scores, keeping up with the horses so fearlessly and persistently that the girl turned in her saddle and looked back at her father in delight.

"I'm certainly as gifted as the Pied Piper, dad! If they follow me to Ruffle Lake I won't permit a shot to be fired."

While she spoke she kept her eyes on her father. Except for a brief good morning at breakfast she had neither looked at nor spoken to Hamil, making no noticeable effort to avoid him, but succeeded in doing it nevertheless.

Like her father and brother and Hamil she was mounted on an unornamental but wiry Tallahassee horse; and she rode cross-saddle, wearing knee-coat and kilts of kahkee and brown leather puttees strapped from under the kneecap to the ankle. Like the others, too, she carried a small shotgun in a saddle boot, and in the web loops across her breast glimmered the metal rims of a dozen cartridges. A brilliant handkerchief knotted loosely around her bare white throat, and a broad Panama turned up in front and resolutely pulled down behind to defy sunstroke, completed a most bewilderingly charming picture, which moved even her father to admiring comment.

"Only," he added, "look before you step over a log when you're afoot. The fangs of a big diamond-back are three-quarters of an inch long, my dear, and they'll go through leather as a needle goes through cambric."

"Thanks, dad—and here endeth the usual lesson."

Cardross said to Hamil: "One scarcely knows what to think about the snakes here. The records of the entire Union show few deaths in a year, and yet there's no scarcity of rattlers, copperheads, and moccasins in this Republic of ours. I know a man, an ornithologist, who for twelve years has wandered about the Florida woods and never saw a rattler. And yet, the other night a Northern man, a cottager, lighted his cigar after dinner and stepped off his veranda on to a rattler."

"Was he bitten?"

"Yes. He died in two hours." Cardross shrugged and gathered up his bridle. "Personally I have no fear; leggings won't help much; besides, a good-sized snake can strike one's hand as it swings; but our cracker guides go everywhere in thin cotton trousers and the Seminoles are barelegged. One hears often enough of escapes, yet very rarely of anybody being bitten. One of my grove guards was struck by a moccasin last winter. He was an awfully sick nigger for a while, but he got over it."

"That's cheerful," said Hamil, laughing.

"Oh, you might as well know. There are plenty of wiseacres who'll tell you that nobody's in danger at these East Coast resorts, and the hotel people will swear solemnly there isn't a serpent in the State; but there are, Hamil, and plenty of them. I've seen rattlers strike without rattling; and moccasins are ugly brutes that won't get out of the way for you and that give no warning when they strike; and all quail hunters in the flat-woods know how their pointers and setters are killed, and every farmer knows that the best watchmen he can have is a flock of guinea-fowl or turkeys or a few hogs loose. The *fact* is that deadly snakes are not rare in many localities; the *wonder* is that scarcely a death is reported in a year. How many niggers die, I don't know; but I know enough, when I'm in the woods or fields, to look every time before I put my foot upon the ground."

"How can you see in the jungle?"

"You've *got* to see. Besides, rattlers are on the edge of thickets, not inside. They've got to have an open space to strike the small furry creatures which they live on. Moccasins affect mud—*look* there!"

Both horses shyed; in front Shiela's mount was behaving badly, but even while she was mastering him she tried at the same time to extract her shotgun from the leather boot. Stent rode up and drew it out for her; Hamil saw her break and load, swing in the saddle, and gaze straight into an evil-looking bog all set with ancient cypress knees and the undulating snaky roots of palmettos.

"A perfectly enormous one, dad!" she called back.

"Wait!" said Cardross; "I want Hamil to see." And to Hamil: "Ride forward; you ought to know what the ugly brutes look like!"

As he drew bridle at Shiela's left the girl, still intent, pointed in silence; but he looked in vain for the snake, mistaking every palmetto root for a serpent, until she leaned forward and told him to sight along her extended arm. Then he saw a dull gray fold without any glitter to it, draped motionless over a palmetto root, and so like the root that he could scarcely believe it anything else.

"That?"

"Yes. It's as thick as a man's arm."

"Is it a moccasin?"

"It is; a cotton-mouth."

The guide drawled: "Ah reckon he's asleep, Miss Cahdhoss. Ah'll make him rare up 'f yew say so."

"Make him rear up," suggested Gray. "And stand clear, Hamil, because Shiela must shoot quick if he slides for the water."

The men backed their nervously snorting horses, giving her room; Stent dismounted, picked up a pig-nut, and threw it accurately. Instantly the fat mud-coloured fold slipped over the root and a head appeared rising straight out of the coils up into the air—a flat and rather small head on a horribly swollen body, stump-tailed, disgusting. The head was looking at them, stretched high, fully a third of the creature in the air. Then, soundlessly, the wide-slitted mouth opened; and Hamil saw its silky white lining.

"Moccasins stand their ground," said the girl, raising her gun. The shot crashed out; the snake collapsed. For fully a minute they watched; not a fold even quivered.

"Struck by lightning," said Gray; "the buzzards will get him." And he drew a folding butterfly net from his saddle boot, affixed ring and gauze bag, and cantered forward briskly in the wake of a great velvety black butterfly which was sailing under the live-oaks above his head.

His father, wishing to talk to Eudo Stent, rode ahead with the guide, leaving Shiela and Hamil to follow.

The latter reined in and waited while the girl leisurely returned the fowling-piece to its holster. Then, together, they walked their horses forward, wading the "branch" which flowed clear as a trout stream out of the swamp on their right.

"It looks drinkable," he said.

"It is, for Crackers; but there's fever in it for you, Mr. Hamil.... Look at Gray! He's missed his butterfly. But it's a rather common one—the black form of the tiger swallow-tail. Just see those zebra-striped butterflies darting like lightning over the palmetto scrub! Gray and I could never catch them until one day we found a ragged one that couldn't fly and we placed it on a leaf; and every time one of those butterflies came our way it paused in its flight for a second and hovered over the ragged one. And that's how Gray and I caught the swift Ajax butterflies for his collection!... I've helped him considerably, if you please; I brought him the mysterious Echo moth from Ormond, and a wonderful little hornet moth from Jupiter Inlet."

She was rattling on almost feverishly, never looking at him, restless in her saddle, shifting bridle, adjusting stirrups, gun-case, knotting and reknotting her neckerchief, all with that desperate attempt at composure which betrays the courage that summons it.

"Shiela, dear!"

"What!" she said, startled into flushed surprise.

"Look at me."

She turned in her saddle, the colour deepening and waning on her white skin from neck to temples; and sustained his gaze to the limit of endurance. Then again in her ears sounded the soft crash of her senses; he swung wide in his stirrups, looking recklessly into her eyes. A delicate sense of intoxication stilled all speech between them for a moment. Then, head bowed, eyes fixed on her bridle hand, the other hand, ungloved, lying hotly unresponsive in his, she rode slowly forward at his side. Face to face with all the mad unasked questions of destiny and fate and chance still before her—all the cold problems of truth and honour still to be discussed with that stirring, painful pulse in her heart which she had known as conscience—silently, head bent, she rode into the west with the man she must send away.

Far to the north-east, above a sentinel pine which marks the outskirts of the flat-woods, streaks like smoke drifted in the sky—the wild-fowl leaving the lagoons. On the Lantana Road they drew bridle at a sign from her; then she wheeled her horse and sat silent in her saddle, staring into the western wilderness.

The character of the country had changed while they had been advancing along this white sandy road edged with jungle; for now west and south the Florida wilderness stretched away, the strange "Flat-woods," deceptively open, almost park-like in their monotony where, as far as the eye could see, glade after glade, edged by the stately vivid green pines, opened invitingly into other glades through endlessly charming perspective. At every step one was prepared to come upon some handsome mansion centring this park—some bridge spanning the shallow crystal streams that ran out of jasmine thickets—some fine driveway curving through the open woods. But this was the wilderness, uninhabited, unplotted. No dwelling stood within its vistas; no road led out or in; no bridge curved over the silently moving waters. West and south-west into the unknown must he go who follows the lure of those peaceful, sunny glades where there are no hills, no valleys, nothing save trees and trees and trees again, and shallow streams with jungle edging them, and lonely lakes set with cypress, and sunny clearings, never made by human hands, where last year's grass, shoulder-high, silvers under the white sun of the South.

Half a hundred miles westward lay the great inland lake; south-west, the Everglades. The Hillsboro trail ran south-west between the upper and lower chain of lakes, over Little Fish Crossing, along the old Government trail, and over the Loxahatchi. Westward no trail lay save those blind signs of the Seminoles across the wastes of open timber and endless stretches of lagoon and saw-grass which is called the Everglades.

On the edge of the road where Hamil sat his horse was an old pump—the last indication of civilisation. He dismounted and tried it, filling his cup with clear sparkling water, neither hot nor cold, and walking through the sand offered it to Shiela Cardross.

"Osceola's font," she nodded, returning from her abstraction; "thank you, I am thirsty." And she drained the cup at her leisure, pausing at moments to look into the west as though the wilderness had already laid its spell upon her.

Then she looked down at Hamil beside her, handing him the cup.

"*In-nah-cahpoor?*" she asked softly; and as he looked up puzzled and smiling: "I asked you, in Seminole, what is the price I have to pay for your cup of water?"

"A little love," he said quietly—"a very little, Shiela."

"I see!—like this water, neither warm nor cold: *nac-ey-tai?*—what do you call it?—oh, yes, sisterly affection." She looked down at him with a forced smile. "*Uncah*" she said, "which in Seminole means 'yes' to your demand.... You don't mind if I relapse into the lake dialect occasionally— do you?—especially when I'm afraid to say it in English." And, gaining confidence, she smiled at him, the faintest hint of tenderness in her eyes. "Neither warm nor cold—*Haiee-Kasapi*!—like this Indian well, Mr. Hamil; but, like it, very faithful—even when in the arid days to come you turn to drink from sweeter springs."

"Shiela!"

"Oh, no—no!" she breathed, releasing her hands; "you interrupt me; I was thinking *ist-ahmah-mahhen*—which way we must go. Listen; we leave the road yonder where Gray's green butterfly net is bobbing above the dead grass: *in-e-gitskah?*—can't you see it? And there are dad and Stent riding in line with that outpost pine—*ho-paiee*! Mount, my cavalier. And"—in a lower voice—"perhaps you also may hear that voice in the wilderness which cried once to the unwise."

As they rode girth-high through the grass the first enchanting glade opened before them, flanked by palmettos and pines. Gray was galloping about in the woods among swarms of yellow and brown butterflies, swishing his net like a polo mallet, and drawing bridle every now and then to examine some specimen and drop it into the cyanide jar which bulged from his pocket.

"I got a lot of those dog's-head fellows!" he called out to Shiela as she came past with Hamil. "You remember that the white ants got at my other specimens before I could mount them."

"I remember," said Shiela; "don't ride too hard in the sun, dear." But Gray saw something ahead and shook out his bridle, and soon left them in the rear once more, riding through endless glades of green where there was no sound except the creak of leather and the continuous popping of those small pods on the seeds of which quail feed.

"I thought there were no end of gorgeous flowers in the semi-tropics," he said, "but there's almost nothing here except green."

She laughed. "The concentration of bloom in Northern hothouses deceives people. The semi-tropics and the tropics are almost monotonously green except where cultivated gardens exist. There are no masses of flowers anywhere; even the great brilliant blossoms make no show because they are widely scattered. You notice them when you happen to come across them in the woods, they are so brilliant and so rare."

"Are there no fruits—those delectable fruits one reads about?"

"There are bitter wild oranges, sour guavas, eatable beach-grapes and papaws. If you're fond of wild cassava and can prepare it so it won't poison you, you can make an eatable paste. If you like oily cabbage, the top of any palmetto will furnish it. But, my poor friend, there's little here to tempt one's appetite or satisfy one's aesthetic hunger for flowers. Our Northern meadows are far more gorgeous from June to October; and our wild fruits are far more delicious than what one finds growing wild in the tropics."

"But bananas, cocoa-nuts, oranges—"

"All cultivated!"

"Persimmons, mulberries—"

"All cultivated when eatable. Everything palatable in this country is cultivated."

He laughed dejectedly, then, again insistent: "But there *are* plenty of wild flowering trees!—magnolia, poinciana, china-berry—"

"All set out by mere man," she smiled—"except the magnolias and dog-wood. No, Mr. Hamil, the riotous tropical bloom one reads about is confined to people's gardens. When you come upon jasmine or an orchid in the woods you notice the colour at once in the green monotony. But think how many acres of blue and white and gold one passes in the North with scarcely a glance! The South is beautiful too, in its way; but it is not that way. Yet I care for it even more, perhaps, than I do for the North—"

The calm, even tenor of the speech between them was reassuring her, although it was solving no problems which, deep in her breast, she knew lay latent, ready to quicken at any instant.

All that awaited to be solved; all that threatened between her and her heart and conscience, now lay within her, quiescent for the moment. And it was from moment to moment now that she was living, blindly evading, resolutely putting off what must come after that relentless self-examination which was still before her.

The transport wagon was now in sight ahead; and Bulow, one of the guides, had released a brace of setters, casting them out among the open pines.

Away raced the belled dogs, jingling into the saw-scrub; and Shiela nodded to him to prepare for a shot as she drew her own gun from its boot and loaded, eyes still following the distant dogs.

To and fro raced the setters, tails low, noses up, wheeling, checking, quartering, cutting up acres and acres—a stirring sight!—and more stirring still when the blue-ticked dog, catching the body-scent, slowed down, flag whipping madly, and began to crawl into the wind.

"You and Shiela!" called out Cardross as they trotted up, guns resting on their thighs. "Gray and I'll pick up the singles."

The girl sprang to the ground, gun poised; Hamil followed her, and they walked across the sandy open where scarcely a tuft of dead grass bristled. It seemed impossible that any living creature bigger than an ant could conceal itself on that bare, arid sand stretch, but the ticked dog was standing rigid, nose pointing almost between his forefeet, and the red dog was backing him, tail like a ramrod, right forefoot doubled, jaws a-slaver.

The girl glanced sideways at Hamil mischievously.

"What are we shooting for, Mr. Hamil?"

"Anything you wish," he said, "but it's yours anyway—all I can give. I suppose I'm going to miss."

"No; you mustn't. If you're out of practice remember to let them get well away. And I won't shoot a match with you this time. Shall I flush?"

"I'll put them up. Are you ready?"

"Quite, thank you."

He stepped up beside the ticked dog, halted, took one more step beyond—whir-r-r! and the startled air was filled with wings; and crack! crack! crack-crack! spoke the smokeless powder.

Two quail stopped in mid-air and pitched downward.

"O Lord!" said Hamil, "they're not my birds. Shiela, how *could* you do such a thing under my very nose and in sight of your relatives and three unfeeling guides!"

"You poor boy'" she said, watching the bevy as he picked up the curious, dark, little Florida quail and displayed them. Then, having marked, she quietly signalled the dogs forward.

"I'm not going," he said; "I've performed sufficiently."

She was not quite sure how much of disappointment lay under his pretence, and rather shyly she suggested that he redeem himself. Gray and his father were walking toward one dog who was now standing; two quail flushed and both fell.

"Come," she said, laying her hand lightly on his arm; "Ticky is pointing and I *will* have you redeem yourself."

So they went forward, shoulder to shoulder; and three birds jumped and two fell.

"Bravo!" she exclaimed radiantly; "I knew my cavalier after all!"

"You held your fire," he said accusingly.

"Ye-s."

"Why?"

"Because—if you—" She raised her eyes half serious, half mockingly: "Do you think I care for—anything—at your expense?"

A thrill passed through him. "Do you think I mind if you are the better of us, you generous girl?"

"I am not a better shot; I really am not.... Look at these birds—both cocks. Are they not funny—these quaint little black quail of the semi-tropics? We'll need all we can get, too. But now that you are your resistless self again I shall cease to dread the alternative of starvation or a resort to alligator tail."

So with a gay exchange of badinage they took their turns when the dogs rounded up singles; and sometimes he missed shamefully, and sometimes he performed with credit, but she never amended his misses nor did more than match his successes, and he thought that in all his life he had never witnessed more faultless field courtesy than this young girl instinctively displayed. Nothing in the world could have touched him more keenly or convinced him more thoroughly. For it is on the firing line that character shows; a person is what he is in the field—even though he sometimes neglects to live up to it in less vital moments.

Generous and quick in her applause, sensitive under his failures, cool in difficulties, yielding instantly the slightest advantage to him, holding her fire when singles rose or where there could be the slightest doubt—that was his shooting companion under the white noon sun that day. He noticed, too, her sweetness with the dogs, her quick encouragement when work was well done, her brief rebuke when the red dog, galloping recklessly down wind, jumped a ground-rattler and came within a hair's breadth of being bitten.

"The little devil!" said Hamil, looking down at the twisting reptile which he had killed with a palmetto stem. "Why, Shiela, he has no rattles at all."

"No, only a button. Dig a hole and bury the head. Fangs are always fangs whether their owner is dead or alive."

So Hamil scooped out a trench with his hunting-knife and they buried the little ground-rattler while both dogs looked on, growling.

Cardross and Gray had remounted; Bulow cast out a brace of pointers for them, and they were already far away. Presently the distant crack of their guns announced that fresh bevies had been found beyond the branch.

The guide, Carter, rode out, bringing Shiela and Hamil their horses and relieving the latter's pockets of a dozen birds; announcing a halt for luncheon at the same time in a voice softly neglectful of I's and R's, and musical with aspirates.

As they followed him slowly toward the wagon which stood half a mile away under a group of noble pines, Hamil began in a low voice:

"I've got to say this, Shiela: I never saw more perfect sportsmanship than yours; and, if only for that, I love you with all my heart."

"What a boyish thing to say!" But she coloured deliciously.

"You don't care whether I love you—that way, do you?" he asked hopefully.

"N-no."

"Then—I can wait."

She turned toward him, confused.

"Wait?" she repeated.

"Yes—wait; all my life, if it must be."

"There is nothing to wait for. Don't say such things to me. I—it's difficult enough for me now—to think what to do—You will not speak to me again that way, will you? Because, if you do, I must send you away.... And that will be—hard."

"Once," he said, "you spoke about men—how they come crashing through the barriers of friendship. Am I like that?"

She hesitated, looked at him.

"There were no barriers."

"No barriers!"

"None—to keep you out. I should have seen to it; I should have been prepared; but you came so naturally into my friendship—inside the barriers—that I opened my eyes and found you there—and remembered, too late, alas—"

"Too late?"

"Too late to shut you out. And you frightened me last night; I tried to tell you—for your own sake; I was terrified, and I told you what I have never before told a living soul—that dreadful, hopeless, nightmare thing—to drive you out of my—my regard—and me from yours."

His face whitened a little under its tan, but the flat jaw muscles tightened doggedly.

"I don't understand—yet," he said. "And when you tell me—for you will tell me sooner or later—it will not change me."

"It *must!*"

He shook his head.

She said in desperation: "You cannot care for me too much because you know that I am—not free."

"Cannot?" He laughed mirthlessly. "I *am* caring for you—loving you—every second more and more."

"That is dishonourable," she faltered.

"Why?"

"You *know!*"

"Yes. But if it does not change me how can I help it?"

"You can help making me care for *you!*"

His heart was racing now; every vein ran fiery riot.

"Is there a chance of *that*, Shiela?"

She did not answer, but the tragedy in her slowly lifted eyes appalled him. Then a rushing confusion of happiness and pain almost stupefied him.

"You must not be afraid," he managed to say while the pulse hammered in his throat, and the tumult of his senses deadened his voice to a whisper.

"I am afraid."

They were near the wagon now; both dismounted under the pines while Bulow came forward to picket their horses. On their way together among the trees she looked up at him almost piteously: "You must go if you talk to me again like this. I could not endure very much of it."

"I don't know what I am going to do," he said in the same curiously deadened voice. "You must tell me more."

"I cannot. I am—uncertain of myself. I can't think clearly when we—when you speak to me—this way. Couldn't you go North before I—before my unhappiness becomes too real—too hard?—couldn't you go before it is too late—and leave me my peace of mind, my common sense!"

He looked around at her. "Yes," he said, "I will go if there is no decent chance for us; and if it is not too late."

"I have my common senses still left. It is not too late."

There was a silence. "I will go," he said very quietly.

"W-when?"

"The day we return."

"Can you leave your work?"

"Yes. Halloran knows."

"And—you *will* go?"

"Yes, if you wish it."

Another silence. Then she shook her head, not looking at him.

"There is no use in going—now."

"Why?"

"Because—because I do not wish it." Her eyes fell lower; she drew a long, unsteady breath. "And because it is too late," she said. "You should have gone before I ever knew you—if I was to be spared my peace of mind."

Gray came galloping back through the woods, followed by his father and Eudo Stent. They were rather excited, having found signs of turkey along the mud of a distant branch; and, as they all gathered around a cold luncheon spread beside the wagon, a lively discussion began concerning the relative chances of "roosting" and "yelping."

Hamil talked as in a dream, scarcely conscious that he was speaking and laughing a great deal. A heavenly sort of intoxication possessed him; a paradise of divine unrealities seemed to surround him—Shiela, the clustering pines, the strange white sunlight, the depthless splendour of the unshadowed blue above.

He heard vaguely the voices of the others, Cardross, senior, rallying Gray on his shooting, Gray replying in kind, the soft Southern voices of the guides at their own repast by the picket line, the stir and whisk and crunch of horses nuzzling their feed.

Specks moved in the dome of heaven—buzzards. Below, through the woods, myriads of robins were flying about, migrants from the North.

Gray displayed his butterflies; nothing uncommon, except a black and green one seldom found north of Miami—but they all bent over the lovely fragile creatures, admiring the silver-spangled Dione butterflies, the great velvety black Turnus; and Shiela, with the point of a dry pine needle, traced for Hamil the grotesque dog's head on the fore wings of those lemon-tinted butterflies which haunt the Florida flat-woods.

"He'd never win at a bench-show," observed her father, lighting his pipe—an out-of-door luxury he clung to. "Shiela, you little minx, what makes you look so unusually pretty? Probably that wild-west rig of yours. Hamil, I hope you gave her a few points on grassing a bird. She's altogether too conceited. Do you know, once, while we were picking up singles, a razor-back boar charged us—or more probably the dogs, which were standing, poor devils. And upon my word I was so rattled that I did the worst thing possible—I tried to kick the dogs loose. Of course they went all to pieces, and I don't know how it might have fared with us if my little daughter had not calmly bowled over that boar at three paces from my shin-bones!"

"Dad exaggerates," observed the girl with heightened colour, then ventured a glance at Hamil which set his heart galloping; and her own responded to the tender pride and admiration in his eyes.

There was more discussion concerning "roosting" versus "yelping" with dire designs upon the huge wild turkey-cock whose tracks Gray had discovered in the mud along the branch where their camp was to be pitched.

Seven hens and youthful gobblers accompanied this patriarch according to Eudo Stent's calculations, and Bulow thought that the Seminole might know the location of the roost; probably deep in some uninviting swamp.

But there was plenty of time to decide what to do when they reached camp; and half an hour later they started, wagon and all, wheels bumping over the exposed tree roots which infinitely bored the well-behaved dogs, squatting forward, heads in a row, every nose twitching at the subtle forest odours that only a dog could detect.

Once they emitted short and quickly stifled yelps as a 'possum climbed leisurely into a small tree and turned to inspect the strange procession which was invading his wilderness. And Shiela and Hamil, riding behind the wagon, laughed like children.

Once they passed under a heronry—a rather odoriferous patch of dead cypress and pines, where the enormous nests bulged in the stark tree-tops;

and once, as they rode out into a particularly park-like and velvety glade, five deer looked up, and then deliberately started to trot across.

"We need that venison!" exclaimed Gray, motioning for his gun which was in the wagon. Shiela spurred forward, launching her mount into a gallop; Hamil's horse followed on a dead run, he tugging madly at the buck-shot shell in his web belt; and away they tore to head the deer. In vain! for the agile herd bounded past far out of shell-range and went crashing on through the jungle of the branch; and Shiela reined in and turned her flushed face to Hamil with a laugh of sheer delight.

"Glorious sight, wasn't it?" said Hamil. "I'm rather glad they got clear of us."

"So am I. There was no chance, but I always try."

"So shall I," he said—"whether there is a chance or not."

She looked up quickly, reading his meaning. Then she bent over the gun that she was breaking, extracted the shells, looped them, and returned the weapon to its holster.

Behind them her father and brother jeered at them for their failure, Gray being particularly offensive in ascribing their fiasco to bad riding and buck-fever.

A little later Shiela's horse almost unseated her, leaping aside and into the jungle as an enormous black snake coiled close in front.

"Don't shoot!" she cried out to Hamil, mastering her horse and forcing him past the big, handsome, harmless reptile; "nobody shoots black snakes or buzzards here. Slip your gun back quickly or Gray will torment you."

However, Gray had seen, and kept up a running fire of sarcastic comment which made Hamil laugh and Shiela indignant.

And so they rode along through the rich afternoon sunshine, now under the clustered pines, now across glades where wild doves sprang up into clattering flight displaying the four white feathers, or pretty little ground doves ran fearlessly between the horses' legs.

Here and there a crimson cardinal, crest lifted, sat singing deliciously on some green bough; now and then a summer tanager dropped like a live coal into the deeper jungle. Great shiny blue, crestless jays flitted over the scrub; shy black and white and chestnut chewinks flirted into sight and out again among the heaps of dead brush; red-bellied woodpeckers, sticking to the tree trunks, turned their heads calmly; gray lizards, big, ugly red-headed lizards, swift slender lizards with blue tails raced across the dry leaves or up tree trunks, making even more fuss and clatter than the noisy cinnamon-tinted thrashers in the underbrush.

Every step into the unknown was a new happiness; there was no silence there for those who could hear, no solitude for those who could see. And he was riding into it with a young companion who saw and heard and loved and understood it all. Nothing escaped her; no frail air plant trailing from the high water oaks, no school of tiny bass in the shallows where their horses splashed through, no gopher burrow, no foot imprint of the little wild things which haunt the water's edge in forests.

Her eyes missed nothing; her dainty close-set ears heard all—the short, dry note of a chewink, the sweet, wholesome song of the cardinal, the thrilling cries of native jays and woodpeckers, the heavenly outpoured melody of the Florida wren, perched on some tiptop stem, throat swelling under the long, delicate, upturned bill.

Void of self-consciousness, sweetly candid in her wisdom, sharing her lore with him as naturally as she listened to his, small wonder that to him the wilderness was paradise, and she with her soft full voice, a native guide. For all around them lay an enchanted world as young as they—the world is never older than the young!—and they "had eyes and they saw; ears had they and they heard"—but not the dead echoes of that warning voice, alas! calling through the ancient wilderness of fable.

CHAPTER XI
PATHFINDERS

Considerably impressed by her knowledge he was careful not to embarrass her by saying so too seriously.

"For a frivolous and fashionable girl who dances cotillions, drives four, plays polo, and reviews her serious adorers by regiments, you're rather perplexing," he said. "Of course you don't suppose that I really believe all you say about these beasts and birds and butterflies."

"What has disturbed your credulity?" she laughed.

"Well, that rabbit which crossed ahead, for one thing. You promptly called it a marsh rabbit!"

"*Lepus palustris*" she nodded, delighted.

"By all means," he retorted, pretending offensive scepticism, "but why a *marsh* rabbit?"

"Because, monsieur, its tail was brown, not white. Didn't you notice that?"

"Oh, it's all very well for you to talk that way, but I've another grievance. All these holes in the sand you call gopher burrows sometimes, sometimes salamander holes. And I saw a thing like a rat run into one of them and a thing like a turtle run into another and I think I've got you now—"

Her delightful laughter made the forest silence musical.

"You poor boy! No wonder your faith is strained. The Crackers call the gopher a salamander, and they also call the land turtle a gopher. Their burrows are alike and usually in the same neighbourhood."

"Well, what I want to know is where you had time to learn all this?" he persisted.

"From my tame Seminole, if you please."

"Your Seminole!"

"Yes, indeed, my dear, barelegged, be-turbaned Seminole, Little Tiger. I am now twenty, Mr. Hamil; for ten years every winter he has been with us on our expeditions. A week before we start Eudo Stent goes to the north-west edge of the Everglades, and makes smoke talk until he gets a brief answer somewhere on the horizon. And always, when we arrive in camp, a Seminole fire is burning under a kettle and before it sits my Little Tiger wearing a new turban and blinking through the smoke haze like a tree-lynx lost in thought."

"Do you mean that this aboriginal admirer of yours has already come out of the Everglades to meet you at your camp?"

"Surely he is there, waiting at this moment," she said. "I'd as soon doubt the stars in their courses as the Seminole, Coacochee. And you will see very soon, now, because we are within a mile of camp."

"Within a mile!" he scoffed. "How do you know? For the last two hours these woods and glades have all looked precisely alike to me. There's no trail, no blaze, no hills, no valleys, no change in vegetation, not the slightest sign that I can discover to warrant any conclusion concerning our whereabouts!"

She threw back her head and laughed deliciously.

"My pale-face brother," she said, "do you see that shell mound?"

"Is that hump of rubbish a shell mound?" he demanded scornfully.

"It certainly is; did you expect a pyramid? Well, then, that is the first sign, and it means that we are very near camp.... And can you not smell cedar smoke?"

"Not a whiff!" he said indignantly.

"Can't you even *see* it?"

"Where in Heaven's name, Shiela?"

Her arm slanted upward across his saddle: "That pine belt is *too* blue; do you notice it now? That is smoke, my obstinate friend."

"It's more probably swamp mist; I think you're only a pretty counterfeit!" he said, laughing as he caught the volatile aroma of burning cedar. But he wouldn't admit that she knew where she was, even when she triumphantly pointed out the bleached skull of an alligator nailed to an ungainly black-jack. So they rode on, knee to knee, he teasing her about her pretended woodcraft, she bantering him; but in his lively skirmishes and her disdainful retorts there was always now an undertone which they both already had begun to detect and listen for: the unconscious note of tenderness sounding at moments through the fresh, quick laughter and gayest badinage.

But under all her gaiety, at moments, too, the dull alarm sounded in her breast; vague warning lest her heart be drifting into deeper currents where perils lay uncharted and unknown.

With every intimate and silent throb of warning she shivered, responsive, masking her growing uncertainty with words. And all the while, deep in her unfolding soul, she was afraid, afraid. Not of this man; not of herself as she had been yesterday. She was afraid of the unknown in her, yet unrevealed, quickening with instincts the parentage of which she knew nothing. What might be these instincts of inheritance, how ominous their power, their trend, she did not know; from whom inherited she could never, never know. Would engrafted and acquired instincts aid her; would training control this unknown heritage from a father and a mother whose very existences must always remain without concrete meaning to her?

Since that dreadful day two years ago when a word spoken inadvertently, perhaps maliciously, by Mrs. Van Dieman, made it necessary that she be told the truth; since the dazed horror of that revelation when, beside herself with grief and shame, she had turned blindly to herself for help; and, childish impulse answering, had hurled her into folly unutterable, she had, far in the unlighted crypt of her young soul, feared this unknown sleeping self, its unfolded intelligence, its passions unawakened.

Through many a night, wet-eyed in darkness, she had wondered whose blood it was that flowed so warmly in her veins; what inherited capacity for good and evil her soul and body held; whose eyes she had; whose hair, and skin, and hands, and who in the vast blank world had given colour to these eyes, this skin and hair, and shaped her fingers, her mouth, her limbs, the delicate rose-tinted nails whitening in the clinched palm as she lay there on her bed at night awake.

The darkness was her answer.

And thinking of these things she sighed unconsciously.

"What is it, Shiela?" he asked.

"Nothing; I don't know—the old pain, I suppose."

"Pain?" he repeated anxiously.

"No; only apprehension. You know, don't you? Well, then, it is nothing; don't ask me." And, noting the quick change in his face—"No, no; it is not what you think. How quickly you are hurt! My apprehension is not about you; it concerns myself. And it is quite groundless. I know what I must do; I *know!*" she repeated bitterly. "And there will always be a straight path to the end; clear and straight, until I go out as nameless as I came in to all this.... Don't touch my hand, please.... I'm trying to think.... I can't, if we are in contact.... And you don't know who you are touching; and I can't tell you. Only two in all the world, if they are alive, could tell you. And they never will tell you—or tell me—why they left me here alone."

With a little shiver she released her hand, looking straight ahead of her for a few moments, then, unconsciously up into the blue overhead.

"I shall love you always," he said. "Right or wrong, always. Remember that, too, when you think of these things."

She turned as though slowly aroused from abstraction, then shook her head.

"It's very brave and boyish of you to be loyal—"

"You speak to me as though I were not years older than you!"

"I can't help it; I am old, old, sometimes, and tired of an isolation no one can break for me."

"If you loved me—"

"How *can* I? You *know* I cannot!"

"Are you afraid to love me?"

She blushed crimson, saying: "If I—if such a misfortune—"

"Such a misfortune as your loving me?"

"Yes; if it came, I would never, never admit it! Why do you say these things to me? Won't you understand? I've tried so hard—so hard to warn you!" The colour flamed in her cheeks; a sort of sweet anger possessed her.

"Must I tell you more than I have told before you can comprehend the utter impossibility of any—love—between us?"

His hand fell over hers and held it crushed.

"Tell me no more," he said, "until you can tell me that you dare to love!"

"What do you mean? Do you mean that a girl does not do a dishonourable thing because she dares not?—a sinful thing because she's afraid? If it were only that—" She smiled, breathless. "It is not fear. It is that a girl *can* not love where love is forbidden."

"And you believe that?"

"Believe it!"—in astonishment.

"Yes; do you believe it?"

She had never before questioned it. Dazed by his impatience, dismayed, she affirmed it again, mechanically. And the first doubt entered as she spoke, confusing her, awakening a swarm of little latent ideas and misgivings, stirring memories of half-uttered sentences checked at her entrance into a room, veiled allusions, words, nods, that she remembered but had never understood. And, somehow, his question seemed a key to this cipher, innocently retained in the unseen brain-cells, stored up without suspicion— almost without curiosity.

For all her recent eloquence upon unhappiness and divorce, it came to her now in some still subtle manner, that she had been speaking concerning things in the world of which she knew nothing. And one of them, perhaps, was love.

Then every instinct within her revolted, all her innate delicacy, all the fastidious purity recoiled before the menace of his question. Love! Was it possible? Was this that she already felt, *love*? Could such treachery to herself, such treason to training and instinct arise within her and she not know it?

Panic-stricken she raised her head; and at sight of him a blind impulse to finish with him possessed her—to crush out that menace—end it for ever—open his eyes to the inexorable truth.

"Lean nearer," she said quietly. Every vestige of blood had left her face.

"Listen to me. Two years ago I was told that I am a common foundling. Under the shock of that—disclosure—I ruined my life for ever.... Don't speak! I mean to check that ruin where it ended—lest it spread to—others. Do you understand?"

"No," he said doggedly.

She drew a steady breath. "Then I'll tell you more if I must. I ruined my life for ever two years ago!... I must have been quite out of my senses—they had told me that morning, very tenderly and pitifully—what you already know. I—it was—unbearable. The world crashed down around me—horror, agonized false pride, sheer terror for the future—"

She choked slightly, but went on:

"I was only eighteen. I wanted to die. I meant to leave my home at any rate. Oh, I know my reasoning was madness, the thought of their charity— the very word itself as my mind formed it—drove me almost insane. I might have known it was love, not charity, that held me so safely in their hearts. But when a blow falls and reason goes—how can a girl reason?"

She looked down at her bridle hand.

"There was a man," she said in a low voice; "he was only a boy then."

Hamil's face hardened.

"Until he asked me I never supposed any man could ever want to marry me. I took it for granted.... He was Gray's friend; I had always known him.... He had been silly sometimes. He asked me to marry him. Then he asked me again.

"I was a débutante that winter, and we were rehearsing some theatricals for charity which I had to go through with.... And he asked me to marry him. I told him what I was and he still wished it."

Hamil bent nearer from his saddle, face tense and colourless.

"I don't know exactly what I thought; I had a dim notion of escaping from the disgrace of being nameless. It was the mad clutch of the engulfed at anything.... Not with any definite view—partly from fright, partly I think for the sake of those who had been kind to a—a foundling; some senseless idea that it was my duty to relieve them of a squalid burden—" She shook her head vaguely: "I don't know exactly—I don't know."

"You married him."

"Yes—I believe so."

"Don't you *know*?"

"Oh, yes," she said wearily, "I know what I did. It was that."

And after he had waited for her in silence for fully a minute she said in a low voice:

"I was very lonely, very, very tired; he urged me; I had been crying. I have seldom cried since. It is curious, isn't it? I can feel the tears in my eyes at night sometimes. But they never fall."

She passed her gloved hand slowly across her forehead and eyes.

"I—married him. At first I did not know what to do; did not realise, understand. I scarcely do yet. I had supposed I was to go to mother and dad and tell them that I had a name in the world—that all was well with me at last. But I could not credit it myself; the boy—I had known him always— went and came in our house as freely as Gray. And I could not convince myself that the thing that had happened was serious—had really occurred."

"How did it occur?"

"I will tell you exactly. We were walking home, all of us, along Fifth Avenue, that winter afternoon. The avenue was gay and densely crowded; and I remember the furs I wore and the western sunset crimsoning the cross-streets, and the early dusk—and Jessie ahead with Cecile and the dogs. And then he said that now was the time, for he was going back to college that same day, and would not return before Easter—and he urged it, and hurried me—and—I couldn't think; and I went with him, west, I believe—yes, the sky was red over the river—west, two blocks, or more.... There was a parsonage. It lasted only a few minutes.... We took the elevated to Fifty-ninth Street and hurried east, almost running. They had just reached the Park and had not yet missed us.... And that is all."

"All?"

"Yes," she said, raising her pale face to his. "What more is there?"

"The—man."

"He was as frightened as I," she said simply, "and he went back to college that same evening. And when I had become still more frightened and a little saner I wrote asking him if it was really true. It was. There seemed to be nothing to do; I had no money, nor had he. And there was no love—because I could not endure even his touch or suffer the least sentiment from him when he came back at Easter. He was a boy and silly. He annoyed me. I don't know why he persisted so; and finally I became thoroughly exasperated.... We did not part on very friendly terms; and I think that was why he did not return to us from college when he graduated. A man offered him a position, and he went away to try to make a place for himself in the world. And after he had gone, somehow the very mention of his name began to chill me. You see nobody knew. The deception became a shame to me, then a dull horror. But, little by little, not seeing him, and being young, after a year the unreality of it all grew stronger, and it seemed as though I were awaking from a nightmare, among familiar things once more.... And for a year it has been so, though at night, sometimes, I still lie awake. But I have been contented—until—*you* came.... Now you know it all."

"All?"

"Every word. And now you understand why I cannot care for you, or you for me."

He said in a deadened voice: "There is a law that deals with that sort of man—"

"What are you saying?" she faltered.

"That you cannot remain bound! Its monstrous. There is a law—"

"I cannot disgrace dad!" she said. "There is no chance that way! I'd rather die than have him know—have mother know—and Jessie and Cecile and Gray! Didn't you understand that?"

"You must tell them nevertheless, and they must help you."

"Help me?"

"To free yourself—"

Flushed with anger and disdain she drew bridle and faced him.

"If *this* is the sort of friendship you bring me, what is your love worth?" she asked almost fiercely. "And—I cared for you—cared for the man I believed you to be; bared my heart to you—wrung every secret from it— thinking you understood! And you turn on me counselling the law, divorce, horrors unthinkable!—because you say you *love* me!... And I tell you that if I loved you—dearly—blindly—I could not endure to free myself at the expense of pain—to them—even for your sake! They took me, nameless, as I was—a—a foundling. If they ever learn what I have done I shall ask their pardon on my knees, and accept life with the man I married. But if they never learn I shall remain with them—always. You have asked me what chance you have. Now you know! It is useless to love me. I cared enough for you to try to kill what you call love last night. I cared enough to-day to strip my heart naked for you—to show you there was no chance. If I have done right or wrong I do not know—but I did it for your sake."

His face reddened painfully, but as he offered no reply she put her horse in motion and rode on, proud little head averted. For a few minutes neither he nor she spoke, their horses pacing neck and neck through the forest. At last he said: "You are right, Shiela; I am not worth it. Forgive me."

She turned, eyes level and fearless. Suddenly her mouth quivered.

"Forgive *me*," she said impulsively; "you are worth more than I dare give you. Love me in your own fashion. I wish it. And I will care for you very faithfully in mine."

They were very young, very hopeless, deeply impressed with one another, and quite inexperienced enough to trust each other. She leaned from her saddle and laid her slim bare hands in both of his, lifting her gaze bravely to his—a little dim of eye and still tremulous of lip. And he looked back, love's tragedy dawning in his gaze, yet forcing the smile that the very young employ as a defiance to destiny and an artistic insult in the face of Fate; that Fate which looks back so placid and unmoved.

"Can you forgive me, Shiela?"

"Look at me?" she whispered.

A few moments later she hastily disengaged her hand.

"There seems to be a fire, yonder," he said; "and somebody seated before it; your Seminole, I think. By Jove, Shiela, he's certainly picturesque!"

A sullen-eyed Indian rose as they rode up, his turban brilliant in the declining sunshine, his fringed leggings softly luminous as woven cloth of gold.

"He—a—mah, Coacochee!" said the girl in friendly greeting. "It is good to see you, Little Tiger. The people of the East salute the Uchee Seminoles."

The Indian answered briefly and with dignity, then stood impassive, not noticing Hamil.

"Mr. Hamil," she said, "this is my old friend Coacochee or Little Tiger; an Okichobi Seminole of the Clan of the Wind; a brave hunter and an upright man."

"Sommus-Kala-ne-sha-ma-lin," said the Indian quietly; and the girl interpreted: "He says, 'Good wishes to the white man.'"

Hamil dismounted, turned and lifted Shiela from her saddle, then walked straight to the Seminole and offered his hand. The Indian grasped it in silence.

"I wish well to Little Tiger, a Seminole and a brave hunter," said Hamil pleasantly.

The red hand and the white hand tightened and fell apart.

A moment later Gray came galloping up with Eudo Stent.

"How are you, Coacochee!" he called out; "glad to see you again! We saw the pine tops blue a mile back."

To which the Seminole replied with composure in terse English. But for Mr. Cardross, when he arrived, there was a shade less reserve in the Indian's greeting, and there was no mistaking the friendship between them.

"Why did you speak to him in his own tongue?" asked Hamil of Shiela as they strolled together toward the palmetto-thatched, open-face camp fronting on Ruffle Lake.

"He takes it as a compliment," she said. "Besides he taught me."

"It's a pretty courtesy," said Hamil, "but you always do everything more graciously than anybody else in the world."

"I am afraid you are biassed."

"Can any man who knows you remain non-partisan?—even your red Seminole yonder?"

"I am proud of that conquest," she said gaily. "Do you know anything about the Seminoles? No? Well, then, let me inform you that a Seminole rarely speaks to a white man except when trading at the posts. They are a very proud people; they consider themselves still unconquered, still in a state of rebellion against the United States."

"What!" exclaimed Hamil, astonished.

"Yes, indeed. All these years of peace they consider only as an armed truce. They are proud, reticent, sensitive, suspicious people; and there are few cases on record where any such thing as friendship has existed between a Seminole and a white man. This is a genuine case; Coacochee is really devoted to dad."

The guides and the wagon had now arrived; camp was already in the confusion and bustle of unloading equipage and supplies; picket lines were established, water-jars buried, blankets spread, guns, ammunition, rods, and saddles ranged in their proper places.

Carter unsheathed his heavy cane-knife and cut palmetto fans for rethatching where required; Eudo Stent looked after the horses; Bulow's axe rang among the fragrant red cedars; the Indian squatted gravely before a characteristic Seminole fire built of logs, radiating like the spokes of a cart-wheel from the centre which was a hub of glowing coals. And whenever it was necessary he simply shoved the burning log-ends toward the centre where kettles were already boiling and sweet potatoes lay amid the white ashes, and a dozen wild ducks, split and skewered and basted with pork, were exhaling a matchless fragrance.

Table-legs, bench-legs, and the bases of all culinary furniture, like the body of the camp, were made out of palmetto logs driven into the ground to support cedar planks for the tops.

And it was seated at one of these tables, under the giant oaks, pines, and palmettos, that Shiela and Hamil ate their first camp-repast together, with Gray and his father opposite.

Never had he tasted such a heavenly banquet, never had he dreamed of such delicacies. Eudo Stent brought panfuls of fried bass, still sizzling under the crisp bacon; and great panniers woven of green palmetto, piled high with smoking sweet potatoes all dusty from the ashes; and pots of coffee and tea, steaming and aromatic.

Then came broiled mallard duck, still crackling from the coals, and coonti bread, and a cold salad of palm cabbage, nut-flavored, delectable. Then in the thermos-jugs were spring water and a light German vintage to mix with it. And after everything, fresh oranges in a nest of Spanish moss.

Red sunlight struck through the forest, bronzing bark and foliage; sombre patches of shade passed and repassed across the table—the shadows of black vultures soaring low above the camp smoke. The waters of the lake burned gold.

As yet the approach of sunset had not stirred the water-fowl to restlessness; dark streaks on the lake gleamed white at moments as some string of swimming ducks turned and the light glinted on throat and breast. Herons stood in the shallows; a bittern, squawking, rose from the saw-grass, circled, and pitched downward again.

"Never had he tasted such a heavenly banquet."

"This is a peaceful place," said Cardross, narrowing eyes watching the lake through the haze of his pipe. "I almost hate to disturb it with a gun-shot; but if we stay here we've got to eat." And, turning toward the guides' table where they lounged over their after-dinner pipes: "Coacochee, my little daughter has never shot a wild turkey. Do you think she had better try this evening or go after the big duck?"

"Pen-ni-chah," said the Seminole quietly.

"He says, 'turkey-gobbler,'" whispered Shiela to Hamil; "'pen-nit-kee' is the word for *hen* turkey. Oh, I *hope* I have a chance. You'll pair with me, won't you?"

"Of course."

Cardross, listening, smiled. "Is it yelping or roosting, Little Tiger?"

"Roost um pen-ni-chah, aw-tee-tus-chee. I-hoo-es-chay."

"He says that we can roost them by and by and that we ought to start now," whispered the girl, slightly excited. "Dad, Mr. Hamil has never shot a wild turkey—"

"Neither have I," observed her father humourously.

"Oh, I forgot! Well, then—why can't we all—"

"Not much! No sitting in swamps for me, but a good, clean, and easy boat in the saw-grass. Gray, are you going after ducks with me or are you going to sit with one hopeful girl, one credulous white man, and one determined red man on a shell heap in a bog and yawn till moonrise? Ducks? Sure! Well, then, we'd better be about it, my son."

The guides rose laughing, and went about their duties, Carter and Bulow to clean up camp, Eudo Stent with Cardross, senior and junior, carrying guns and shell cases down to the landing where the boats lay; and Shiela and Hamil to mount the two fresh led-horses and follow the Seminole into the forest.

"Shame on your laziness, dad!" said Shiela, as Cardross looked after her in pretended pity; "anybody can shoot ducks from a boat, but it takes real hunters to stalk turkeys! I suppose Eudo loads for you and Gray pulls the triggers!"

"The turkey you get will be a water-turkey," observed Cardross; "or a fragrant buzzard. Hamil, I'm sorry for you. I've tried that sort of thing myself when younger. I'm still turkeyless but wiser."

"You'd better bring Eudo and let us help you to retrieve yourself!" called back Shiela.

But he refused scornfully, and she waved them adieu; then, settling in her stirrups, turned smilingly to Hamil who brought his horse alongside.

"Dad is probably right; there's not much chance for us this way. But if there is a chance Little Tiger will see that we get it. Anyway, you can try the ducks in the morning. You don't mind, do you?"

He tried to be prudent in his reply.

CHAPTER XII
THE ALLIED FORCES

Through the glades the sun poured like a red searchlight, and they advanced in the wake of their own enormous shadows lengthening grotesquely with every stride. Tree trunks and underbrush seemed afire in the kindling glory; the stream ran molten.

Then of a sudden the red radiance died out; the forest turned ashy; the sun had set; and on the wings of silence already the swift southern dusk was settling over lake and forest. A far and pallid star came out in the west; a cat-owl howled.

At the edge of an evil-looking cypress "branch" they dismounted, drew gun from saddle-boot, and loaded in silence while the Indian tethered the horses.

Then through the thickening twilight they followed the Seminole in file, Hamil bringing up the rear.

Little Tiger had left turban, plume, and leggings in camp; the scalp-lock bobbed on his head, bronzed feet and legs were bare; and, noiseless as a cypress shadow in the moonlight, he seemed part of it all, harmonious as a wild thing in its protective tints.

A narrow tongue of dry land scarcely three inches above the swamp level was the trail they followed. All around tall cypress trees, strangely buttressed at the base, rose pillar-like into obscurity as though supporting the canopy of dusk. The goblin howling of the big cat-owl pulsated through the silence; strange gleams and flashes stirred the surface of the bog. Once, close ahead, a great white bird, winged like an angel, rose in spectral silence through the twilight.

"Did you see!" she breathed, partly turning her head.

"Good heavens, yes! What was it; the archangel Michael?"

"Only a snowy heron."

The Seminole had halted and laid his hand flat on the dead leaves under a gigantic water-oak.

"A-po-kes-chay," he whispered; and Shiela translated close to Hamil's ear: "He says that we must all sit down here—" A sudden crackle in the darkness stilled her voice.

"Im-po-kit-chkaw?" she asked. "Did you hear that? No-ka-tee; what is it?"

"Deer walk," nodded the Seminole; "sun gone down; moon come. Bimeby roost um turkey. Li-kus-chay! No sound."

Shiela settled quietly on the poncho among the dead leaves, resting her back against the huge tree trunk. Hamil warily sank into position beside her; the Indian stood for a while, head raised, apparently gazing at the tree-tops, then, walking noiselessly forward a dozen yards, squatted.

Shiela opened the conversation presently by whispering that they must not speak.

And the conversation continued, fitfully in ghostly whispers, lips scarcely stirring close to one another's ears.

As for the swamp, it was less reticent, and began to wake up all around them in the darkness. Strange creaks and quacks and croaks broke out, sudden snappings of twigs, a scurry among dead leaves, a splash in the water, the far whir of wings. There were no insect noises, no resonant voices of bull-frogs; weird squeaks arose at intervals, the murmuring complaint of water-fowl, guttural quack of duck and bittern—a vague stirring everywhere of wild things settling to rest or awaking. There were things moving in the unseen ooze, too, leaving sudden sinuous trails in the dim but growing lustre that whitened above the trees—probably turtles, perhaps snakes.

She leaned almost imperceptibly toward him, and he moved his shoulder close to hers.

"You are not nervous, Shiela?"

"Indeed I am."

"Why on earth did you come?"

"I don't know. The idea of snakes in darkness always worries me.... Once, waking in camp, reaching out through the darkness for the water-bottle, I laid my hand on an exceedingly chilly snake. It was a harmless one, but I nearly died.... And here I am back again. Believe me, *no* burnt child ever dreaded the fire enough to keep away from it. I'm a coward, but not enough of a one to practise prudence."

He laughed silently. "You brave little thing! Every moment I am learning more and more how adorable you are—"

"Do men adore folly?"

"Your kind of folly. Are you cold?"

"No; only foolish. There's some sort of live creature moving rather close to me—hush! Don't you hear it?"

But whatever it was it went its uncanny way in darkness and left them listening, her small hand remaining loosely in his.

"What on earth is the matter now, Shiela?" he whispered, feeling her trembling.

"Nothing. They say a snake won't strike you if you hold your breath. Its nonsense, but I was trying it.... What is that ring I feel on your hand?"

"A signet; my father's." He removed it from his little finger, tried it on all of hers.

"Is it too large?"

"It's a little loose.... You don't wish me to wear it, do you?... Your *father's*? I'd rather not.... Do you really wish it? Well, then—for a day—if you ask me."

Her ringed hand settled unconsciously into his again; she leaned back against the tree, and he rested his head beside hers.

"Are you afraid of wood-ticks, Mr. Hamil? I am, horribly. We're inviting all kinds of disaster—but isn't it delicious! Look at that whitish light above the trees. When the moon outlines the roosting-tree we'll know whether our labour is lost. But I wouldn't have missed it for all the mallard on Ruffle Lake. Would you? Are you contented?"

"Where you are is contentment, Shiela."

"How nice of you! But there is always that sweet, old-fashioned, boyish streak in you which shows true colour when I test you. Do you know, at times, you seem absurdly young to me."

"That's a pleasant thing to say."

Their shoulders were in contact; she was laughing without a sound.

"At times," she said, "you are almost what young girls call cunning!"

"By heavens!" he began indignantly, but she stilled his jerk of resentment with a quick pressure.

"Lie still! For goodness' sake don't make the leaves rustle, silly! If there's a flock of turkeys in any of those cypress tops, you may be sure that every separate bird is now looking straight in our direction.... I won't torment you any more; I dare not. Little Tiger turned around; did you notice? He'd probably like to scalp us both."

But the Indian had resumed his motionless study of the darkness, squatted on his haunches as immobile as a dead stump.

Hamil whispered: "Such a chance to make love to you! You dare not move. And you deserve it for tormenting me."

"If you did such a thing—"

"Yes?"

"Such a thing as that—"

"Yes?"

"But you wouldn't."

"Why, Shiela, I'm doing it every minute of my life!"

"Now?"

"Of course. It goes on always. I couldn't prevent it any more than I could stop my pulses. It just continues with every heart-beat, every breath, every word, every silence—"

"Mr. Hamil!"

"Yes?"

"That *does* sound like it—a little; and you must stop!"

"Of course I'll stop saying things, but *that* doesn't stop with my silence. It simply goes on and on increasing every—"

"Try silence," she said.

Motionless, shoulder to shoulder, the pulsing moments passed. Every muscle tense, she sat there for a while, fearful that he could hear her heart beating. Her palm, doubled in his, seemed to burn. Then little by little a subtle relaxation stole over her; dreamy-eyed she sank back and looked into the darkness. A sense of delicious well-being possessed her, enmeshing thought in hazy lethargy, quieting pulse and mind.

Through it she heard his voice faintly; her own seemed unreal when she answered.

He said: "Speaking of love; there is only one thing possible for me, Shiela—to go on loving you. I can't kill hope, though there seems to be none. But there's no use in saying so to myself for it is one of those things no man believes. He may grow tired of hoping, and, saying there is none, live on. But neither he nor Fate can destroy hope any more than he can annihilate his soul. He may change in his heart. That he cannot control. When love goes no man can stay its going."

"Do you think yours will go?"

"No. That is a lover's answer."

"What is a sane man's answer?"

"Ask some sane man, Shiela."

"I would rather believe you."

"Does it make you happy?"

"Yes."

"You wish me to love you?"

"Yes."

"You would love me—a little—if you could?"

She closed her eyes.

"Would you?" he asked again.

"Yes."

"But you cannot."

She said, dreamily: "I don't know. That is a dreadful answer to make. But I don't know what is in me. I don't know what I am capable of doing. I wish I knew; I wish I could tell you."

"Do you know what I think, Shiela?"

"What?"

"It's curious—but since I have known you—and about your birth—the idea took shape and persisted—that—that—"

"What?" she asked.

"That, partly perhaps because of your physical beauty, and because of your mind and its intelligence and generosity, you embodied something of that type which this nation is developing."

"That is curious," she said softly.

"Yes; but you give me that impression, as though in you were the lovely justification of these generations of welding together alien and native to make a national type, spiritual, intelligent, wholesome, beautiful.... And I've fallen into the habit of thinking of you in that way—as thoroughly human, thoroughly feminine, heir to the best that is human, and to its temptations too; yet, somehow, instinctively finding the right way in life, the true way through doubt and stress.... Like the Land itself—with perhaps the blood of many nations in your veins.... I don't know exactly what I'm trying to say—"

"*I* know."

"Yes," he whispered, "you do know that all I have said is only a longer way of saying that I love you."

"Through stress and doubt," she murmured, "you think I will find the way?—with perhaps the blood of many nations in my veins, with all their transmitted emotions, desires, passions for my inheritance?... It is my only heritage. They did not even leave me a name; only a capacity for every human error, with no knowledge of what particular inherited failing I am to contend with when temptation comes. Do you wonder I am sometimes lonely and afraid?"

"You darling!" he said under his breath.

"Hush; that is forbidden. You know perfectly well it is. *Are* you laughing? That is very horrid of you when I'm trying *so* hard not to listen when you use forbidden words to me. But I heard you once when I should not have heard you. Does that seem centuries ago? Alas for us both, Ulysses, when I heard your voice calling me under the Southern stars! Would you ever have spoken if you knew what you know now?"

"I would have told you the truth sooner."

"Told me what truth?"

"That I love you, Calypso."

"You always answer like a boy! Ah, well I—if you knew how easily a girl believes such answers!"

He bent his head, raising her bare fingers to his lips. A tiny shock passed through them both; she released her hand and buried it in the folds of her kilt.

There was a pale flare of moonlight behind the forest; trunks and branches were becoming more distinct. A few moments later the Indian, bending low, came creeping back without a sound, and straightened up in the fathomless shadow of the oak, motioning Shiela and Hamil to rise.

"Choo-lee," he motioned with his lips; "Ko-la-pa-kin!"

Lips close to Hamil's ear she whispered: "He says that there are seven in that pine. Can you see them?"

He strained his eyes in vain; she had already found them and now stood close to his shoulder, whispering the direction.

"I can't make them out," he said. "Don't wait for me, but take your chance at once."

"Do you think I would do that?"

"You *must*! You have never shot a turkey—"

"Hush, silly. What pleasure would there be in it without you? Try to see them; look carefully. All those dark furry blotches against the sky are pine leaves, but the round shadowy lumps are turkeys; one is quite clearly silhouetted, now; even to his tail—"

"I believe I *do* see!" murmured Hamil. "By Jove, yes! Shiela, you're an angel to be so patient."

"I'll take the top bird," she whispered. "Are you ready? We must be quick."

"Ready," he motioned.

Then in the dim light one of the shadowy bunches rose abruptly, standing motionless on the branch, craning a long neck into the moonlight.

"Fire!" she whispered; and four red flashes in pairs split the gloom wide open for a second. Then roaring darkness closed about them.

Instantly the forest resounded with the thunderous racket of heavy wings as the flock burst into flight, clattering away through leafy obscurity; but under the uproar of shot and clapping wings sounded the thud and splash of something heavy crashing earthward; and the Indian, springing from root to tussock, vanished into the shadows.

"Two down!" said the girl, unsteadily. "Oh, I am so thankful that you got yours!"

They exchanged excited handclasps of mutual congratulation. Then he said:

"Shiela, you dear generous girl, I don't believe I hit anything, but I'll bet that you got a turkey with each barrel!"

"Foolish boy! Of course you grassed your bird! It wasn't a wing shot, but we took what fate sent us. Nobody can choose conditions on the firing line. We did our best, I think."

"Wise little Shiela! Her philosophy is as fascinating as it is sound!" He looked at her half smiling, partly serious. "You and I are on life's firing line, you know."

"Are we?"

"And under the lively fusillade of circumstances."

"Are we?"

He said: "It will show us up as we are.... I am afraid for us both."

"If you are—don't tell me."

"It is best to know the truth. We've got to stay on the firing line anyway. We might as well know that we are not very sure of ourselves. If the fear of God doesn't help us it will end us. But—" He walked up to her and took both her hands frankly. "We'll try to be good soldiers; won't we?"

"Yes."

"And good comrades—even if we can't be more?"

"Yes."

"And help each other under fire?"

"Yes."

"You make me very happy," he said simply; and turned to the Seminole who was emerging from obscurity, shoulders buried under a mass of bronzed feathers from which dangled two grotesque heads.

One was a gobbler—a magnificent patriarch; and Shiela with a little cry of delight turned to Hamil: "That's yours! I congratulate you with all my heart!"

"No, no!" he protested, "the gobbler fell to you—"

"It is *yours*!" she repeated firmly; "mine is this handsome, plump hen—"

"I *won't* claim that magnificent gobbler! Little Tiger, didn't Miss Cardross shoot this bird?"

"Gobbler top bird," nodded the Seminole proudly.

"You fired at the top bird, Shiela! That settles it! I'm perfectly delighted over this. Little Tiger, you stalked them beautifully; but how on earth you ever managed to roost them in the dark I can't make out!"

"See um same like tiger," nodded the pleased Seminole. And, to Shiela: "Pen-na-waw-suc-chai! I-hoo-es-chai." And he lighted his lantern.

"He says that the turkeys are all gone and that we had better go too, Mr. Hamil. What a perfect beauty that gobbler is! I'd much rather have him mounted than eat him. Perhaps we can do both. Eudo skins very skilfully and there's plenty of salt in camp. Look at that mist!"

And so, chattering away in highest spirits they fell into file behind the Seminole and his lantern, who, in the thickening fog, looked like some slim luminous forest-phantom with great misty wings atrail from either shoulder.

Treading the narrow way in each other's footsteps they heard, far in the darkness, the gruesome tumult of owls. Once the Indian's lantern flashed on a snake which rose quickly from compact coils, hissing and distending its neck; but for all its formidable appearance and loud, defiant hissing the Indian picked up a palmetto fan and contemptuously tossed the reptile aside into the bog.

"It's only a noisy puff-adder," said Shiela, who had retreated very close against Hamil, "but, oh, I don't love them even when they are harmless." And rather thoughtfully she disengaged herself from the sheltering arm of that all too sympathetic young man, and went forward, shivering a little as the hiss of the enraged adder broke out from the uncongenial mud where he had unwillingly landed.

And so they came to their horses through a white mist which had thickened so rapidly that the Indian's lantern was now only an iridescent star ringed with rainbows. And when they had been riding for twenty minutes Little Tiger halted them with lifted lantern and said quietly:

"Chi-ho-ches-chee!"

"Wh-at!" exclaimed the girl, incredulous.

"What did he say?" asked Hamil.

"He says that he is lost!"

Hamil stared around in dismay; a dense white wall shut out everything; the Indian's lantern at ten paces was invisible; he could scarcely see Shiela unless she rode close enough to touch his elbow.

"Catch um camp," observed Little Tiger calmly. "Loose bridle! Bimeby catch um camp. One horse lead. No be scared."

So Hamil dismounted and handed his bridle to the Indian; then Shiela cast her own bridle loose across the pommel, and touching her horse with both heels, rode forward, hands in her jacket pockets. And Hamil walked beside her, one arm on the cantle.

Into blank obscurity the horse moved, bearing to the left—a direction which seemed entirely wrong.

"Catch um camp," came the Indian's amused voice through the mist from somewhere close behind.

"It doesn't seem to me that this is the right direction," ventured Shiela doubtfully. "Isn't it absurd? Where are you, Mr. Hamil? Come closer and keep in touch with my stirrup. I found you in a fog and I really don't want to lose you in one."

She dropped one arm so that her hand rested lightly on his shoulder.

"This is not the first mist we've been through together," he said, laughing.

"I was thinking of that, too. They say the gods arrive and go in a mist. Don't go."

They moved on in silence, the horse stepping confidently into the crowding fog. Once Hamil stumbled over a root and Shiela's hand slipped around his neck, tightening a moment. He straightened up; but her hand slid back to his coat sleeve, resting so lightly that he could scarce feel the touch.

Then the horse stumbled, this time over the tongue of the camp wagon. Little Tiger was right; the horse had brought them back.

Hamil turned; Shiela swung one leg across the pommel and slipped from her saddle into his arms.

"Have you been happy, Shiela?"

"You know I have.... But—you must release me."

"Perfectly happy?"

"Ah, yes. Don't you know I have?" ... And in a low voice: "Release me now—for both our sakes."

She did not struggle nor did he retain her by perceptible force.

"Won't you release me?"

"Must I?"

"I thought you promised to help me—on the firing line?" She forced a little laugh, resting both her hands on his wrists against her waist. "You said," she added with an effort at lightness, "that we are under heavy fire now."

"The fire of circumstances?"

"The cross-fire—of temptation.... Help me."

His arms fell; neither moved. Then a pale spark grew in the mist, brighter, redder, and, side by side, they walked toward it.

"What luck!" cried Gray, lifting a blazing palmetto fan above his head. "We got ten mallard and a sprig! Where's your game? We heard you shoot four times!"

Shiela laughed as the Seminole loomed up in the incandescent haze of the camp fire, buried in plumage.

"Dad! Dad! Where are you? Mr. Hamil has shot a magnificent wild turkey!"

"Well, upon my word!" exclaimed Cardross, emerging from his section; "the luck of the dub is proverbial! Hamil, what the deuce do you mean by it? That's what' I want to know! O Lord! *Look* at that gobbler! Shiela, did you let this young man wipe both your eyes?"

"Mine? Oh, I almost forgot. You see I shot one of them."

"Which?"

"It happened to be the gobbler," she said. "It was a mere chance in the dark.... And—if my section is ready, dad—I'm a little tired, I think. Good night, everybody; good night, Mr. Hamil—and thank you for taking care of me."

Cardross, enveloped in blankets, glanced at Hamil.

"Did you ever know anybody so quick to give credit to others? It's worth something to hear anybody speak in that fashion."

"That is why I did not interrupt," said Hamil.

Cardross looked down at the dying coals, then directly at the silent young fellow—a long, keen glance; then his gaze fell again on the Seminole fire.

"Good night, sir," said Hamil at last.

"Good night, my boy," replied the older man very quietly.

CHAPTER XIII
THE SILENT PARTNERS

Late one evening toward the end of the week a somewhat battered camping party, laden with plump, fluffy bunches of quail, and plumper strings of duck, wind-scorched, sun-burnt, brier-torn and trail-worn, re-entered the *patio* of the Cardross villa, and made straight for shower-bath, witch-hazel, fresh pyjamas, and bed.

In vain Jessie Carrick, Cecile, and their mother camped around Shiela's bed after the tray was removed, and Shiela's flushed face, innocent as usual of sunburn, lay among the pillows, framed by the brown-gold lustre of her hair.

"We had *such* a good time, mother; Mr. Hamil shot a turkey," she said sleepily. "Mr. Hamil—Mr. H-a-m-i-l"—A series of little pink yawns, a smile, a faint sigh terminated consciousness as she relaxed into slumber as placid as her first cradle sleep. So motionless she lay, bare arms wound around the pillow, that they could scarcely detect her breathing save when the bow of pale-blue ribbon stirred on her bosom.

"The darling!" whispered Mrs. Carrick; "look at that brier mark across her wrist!—our poor little worn-out colleen!"

"She was not too far gone to mention Garret Hamil," observed Cecile.

Mrs. Cardross looked silently at Cecile, then at the girl on the bed who had called her mother. After a moment she bent with difficulty and kissed the brier-torn wrist, wondering perhaps whether by chance a deeper wound lay hidden beneath the lace-veiled, childish breast.

"Little daughter—little daughter!" she murmured close to the small unheeding ear. Cecile waited, a smile half tender, half amused curving her parted lips; then she glanced curiously at Mrs. Carrick. But that young matron, ignoring the enfant terrible, calmly tucked her arm under her mother's; Cecile, immersed in speculative thought, followed them from the room; a maid extinguished the lights.

In an hour the Villa Cardross was silent and dark, save that, in the moonlight which struck through the panes of Malcourt's room, an unquiet shadow moved from window to window, looking out into the mystery of night.

The late morning sun flung a golden net across Malcourt's bed; he lay asleep, dark hair in handsome disorder, dark eyes sealed—too young to wear that bruised, loose mask so soon with the swollen shadows under lid and lip. Yet, in his unconscious features there was now a certain simplicity almost engaging, which awake, he seemed to lack; as though latent somewhere within him were qualities which chance might germinate into nobler growth. But chance, alone, is a poor gardener.

Hamil passing the corridor as the valet, carrying a tray, opened Malcourt's door, glanced in at him; and Malcourt awoke at the same moment, and sat bolt upright.

"Hello, Hamil!" he nodded sleepily, "come in, old fellow!" And, to the valet: "No breakfast for me, thank you—except grape-fruit!—unless you've brought me a cuckootail? Yes? No? Stung! Never mind; just hand me a cigarette and take away the tray. It's a case of being a very naughty boy, Hamil. How are you anyway, and what did you shoot?"

Hamil greeted him briefly, but did not seem inclined to enter or converse.

Malcourt yawned, glanced at the grape-fruit, then affably at Hamil.

"I say," he began, "hope you'll overlook my rotten behaviour last time we met. I'd been dining at random, and I'm usually a brute when I do that."

"Oh, it's all right," said Hamil, looking at the row of tiny Chinese idols on the mantel.

"No rancour?"

"No. Only—why do you do it, Malcourt?"

"Why do I do which? The wheel or the lady?"

"Oh, the whole bally business? It isn't as if you were lonely and put to it. There are plenty of attractive girls about, and anybody will take you on at Bridge. Of course it's none of my affair—but we came unpleasantly close to a quarrel—which is my only excuse."

Malcourt looked at him thoughtfully. "Hamil, do you know, I've always liked you a damn sight better than you've liked me."

Hamil said, laughing outright: "I never saw very much of you to like or dislike."

Malcourt smiled, stretched his limbs lazily, and lighted a cigarette.

"As a matter of fact," he said, "you think I'm worse than I am, but I *know* you are worse than you think, because I couldn't even secretly feel friendly toward a prig. You've had a less battered career than I; you are, in consequence, less selfish, less ruthless, less cynical concerning traditions and illusions. You've something left to stick to; I haven't. You are a little less intelligent than I, and therefore possess more natural courage and credulity. Outside of these things we are more or less alike, Hamil. Hope you don't mind my essay on man."

"No," said Hamil, vastly amused.

"The trouble with me," continued Malcourt, "is that I possess a streak of scientific curiosity that you lack; which is my eternal undoing and keeps me poor and ignobly busy. I ought to have leisure; the world should see to it that I have sufficient leisure and means to pursue my studies in the interest of social economy. Take one of my favourite experiments, for example. I see a little ball rattling around in a wheel. Where will that ball stop? You, being less intellectual than I, don't care where it stops. *I* do. Instantly my scientific curiosity is aroused; I reason logically; I evolve an opinion; I back that opinion; and I remain busy and poor. I see a pretty woman. Is she responsive or unresponsive to intelligently expressed sentiment? I don't know. *You* don't care. *I* do. My curiosity is piqued. She becomes to me an abstract question which scientific experiment alone can elucidate—"

Hamil, leaning on the footboard of the bed, laughed and straightened up.

"All right, Malcourt, if you think it worth while—"

"What pursuit, if you please, is worthier than logical and scientific investigations?"

"Make a lot of honest money and marry some nice girl and have horses and dogs and a bully home and kids. Look here, as Wayward says, you're not the devilish sort you pretend to be. You're too young for one thing. I never knew you to do a deliberately ungenerous act—"

"Like most rascals I'm liable to sentimental generosity in streaks? Thanks. But, somehow, I'm so damned intelligent that I can never give myself any credit for relapsing into traditional virtues. Impulse is often my executive officer; and if I were only stupid I'd take great comfort out of it."

Hamil walked toward the door, stopping on the threshold to say: "Well, I'll tell you one thing, Malcourt; I've often disliked you at times; but I don't now. And I don't exactly know why."

"I do."

"Why?"

"Oh, because you've forgiven me. Also—you think I've a better side."

"Haven't you?"

"My son," said Malcourt, "if somebody'll prove it to me I might sleep better. Just at present I'm ready for anything truly criminal. There was a killing at the Club all right. I assumed the rôle of the defunct. Now I haven't any money; I've overdrawn my balance and my salary; Portlaw is bilious, peevish, unapproachable. If I asked you for a loan I'd only fall a victim again to my insatiable scientific curiosity. So I'll just lie here and browse on cigarettes and grape-fruit until something happens—"

"If you need any money—"

"I told you that we are more or less alike," nodded Malcourt. "Your offer is partly traditional, partly impulsive, altogether ill-considered, and does your intelligence no credit!"

Hamil laughed.

"All the same it's an offer," he said, "and it stands. I'm glad I know you better, Malcourt. I'll be sorry instead of complacently disgusted if you never pan out; but I'll bet you do, some time."

Malcourt looked up.

"I'm ass enough to be much obliged," he said. "And now, before you go, what the devil did you shoot in the woods?"

"Miss Cardross got a gobbler—about the biggest bird I ever saw. Eudo Stent skinned it and Mr. Cardross is going to have it set up in New York. It's a wonderful—"

"Didn't *you* shoot anything?"

"Oh, I assassinated a few harmless birds," said Hamil absently; and walked out into the corridor. "I've got to go over a lot of accumulated letters and things," he called back. "See you later, Malcourt."

There was a mass of mail, bills, plans, and office reports for him lying on the hall table. He gathered these up and hastened down the stairway.

On the terrace below he found Mrs. Cardross, and stopped to tell her what a splendid trip they had, and how beautifully Shiela had shot.

"You did rather well yourself," drawled Mrs. Cardross, with a bland smile. "Shiela says so."

"Oh, yes, but my shooting doesn't compare with Shiela's. I never knew such a girl; I never believed they existed—"

"They are rare," nodded the matron. "I am glad everybody finds my little daughter so admirable in the field."

"Beyond comparison in the field and everywhere," said Hamil, with a cordiality so laboriously frank that Mrs. Cardross raised her eyes—an instant only—then continued sorting the skeins of silk in her voluminous lap.

Shiela appeared in sight among the roses across the lawn; and, as Mr. Cardross came out on the terrace to light his after-breakfast cigar, Hamil disappeared in the direction of the garden where Shiela now stood under the bougainvillia, leisurely biting into a sapodilla.

Mrs. Cardross nodded to her white-linen-clad husband, who looked very handsome with the silvered hair at his temples accentuating the clear, deep tan of his face.

"You are burnt, Neville. Did you and the children have a good time?"

"A good time! Well, just about the best in my life—except when I'm with you. Too bad you couldn't have been there. Shiela shoots like a demon. You ought to have seen her among the quail, and later, in the saw-grass, pulling down mallard and duskies from the sky-high overhead range! I tell you, Amy, she's the cleverest, sweetest, cleanest sportsman I ever saw afield. Gray, of course, stopped his birds very well. He has a lot of butterflies to show you, and—'longicorns,' I believe he calls those beetles with enormous feelers. Little Tiger is a treasure; Eudo and the others did well—"

"And Mr. Hamil?" drawled his wife.

"I *like* him. It's a verdict, dear. You were quite right; he *is* a nice boy— rather a lovable boy. I've discovered no cloven hoof about him. He doesn't shoot particularly well, but his field manners are faultless."

His wife, always elaborately upholstered, sat in her wide reclining chair, plump, jewelled fingers busy with a silk necktie for Hamil, her pretty blue eyes raised at intervals to scan her husband's animated features.

"Does Gray like him as much as ever, Neville?"

"O Lord, Gray adores him, and I like him, and you knit neckties for him, and Jessie doses him, and Cecile quotes him—"

"And Shiela?"

"Oh, Shiela seems to like him," said Cardross genially. His wife raised her eyes, then calmly scrutinized her knitting.

"And Mr. Hamil?"

"What about him, dear?"

"Does he seem to like Shiela?"

Her husband glanced musingly out over the lawn where, in their white flannels, Shiela and Hamil were now seated together under a brilliant Japanese lawn umbrella, examining the pile of plans, reports and blueprints which had accumulated in Hamil's office since his absence.

"He—seems to like her," nodded Cardross, "I'm sure he does. Why not?"

"They were together a good deal, you said last night."

"Yes; but either Gray or I or one of the guides—"

"Of course. Then you don't think—"

Cardross waited and finally looked up. "What, dear?"

"That there is anything more than a sensible friendship—"

"Between Shiela and Garret Hamil?"

"Yes; we were not discussing the Emperor of China."

Cardross laughed and glanced sideways at the lawn umbrella.

"I—don't—know."

His wife raised her brows but not her head.

"Why, Neville?"

"Why what?"

"Your apparent doubt as to the significance of their friendship."

"Dear—I don't know much about those things."

His wife waited.

"Hamil is so nice to everybody; and I've not noticed how he is with other young girls," continued her husband restlessly. "He does seem to tag after Shiela.... Once or twice I thought—or it seemed to me—or rather—"

His wife waited.

"Well, he seemed rather impressed by her field qualities," concluded Cardross weakly.

His wife waited.

Her husband lit a cigar very carefully: "That's all I noticed, dear."

Mrs. Cardross laid the narrow bit of woven blue silk on her knee and smoothed it reflectively.

"Neville!"

"Yes, dear."

"I wonder whether Mr. Hamil has heard."

Her husband did not misunderstand. "I think it likely. That old harridan—"

"*Please*, Neville!"

"Well, then, Mrs. Van Dieman has talked ever since you and Shiela sat on the aspirations of her impossible son."

"You think Mr. Hamil knows?"

"Why not? Everybody does, thanks to that venomous old lady and her limit of an offspring."

"And in spite of that you think Mr. Hamil might be seriously impressed?"

"Why not?" repeated Cardross. "She's the sweetest, cleanest-cut sportsman—"

"Dear, a field-trial is not what we are discussing."

"No, of course. But those things count with a man. And besides, admitting that the story is all over Palm Beach and New York by this time, is there a more popular girl here than our little Shiela? Look at the men— troops of 'em! Alex Anan knew when he tried his luck. You had to tell Mr. Cuyp, but Shiela was obliged to turn him down after all. It certainly has not intimidated anybody. Do you remember two years ago how persistent Louis Malcourt was until you squelched him?"

"Yes; but he didn't know the truth then. He acts sometimes as though he knew it now. I don't think he would ask Shiela again. And, Neville, if Mr. Hamil does not know, and if you think there is the slightest chance of Shiela becoming interested in him, he ought to be told—indirectly. Unhappiness for both might lie in his ignorance."

"Shiela would tell him before he—"

"Of course. But—it might then be too late for her—if he prove less of a man than we think him! He comes from a family whose connections have always thought a great deal of themselves—in the narrower sense; a family not immune from prejudice. His aunt, Miss Palliser, is very amiable; but, dear, we must not make the mistake that she could consider Shiela good enough for her nephew. One need not be a snob to hesitate under the pitiful circumstances."

"If I know Hamil, he'll ask little advice from his relatives—"

"But he will receive plenty, Neville."

Cardross shrugged. "Then it's up to him, Amy."

"Exactly. But do you wish to have our little Shiela in a position where her declared lover hesitates? And so I say, Neville, that it is better for her that Mr. Hamil should know the truth in ample time to reconsider any sentiment before he utters it. It is only fair to him and to Shiela. That is all."

"Why do you say all this now, dearest? Have you thought—"

"Yes, a little. The child is fond of him. I did think she once cared for Louis—as a young girl cares for a boy. But we couldn't permit her to take any chances, poor fellow!—his family record is sadly against him. No; we did right, Neville. And now, at the first sign, we must do right again between Shiela and this very lovable boy who is making your park for you."

"Of course," said Cardross absently, "but the man who hesitates because of what he learns about Shiela isn't worth enlightening." He looked out across the lawn. "I hope it happens," he said. "And, by the way, dear, I've got to go to town."

"O Neville!"

"Don't worry; I'm not going to contract pneumonia—"

"When are you going?"

"To-morrow, I think."

"Is it anything that bothers you?"

"No, nothing in particular. I have a letter from Acton. There seems to be some uncertainty developing in one or two business quarters. I thought I'd see for myself."

"Are you worrying?"

"About what?"

"About the Shoshone Securities Company?"

"Not exactly worrying."

She shook her head, but said nothing more.

During February the work on the Cardross estate developed sufficiently to become intensely interesting to the family. A vast circular sunken garden, bewitchingly formal, and flanked by a beautiful terrace and balus trade of coquina, was approaching completion between the house and an arm of the lagoon. The stone bridge over the water remained unfinished, but already, across it, miles of the wide forest avenue stretched straight away, set at intervals by carrefours centred with fountain basins from which already tall sparkling columns of water tumbled up into the sunshine.

But still the steam jets puffed up above the green tree-tops; and the sickening whine of the saw-mill, and the rumble of traction engines over rough new roads of shell, and the far racket of chisel and hammer on wood and stone continued from daylight till dark.

Every day brought to Hamil new questions, new delays, vexations of lighting, problems of piping and drainage. Contractors and sub-contractors beset him; draughtsmen fairly buried him under tons of drawings and blue-prints. All of which was as nothing compared to the labour squabbles and endless petty entanglements which arose from personal jealousy or political vindictiveness, peppered with dark hints of peonage, threats, demands, and whispers of graft.

The leasing of convict labour for the more distant road work also worried him, but the sheriffs of Dade and Volusia were pillars of strength and comfort to him in perplexity—lean, soft-spoken, hawk-faced gentlemen, gentle and incorruptible, who settled scuffles with a glance, and local riots with a deadly drawl of warning which carried conviction like a bullet to the "bad" nigger of the blue-gum variety, as well as to the brutish white autocrat of the turpentine camps.

That the work progressed so swiftly was wonderful, even with the unlimited means of Neville Cardross to back his demands for haste. And it might have been impossible to produce any such results in so short a period had there not been contractors in the vicinity who were accustomed to handle vast enterprises on short notice. Some of these men, fortunately for Hamil, had been temporarily released from sections of the great Key West Line construction; and these contractors with their men and materials were immediately available for the labour in hand.

So all though February work was rushed forward; and March found the sunken garden in bloom, stone-edged pools full of lotus and lilies, orange trees blossoming in a magnificent sweep around the balustrade of the terrace, and, beyond, the graceful stone bridge, passable but not quite completed. Neither were the great systems of pools, fountains, tanks, and lakes completed by any means, but here and there foaming jets trembled and glittered in the sunlight, and here and there placid reaches, crystal clear, reflected the blue above.

As for Palm Beach, visitors and natives had watched with liveliest interest the development of the great Cardross park. In the height of the season visits to the scene of operations were made functions; tourists and residents gathered in swarms and took tea and luncheon under the magnificent live-oaks of the hammock.

Mrs. Cardross herself gave a number of lawn fêtes with the kindly intention of doing practical good to Hamil, the success of whose profession was so vitally dependent upon the approval and personal interest of wealth and fashion and idleness.

Shiela constantly tormented him about these functions for his benefit, suggesting that he attire himself in a sloppy velvet jacket and let his hair grow and his necktie flow. She pretended to prepare placards advertising Hamil's popular parks for poor people at cut rates, including wooden horses and a barrel-organ.

"An idea of mine," she suggested, glancing up from the writing-pad on her knees, "is to trim a dozen alligators with electric lights and turn them loose in our lake. There's current enough in the canal to keep the lights going, isn't there, Mr. Hamil? Incandescent alligators would make Luna Park look like a bog full of fireflies—"

"O Shiela, let him alone," protested Mrs. Carrick. "For all you know Mr. Hamil may be dreadfully sensitive."

"I'll let him alone if he'll let his beard grow horrid and silky and permit us to address him as Cher maître—"

"I won't insist on that if you'll call me by my first name," said Hamil mischievously.

"I never will," returned the girl. Always when he suggested it, the faint pink of annoyed embarrassment tinted Shiela's cheeks. And now everybody in the family rallied her on the subject, for they all had come to call him Garry by this time.

"Don't I always say 'Shiela' to you?" he insisted.

"Yes, you do and nobody was consulted. I informed my mother, but she doesn't seem to resent it. So I am obliged to. Besides I don't like your first name."

Mrs. Cardross laughed gently over her embroidery; Malcourt, who was reading the stock column in the *News*, turned and looked curiously at Hamil, then at Shiela. Then catching Mrs. Carrick's eye:

"Portlaw is rather worried over the market," he said. "I think he's going North in a day or two."

"Why, Louis!" exclaimed Mrs. Cardross; "then you will be going, too, I suppose."

"His ways are my ways," nodded Malcourt. "I've been here too long anyway," he added in a lower voice, folding the paper absently across his knees. He glanced once more at Shiela, but she had returned to her letter writing.

Everybody spoke of his going in tones of civil regret—everybody except Shiela, who had not even looked at him. Cecile's observations were plainly perfunctory, but she made them nevertheless, for she had begun to take the same feminine interest in Malcourt that everybody was now taking in view of his very pronounced attentions to Virginia Suydam.

All the world may not love a lover, but all the world watches him. And a great many pairs of bright eyes and many more pairs of faded ones were curiously following the manoeuvres of Louis Malcourt and Virginia Suydam.

Very little of what these two people did escaped the social Argus at Palm Beach—their promenades on the verandas of the two great hotels, their appearance on the links and tennis-courts together, their daily encounter at the bathing-hour, their inevitable meeting and pairing on lawn, in ballroom, afloat, ashore, wherever young people gathered under the whip of light social obligations or in pursuit of pleasure.

And they were discussed. She being older than he, and very wealthy, the veranda discussions were not always amiable; but nobody said anything very bitter because Virginia was in a position to be socially respected and the majority of people rather liked Malcourt. Besides there was just enough whispering concerning his performances at the Club and the company he kept there to pique the friendly curiosity of a number of fashionable young matrons who are always prepossessed in favour of a man at whom convention might possibly one day glance askance.

So everybody at Palm Beach was at least aware of the affair. Hamil had heard of it from his pretty aunt, and had been thoroughly questioned. It was very evident that Miss Palliser viewed the proceedings with dismay for she also consulted Wayward, and finally, during the confidential retiring-hour, chose the right moment to extract something definite from Virginia.

But that pale and pretty spinster was too fluently responsive, admitting that perhaps she had been seeing a little too much of Malcourt, protesting it to be accidental, agreeing with Constance Palliser that more discretion should be exercised, and promising it with a short, flushed laugh.

And the next morning she rode to the Inlet with Malcourt, swam with him to the raft, and danced with him until dawn at "The Breakers."

Mrs. Cardross and Jessie Carrick bent over their embroidery; Shiela continued her letter writing with Gray's stylographic pen; Hamil, booted and spurred, both pockets stuffed with plans, paced the terrace waiting for his horse to be brought around; Malcourt had carried himself and his newspaper to the farther end of the terrace, and now stood leaning over the balustrade, an unlighted cigarette between his lips.

"I suppose you'll go to Luckless Lake," observed Hamil, pausing beside Malcourt in his walk.

"Yes. There's plenty to do. We stripped ten thousand trout in October, and we're putting in German boar this spring."

"I should think your occupation would be fascinating."

"Yes? It's lonely, too, until Portlaw's camp parties begin. I get an overdose of nature at times. There's nobody of my own ilk there except our Yale and Cornell foresters. In winter it's deadly, Hamil, deadly! I don't shoot, you know; it's deathly enough as it is."

"I don't believe I'd find it so."

"You think not, but you would. That white solitude may be good medicine for some, but it makes me furious after a while, and I often wish that the woods and the deer and the fish and I myself and the whole devilish outfit were under the North Pole and frozen solid! But I can't afford to pick and choose. If I looked about for something else to do I don't believe anybody would want me. Portlaw pays me more than I'm worth as a Harvard post-graduate. And if that is an asset it's my only one."

Hamil, surprised at his bitterness, looked at him with troubled eyes. Then his eyes wandered to Shiela, who had now taken up her embroidery.

"I can't help it," said Malcourt impatiently; "I like cities and people. I always liked people. I never had enough of people. I never had any society as a boy; and, Hamil, you can't imagine how I longed for it. It would have been well for me to have had it. There was never any in my own home; there was never anything in my home life but painful memories of domestic trouble and financial stress. I was for a while asked to the homes of schoolmates, but could offer no hospitality in return. Sensitiveness and humiliation have strained the better qualities out of me. I've been bruised dry."

He leaned on his elbows, hands clasped, looking out into the sunlight where myriads of brilliant butterflies were fluttering over the carpet of white phlox.

"Hamil," he said, "whatever is harsh, aggressive, cynical, mean, sneering, selfish in me has been externally acquired. You scrape even a spineless mollusc too long with a pin, and the irritation produces a defensive crust. I began boy-like by being so damned credulous and impulsive and affectionate and tender-hearted that even my kid sister laughed at me; and she was only three years older than I. Then followed that period of social loneliness, the longing for the companionship of boys and girls—girls particularly, in spite of agonies of shyness and the awakening terrors of shame when the domestic troubles ended in an earthquake which gave me to my father and Helen to my mother, and a scandal to the newspapers.... O hell! I'm talking like an autobiography! Don't go, if you can stand it for a moment longer; I'm never likely to do it again."

Hamil, silent and uncomfortable, stood stiffly upright, gloved hands resting on the balustrade behind him. Malcourt continued to stare at the orange-and-yellow butterflies dancing over the snowy beds of blossoms.

"In college it was the same," he said. "I had few friends—and no home to return to after—my father-died." He hesitated as though listening. Whenever he spoke of his father, which was seldom, he seemed to assume that curious listening attitude; as though the man, dead by his own hand, could hear him....

"Wayward saw me through. I've paid him back what he spent on me. You know his story; everybody does. I like him and sponge on him. We irritate each other; I'm a beast to resent his sharpness. But he's not right when he says I never had any illusions.... I had—and have.... I do beastly things, too.... Some men will do anything to crush out the last quiver of pride in them.... And the worst is that, mangled, torn, mine still palpitates—like one of your wretched, bloody quail gaping on its back! By God! At least, I couldn't do *that*!—*Kill* for pleasure!—as better men than I do. And better women, too!... What am I talking about? I've done worse than that on impulse—meaning well, like other fools."

Malcourt's face had become drawn, sallow, almost sneering; but in the slow gaze he turned on Hamil was that blank hopelessness which no man can encounter and remember unmoved.

"Malcourt," he said, "you're morbid. Men like you; women like you—So do I—now—"

"It's too late. I needed that sort of thing when I was younger. Kindness arouses my suspicion now. Toleration is what it really is. I have no money, no social position here—or abroad; only a thoroughly discredited name in two hemispheres. It took several generations for the Malcourts to go to the devil; but I fancy we'll all arrive on time. What a reunion! I hate the idea of family parties, even in hell."

He straightened up gracefully and lighted his cigarette; then the easy smile twitched his dry lips again and he nodded mockingly at Hamil:

"Count on my friendship, Hamil; it's so valuable. It has already quite ruined one person's life, and will no doubt damage others before I flicker out."

"What do you mean, Malcourt?"

"What I say, old fellow. With the best intentions toward self-sacrifice I usually do irreparable damage to the objects of my regard. Beware my friendship, Hamil. There's no luck in it or me.... But I do like you."

He laughed and sauntered off into the house as Hamil's horse was brought around; and Hamil, traversing the terrace, mounted under a running fire of badinage from Shiela and Cecile who had just come from the tennis-courts to attempt some hated embroidery for the charity fair then impending.

So he rode away to his duties in the forest, leaving a placid sewing-circle on the terrace. From which circle, presently, Shiela silently detached herself, arms encumbered with her writing materials and silks. Strolling aimlessly along the balustrade for a while, watching the bees scrambling in the scarlet trumpet-flowers, she wandered into the house and through to the cool patio.

For some days, now, after Hamil's daily departure, it had happened that an almost unendurable restlessness akin to suspense took possession of her; a distaste and impatience of people and their voices, and the routine of the commonplace.

To occupy herself in idleness was an effort; she had no desire to. She had recently acquired the hammock habit, lying for hours in the coolness of the patio, making no effort to think, listening to the splash of the fountain, her book or magazine open across her breast. When people came she picked up the book and scanned its pages; sometimes she made pretence of sleeping.

But that morning, Malcourt, errant, found her reading in her hammock. Expecting him to pass his way as usual, she nodded with civil indifference, and continued her reading.

"I want to ask you something," he said, "if I may interrupt you."

"What is it, Louis?"

"May I draw up a chair?"

"Why—if you wish. Is there anything I can do for you? "—closing her book.

"Is there anything I can do for *you*, Shiela?"

A tinge of colour came into her cheeks.

"Thank you," she said in curt negation.

"Are you quite sure?"

"Quite. What do you mean?"

"There is one thing I might do for your sake," he smiled—"blow my bally brains out."

She said in a low contemptuous voice: "Better resort to that for your own sake than do what you are doing to Miss Suydam."

"What am I doing to Miss Suydam?"

"Making love to her."

He sat, eyes idly following the slight swaying motion of her hammock, the smile still edging his lips.

"Don't worry about Miss Suydam," he said; "she can take care of herself. What I want to say is this: Once out of mistaken motives—which nobody, including yourself, would ever credit—I gave you all I had to give—my name.... It's not much of a name; but I thought you could use it. I was even fool enough to think—other things. And as usual I succeeded in injuring where I meant only kindness. Can you believe that?"

"I—think you meant it kindly," she said under her breath. "It was my fault, Louis. I do not blame you, if you really cared for me. I've told you so before."

"Yes, but I was ass enough to think *you* cared for *me*."

She lay in her hammock, looking at him across the crimson-fringed border.

"There are two ways out of it," he said; "one is divorce. Have you changed your mind?"

"What is the other?" she asked coldly.

"That—if you could ever learn to care for me—we might try—" He stopped short.

For two years he had not ventured such a thing to her. The quick, bright anger warned him from her eyes. But she said quietly: "You know that is utterly impossible."

"Is it impossible. Shiela?"

"Absolutely. And a trifle offensive."

He said pleasantly: "I was afraid so, but I wanted to be sure. I did not mean to offend you. People change and mature in two years.... I suppose you are as angrily impatient of sentiment in a man as you were then."

"I cannot endure it—"

Her voice died out and she blushed furiously as the memory of Hamil flashed in her mind.

"Shiela," he said quietly, "now and then there's a streak of misguided decency in me. It cropped out that winter day when I did what I did. And I suppose it's cropping up now when I ask you, for your own sake, to get rid of me and give yourself a chance."

"How?"

"Legally."

"I cannot, and you know it."

"You are wrong. Do you think for one moment that your father and mother would accept the wretched sacrifice you are making of your life if they knew—"

"The old arguments again," she said impatiently.

"There is a *new* argument," said Malcourt, staring at her.

"What new argument?"

"Hamil."

Then the vivid colour surged anew from neck to hair, and she rose in the hammock, bewildered, burning, incensed.

"If it were true," she stammered, leaning on one arm, "do you think me capable of disgracing my own people?"

"The disgrace will be mine and yours. Is not Hamil worth it?"

"No man is worth any wrong I do to my own family!"

"You are wronging more people than your own, Shiela—"

"It is not true!" she said breathlessly. "There is a nobler happiness than one secured at the expense of selfishness and ingratitude. I tell you, as long as I live, I will not have them know or suffer because of my disgraceful escapade with you! You probably meant well; I must have been crazy, I think. But we've got to endure the consequences. If there's unhappiness and pain to be borne, we've got to bear it—we alone—"

"And Hamil. All three of us."

She looked at him desperately; read in his cool gaze that she could not deceive him, and remained silent.

"What about Hamil's unhappiness?" repeated Malcourt slowly.

"If—if he has any, he requires no instruction how to bear it."

Malcourt nodded, then, with a weary smile: "I do not plead with you for my own chance of happiness. Yet, you owe me something, Shiela."

"What?"

"The right to face the world under true colours. You owe me that."

She whitened to the lips. "I know it."

"Suppose I ask for that right?"

"I have always told you that, if you demanded it, I would take your name openly."

"Yes; but now you admit that you love Hamil."

"Love! Love!" she repeated, exasperated. "What has that got to do with it? I know what the law of obligation is. You meant to be generous to me and you ruined your own life. If your future career requires me to publicly assume your name and a place in your household, I've told you that I'll pay that debt."

"Very well. When will you pay it?"

She blanched pitifully.

"When you insist, Louis."

"Do you mean you would go out there to the terrace, *now!*—and tell your mother what you've done?"

"Yes, if I must," she answered faintly.

"In other words, because you think you're in my debt, you stand ready to acknowledge, on demand, what I gave you—my name?"

Her lips moved in affirmation, but deep in her sickened eyes he saw terror unspeakable.

"Well," he said, looking away from her, "don't worry, Shiela. I'm not asking that of you; in fact I don't want it. That's not very complimentary, but it ought to relieve you.... I'm horribly sorry about Hamil; I like him; I'd like to do something for him. But if I attempted anything it would turn out all wrong.... As for you—well, you are plucky. Poor little girl! I wish I could help you out—short of a journey to eternity. And perhaps I'll take that before very long," he added gaily; "I smoke too many cigarettes. Cheer up, Shiela, and send me a few thousand for Easter."

He rose, gracefully as always, picked up the book from where it lay tumbled in the netting of the hammock, glanced casually through a page or two.

Still scanning the print, he said:

"I wanted to give you a chance; I'm going North in a day or two. It isn't likely we'll meet again very soon.... So I thought I'd speak.... And, if at any time you change your ideas—I won't oppose it."

"Thank you, Louis."

He was running over the pages rapidly now, the same unchanging smile edging his lips.

"The unexpected sometimes happens, Shiela—particularly when it's expected. There are ways and ways—particularly when one is tired—too tired to lie awake and listen any longer, or resist.... My father used to say that anybody who could use an anæsthetic was the equal of any graduate physician—"

"Louis! What do you mean?"

But his head was bent again in that curious attitude of listening; and after a moment he made an almost imperceptible gesture of acquiescence, and turned to her with the old, easy, half-impudent, half-challenging air.

"Gray has a butterfly in his collection which shows four distinct forms. Once people thought these forms were distinct species; now they know they all are the same species of butterfly in various suits of disguise— just as you might persuade yourself that unhappiness and happiness are radically different. But some people find satisfaction in being unhappy, and some find it in being happy; and as it's all only the gratification of that imperious egotism we call conscience, the specific form of all is simply ethical selfishness."

He laughed unrestrainedly at his own will-o'-the-wisp philosophy, looking very handsome and care-free there where the noon sun slanted across the white arcade all thick with golden jasmine bloom.

And Shiela, too intelligent to mistake him, smiled a little at his gay perversity.

He met Portlaw, later, at the Beach Club for luncheon; and, as the latter looked particularly fat, warm, and worried, Malcourt's perverse humour remained in the ascendant, and he tormented Portlaw until that badgered gentleman emitted a bellow of exasperation.

"What on earth's the matter?" asked Malcourt in pretended astonishment. "I thought I was being funny."

"Funny! Does a man want to be prodded with wit at his own expense when the market is getting funnier every hour—at his expense? Go and look at the tape if you want to know why I don't enjoy either your wit or this accursed luncheon."

"What's happening, Portlaw?"

"I wish you'd tell me."

"Muck-raking?"

"Partly, I suppose."

"Administration?"

"People say so. I don't believe it. There's a rotten lot of gambling going on. How do I know what's the matter?"

"Perhaps there isn't anything the matter, old fellow."

"Well, there is. I can sniff it 'way down here. And I'm going home to walk about and listen and sniff some more. Sag, sag, sag!—that's what the market has been doing for months. Yet, if I sell it short, it rallies on me and I'm chased to cover. I go long and the thing sags like the panties on that French count, yonder.... Who's the blond girl with him?"

"Hope springs eternal in the human beast," observed Malcourt. "Hope is a bird, Porty, old chap—"

"Hope is a squab," growled Portlaw, swallowing vast quantities of claret, "all squashy and full of pin-feathers. That's what hope is. It needs a thorough roasting, and it's getting it."

"Exquisite metaphor," mused Malcourt, gazing affably at the rather blond girl who crumbled her bread and looked occasionally and blankly at him, occasionally and affectionately at the French count, her escort, who was consuming lobster with characteristic Gallic thoroughness and abandon.

"The world," quoted Malcourt, "is so full of a number of things. You're one of 'em, Portlaw; I'm several.... Well, if you're going North I'd better begin to get ready."

"What have you got to do?"

"One or two friends of mine who preside in the Temple of Chance yonder. Oh, don't assume that babyish pout! I've won enough back to keep going for the balance of the time we remain."

Portlaw, pleased and relieved, finished his claret.

"You've a few ladies to take leave of, also," he said briskly.

"Really, Portlaw!"—in gentle admonition.

"Haw! Haw!" roared Portlaw, startling the entire café; "you'd better get busy. There'll be a run on the bank. There'll be a waiting line before Malcourt & Co. opens for business, each fair penitent with her little I.O.U. to be cashed! Haw! Haw! Sad dog! Bad dog! The many-sided Malcourt! Come on; I've got a motor across the—"

"And I've an appointment with several superfluous people and a girl," said Malcourt drily. Then he glanced at the blond companion of the count who continued crumbling bread between her brilliantly ringed fingers as though she had never before seen Louis Malcourt. The price of diamonds varies. Sometimes it is merely fastidious observance of convention and a sensitive escort. It all depends on the world one inhabits; it does indeed.

CHAPTER XIV
STRATEGY

An hour or two later that afternoon Wayward and Constance Palliser, Gussie Vetchen, and Livingston Cuyp gazed with variously mingled sentiments upon the torpid saurians belonging to one Alligator Joe in an enclosure rather remote from the hotel.

Vetchen bestowed largess upon the small, freckled boy attendant; and his distinguished disapproval upon the largest lady-crocodile which, with interlocked but grinning jaws, slumbered under a vertical sun in monochromatic majesty.

"One perpetual and gigantic simper," he said, disgusted.

"Rather undignified for a thing as big as that to lay eggs like a hen," observed Cuyp, not intending to be funny.

Wayward and Miss Palliser had wandered off together to inspect the pumps. Vetchen, always inquisitive, had discovered a coy manatee in one tank, and was all for poking it with his walking-stick until he saw its preposterous countenance emerge from the water.

"Great heavens," he faltered, "it looks like a Dutch ancestor of Cuyp's!"

Cuyp, intensely annoyed, glanced at his watch.

"Where the mischief did Miss Suydam and Malcourt go?" he asked Wayward. "I say, Miss Palliser, you don't want to wait here any longer, do you?"

"They're somewhere in the labyrinth," said Wayward. "Their chair went that way, didn't it, boy?"

"Yeth, thir," said the small and freckled attendant.

So the party descended the wooden incline to where their sleepy black chairmen lay on the grass, waiting; and presently the two double chairs wheeled away toward that amusing maze of jungle pathways cut through the impenetrable hammock, and popularly known as the labyrinth.

But Miss Suydam and Mr. Malcourt were not in the labyrinth. At that very moment they were slowly strolling along the eastern dunes where the vast solitude of sky and sea seemed to depress even the single white-headed eagle standing on the wet beach, head and tail adroop, motionless, fish-gorged. No other living thing was in sight except the slim, blue dragon-flies, ceaselessly darting among the beach-grapes; nothing else stirred except those two figures on the dunes, moving slowly, heads bent as though considering the advisability of every step in the breaking sands. There was a fixed smile on the girl's lips, but her eyes were mirthless, almost vacant.

"So you've decided to go?" she said.

"Portlaw decides that sort of thing for me."

"It's a case of necessity?"

Malcourt answered lightly: "He intends to go. Who can stop a fat and determined man? Besides, the season is over; in two weeks there will be nobody left except the indigenous nigger, the buzzards, and a few cast-off summer garments—"

"And a few cast-off winter memories," she said. "You will not take any away with you, will you?"

"Do you mean clothes?"

"Memories."

"I'll take some."

"Which?"

"All those concerning you."

"Thank you, Louis." They had got that far. And a trifle farther, for her hand, swinging next his, encountered it and their fingers remained interlocked. But there was no change of expression in her pretty, pale face as, head bent, shoulder to shoulder with him, she moved thoughtfully onward along the dunes, the fixed smile stamped on her lips.

"What are you going to do with your memories?" she asked. "Pigeon-hole and label them? Or fling them, like your winter repentance, in the Fire of Spring?"

"What are you going to do with yours, Virginia?"

"Nothing. They are not disturbing enough to destroy. Besides, unlike yours, they are my first memories of indiscretions, and they are too new to forget easily, too incredible yet to hurt. A woman is seldom hurt by what she cannot understand."

He passed one arm around her supple waist; they halted; he turned her toward him.

"What is it you don't understand?"

"This."

"My kissing you? Like this?"

She neither avoided nor returned the caress, looking at him out of impenetrable eyes more green than blue like the deep sea under changing skies.

"Is this what you don't understand, Virginia?"

"Yes; that—and your moderation."

His smile changed, but it was still a smile.

"Nor I," he said. "Like our friend, Warren Hastings, I am astonished. But there our resemblance ends."

The eagle on the wet sands ruffled, shook his silvery hackles, and looked around at them. Then, head low and thrust forward, he hulked slowly toward the remains of the dead fish from which but now he had retired in the disgust of satiation.

Meanwhile Malcourt and Miss Suydam were walking cautiously forward again, selecting every footstep as though treading on the crumbling edges of an abyss.

"It's rather stupid that I never suspected it," she said, musing aloud.

"Suspected what?"

"The existence of this other woman called Virginia Suydam. And I might have been mercifully ignorant of her until I died, if you had not looked at me and seen us both at once."

"We all are that way."

"Not all women, Louis. Have you found them so? You need not answer. There is in you, sometimes, a flash of infernal chivalry; do you know it? I can forgive you a great deal for it; even for discovering that other and not very staid person, so easily schooled, easily taught to respond; so easily thrilled, easily beguiled, easily caressed. Why, with her head falling back on your shoulder so readily, and her lips so lightly persuaded, one can scarcely believe her to have been untaught through all these years of dry convention and routine, or unaware of that depravity, latent, which it took your unerring faith and skill to discover and develop."

"How far have I developed it?"

She bent her delicate head: "I believe I have already admitted your moderation."

He shivered, walking forward without looking at her for a pace or two, then halted.

"Would you marry me?" he asked.

"I had rather not. You know it."

"Why?—once again."

"Because of my strange respect for that other woman that I am—or was."

"Which always makes me regret my—moderation," he said, wincing under the lash of her words. "But I'm not considering you! I'm considering the peace of mind of that other woman—not yours!" He took her in his arms, none too gently. "Not yours. I'd show no mercy to *you*\ There is only one kind of mercy you'd understand. Look into my eyes and admit it."

"Yes," she said.

"But your other self understands!"

"Why don't you destroy her?"

"And let her die in her contempt for me? You ask too much—Virginia-that-I-know. If that other Virginia-that-I-don't-know loved me, I'd kill *this* one, not the other!"

"Do you care for that one, Louis?"

"What answer shall I make?"

"The best you can without lying."

"Then"—and being in his arms their eyes were close—"then I think I could love her if I had a chance. I don't know. I can deny myself. They say that is the beginning. But I seldom do—very seldom. And that is the best answer I can give, and the truest."

"Thank you.... And so you are going to leave me?"

"I am going North. Yes."

"What am I to do?"

"Return to your other self and forget me."

"Thank you again.... Do you know, Louis, that you have never once by hint or by look or by silence suggested that it was I who deliberately offered you the first provocation? That is another flicker of that infernal chivalry of yours."

"Does your other self approve?" he said, laughing.

"My other self is watching us both very closely, Louis. I—I wish, sometimes, she were dead! Louis! Louis! as I am now, here in your arms, I thought I had descended sufficiently to meet you on your own plane. But— you seem higher up—at moments.... And now, when you are going, you tell my other self to call in the creature we let loose together, for it will have no longer any counterpart to caress.... Louis! I *do* love you; how can I let you go! Can you tell me? What am I to do? There are times—there are moments when I cannot endure it—the thought of losing the disgrace of your lips— your arms—the sound of your voice. Don't go and leave me like this—don't go—"

Miss Suydam's head fell. She was crying.

The eagle on the wet beach, one yellow talon firmly planted on its offal, tore strip after strip from the quivering mass. The sun etched his tinted shadow on the sand.

When the tears of Miss Suydam had been appropriately dried, they turned and retraced their steps very slowly, her head resting against his shoulder, his arm around her thin waist, her own hand hanging loosely, trailing the big straw hat and floating veil.

They spoke very seldom—very, very seldom. Malcourt was too busy thinking; Virginia too stunned to realise that, it was, now, her other austere self, bewildered, humiliated, desperate, which was walking amid the solitude of sky and sea with Louis Malcourt, there beneath the splendour of the westering sun.

The eagle, undisturbed, tore at the dead thing on the beach, one yellow talon embedded in the offal.

Their black chair-boy lay asleep under a thicket of Spanish bayonet.

"Arise, O Ethiope, and make ready unto us a chariot!" said Malcourt pleasantly; and he guided Virginia into her seat while the fat darky climbed up behind, rubbing slumber from his rolling and enormous eyes.

Half-way through the labyrinth they met Miss Palliser and Wayward.

"Where on earth have you been?" asked Virginia, so candidly that Wayward, taken aback, began excuses. But Constance Palliser's cheeks turned pink; and remained so during her silent ride home with Wayward.

Lately the world had not been spinning to suit the taste of Constance Palliser. For one thing Wayward was morose. Besides he appeared physically ill. She shrank from asking herself the reason; she might better have asked him for her peace of mind.

Another matter: Virginia, the circumspect, the caste-bound, the intolerant, the emotionless, was displaying the astounding symptoms peculiar to the minx! And she had neither the excuse of ignorance nor of extreme youth. Virginia was a mature maiden, calmly cognisant of the world, and coolly alive to the doubtful phases of that planet. And why on earth she chose to affiche herself with a man like Malcourt, Constance could not comprehend.

And another thing worried the pretty spinster—the comings, goings, and occult doings of her nephew with the most distractingly lovely and utterly impossible girl that fate ever designed to harass the soul of any young man's aunt.

That Hamil was already in love with Shiela Cardross had become painfully plainer to her every time she saw him. True, others were in love with Miss Cardross; that state of mind and heart seemed to be chronic at Palm Beach. Gussie Vetchen openly admitted his distinguished consideration, and Courtlandt Classon toddled busily about Shiela's court, and even the forlorn Cuyp had become disgustingly unfaithful and no longer wrinkled his long Dutch nose into a series of white corrugations when Wayward took Miss Palliser away from him. Alas! the entire male world seemed to trot in the wake of this sweet-eyed young Circe, emitting appealingly gentle and propitiating grunts.

"The very deuce is in that girl!" thought Constance, exasperated; "and the sooner Garry goes North the better. He's madly unhappy over her.... Fascinating little thing! I can't blame him too much—except that he evidently realises he can't marry such a person—"

The chair rolled into the hotel grounds under the arch of jasmine. The orchestra was playing in the colonnade; tea had been served under the cocoa-nut palms; pretty faces and gay toilets glimmered familiarly as the chair swept along the edge of the throng.

"Tell the chair-boy that we'll tea here, Jim," said Miss Palliser, catching sight of her nephew and the guilty Circe under whose gentle thrall Hamil was now boldly imbibing a swizzle.

So Wayward nodded to the charioteer, the chair halted, and he and Constance disembarked and advanced across the grass to exchange amenities with friends and acquaintances. Which formalities always fretted Wayward, and he stood about, morose and ungracious, while Constance floated prettily here and there, and at last turned with nicely prepared surprise to encounter Shiela and Hamil seated just behind her.

The younger girl, rising, met her more than half-way with gloved hand frankly offered; Wayward turned to Hamil in subdued relief.

"Lord! I've been looking at those confounded alligators and listening to Vetchen's and Cuyp's twaddle! Constance wouldn't talk; and I'm quite unfit for print. What's that in your glass, Garry?"

"A swizzle—"

"Anything in it except lime-juice and buzz?"

"Yes—"

"Then I won't have one. Constance! Are you drinking tea?"

"Do you want some?" she asked, surprised.

"Yes, I do—if you can give me some without asking how many lumps I take—like the inevitable heroine in a British work of fiction—"

"Jim, what a bear you are to-day!" And to Shiela, who was laughing: "He snapped and growled at Gussie Vetchen and he glared and glowered at Livingston Cuyp, and he's scarcely vouchsafed a word to me this afternoon except the civility you have just heard. Jim, I *will* ask you how many lumps—"

"O Lord! Britain triumphant! Two—I think; ten if you wish, Constance— or none at all. Miss Cardross, you wouldn't say such things to me, would you?"

"Don't answer him," interposed Constance; "if you do you'll take him away, and I haven't another man left! Why are you such a dreadful devastator, Miss Cardross?... Here's your tea, James. Please turn around and occupy yourself with my nephew; I'd like a chance to talk to Miss Cardross."

The girl had seated herself beside Miss Palliser, and, as Wayward moved over to the other table, she gave him a perverse glance, so humourous and so wholly adorable that Constance Palliser yielded to the charm with an amused sigh of resignation.

"My dear," she said, "Miss Suydam and I are going North very soon, and we are coming to see your mother at the first opportunity."

"Mother expects you," said the girl simply. "I did not know that she knew Miss Suydam—or cared to."

Something in the gentle indifference of the words sent the conscious blood pulsing into Miss Palliser's cheeks. Then she said frankly:

"Has Virginia been rude to you?"

"Yes—a little."

"Unpardonably?"

"N-no. I always can pardon."

"You dear!" said Constance impulsively. "Listen; Virginia does snippy things at times. I don't know why and she doesn't either. I know she's sorry she was rude to you, but she seems to think her rudeness too utterly unpardonable. May I tell her it isn't?"

"If you please," said Shiela quietly.

Miss Palliser looked at her, then, succumbing, took her hand in hers.

"No wonder people like you, Miss Cardross."

"Do *you*?"

"How could I escape the popular craze?" laughed Miss Palliser, a trifle embarrassed.

"That is not an answer," returned Shiela, the smile on her red lips faintly wistful. And Constance surrendered completely.

"You sweet, cunning thing," she said, "I do like you. You are perfectly adorable, for one reason; for the other, there is something—a nameless something about you—"

"Quite—nameless," said the girl under her breath.

A little flash of mist confused Miss Palliser's eyesight for a moment; her senses warned her, but her heart was calling.

"Dear," she said, "I could love you very easily."

Shiela looked her straight in the eyes.

"What you give I can return; no more, no less—"

But already Constance Palliser had lifted the girl's smooth hand to her lips, murmuring: "Pride! pride! It is the last refuge for social failures, Shiela. And you are too wise to enter there, too sweet and wholesome to remain. Leave us our obsolete pride, child; God knows we need something in compensation for all that you possess."

Later they sipped their tea together. "I always wanted you to like me," said the girl. Her glance wandered toward Hamil so unconsciously that Constance caught her breath. But the spell was on her still; she, too, looked at Hamil; admonition, prejudice, inculcated precept, wavered hazily.

"Because I care so much for Mr. Hamil," continued the girl innocently.

For one instant, in her inmost intelligence, Miss Palliser fiercely questioned that innocence; then, convinced, looked questioningly at the girl beside her. So questioningly that Shiela answered:

"What?"—as though the elder woman had spoken.

"I don't know, dear.... Is there anything you—you cared to ask me?—say to me?—tell me?—perhaps—"

"About what?"

So fearless and sweet and true the gaze that met her own that Constance hesitated.

"About Mr. Hamil?"

The girl looked at her; understood her; and the colour mounted to her temples.

"No," she said slowly, "there is nothing to tell anybody.... There never will be."

"I wish there were, child." Certainly Constance must have gone quite mad under the spell, for she had Shiela's soft hands in hers again, and was pressing them close between her palms, repeating: "I am sorry; I am, indeed. The boy certainly cares for you; he has told me so a thousand times without uttering a word. I have known it for weeks—feared it. *Now* I wish it. I am sorry."

"Mr. Hamil—understands—" faltered Shiela; "I—I care so much for him—so much more than for any other man; but not in the way you—you are kind enough to—wish—"

"*Does* he understand?"

"Y-yes. I think so. I think we understand each other—thoroughly. But"—she blushed vividly—"I—did not dream that *you* supposed—"

Miss Palliser looked at her searchingly.

"—But—it has made me very happy to believe that you consider me—acceptable."

"Dearest child, it is evident that *we* are the unacceptable ones—"

"Please don't say that—or think it. It is absurd—in one sense.... Are we to be friends in town? Is that what you mean?"

"Indeed we are, if you will."

Miss Cardross nodded and withdrew her hands as Virginia and Malcourt came into view across the lawn.

Constance, following her glance, saw, and signalled silent invitation; Malcourt sauntered up, paid his respects airily, and joined Hamil and Wayward; Virginia spoke in a low voice to Constance, then, leaning on the back of her chair, looked at Shiela as inoffensively as she knew how. She said:

"I am very sorry for my rudeness to you. Can you forgive me, Miss Cardross?"

"Yes.... Won't you have some tea?"

Her direct simplicity left Virginia rather taken aback. Perhaps she expected some lack of composure in the girl, perhaps a more prolix acceptance of honourable amends; but this terse and serene amiability almost suggested indifference; and Virginia seated herself, not quite knowing how she liked it.

Afterward she said to Miss Palliser:

"Did you ever see such self-possession, my dear? You know I might pardon my maid in exactly the same tone and manner."

"But you wouldn't ask your maid to tea, would you?" said Constance, gently amused.

"I might, if I could afford to," she nodded listlessly. "I believe that girl could do it without disturbing her Own self-respect or losing caste below stairs or above. As for the Van Dieman—just common cat, Constance."

Miss Palliser laughed. "Shiela Cardross refused the Van Dieman son and heir—if you think that might be an explanation of the cattishness."

"Really?" asked Virginia, without interest. "Where did you hear that gossip?"

"From our vixenish tabby herself. The thin and vindictive are usually without a real sense of humour. I rather suspected young Jan Van Dieman's discomfiture. He left, you know, just after Garret arrived," she added demurely.

Virginia raised her eyes at the complacent inference; but even curiosity seemed to have died out in her, and she only said, languidly:

"You think she cares for Garret? And you approve?"

"I think I'd approve if she did. Does that astonish you?"

"Not very much."

Virginia seemed to have lost all spirit. She laughed rarely, nowadays. She was paler, too, than usual—paler than was ornamental; and pallor suited her rather fragile features, too. Also she had become curiously considerate of other people's feelings—rather subdued; less ready in her criticisms; gentler in judgments. All of which symptoms Constance had already noted with incredulity and alarm.

"Where did you and Louis Malcourt go this afternoon?" she asked, unpegging her hair.

"Out to the beach. There was nothing there except sky and water, and a filthy eagle dining on a dead fish."

Miss Palliser waited, sitting before her dresser; but as Virginia offered no further information she shook out the splendid masses of her chestnut hair and, leaning forward, examined her features in the mirror with minute attention.

"It's strange," she murmured, half to herself, "how ill Jim Wayward has been looking recently. I can't account for it."

"I can, dear," said Virginia gently.

Constance turned in surprise.

"How?"

"Mr. Malcourt says that he is practising self-denial. It hurts, you know."

"What!" exclaimed Constance, flushing up.

"I said that it hurts."

"Such a slur as that harms Louis Malcourt—not Mr. Wayward!" returned Constance hotly.

Virginia repeated: "It hurts—to kill desire. It hurts even before habit is acquired ... they say. Louis Malcourt says so. And if that is true—can you wonder that poor Mr. Wayward looks like death? I speak in all sympathy and kindness—as did Mr. Malcourt."

So *that* was it! Constance stared at her own fair face in the mirror, and deep into the pained brown eyes reflected there. The eyes suddenly dimmed and the parted mouth quivered.

So that was the dreadful trouble!—the explanation of the recent change in him—the deep lines of pain from the wing of the pinched nostril—the haunted gaze, the long, restless silences, the forced humour and its bitter flavour tainting voice and word!

And she had believed—feared with a certainty almost hopeless—that it was his old vice, slowly, inexorably transforming what was left of the man she had known so long and cared for so loyally through all these strange, confusing years.

From the mirror the oval of her own fresh unravaged face, framed in the burnished brown of her hair, confronted her like a wraith of the past; and, dreaming there, wide-eyed, expressionless, she seemed to see again the old-time parlour set with rosewood; and the faded roses in the carpet; and, through the half-drawn curtains, spring sunlight falling on a boy and a little girl.

Virginia, partly dressed for dinner, rose and went to the window, frail restless hands clasped behind her back, and stood there gazing out at the fading daylight. Perhaps the close of day made her melancholy; for there were traces of tears on her lashes; perhaps it suggested the approaching end of a dream so bright and strange that, at times, a dull pang of dread stilled her heart—checking for a moment its heavy beating.

Light died in the room; the panes turned silvery, then darker as the swift Southern night fell over sea, lagoon, and forest.

Far away in the wastes of dune and jungle the sweet flute-like tremolo of an owl broke out, prolonged infinitely. From the dark garden below, a widow-bird called breathlessly, its ghostly cry, now a far whisper in the night, now close at hand, husky, hurried, startling amid the shadows. And, whir! whir-r-r! thud! came the great soft night-moths against the window screens where sprays of silvery jasmine clung, perfuming all the night.

Still Constance sat before the mirror which was now invisible in the dusk, bare elbows on the dresser's edge, face framed in her hands over which the thick hair rippled. And, in the darkness, her brown eyes closed— perhaps that they might behold more clearly the phantoms of the past together there in an old-time parlour, where the golden radiance of suns long dead still lingered, warming the faded roses on the floor.

And after a long while her maid came with a card; and she straightened up in her chair, gathered the filmy robe of lace, and, rising, pressed the electric switch. But Virginia had returned to her own room to bathe her eyelids and pace the floor until she cared to face the outer world once more and, for another hour or two, deceive it.

CHAPTER XV
UNDER FIRE

Meanwhile Constance dressed hastily, abetted by the clever maid; for Wayward was below, invited to dine with them. Malcourt also was due for dinner, and, as usual, late.

In fact, he was at that moment leisurely tying his white neckwear in his bed-chamber at Villa Cardross. And sometimes he whistled, tentatively, as though absorbed in mentally following an elusive air; sometimes he resumed a lighted cigarette which lay across the gilded stomach of a Chinese joss, sending a thin, high thread of smoke to the ceiling. He had begun his collection with one small idol; there were now nineteen, and all hideous.

"The deuce! the deuce!" he murmured, rejecting the tie and trying another one; "and all the things I've got to do this blessed night!... Console the afflicted—three of them; dine with one, get to "The Breakers" and spoon with another—get to the Club and sup with another!—the deuce! the deuce! the—"

He hummed a bar or two of a new waltz, took a puff at his cigarette, winked affably at the idol, put on his coat, and without a second glance at the glass went out whistling a lively tune.

Hamil, dressed for dinner, but looking rather worn and fatigued, passed him in the hall.

"You've evidently had a hard day," said Malcourt; "you resemble the last run of sea-weed. Is everybody dining at this hour?"

"I dined early with Mrs. Cardross. Mrs. Carrick has taken Shiela and Cecile to that dinner dance at the O'Haras'. It's the last of the season. I thought you might be going later."

"Are you?"

"No; I'm rather tired."

"I'm tired, too. Hang it! I'm always tired—but only of Bibi. Quand même! Good night.... I'll probably reappear with the dicky-birds. Leave your key under that yellow rose-bush, will you? I can't stop to hunt up mine. And tell them not to bar and chain the door; that's a good fellow."

Hamil nodded and resumed his journey to his bedroom. There he transferred a disorderly heap of letters, plans, contracts, and blue-prints from his bed to a table, threw a travelling rug over the bed, lay down on it, and lighted a cigar, closing his eyes for a moment. Then he opened them wearily.

He did not intend to sleep; there was work waiting for him; that was why he left the electric bulbs burning as safeguard against slumber.

For a while he smoked, flat on his back; his cigar went out twice and he relighted it. The third time he was deciding whether or not to set fire to it again—he remembered that—and remembered nothing more, except the haunted dreams in which he followed *her*, through sad and endless forests, gray in deepening twilight, where he could neither see her face nor reach her side, nor utter the cry which strained in his throat.... On, on, endlessly struggling onward in the thickening darkness, year after year, the sky a lowering horror, the forest, no longer silent, a twisting, stupefying confusion of sound, growing, increasing, breaking into a hellish clamour!—

Upright on his bed he realised that somebody was knocking; and he slid to the floor, still stupid and scarcely convinced.

"Mrs. Carrick's compliments, and is Mr. Hamil quite well bein' as the lights is burnin' an' past two o'clock, sir?" said the maid at the door.

"Past *two*! O Lord! Please thank Mrs. Carrick, and say that I am going to do a little work, and that I am perfectly well."

He closed the door and looked around him in despair: "All that stuff to verify and O.K.! What an infernal ass I am! By the nineteen little josses in Malcourt's bedroom I'm so many kinds of a fool that I hate to count up beyond the dozen!"

Stretching and yawning alternately he eyed the mass of papers with increasing repugnance; but later a cold sponge across his eyes revived him sufficiently to sit down and inspect the first document. Then he opened the ink-well, picked up a pen, and began.

For half an hour he sat there, now refreshed and keenly absorbed in his work. Once the stairs outside creaked, and he raised his head, listening absently, then returned to the task before him with a sigh.

All his windows were open; the warm night air was saturated with the odour of Bermuda lilies. Once or twice he laid down his pen and stared out into the darkness as a subtler perfume grew on the breeze—the far fragrance of china-berry in bloom; Calypso's breath!

Then, in the silence, the heavy throb of his heart unnerved his hand, rendering his pen unsteady as he signed each rendered bill: "O.K. for $— —," and affixed his signature, "John Garret Hamil, Architect."

The aroma of the lilies hung heavy in the room, penetrating as the scent of Malcourt's spiced Chinese gums afire and bubbling. And he thought again of Malcourt's nineteen little josses which he lugged about with him everywhere from some occult whim, and in whose gilt-bronze laps he sometimes burned cigarettes, sometimes a tiny globule of aromatic gum, pretending it propitiated the malice-brooding gods.

And, thinking of Malcourt, suddenly he remembered the door-key. Malcourt could not get in without it. And the doors were barred and chained.

Slipping the key into his pocket he opened his door, and, treading quietly through the silent house, descended to the great hall. With infinite precaution he fumbled for the chains; they were dangling loose. Somebody, too, had drawn the heavy bars, but the door itself was locked.

So he cautiously unlocked it, and holding the key in his hand, let himself out on the terrace.

And at the same moment a shadowy figure turned in the starlight to confront him.

"Shiela!"

"Is that you, Mr. Hamil?"

"Yes. What on earth are you—"

"Hush! What are *you* doing down here?"

"Louis Malcourt is out. I forgot to leave a key for him under the yellow rose—"

"Under the rose—and yellow at that! The mysteries of the Rosicrucians pale into insignificance beside the lurid rites of Mr. Malcourt and Mr. Hamil—under the yellow rose! Proceed, my fearsome adept, and perform the occult deed!"

Hamil descended the terrace to the new garden, hung the key to a brier under the fragrant mass of flowers, and glanced up at Shiela, who, arms on the balustrade above him, was looking down at the proceedings.

"Is the dread deed done?" she whispered.

"If you don't believe it come down and see."

"I? Come down? At *two* in the morning?"

"It's half-past two."

"Oh," she said, "if it's half-past two I might think of coming down for a moment—to look at my roses.... Thank you, Mr. Hamil, I can see my way very clearly. I can usually see my own way clearly—without the aid of your too readily offered hand.... Did you ever dream of such an exquisitely hot night! That means rain, doesn't it?—with so many fragrances mingling? The odour of lilies predominates, and I think some jasmine is in the inland wind, but my roses are very sweet if you only bend down to them. A rose is always worth stooping for."

She leaned over the yellow blossoms, slender, spirit-white in the starlight, and brushed her fresh young face with the silken petals.

"So sweet," she said; "lean down and worship my young roses, you unappreciative man!"

For a few minutes she strolled along the paths of the new garden he had built, bending capriciously here and there to savour some perfect blossom. The night was growing warmer; the sea breeze had died out, and a hot wind blew languidly from the west.

"You know," she said, looking back at him over her shoulder, "I don't want to go to bed."

"Neither do I, and I'm not going."

"But I'm going.... I wonder why I don't want to? Listen! Once—after I was a protoplasm and a micro-organism, and a mollusc, and other things, I probably was a predatory animal—nice and sleek with velvet feet and shining incandescent eyes—and very, very predatory.... That's doubtless why I often feel so deliciously awake at night—with a tameless longing to prowl under the moon.... And I think I'd better go in, now."

"Nonsense," he said, "I'm not going to bed yet."

"Oh! And what difference might that make to me? You are horridly conceited; do you know it?"

"Please stay, Calypso. It's too hot to sleep."

"No; star-prowling is contrary to civilized custom."

"But every soul in the house is sound asleep—"

"I should hope so! And you and I have no business to be out here."

"Do little observances of that sort count with you and me?"

"They don't," she said, shaking her head, "but they ought to. I *want* to stay. There is no real reason why I shouldn't—except the absurd fear of being caught unawares. Perhaps, perhaps I might stay for ten more minutes.... Oh, the divine beauty of it all! How hot it is!—the splash of the fountains seems to cool things a little—and those jagged, silvery reflections of the stars, deep, deep in the pool there.... Did you see that fish swirl to the surface? Hark! What was that queer sound?"

"Some night bird crying in the marshes. It will rain to-morrow; the wind is blowing from the hammock; that's why it's hot to-night; can you detect the odour of wild sweet-bay?"

"Yes—at moments. And I can just hear the surf—calling, calling 'Calypso!' as you called me once.... I *must* go, now."

"To the sea or the house?" he asked, laughing.

She walked a few paces toward the house, halted, and looked back audaciously.

"I'd go to the sea—only I'm afraid I'd be found out.... Isn't it all too stupid! Where convention is needless and one's wish is so harmless why should a girl turn coward at the fear of somebody discovering how innocently happy she is trying to be with a man!... It makes me very impatient at times." ... She turned, hesitated, stepped nearer and looked him in the face, daringly perverse.

"I want to go with you!... Have we not passed through enough together to deserve this little unconventional happiness?" She was breathing more quickly. "I *will* go with you if you wish."

"To the sea?"

"Yes. It is only a half mile by the hammock path. The servants are awake at six. Really, the night is too superb to waste—alone. But we must get back in time, if I go with you."

"Have you a key?"

"Yes, here in my gloves"—stripping them from her bare arms. "Can you put them into your pocket with the key?... And I'll pin up my skirt to get it out of the way.... What? Do you think it's a pretty gown? I did not think you noticed it. I've danced it to rags.... And will you take this fan, please? No, I'll wear the wrap—it's only cobweb weight."

She had now pinned up her gown to walking-skirt length; her slim feet were sheathed in silken dancing gear; and she bent over to survey them, then glanced doubtfully at Hamil, who shook his head.

"Never mind," she said resolutely; "only we can't walk far on the beach; I could never keep them on in the dune sands. Are you ready, O my tempter?"

Like a pair of guilty ghosts they crossed the shadowy garden, skirted the dark orange groves, and instead of entering the broad palm-lined way that led straight east for two miles to the sea, they turned into the sinuous hammock path which, curving south, cut off nearly a mile and a half.

"It's rather dark," she said.

They walked for a few minutes in silence; and, at first, she could not understand why he insisted on leading, because the path was wide enough for both.

"I *will* not proceed in this absurd manner," she said at last—"like an Indian and his faithful squaw. Why on earth do you—"

And it flashed across her at the same instant.

"Is *that* why?"—imperiously abrupt.

"What?" he asked, halting.

She passed her arm through his, not gently, but her laughing voice was very friendly:

"If we jump a snake in the dark, my friend, we jump him *together*! It's like you, but your friend Shiela won't permit it."

"Oh, it's only a conventional precaution—"

"Yes? Well, we'll take chances together.... Suppose—by the wildest and weirdest stretch of a highly coloured imagination you jumped a rattler?"

"Nonsense—"

"*Suppose* you did?"

He said, sobered: "It would be horribly awkward for you to explain. I forgot about—"

"Do you think I meant *that*! Do you think I'd care what people might say about our being here together? I—I'd *want* them to know it! What would I care—about—anything—then!"

Through the scorn in her voice he detected the awakened emotion; and, responsive, his pulse quickened, beating hard and heavy in throat and breast.

"I had almost forgotten," he said, "that we might dare look at things that way.... It all has been so—hopeless—lately—"

"What?... Yes, I understand."

"Do you?—my trying to let you alone—trying to think differently—to ignore all that has been said?"

"Yes.... This is no time to bring up such things." Her uneven breathing was perceptible to him as she moved by his side through the darkness, her arm resting on his.

No, this was no time to bring up such things. They knew it. And she, who in the confidence of her youth had dared to trust her unknown self, listened now to the startled beating of her heart at the first hint of peril.

"I wish I had not come," she said.

He did not ask her why.

"You are very silent—you have been so for days," she added; then, too late, knew that once more her tongue had betrayed her. "Don't answer me," she whispered.

"Why not?"

"Because what I say is folly.... I—I must ask you to release my hands.... You know it is only because I think it safer for—us; don't you?"

"What threatens *you*. Calypso?"

"Nothing.... I told you once that I am afraid—even in daylight. Ask yourself what I fear here under the stars with you."

"You fear *me*?"—managing to laugh.

"No; I dread your ally—my unknown self—in arms eternally to fight for you," she answered with forced gaiety. "Shall we kill her to-night? She deserves no consideration at our hands."

"Dear—"

"Hush! That is not the countersign on the firing line. Besides it is treachery, because to say that word is aiding, abetting, and giving information and comfort to our enemies. Our enemies, remember, are our other and stealthy selves." Her voice broke unsteadily. "I am trying so hard," she breathed, "but I cannot think clearly unless you help me. There is mutiny threatening somewhere."

"I have tried, too," he said.

"I know you have. Do you suppose I have been untouched by your consideration for me all these long days—your quiet cheerfulness—your dear unselfishness—the forbidden word!—but what synonym am I to use?... Oh, I know, I know what you are doing, thinking, feeling—believe me—believe me, I know! And—it is what you must do, of course. But—if you only did not show it so plainly—the effort—the strain—the hurt—"

"Do I show it?" he asked, chagrined. "I did not know that."

"Only to me—because I know. And I remember how young you were—that first day. Your whole expression has changed.... And I know why.... At times it scarcely seems that I can bear it—when I see your mouth laughing at the world and your eyes without mirth—dead—and the youth in you so altered, so quenched, so—forgive me!—so useless—"

"To what better use could I devote it, Shiela?"

"Oh, you don't know!—you don't know!—You are free; there are other women, other hopes—try to understand what freedom means!"

"It means—*you,,* Shiela."

She fell silent; then:

"Wherever I turn, whatever I say—all paths and words lead back again to you and me. I should not have come."

The hard, hammering pulse in his throat made it difficult for him to speak; but he managed to force an unsteady laugh; "Shiela, there is only one way for me, now—to fire and fall back. I've got to go up to Portlaw's camp anyhow—"

"And after that?"

"Mrs. Ascott wants a miniature Versailles. I'll show you the rough sketches—"

"And after that?"

"I've one or two promises—"

"And afterward?"

"Nothing."

"You will never—see me—again. Is that what 'nothing' means?"

They walked on in silence. The path had now become palely illumined; the sound of the surf was very near. Another step or two and they stood on the forest's edge.

A spectral ocean stretched away under the stars; ghostly rollers thundered along the sands. North and south dunes glimmered; and the hot fragrance of sweet-bay mingled with the mounting savour of the sea.

She looked at the sea, the stars, blindly, lips apart, teeth closed, her arm still resting on his.

"Nothing," she repeated under her breath; "that was the best answer.... Don't touch my hand!... I was mad to come here.... How close and hot it is! What is that new odour—so fresh and sweet—"

"China-berry in bloom—"

"Is it?"

"I'm not sure; once I thought it was—you; the fragrance of your hair and breath—Calypso."

"When did you think that?"

"Our first night together."

She said: "I think this is our last."

He stood for a while, motionless; slowly raised his head and looked straight into her eyes; took her in his arms; holding her loosely.

White of cheek and lip, rigid, her eyes met his in breathless suspense. Fear widened them; her hands tightened on his wrists behind her.

"Will you love me?"

"No!" she gasped.

"Is there no chance?"

"No!"

Her heart was running riot; every pulse in rebellion. A cloud possessed her senses, through which her eyes fought desperately for sight.

"Give me a memory—to carry through the years," he said unsteadily.

"No."

"Not one?"

"No!"

"To help us endure?"

Suddenly she turned in his arms, covering her eyes with both hands.

"Take—what—you wish—" she panted.

He touched one slim rigid finger after another, but they clung fast to the pallid face. Time and space reeled through silence. Then slowly, lids still sealed with desperate white hands, her head sank backward.

Untaught, her lips yielded coldly; but the body, stunned, swayed toward him as he released her; and, his arm supporting her, they turned blindly toward the path. Without power, without will, passive, dependent on his strength, her trembling knees almost failed her. She seemed unconscious of his lips on her cheek, on her hair—of her cold hands crushed in his, of the words he uttered—senseless, broken phrases, questions to which her silence answered and her closed lids acquiesced. If love was what he was asking for, why did he ask? He had his will of her lips, her hair, her slim fragrant hands; and now of her tears—for the lashes were wet and the mouth trembled. Her mind was slowly awaking to pain.

With it, far within her in unknown depths, something else stirred, stilling her swelling heart. Then every vein in her grew warm; and the quick tears sprang to her eyes.

"Dearest—dearest—" he whispered. Through the dim star-pallor she turned toward him, halted, passing her finger-tips across her lashes.

"After all," she said, "it was too late. If there is any sin in loving you it happened long ago—not to-night.... It began from the—the beginning. Does the touch of your lips make me any worse?... But I am not afraid—if you wish it—now that I know I always loved you."

"Shiela! Shiela, little sweetheart—"

"I love you so—I love you so," she said. "I cannot help it any more than I could in dreams—any more than I could when we met in the sea and the fog.... Should I lie to myself and you? I know I can never have you for mine; I know—I know. But if you will be near me when you can—if you will only be near—sometimes—"

She pressed both his hands close between hers.

"Dear—can you give up your freedom for a girl you cannot have?"

"I did so long since."

She bent and laid her lips on his hands, gravely.

"I must say something—that disturbs me a little. May I? Then, there are perils—warnings—veiled hints.... They mean nothing definite to me.... Should I be wiser?... It is difficult to say—senseless—showing my ignorance, but I thought if there were perils that I should know about—that could possibly concern me, now, you would tell me, somehow—in time—"

For a moment the revelation of her faith and innocence—the disclosure of how strange and lost she felt in the overwhelming catastrophe of forbidden love—how ignorant, how alone, left him without a word to utter.

She said, still looking down at his hands held between her own:

"A girl who has done what I have done, loses her bearings.... I don't know yet how desperately bad I am. However, one thing remains clear—only one—that no harm could come to—my family—even if I have given myself to you. And when I did it, only the cowardly idea that I was wronging myself persisted. If that is my only sin—you are worth it. And if I committed worse—I am not repentant. But—dear, what you have done to me has so utterly changed me that—things that I never before heeded or comprehended trouble me. Yesterday I could not have understood what to-night I have done. So, if there lies any unknown peril in to-morrow, or the days to come—if you love me you will tell me.... Yet I cannot believe in it. Dearly as I love you I would not raise one finger to comfort you at *their* expense. I would not go away with you; I would not seek my freedom for your sake. If there is in my love anything base or selfish I am not conscious of it. I cannot marry you; I can only live on, loving you. What danger can there be in that for you and me?"

"None," he said.

She sighed happily, lifted her eyes, yielded to his arms, sighing her heart out, lips against his.

Somewhere in the forest a bird awoke singing like a soul in Paradise.

CHAPTER XVI
AN ULTIMATUM

With the beginning of March the end of the so-called social season, south of Jupiter Light, is close at hand. First, the great winter hotels close; then, one by one, doors and gates of villa and cottage are locked, bright awnings and lawn shades furled and laid away, blinds bolted, flags lowered. All summer long villa and caravansary alike stand sealed and silent amid their gardens, blazing under the pale fierce splendour of an unclouded sky; tenantless, save where, beside opened doors of quarters, black recumbent figures sprawl asleep, shiny faces fairly sizzling in the rays of a vertical sun.

The row of shops facing the gardens, the white streets, quay, pier, wharf are deserted and silent. Rarely a human being passes; the sands are abandoned except by some stray beach-comber; only at the station remains any sign of life where trains are being loaded for the North, or roll in across the long draw-bridge, steaming south to that magic port from which the white P. and O. steamers sail away into regions of eternal sunshine.

So passes Palm Beach into its long summer sleep; and the haunts of men are desolate. But it is otherwise with the Wild.

Night and the March moon awake the winter-dormant wilderness from the white man's deadening spell. Now, unrestrained, the sound of negro singing floats inland on the sea-wind from inlet, bar, and glassy-still lagoon; great, cumbersome, shadowy things lumber down to tidewater—huge turtles on egg-laying intent. In the dune-hammock the black bear, crab-hungry, awakes from his December sleep and claws the palmetto fruit; the bay lynx steals beachward; a dozen little deaths hatch from the diamond-back, alive; and the mean gray fox uncurls and scratches ticks, grinning, red-gummed, at the moon.

Edging the Everglades, flat-flanked panthers prowl, ears and tail-tips twitching; doe and buck listen from the cypress shades; the razor-back clatters his tusks, and his dull and furry ears stand forward and his dull eyes redden. Then the silver mullet leap in the moonlight, and the tiger-owl floats soundlessly to his plunging perch, and his daring yellow glare flashes even when an otter splashes or a tiny fawn stirs.

And very, very far away, under the stars, rolls the dull bull-bellow of the 'gator, labouring, lumbering, clawing across the saw-grass seas; and all the little striped pigs run, bucking madly, to their dangerous and silent dam who listens, rigid, horny nose aquiver in the wind.

So wakes the Wild when the white men turn northward under the March moon; and, as though released from the same occult restraint, tree and shrub break out at last into riotous florescence: swamp maple sets the cypress shade afire; the cassava lights its orange elf-lamps; dogwood snows in the woods; every magnolia is set with great white chalices divinely scented, and the Royal Poinciana crowns itself with cardinal magnificence.

All day long brilliant butterflies hover on great curved wings over the jungle edge; all day long the cock-quail whistles from wall and hedge, and the crestless jays, sapphire winged, flit across the dunes. Red-bellied woodpeckers gossip in live-oak, sweet-gum, and ancient palm; gray squirrels chatter from pine to bitter-nut; the iridescent little ground-doves, mated for life, run fearlessly under foot or leap up into snapping flight with a flash of saffron-tinted wings. Under the mangroves the pink ajajas preen and wade; and the white ibis walks the woods like a little absent-minded ghost buried in unearthly reverie.

Truly when madam closes her Villa Tillandsia, and when Coquina Court is bereft of mistress and household—butler, footman, maid, and flunky; and when Tsa-na Lah-ni is abandoned by its handsome chatelaine, and the corridors of the vast hotels are dark, it is fashion, not common sense that stirs the flock of gaily gregarious immigrants into premature northern flight; for they go, alas! just as the southland clothes itself in beauty, and are already gone when the Poinciana opens, leaving Paradise to blossom for the lesser brothers of the woodland and the dark-skinned children of the sun.

The toddling Moses of the Exodus, as usual, was Courtlandt Classon; the ornamental Miriam, Mrs. O'Hara; and the children of the preferred stock started North with cymbals and with dances, making a joyful noise, and camping en route at Ormond—vastly more beautiful than the fashion-infested coral reef from which they started—at Saint Augustine, on corporate compulsion, at the great inns of Hampton, Hot Springs, and Old Point, for fashion's sake—taking their falling temperature by degrees—as though any tropic could compare with the scorching suffocation of Manhattan town.

Before the Beach Club closed certain species of humanity left in a body, including a number of the unfledged, and one or two pretty opportunists. Portlaw went, also Malcourt.

It required impudence, optimism, and executive ability for Malcourt to make his separate adieux and render impartial justice on each occasion.

There was a girl at "The Breakers" who was rather apt to slop over, so that interview was timed for noon, when the sun dries up everything very quickly, including such by-products as tears.

Then there was Miss Suydani to ride with at five o'clock on the beach, where the chain of destruction linked mullet and osprey and ended with the robber eagle—and Malcourt—if he chose.

But here there were no tears for the westering sun to dry, only strangely quenched eyes, more green than blue, for Malcourt to study, furtively; only the pale oval of a face to examine, curiously, and not too cynically; and a mouth, somewhat colourless, to reassure without conviction—also without self-conviction. This was all—except a pair of slim, clinging hands to release when the time came, using discretion—and some amiable firmness if required.

They were discussing the passing of the old régime, for lack of a safer theme; and he had spoken flippantly of the decadence of the old families— his arm around her and her pale cheek against his shoulder.

She listened rather absently; her heart was very full and she was thinking of other matters. But as he continued she answered at length, hesitating, using phrases as trite and quaintly stilted as the theme itself, gently defending the old names he sneered at. And in her words he savoured a certain old-time flavour of primness and pride—a vaguely delicate hint of resentment, which it amused him to excite. Pacing the dunes with her waist enlaced, he said, to incite retort:

"The old families are done for. Decadent in morals, in physique, mean mentally and spiritually, they are even worse off than respectfully cherished ruins, because they are out of fashion; they and their dingy dwellings. Our house is on the market; I'd be glad to see it sold only Tressilvain will get half."

"In you," she said, "there seems to be other things, besides reverence, which are out of fashion."

He continued, smilingly: "As the old mansions disappear, Virginia, so disintegrate those families whose ancestors gave names to the old lanes of New Amsterdam. I reverence neither the one nor the other. Good riddance! The fit alone survive."

"I still survive, if you please."

"Proving the rule, dear. But, yourself excepted, look at the few of us who chance to be here in the South. Look at Courtlandt Classon, intellectually destitute! Cuyp, a mental brother to the ox; and Vetchen to the ass; and

Mrs. Van Dieman to somebody's maidservant—that old harridan with all the patrician distinction of a Dame des Halles—"

"Please, Louis!"

"Dear, I am right. Even Constance Palliser, still physically superb, but mentally morbid—in love with what once was Wayward—with the ghost she raised in her dead girlhood, there on the edge of yesterday—"

"Louis! Louis! And *you*! What were you yesterday? What are you to-day?"

"What do I care what I was and am?—Dutch, British, burgher, or cavalier?—What the deuce do I care, my dear? The Malcourts are rotten; everybody knows it. Tressilvain is worse; my sister says so. As I told you, the old families are done for—all except yours—"

"I am the last of mine, Louis."

"The last and best—"

"Are you laughing?"

"No; you are the only human one I've ever heard of among your race—the sweetest, soundest, best—"

"I?... What you say is too terrible to laugh at. I—guilty in mind—unsound—contaminated—"

"Temporarily. I'm going to-night. Time and absence are the great antiseptics. When the corrupt cause disappears the effect follows. Cheer up, dear; I take the night train."

But she only pressed her pale face closer to his shoulder. Their interlocked shadows, huge, fantastic, streamed across the eastern dunes as they moved slowly on together.

"Louis!"

"Yes?"

She could not say it. Close to the breaking point, she was ready now to give up to him more than he might care for—the only shred left which she had shrunk from letting him think was within his reach for the asking—her name.

Pride, prejudice, had died out in the fierce outbreak of a heart amazingly out of place in the body of one who bore her name.

Generations of her kinsmen, close and remote, had lived in the close confines of narrow circles—narrow, bloodless, dull folk, almost all distantly related—and they had lived and mated among themselves, coldly defiant of that great law which dooms the over-cultivated and inbred to folly and extinction.

Somewhere, far back along the race-line, some mongrel ancestor had begun life with a heart; and, unsuspected, that obsolete organ had now reappeared in her, irritating, confusing, amazing, and finally stupefying her with its misunderstood pulsations.

At first, like a wounded creature, consciousness of its presence turned her restless, almost vicious. Then from cynicism to incredulity she had passed the bitter way to passion, and the shamed recoil from it; to recklessness, and the contempt for it, and so through sorrow and humility to love—if it were love to endure the evil in this man and to believe in the good which he had never yet revealed to her save in a half-cynical, half-amused content that matters rest in *statu quo*.

"The trouble with us," mused Malcourt, lazily switching the fragrant beach-grapes with his riding-crop, "is inbreeding. Yes, that's it. And we know what it brings to kings and kine alike. Tressilvain is half-mad, I think. And we are used up and out of date.... The lusty, jewelled bacchantes who now haunt the inner temple kindle the social flames with newer names than ours. Few of us count; the lumbering British or Dutch cattle our race was bred from, even in these brief generations, have become decadent and barren; we are even passing from a fashion which we have neither intellect to sustain nor courage to dictate to. It's the raw West that is to be our Nemesis, I think.... 'Mix corpuscles or you die!'—that's what I read as I run—I mean, saunter; the Malcourts never run, except to seed. My, what phosphorescent perversion! One might almost mistake it for philosophy.... But it's only the brilliancy of decay, Virginia; and it's about time that the last Malcourt stepped down and out of the scheme of things. My sister is older, but I don't mind going first—even if it is bad manners."

"Is that why you have never asked me to marry you?" she said, white as a ghost.

Startled to silence he walked on beside her. She had pressed her pallid face against his shoulder again; one thin hand crushed her gloves and riding-crop into her hip, the other, doubled, left in the palm pale imprints of her fingers.

"Is *that* the reason?" she repeated.

"No, dear."

"Is it because you do not care for me—enough?"

"Partly. But that is easily remedied."

"Or"—with bent head—"because you think too—lightly—of me—"

"No! That's a lie anyway."

"A—a lie?"

"Yes. You lie to yourself if you think that! You are *not* that sort. You are not, and you never were and never could be. Don't you suppose I know?"—almost with a sneer: "I won't have it—nor would you! It is you, not I, who have controlled this situation; and if you don't realise it I do. I never doubted you even when you prattled to me of moderation. *I* know that you were not named with your name in mockery, or in vain."

Dumb, thrilled, understanding in a blind way what this man had said, dismayed to find safety amid the elements of destruction, a sudden belief in herself—in him, too, began to flicker. "Had the still small flame been relighted for her? Had it never entirely died?"

"If—you will have me, Louis," she whispered.

"I don't love you. I'm rather nearer than I ever have been just now. But I am not in love."

"Could you ever—"

"Yes."

"Then—why—"

"I'll tell you why, some day. Not now."

They had come to where their horses were tied. He put her up, adjusted boot-strap and skirt, then swung gracefully aboard his own pie-faced Tallahassee nag, wheeling into the path beside her.

"The world," observed Malcourt, using his favourite quotation, "is *so* full of a number of things—like you and me and that coral snake yonder.... It's very hard to make a coral snake bite you; but it's death if you succeed.... Whack that nag if he plunges! Lord, what a nose for sarpints horses have! Hamil was telling me—by the way, there's nothing degenerate about our distant cousin, John Garret Hamil; but he's not pure pedigree. However, I'd advise him to marry into some fresh, new strain—"

"He seems likely to," said Virginia.

After a moment Malcourt looked around at her curiously.

"Do you mean Shiela Cardross?"

"Obviously."

"You think it safe?"—mockingly.

"I wouldn't care if I were a man."

"Oh! I didn't suppose that a Suydam could approve of her."

"I do now—with envy.... You are right about the West. Do you know that it seems to me as though in that girl all sections of the land were merged, as though the freshest blood of all nations flowing through the land had centred and mingled to produce that type of physical perfection! It is a curious idea—isn't it, Louis?—to imagine that the brightest, wholesomest, freshest blood of the nations within this nation has combined to produce such a type! Suppose it were so. After all is it not worth dispensing with a few worn names to look out at the world through those fearless magnificent eyes of hers—to walk the world with such limbs and such a body? Did you ever see such self-possession, such superb capacity for good and evil, such quality and texture!... Oh, yes, I am quite crazy about her—like everybody and John Garret Hamil, third."

"Is he?"

She laughed. "Do you doubt it?"

Malcourt drew bridle, fished for his case, and lighted a cigarette; then he spurred forward again, alert, intent, head partly turned in that curious attitude of listening, though Virginia was riding now in pensive silence.

"Louis," she said at last, "what is it you hear when you seem to listen that way. It's uncanny."

"I'll tell *you*," he said. "My father had a very pleasant, persuasive voice.... I was fond of him.... And sometimes I still argue with him—in the old humourous fashion—"

"What?"—with a shiver.

"In the old amusing way," continued Malcourt quietly. "Sometimes he makes suggestions to me—curious suggestions—easy ways out of trouble— and I listen—as you noticed."

The girl looked at him, reined up closer, and bent forward, looking him intently in the eyes.

"Well, dear?" inquired Malcourt, with a smile.

But she only straightened up in her saddle, a chill creeping in her veins.

A few moments later he suggested that they gallop. He was obliged to, for he had other interviews awaiting him. Also Portlaw, in a vile humour with the little gods of high and low finance.

One of these interviews occurred after his final evening adieux to the Cardross family and to Hamil. Shiela drove him to the hotel in Gray's motor, slowly, when they were out of sight, at Malcourt's request.

"I wanted to give you another chance," he said. "I'm a little more selfish, this time—because, if I had a decent opportunity I think I'd try to fall in love with somebody or other—"

She flushed painfully, looking straight ahead over the steering-wheel along the blinding path of the acetylenes.

"I am very sorry," she said, "because I had—had almost concluded to tell them—everything."

"What!" he asked, aghast.

Her eyes were steadily fixed on the fan-shaped radiance ahead which played fantastically along the silvery avenue of palms and swept the white road with a glitter like moonlight streaming over snow.

"You mean you are ready for your freedom, Shiela?"

"No."

"*What* do you mean?"

"That—it may be best—best—to tell them ... and face what is left of life, together."

"You and I?"

"Yes."

He sat beside her, dumb, incredulous, nimble wits searching for reasons. What was he to reckon with in this sudden, calm suggestion of a martyrdom with him? A whim? Some occult caprice?—or a quarrel with Hamil? Was she wearied of the deception? Or distrustful of herself, in her new love for Hamil, lest she be tempted to free herself after all? Was she already at that point where, desperate, benefits forgot, wavering between infatuation and loyalty, she turned, dismayed, to the only course which must crush temptation for ever?

"Is that it?" he asked.

"What?" Her lips moved, forming the word without sound.

"Is it because you are so sorely tempted to free yourself at their expense?"

"Partly."

"You poor child!"

"No child now, Louis.... I have thought too deeply, too clearly. There is no childhood left in me. I *know* things.... You will help me, won't you—if I find I need you?"

"Need *me*, Shiela?"

"I may," she said excitedly; "you can't tell; and I don't know. It is all so confused. I thought I knew myself but I seem to have just discovered a devil looking back at me out of my own reflected eyes from my own mirror!"

"What an exaggerated little thing you are!" he said, forcing a laugh.

"Am I? It must be part of me then. I tell you, since that day they told me what I am, I have wondered what else I might be. I don't know, but I'm watching. There are changes—omens, sinister enough to frighten me—"

"Are you turning morbid?"

"I don't know, Louis. Am I? How can I tell? Whom am I to ask? I *could* ask my own mother if I had one—even if it hurt her. Mothers are made for pain—as we young girls are. Miserable, wretched, deceitful, frightened as I am I *could* tell her—tell her all.... The longing to have her, to tell her has become almost—almost unendurable—lately.... I have so much need of her.... You don't know the desolation of it—and the fear! I beg your pardon for talking this way. It's over now. You see I am quite calm."

"Can't you confide in your—other mother—"

"I have no right. She did not bear me."

"It is the same as though you were her own; she feels so—"

"She cannot feel so! Nor can I. If I could I would take my fears and sorrows and my sins to her. I could take them to my own mother, for both our sakes; I cannot, to her, for my own sake alone. And never can."

"Then—I don't understand! You have just suggested telling her about ourselves, haven't you?"

"Yes. But not that it has been a horror—a mistake. If I tell her—if I think it necessary—best—to tell them, I—it will be done with mask still on—cheerfully—asking pardon with a smile—I do not lack that kind of courage. I can do that—if I must."

"There will be a new ceremony?"

"If they wish.... I can't—can't talk of it yet, unless I'm driven to it—"

He looked quietly around at her. "What drives you, Shiela?"

Her eyes remained resolutely fixed on the road ahead, but her cheeks were flaming; and he turned his gaze elsewhere, thoughtful, chary of speech, until at last the lights of the station twinkled in the north.

Then he said, carelessly friendly: "I'll just say this: that, being of no legitimate use to anybody, if you find any use for me, you merely need to say so."

"Thank you, Louis."

"No; I thank you! It's a new sensation—to be of legitimate use to anybody. Really, I'm much obliged."

"Don't speak so bitterly—"

"Not at all. Short of being celestially translated and sinlessly melodious on my pianola up aloft, I had no hope of ever being useful to you and Hamil—"

She turned a miserable and colourless face to his and he ceased, startled at the tragedy in such young eyes.

Then he burst out impulsively: "Oh, why don't you cut and run with him! Why, you little ninny, if I loved anybody like that I'd not worry over the morals of it!"

"What!" she gasped.

"Not I! Make a nunnery out of me if you must; clutch at me for sanctuary, if you want to; I'll stand for it! But if you'll listen to me you'll give up romantic martyrdom and sackcloth, put on your best frock, smile on Hamil, and go and ask your mother for a bright, shiny, brand-new divorce."

Revolted, incensed, eyes brilliant with anger, she sat speechless and rigid, clutching the steering-wheel as he nimbly descended to the platform.

"Good-bye, Shiela," he said with a haggard smile. "I meant well—as usual."

Something about him as he stood there alone in the lamp's white radiance stilled her anger by degrees.

"Good-bye," she said with an effort.

He nodded, replaced his hat, and turned away.

"Good-bye, Louis," she said more gently.

He retraced his steps, and stood beside the motor, hat off. She bent forward, generous, as always, and extended her hand.

"What you said to me hurt," she said. "Do you think it would not be easy for me to persuade myself? I believe in divorce with all my heart and soul and intelligence. I *know* it is right and just. But not for me.... Louis—how can I do this thing to them? How can I go to them and disclose myself as a common creature of common origin and primitive impulse, showing the

crack in the gay gilding and veneer they have laboured to cover me with?...
I cannot.... I could endure the disgrace myself; I cannot disgrace them. Think
of the ridicule they would suffer if it became known that for two years I
had been married, and now wanted a public divorce? No! No! There is
nothing to do, nothing to hope for.... If it is—advisable—I will tell them, and
take your name openly.... I am so uncertain, so frightened at moments—so
perplexed. There is no one to tell me what to do.... And, believe me, I am
sorry for you—I am deeply, deeply sorry! Good-bye."

"And I for you," he said. "Good-bye."

She sat in her car, waiting, until the train started.

CHAPTER XVII
ECHOES

Some minutes later, on the northward speeding train, he left Portlaw playing solitaire in their own compartment, and, crossing the swaying corridor, entered the state-room opposite. Miss Wilming was there, reading a novel, an enormous bunch of roses, a box of bonbons, and a tiny kitten on the table before her. The kitten was so young that it was shaky on its legs, and it wore very wide eyes and a blue bow.

"Hello, Dolly," he said pleasantly. She answered rather faintly.

"What a voice—like the peep of an infant sparrow! Are you worrying?"

"A little."

"You needn't be. Alphonse will make a noise, of course, but you needn't mind that. The main thing in life is to know what you want to do and do it. Which I've never yet done in my life. Zut! Zut!!—as our late Count Alphonse might say. And he'll say other remarks when he finds you've gone, Dolly." And Malcourt, who was a mimic, shrugged and raised his arms in Gallic appeal to the gods of wrath, until he mouthed his face into a startling resemblance to that of the bereft nobleman.

Then he laughed a little—not very heartily; then, in a more familiar rôle, he sat down opposite the girl and held up one finger of admonition and consolation.

"The main thing, Dolly, was to get clear of him—and all that silly business. Yes? No? Bon!... And now everything is cleared up between us, and I've told you what I'd do—if you really wanted a chance. I believe in chances for people."

The girl, who was young, buried her delicate face in the roses and looked at him. The kitten, balanced on tiny, wavering legs, stared hard at him, too. He looked from girl to kitten, conscious of the resemblance, and managed to smother a smile.

"You said," he repeated severely, "that you wanted a chance. I told you what I could and would do; see that you live and dress decently, stand for your musical, dramatic, athletic, and terpsichorean education and drilling—but not for one atom of nonsense. Is that clear?"

She nodded.

"Not one break; not one escapade, Dolly. It's up to you."

"I know it."

"All right, then. What's passed doesn't count. You start in and see what you can do. They say they drag one about by the hair at those dramatic schools. If they do, you've got to let 'em. Anyway, things ought to come easier to you than to some, for you've got a corking education, and you don't drink sloe-gin, and you don't smoke."

"And I *can* cook," added the girl gravely, looking at her childish ringless hands. The rings and a number of other details had been left behind addressed to the count.

"The trouble will be," said Malcourt, "that you will miss the brightness and frivolity of things. That kitten won't compensate."

"Do you think so? I haven't had very much of anything—even kittens," she said, picking up the soft ball of fur and holding it under her chin.

"You missed the frivolous in life even before you had it. You'll miss it again, too."

"But I've had it now."

"That doesn't count. The capacity for frivolity is always there. You are reconciled just now to other things; that man is a beast all right. Oh, yes; this is reaction, Dolly. The idea is to hang on to this conservatism when it becomes stupid and irksome; when you're tired and discouraged, and when you want to be amused and be in bright, attractive places; and when you're lonesome—"

"Lonesome?"

"Certainly you'll be lonesome if you're good."

"Am I not to see you?"

"I'll be in the backwoods working for a living—"

"Yes, but when you come to New York?"

"Sure thing."

"Often?"

"As often as it's advisable," he said pleasantly. "I want you to make friends at school; I want you to have lots of them. A bachelor girl has got to have 'em.... It's on your account and theirs that I don't intend to have anybody make any mistake about me.... Therefore, I'll come to see you when you've a friend or two present. It's fairer to you. *Now* do you understand me, Dolly?"

"Yes."

"Is it agreeable?"

"Y-es." And, flushing: "But I did not mistake you, Louis; and there is no reason not to come, even if I am alone."

He laughed, lighted a cigarette, and stroked the kitten.

"It's an amusing experiment, anyway," he said.

"Have you never tried it before?"

"Oh, yes, several times."

"Were the several times successes?"

"Not one!" he said, laughing. "It's up to you, Dolly, to prove me a bigger ass than I have been yet—or the reverse."

"It lies with me?" she asked.

"Certainly. Have I ever made love to you?"

"No."

"Ever even kissed you?"

"No."

"Ever been a brute?"

"No.... You are not very careful in speaking to me sometimes. Once—at the Club—when Mr. Hamil—"

"I *was* brutal. I know it. Do you want my respect?"

"Y-es."

"Earn it," he said drily.

The girl leaned back in her corner, flushed, silent, thoughtful; and sometimes her eyes were fixed on vacancy, sometimes on him where he sat in the opposite seat staring out into the blurred darkness at the red eye of the beacon on Jupiter Light which turned flaring, turned again, dwindling to a spark, and went out.

"Of what are you thinking?" she asked, noticing his frown.

He did not reply; he was thinking of Shiela Cardross. And, frowning, he picked up the kitten, very gently, and flattered it until it purred.

"It's about as big as a minute," said the girl, softly touching the tiny head.

"There *are* minutes as big as elephants, too," he said, amused. "Nice pussy!" The kitten, concurring in these sentiments, purred with pleasure.

A little later he sauntered back to his own compartment, and, taking out a memorandum, made some figures.

"Is that girl aboard?" asked Portlaw, looking up from the table, his fat hands full of cards.

"Yes, I believe so."

"Well, that's a deuce of a thing to do."

"What?"—absently.

"What! Why, to travel about the country with the nucleus of a theatrical troupe on your hands—"

"She wanted another chance. Few get it."

"Very well, son, if you think you can afford to endow a home for the frivolously erring!—And the chances are she'll turn on you and scratch."

"Yes—the chances favour that."

"She won't understand it; that sort never understands decency in a man."

"Do you think it might damage my reputation to be misunderstood?" sneered Malcourt. "I've taken a notion to give her a chance and I'm going to do it."

Portlaw spread out his first row of cards. "You know what everybody will think, I suppose."

Malcourt yawned.

Presently Portlaw began in a babyish-irritated voice: "I've buried the deuce and trey of diamonds, and blocked myself—"

"Oh, *shut* up!" said Malcourt, who was hastily scribbling a letter to Virginia Suydam.

He did not post it, however, until he reached New York, being very forgetful and busy in taking money away from the exasperated Portlaw through the medium of double dummy. Also he had a girl, a kitten, and other details to look after, and several matters to think over. So Virginia's letter waited.

Virginia waited, too. She had several headaches to keep inquiring friends at a distance, for her eyes were inclined to redness in those days, and she developed a pronounced taste for the solitude of the chapel and churchly things.

So when at length the letter arrived, Miss Suydam evaded Constance and made for the beach; for it was her natural instinct to be alone with Malcourt, and the instinct unconsciously included even his memory.

Her maid was packing; Constance Palliser's maid was also up to her chin in lingerie, and Constance hovered in the vicinity. So there was no privacy there, and that was the reason Virginia evaded them, side-stepped Gussie Vetchen at the desk, eluded old Classon in the palm room, and fled like a ghost through the empty corridors as though the deuce were at her heels instead of in her heart.

The heart of Virginia was cutting up. Alone in the corridors she furtively glanced at the letter, kissed the edge of the envelope, rolled and tucked it away in her glove, and continued her flight in search of solitude.

The vast hotel seemed lonely enough, but it evidently was too populous to suit Miss Suydam. Yet few guests remained, and the larger caravansary was scheduled to close in another day or two, the residue population to be transferred to "The Breakers."

The day was piping hot but magnificent; corridor, piazza, colonnade, and garden were empty of life, except for a listless negro servant dawdling here and there. Virginia managed to find a wheel-chair under the colonnade and a fat black boy at the control to propel it; and with her letter hidden in her glove, and her heart racing, she seated herself, parasol tilted, chin in the air, and the chair rolled noiselessly away through the dazzling sunshine of the gardens.

On the beach some barelegged children were wading in the surf's bubbling ebb, hunting for king-crabs; an old black mammy, wearing apron and scarlet turban, sat luxuriously in the burning sand watching her thin-legged charges, and cooking the "misery" out of her aged bones. Virginia could see nobody else, except a distant swimmer beyond the raft, capped with a scarlet kerchief. This was not solitude, but it must do.

So she dismissed her chair-boy and strolled out under the pier. And, as nobody was there to interrupt her she sat down in the sand and opened her letter with fingers that seemed absurdly helpless and unsteady.

"On the train near Jupiter Light," it was headed; and presently continued:

> "I am trying to be unselfishly honest with you to see how it feels. First—about my loving anybody. I never have; I have

on several occasions been prepared to bestow heart and hand—been capable of doing it—and something happened every time. On one of these receptive occasions the thing that happened put me permanently out of business. I'll tell you about that later.

"What I want to say is that the reason I don't love you is not because I can't, but because I won't! You don't understand that. Let me try to explain. I've always had the capacity for really loving some woman. I was more or less lonely and shy as a child and had few playmates—very few girls of my age. I adored those I knew—but—well, I was not considered to be a very desirable playmate by those parents who knew the Malcourt history.

"One family was nice to me—some of them. I usually cared a great deal for anybody who was nice to me.

"The point of all this biography is that I'm usually somewhat absurdly touched by the friendship of an attractive woman of my own sort—or, rather, of the sort I might have been. That is my attitude toward you; you are amiable to me; I like you.

"Now, why am I not in love with you? I've told you that it's because I will not let myself be in love with you. Why?

"Dear—it's just because you *have* been nice to me. Do you understand? No, you don't. Then—to go back to what I spoke of—I am not free to marry. I am married. Now you know. And there's no way out of it that I can see.

"If I were in love with you I'd simply take you. I am only your friend—and I can't do you that injury. Curious, isn't it, how such a blackguard as I am can be so fastidious!

"But that's the truth. And that, too, may explain a number of other matters.

"So you see how it is, dear. The world *is* full of a number of things. One of them signs himself your friend,

"LOUIS MALCOURT."

Virginia's eyes remained on the written page long after she had finished reading. They closed once or twice, opened again, blue-green, expressionless. Looking aloft after a while she tried to comprehend that the sky was still overhead; but it seemed to be a tricky, unsteady, unfamiliar sky, wavering, crawling across space like the wrinkled sea beneath it. Confused, she turned, peering about; the beach, too, was becoming unstable; and, through the sudden rushing darkness that obscured things, she tried to rise, then dropped full length along the sand.

A few seconds later—or perhaps minutes, or perhaps hours—she found herself seated perfectly conscious, mechanically drying the sea-water from her wet face; while beside her knelt a red-capped figure in wet bathing-dress, both hands brimming with sea-water which ran slowly between the delicate fingers and fell, sparkling.

"Do you feel better?" asked Shiela gently.

"Yes," she said, perfectly conscious and vaguely surprised. Presently she looked down at her skirts, groped about, turned, searching with outstretched fingers. Then her eyes fell on the letter. It lay on the sand beside her sunshade, carefully weighted with a shell.

Neither she nor the girl beside her spoke. Virginia adjusted her hat and veil, sat motionless for a few moments, then picked up the water-stained letter and, rolling it, placed it in her wet glove. A slow flame burned in her pallid cheeks; her eyes remained downcast.

Shiela said with quick sympathy: "I never fainted in my life. Is it painful?"

"No—it's only rather horrid.... I had been walking in the sun. It is very hot on the beach, I think; don't you?"

"Very," said the girl gravely.

Virginia, head still bent, was touching her wet lace waist with her wetter gloves.

"It was very good of you," she said, in a low voice—"and quite stupid of me."

Shiela straightened to her full height and stood gravely watching the sea-water trickle from her joined palms. When the last shining drop had fallen she looked questioningly at Miss Suydam.

"I'm a little tired, that is all," said Virginia. She rose rather unsteadily and took advantage of Shiela's firm young arm, which, as they progressed, finally slipped around Miss Suydam's waist.

Very slowly they crossed the burning sands together, scarcely exchanging a word until they reached the Cardross pavilion.

"If you'll wait until I have my shower I'll take you back in my chair," said Shiela. "Come into my own dressing-room; there's a lounge."

Virginia, white and haggard, seated herself, leaning back languidly against the wall and closing her heavy eyes. They opened again when Shiela came back from the shower, knotting in the girdle of her snowy bath-robe, and seated herself while her maid unloosed the thick hair and rubbed it till the brown-gold lustre came out like little gleams of sunlight, and the ends of the burnished tresses crisped and curled up on the smooth shoulders of snow and rose.

Virginia's lips began to quiver; she was fairly flinching now under the pitiless contrast, fascinated yet shrinking from the splendid young creature before her, resting there aglow in all the vigourous beauty of untainted health.

And from the mirror reflected, the clear eyes smiled back at her, seeming to sear her very soul with their untarnished loveliness.

"Suppose you come and lunch with me?" said Shiela. "I happen to be quite alone. My maid is very glad to do anything for you. Will you come?"

"Yes," said Virginia faintly.

An hour later they had luncheon together in the jasmine arbour; and after that Virginia lay in the hammock under the orange-trees, very still, very tired, glad of the silence, and of the soft cool hand which covered hers so lightly, and, at rare intervals, pressed hers more lightly still.

Shiela, elbow on knee, one arm across the hammock's edge, chin cupped in her other palm, sat staring at vacancy beside the hammock where Virginia lay. And sometimes her partly doubled fingers indented her red lower lip, sometimes they half framed the oval face, as she sat lost in thought beside the hammock where Virginia lay so pale and still.

Musing there in the dappled light, already linked together by that subtle sympathy which lies in silence and in a common need of it, they scarcely stirred save when Shiela's fingers closed almost imperceptibly on Virginia's hand, and Virginia's eyelids quivered in vague response.

In youth, sadness and silence are near akin. That was the only kinship they could claim—this slim, pale scion of a worn-out line, and the nameless, parentless girl beside her. This kinship was their only bond—unadmitted, uncomprehended by themselves; kinship in love, and the sadness of it; in love, and the loneliness of it; love—and the long hours of waiting; night, and the tears of it.

The sun hung low behind the scented orange grove before Virginia moved, laying her thin cheek on Shiela's hand.

"Did you see—that letter—in the sand?" she whispered.

"Yes."

"The writing—you knew it?... Answer me, Shiela."

"Yes, I knew it."

Virginia lay very still for a while, then covered her face with both hands.

"Oh, my dear, my dear!" breathed Shiela, bending close beside her.

Virginia lay motionless for a moment, then uncovered her face.

"It is strange," she said, in a colourless, almost inaudible voice. "You see I am simply helpless—dependent on your mercy.... Because a woman does not faint over—nothing."

The deep distress in Shiela's eyes held her silent for a space. She looked back at her, then her brooding gaze shifted to the laden branches overhead, to the leafy vistas beyond, to the ground where the golden fruit lay burning in the red, level rays of the western sun.

"I did not know he was married," she said vacantly.

Swift anger burned in Shiela's cheeks.

"He was a coward not to tell you—"

"He was honourable about it," said Virginia, in the same monotonous voice. "Do you think I am shameless to admit it? Perhaps I am, but it is fairer to him. As you know this much, you should know the truth. And the truth is that he has never said he loved me."

Her face had become pinched and ghastly, but her mouth never quivered under this final humiliation.

"Did you ever look upon a more brazen and defenceless woman—" she began—and then very quietly and tearlessly broke down in Shiela's tender arms, face hidden on the young girl's breast.

And Shiela's heart responded passionately; but all she could find to say was: "Dear—I know—indeed, indeed I know—believe me I know and understand!" And all she could do was to gather the humbled woman into her arms until, her grief dry-spent, Virginia raised her head and looked at Shiela with strange, quenched, tearless eyes.

"We women are very helpless, very ignorant," she said, "even the worst of us. And I doubt if in all our lives we are capable of the harm that one man refrains from doing for an hour.... And that, I think, is our only compensation.... What theirs may be I do not know.... Dear, I am perfectly able to go, now.... I think I see your mother coming."

They walked together to the terrace where Mrs. Cardross had just arrived in the motor; and Shiela, herself shaken, wondered at the serene poise with which Virginia sustained ten minutes of commonplaces and then made her final adieux, saying that she was leaving on the morning train.

"May we not see each other in town?" she added amiably; and, to Shiela: "You will let me know when you come North? I shall miss you until you come."

Mrs. Cardross sent her back in the motor, a trifle surprised at any intimacy between Shiela and Virginia. She asked a frank question or two and then retired to write to Mrs. Carrick, who, uneasy, had at last gone North to find out what financial troubles were keeping both her husband and her father so long away from this southland that they loved so well.

Hamil, who was to leave for the North with his aunt and Virginia early next morning, returned from the forest about sundown, reeking as usual of the saddle, and rested a moment against the terrace balustrade watching Mrs. Cardross and Shiela over their tea.

"That boy is actually ill," said the sympathetic matron. "Why don't you give him some tea, Shiela? Or would you rather have a little wine and a biscuit, Garret—?"

"And a few pills," added Shiela gravely. "I found a box of odds and ends—powders, pills, tablets, which he might as well finish—"

"Shiela! Garret is *ill!*"

Hamil, busy with his Madeira and biscuit, laughed. He could not realise he was on the eve of leaving, nor could Shiela.

"Never," said he to the anxious lady, "have I felt better in my life; and I'm sure it is due to your medicines. It's all very well for Shiela to laugh at quinine; mosquitoes don't sting her. But I'd probably be an item in one of those phosphate beds by this time if you hadn't taken care of me."

Shiela laughed; Hamil in excellent humour went off to dress. Everybody seemed to be in particularly good spirits that evening, but later, after dinner, Gray spoke complainingly of the continued absence of his father.

"As for Acton Carrick, he's the limit," added Gray disgustedly. "He hasn't been here this winter except for a day or two, and then he took the train from Miami straight through to New York. I say, Hamil, you'll look him up and write us about him, won't you?"

Shiela looked at Hamil.

"Do you understand anything about financial troubles?" she asked in a bantering voice.

"I've had some experience with my own," he said.

"Well, then, what is the matter with the market?"

"Shall I whisper it?"

"If you are prepared to rhyme it. I dare you!"

It was the rule of the house that anybody was privileged to whisper at table provided they put what they had to communicate into rhyme.

So he thought busily a moment, then leaned over very gravely and whispered close to her ear:

> "Tis money makes the market go;
> When money's high the market's low;
> When money's low the market's right,
> And speculators sleep at night.
> But, dear, there is another mart,
> Where ticks the ticker called my heart;
> And there exhaustless funds await,
> To back my bankrupt trust in Fate;
> For you will find, as I have found,
> The old, old logic yet is sound,
> And love still makes the world go round."

"I always knew it," said Shiela contemptuously.

"Knew what, dear?" asked her mother, amused.

"That Mr. Hamil writes those sickening mottoes for Christmas crackers."

"There are pretty ones in them—sometimes," said Cecile, reminiscently spearing a big red strawberry which resembled the popular and conventional conception of a fat human heart.

Gray, still serious, said: "Unless we are outside of the danger zone I think father ought to teach me something about business."

"If we blow up," observed Cecile, "I'll do clever monologues and support everybody. I'd like that. And Shiela already writes poetry—"

"Nonsense!" said Shiela, very pink.

"Shiela! You do!"

"I did in school—" turning pinker under Hamil's tormenting gaze.

"And you do yet! I found an attempt on the floor—in your flowing penmanship," continued the pitiless younger sister. "What is there to blush about? Of course Phil and I were not low enough to read it, but I'll bet it was about somebody we all know! Do you want to bet—Garry?"

"Cecile!" said her mother mildly.

"Yes, mother—I forgot that I'm not allowed to bet, but if I was—"

Shiela, exasperated, looked at her mother, who shook her head and rose from the table, taking Hamil's arm.

"You little imp!" breathed Shiela fiercely to Cecile, "if you plague me again I'll inform Mr. Hamil of what happened to you this morning."

"I don't care; Garry is part of the family," retorted Cecile, flushed but defiant and not exactly daring to add: "or will be soon." Then she put both arms around Shiela, and holding her imprisoned:

"*Are* you in love?—you darling!" she whispered persuasively. "Oh, don't commit yourself if you feel *that* way!... And, O Shiela, you should have seen Phil Gatewood following me in love-smitten hops when I wouldn't listen! My dear, the creature managed to plant both feet on my gown as I fled, and the parquet is *so* slippery and the gown so flimsy and, oh, there was a dreadful ripping sound and we both went down—"

Shiela was laughing now, holding her sister's gesticulating hands, as she rattled on excitedly:

"I got to my feet in a blaze of fury, holding my gown on with both hands—"

"Cissy!"

"And he gave one horror-stricken look and ran—"

Swaying there together in the deserted dining-room, they gave way to uncontrolled laughter. Laughter rang out from the living-room, too, where Gray was informing Mrs. Cardross and Hamil of the untoward climax to a spring-time wooing; and when Shiela and Cecile came in the latter looked suspiciously at Hamil, requesting to know the reason of his mirth.

"Somebody will have to whisper it to you in rhyme," said Hamil; "it's not fit for prose, Cissy."

Mrs. Cardross retired early. Gray went for a spin in his motor. Cecile, mischievously persuaded that Hamil desired to have Shiela to himself for half an hour, stifled her yawns and bedward inclinations and remained primly near them until Gray returned.

Then the four played innocuous Bridge whist until Cecile's yawns could no longer be disguised; and finally Gray rose in disgust when she ignored the heart-convention and led him an unlovely spade.

"How many kinds of a chump can you be in one day?" asked her wrathful brother.

"Pons longa, vita brevis," observed Hamil, intensely amused. "Don't sit on her, Gray."

"O dear! O dear!" said Cecile calmly, "I'd rather be stepped on again than sat on like that!"

"You're a sweet little thing anyway," said Hamil, "even if you do fall down in Bridge as well as otherwise—"

"Shiela! You told Garret!"

"Cunning child," said Hamil; "make her dance the baby-dance, Shiela!" And he and her sister and brother seized her unwilling hands and compelled her to turn round and round, while they chanted in unison:

> "Cissy's Bridge is falling down,
> Falling down,
> Falling down,
> Cissy's gown is falling down,
> My
> Fair
> Lady!"

"Garry, stop it!... It's only an excuse to hold Shiela's hand—"

But Shiela recited very gravely:

> "Father's in Manhattan town,
> Hunting up our money;
> Philip's in the music-room,
> Calling Cis his honey;
> Cissy's sprinting through the hall,
> Trying to be funny—"

"I *won't* dance!" cried Cecile. But they sang insultingly:

> "Rock-a-by Cissy!
> Philip *will* slop!
> Cissy is angry,
> For Philip won't stop."

> "If dresses are stepped upon,
> Something will fall,
> Down will come petticoat, Cissy, and all!"

"O Garry, how *can* you!"

"Because you've been too gay lately; you're marked for discipline, young lady!"

"Who told you? Shiela?—and it *was* my newest, dearest, duck of a gown!... The situation was perfectly horrid, too. What elephants men are!"

"You know, I'd accept him if I were you—just to teach him the value of gowns," suggested Hamil.

But Shiela said seriously: "Phil Gatewood is a nice boy. We all knew that he was going to ask you. You acted like a ninny, Cis."

"With my gown half off!—what would *you* have done?" demanded the girl hotly.

"Destroyed him," admitted Shiela, "in one way or another, dear. And now I am going to bed—if everybody has had enough of Cissy's Bridge—"

"Me for the hay," observed Gray emphatically.

So they all went up the stairway together, lingering a few moments on the landing to say good night.

Cecile retired first, bewailing the humiliation of not having a maid of her own and requesting Shiela to send hers as she was too sleepy to undress.

Gray caught sight of a moth fluttering around the electric lights and made considerable noise securing the specimen. After which he also retired, cyanide jar containing the victim tucked under his arm.

CHAPTER XVIII
PERIL

Shelia, standing by the lamplit table and resting one slim hand on the edge of it, waited for Hamil to give the signal for separation.

Instead he said: "Are you really sleepy?"

"No."

"Then—"

"I dare not—to-night."

"For any particular reason?"

"For a thousand.... One is that I simply can't believe you are really going North to-morrow. Why do you?" She had asked it nearly a thousand times.

"I've got to begin Portlaw's park; and, besides, my work here is over—"

"Is that all you care about me? Oh, you are truly like the real Ulysses:

"Now toils the hero, trees on trees o'erthrown
Fall crackling round him, and the forests groan!"

Do you remember, in the Odyssey, when poor Calypso begs him to remain?

"Thus spoke Calypso to her god-like guest:
'This shows thee, friend, by old experience taught,
And learn'd in all the wiles of human thought,
How prone to doubt, how cautious are the wise!
Thus wilt thou leave me? Are we thus to part?
Is Portlaw's Park the passion of thy heart?'"

Laughing, he answered in the Grecian verse:

"Whatever the gods shall destine me to bear,
'Tis mine to master with a constant mind;
Inured to peril, to the worst resigned,
Still I can suffer; their high will be done."

From the soft oval of her face the smile faded, but her voice was still carelessly gay:

"And so he went away. But, concerning his nymph, Calypso, further Homer sayeth not. Yet—in the immortal verse it chanced to be he, not she, who was—married.... And I think I'll retire now—if you have nothing more agreeable to say to me—"

"I have; in the garden—"

"No, I dare not risk it to-night. The guards are about—"

"It is my last night here—"

"We will see each other very soon in New York. And I'll be up in the morning to drive you to the station—"

"But, Shiela, dear—"

"There was a bad nigger hanging around the groves last night and our patrols are out.... No, it's too risky. Besides—"

"Besides—what?"

"I've been thinking."

He said, tenderly impatient:

"You little witch of Ogygia, come into the *patio* then, and do your thinking and let me make love to you."

But she would not raise her eyes, standing there in the rose lamplight, the perverse smile still edging her lips.

"Calypso," he repeated persuasively.

"No.... Besides, I have nothing to offer you, Ulysses.... You remember what the real Calypso offered the real Ulysses if he'd remain with her in Ogygia?"

"Eternal youth and love?" He bent over the table, moving his hand to cover hers where it rested in the lamplight. "You have given me eternity in love already," he said.

"Have I?" But she would not lift her eyes.... "Then why make love to me if you have it ready-made for you?"

"Will you come?"

And she, quoting the Odyssey again:

"Swear, then, thou mean'st not what my soul forebodes;
Swear by the solemn oath that binds the gods!"

And in turn he quoted:

"Loved and adored, O goddess as thou art,
Forgive the weakness of a human heart."

But she said with gay audacity, "I have nothing to forgive you—yet."

"Are you challenging me? Because I am likely to take you into my arms at any moment if you are."

"Not *here*—Garry!"—looking up in quick concern, for his recklessness at times dismayed her. Considering him doubtfully she made up her mind that she was safe, and her little chin went up in defiance.

"The hammock's in the *patio*," he said.

"There's moonlight there, too. No, thank you—with Cissy wakeful and her windows commanding every nook!... Besides—as I told you, I've been thinking."

"And what have you concluded?"

Delicate straight nose in the air, eyebrows arched in airy disdain, she stood preoccupied with some little inward train of thought that alternately made grave and gay the upcurled corners of her lips.

"About this question of—ah—love-making—" dropping her eyes in pretence of humility.

"It is no longer a question, you know."

She would *not* look up; her lashes seemed to rest on the bloom of the rounded cheek as though the lids were shut, but there came from the shadows between the lids a faint glimmer; and he thought of that first day when from her lifted gaze a thousand gay little demons seemed to laugh at him.

"I've been thinking," she remarked, "that this question of making love to me should be seriously discussed."

"That's what I've been asking you to do in the *patio*—"

"I've been thinking, with deep but rather tardy concern, that it is not the best policy for me to be—courted—any more."

She glanced up; her entire expression had suddenly altered to a gravity unmistakable.

"What has happened?" he asked.

"Can *you* tell *me*? I ask you, Garry, what has happened?"

"I don't understand—"

"Nor I.... Because that little fool you kissed—so many, many centuries ago—is not this disillusioned woman who is standing here!... May I be a little bit serious with you?"

"Of course," he said, amused; "come out on the east balcony and tell me what troubles you."

She considered him, smilingly suspicious of his alacrity.

"I don't think we had better go to the balcony." "Shiela, can't you ever get over being ashamed when I make love to you?"

"I don't want to get over it, Garry."

"Are you still afraid to let me love you?"

Her mouth curved gravely as a perplexed child's; she looked down at the table where his sun-burnt hand now lay lightly across hers.

"I wished to speak to you about myself—if, somehow you could help me to say what—what is very difficult for a girl to say to a man—even when she loves him.... I don't think I can say it, but I'll try."

"Then if you'll come to the balcony—"

"No, I can't trust you—or myself—unless we promise each other."

"Have I got to do that again?"

"Yes, if I am to go with you. I promise! Do you?"

"If I must," he said with very bad grace—so ungraciously in fact that as they passed from the eastern corridor on to the Spanish balcony she forgot her own promise and slipped her hand into his in half-humourous, half-tender propitiation.

"Are you going to be disagreeable to me, Garry?"

"You darling!" he said; and, laughing, yet secretly dismayed at her own perversion, she hurriedly untwisted her fingers from his and made a new and fervid promise to replace the one just broken.

The moonlight was magnificent, silvering forest, dune, and chaparral. Far to the east a thin straight gleam revealed the sea.

She seated herself under the wall, lying back against it; he lay extended on the marble shelf beside her, studying the moonlight on her face.

"What was it you had to tell me, Shiela? Remember I am going in the morning."

"I've turned cowardly; I cannot tell you.... Perhaps later.... Look at the Seminole moon, Garry. They have such a pretty name for it in March—Tau-sau-tchusi—'Little Spring Moon'! And in May they call it the 'Mulberry Moon'—Kee-hassi, and in November it is a charming name—Hee-wu-li—'Falling Leaf Moon'!—and August is Hyothlucco—'Big Ripening Moon.' ... Garry, this moonlight is filling my veins with quicksilver. I feel very restless, very heathenish." ... She cast a slanting side-glance at him, lips parting with soundless laughter; and in the witchery of the moon she seemed exquisitely unreal, head tipped back, slender throat and shoulders snow-white in the magic lustre that enveloped them.

Resting one bare arm on the marble she turned, chin on shoulder, looking mischievously down at him, lovely, fresh, perfect as the Cherokee roses that spread their creamy, flawless beauty across the wall behind her.

Imperceptibly her expression changed to soft friendliness, to tenderness, to a hint of deeper emotion; and her lids drooped a little, then opened gravely under the quick caress of his eyes; and very gently she moved her head from side to side as reminder and refusal.

"Another man's wife," she said deliberately.... "Thy neighbour's wife.... That's what we've done!"

Like a cut of a whip her words brought him upright to confront her, his blood tingling on the quick edge of anger.

For always, deep within him, lay that impotent anger latent; always his ignorance of this man haunted him like the aftermath of an ugly dream. But of the man himself she had never spoken since that first day in the wilderness. And then she had not named him.

Her face had grown very serious, but her eyes remained unfathomable under his angry gaze.

"Is there any reason to raise that spectre between us?" he demanded.

"Dear, has it ever been laid?" she asked sorrowfully.

The muscles in his cheeks tightened and his eyes narrowed unpleasantly. Only the one feature saved the man from sullen commonness in his suppressed anger—and that was his boyish mouth, clean, sweet, nobly moulded, giving the lie to the baffled brutality gleaming in the eyes. And the spark died out as it had come, subdued, extinguished when he could no longer sustain the quiet surprise of her regard.

"How very, very young you are after all," she said gently. "Come nearer. Lift your sulky, wicked head. Now ask my pardon for not understanding."

"I ask it.... But when you speak of him—"

"Hush. He is only a shadow to you—scarcely more to me. He must remain so. Do you not understand that I wish him to remain a shadow to you—a thing without substance—without a name?"

He bent his head, nodding almost imperceptibly.

"Garry?"

He looked up in response.

"There is something else—if I could only say it.... I might if you would close your eyes." ... She hesitated, half-fearful, then drew his head down on her knees, daintily, using her finger-tips only in the operation.

"Are you listening to what I am trying to tell you?"

"Yes, very intently."

"Then—it's about my being afraid—of love.... Are you listening?... It is very difficult for me to say this.... It is about my being afraid.... I used to be when I did not know enough to be. And now, Garry, when I am less ignorant than I was—when I have divined enough of my unknown self to be afraid—dearest, I am not."

She bent gently above the boyish head lying face downward on her knees—waited timidly for some response, touched his hair.

"I am listening," he nodded.

She said: "My will to deny you, my courage to control myself seem to be waning. I love you so; and it is becoming so much worse, such a blind, unreasoning love.... And—do you think it will grow so much worse that I could be capable of anything ignoble? Do you think I might be mad enough to beg my freedom? I—I don't know where it is leading me, dear. Do you? It is that which bewilders me—that I should love you so—that I should not be afraid to love you so.... Hush, dear! Don't speak—for I shall never be able to tell you this if you speak, or look at me. And I want to ask you a question. May I? And will you keep your eyes covered?"

"Yes."

"Then—there are memories which burn my cheeks—hush!—I do not regret them.... Only, what am I changing into that I am capable of forgetting—everything—in the happiness of consenting to things I never dreamed of—like this"—bending and laying her lips softly against his cheek.... "That was wrong; it ought to frighten me. But it does not."

He turned, looking up into the flushed young face and drew it closer till their cheeks touched.

"Don't look at me! Why do you let me drift like this? It is madness—to give up to each other the way we do—"

"I wish we could give up the world for each other."

"I wish so too. I would—except for the others. Do you suppose I'd hesitate if it were not for them?"

They looked at each other with a new and subtler audacity.

"You see," she said with a wistful smile, "*this* is not Shiela Cardross who sits here smiling into those brown eyes of yours. I think I died before you ever saw me; and out of the sea and the mist that day some changeling crept into your boat for your soul's undoing. Do you remember in Ingoldsby— 'The cidevant daughter of the old Plantagenet line '?"

They laughed like children.

"Do you think our love-tempted souls are in any peril?" he asked lightly.

The question arrested her mirth so suddenly that he thought she must have misunderstood.

"What is it, Shiela?" he inquired, surprised.

"Garry—will you tell me something—if you can?... Then, what does it mean, the saying—'souls lost through love'? Does it mean what we have done?—because I am married? Would people think our souls lost—if they knew?"

"No, you blessed child!"

"Well, how can—"

"It's a lie anyway," he said. "Nothing is lost through love. It is something very different they mean."

"Yes," she said calmly, "something quite inconceivable, like 'Faust' and 'The Scarlet Letter,' ... I *thought* that was what they meant!"

Brooding over him, silent, pensive, clear eyes fearlessly meeting his, she drifted into guiltless retrospection.

"After all," she said, "except for letting everybody know that we belong to each other this is practically like marriage. Look at that honeymoon up there, Garry.... If, somehow, they could think we are engaged, and would let us alone for the rest of our lives, it would not matter.... Except I should like to have a house alone with you."

And she stooped, resting her cheek lightly against his, eyes vaguely sweet in the moonlight.

"I love you so," she murmured, as though to herself, "and there seems no end to it. It is such a hopeless sequence when yesterday's love becomes to-day's adoration and to-morrow's worship. What am I to do? What is the use of saying I am not free to love you, when I do?" She smiled dreamily. "I was silly enough to think it impossible once. Do you remember?"

"You darling!" he whispered, adoring her innocence. Then as he lay, head cradled on her knees, looking up at her, all unbidden, a vision of the future in its sharp-cut ominous desolation flashed into his vision—the world without her!—the endless stretch of time—youth with no meaning, effort wasted, attainment without desire, loneliness, arid, terrible days unending.

"It is too—too senseless!" he breathed, stumbling to his feet as the vague, scarcely formulated horror of it suddenly turned keen and bit into him as he began to realise for the first time something of what it threatened.

"What is it, Garry?" she asked in gentle concern, as he stood looking darkly at her. "Is it time to go? You are tired, I know." She rose and opened the great glass doors. "You poor tired boy," she whispered, waiting for him. And as he did not stir: "What is the matter, Garry?"

"Nothing. I am trying to understand that our winter is ended."

She nodded. "Mother and Gray and Cecile and I go North in April.... I wish we might stay through May—that is, if you—" She looked at him in silent consternation. "Where will *you* be!"

He said in a sullen voice: "That is what I was thinking of—our separation.... Do you realise that it is almost here?"

"No," she said faintly, "I cannot."

He moved forward, opening the glass doors wider; she laid one hand on his arm as though to guide herself; but the eastern corridors were bright with moonlight, every corner illuminated.

They were very silent until they turned into the south corridor and reached her door; and there he suddenly gave way to his passionate resentment, breaking out like a spoiled boy:

"Shiela, I tell you it's going to be unendurable! There must be some way out, some chance for us.... I *don't* mean to ask you to do what is—what you consider dishonourable. You wouldn't do it anyway, whether or not I asked you—"

"But don't ask me," she said, turning very white. "I don't know what I am capable of if I should ever see you suffer!"

"You *couldn't* do it!" he repeated; "it isn't in you to take your happiness at their expense, is it? You say you know how they would feel; I don't. But if you're asking for an annulment—"

"What? Do you mean divorce?"

"No.... That is—different—"

"But what—"

"You dear," he said, suddenly gentle, "you have never been a—wife; and you don't know it."

"Garry, are you mad?"

"Shiela, dear, some day will you very quietly ask some woman the difference between divorce and annulment?"

"Y-yes, if you wish.... Is it something you mayn't tell me, Garry?"

"Yes.... I don't know! You sometimes make me feel as though I could tell you anything.... Of course I couldn't ... you darling!" He stepped nearer. "You are so good and sweet, so utterly beyond evil, or the vaguest thought of it—"

"Garry—I am *not*! And you know it!"

He only laughed at her.

"You *don't* think I am a horrid sort of saint, do you?"

"No, not the horrid sort—"

"Garry! How can you say such things when I'm half ready now to run away with you!"

The sudden hint of fire in her face and voice, and something new in her eyes, sobered him.

"Now do you know what I am?" she said, breathing unevenly and watching him. "Only one thing keeps me respectable. I'd go with you; I'd live in rags to be with you. I ask nothing in the world or of the world except you. You could make me what you pleased, mould me—mar me, I believe— and I would be the happiest woman who ever loved. *That* is your saint!"

Flushed with her swift emotion, she stood a minute facing him, then laid her hand on the door knob behind her, still looking him in the eyes. Behind her the door slowly swung open under the pressure.

His own self-control was fast going; he dared not trust himself to speak lest he break down and beg for the only chance that her loyalty to others forbade her to take. But the new and deeper emotion which she had betrayed had awakened the ever-kindling impatience in him, and now, afire, he stood looking desperately on all he must for ever lose, till the suffering seemed unendurable in the checked violence of his revolt.

"Good night," she whispered sorrowfully, as the shadow deepened on his altered face.

"Are you going!"

"Yes.... And, somehow I feel that perhaps it is better not to—kiss me to-night. When I see you—this way—Garry, I could find it in me to do anything—almost.... Good night."

Watching him, she waited in silence for a while, then turned slowly and lighted the tiny night-lamp on the table beside her bed.

When she returned to the open door there was no light in the hall. She heard him moving somewhere in the distance.

"Where are you, Garry?"

He came back slowly through the dim corridor.

"Were you going without a word to me?" she asked.

He came nearer and leaned against the doorway.

"You are quite right," he said sullenly. "I've been a fool to let us drift in this way. I don't know where we're headed for, and it's time I did."

"What do you mean?"—in soft consternation.

"That there is no hope left for us—and that we are both pretty young, both in love, both close to desperation. At times I tell you I feel like a cornered beast—feel like showing my teeth at the world—like tearing you from it at any cost. I'd do it, too, if it were not for your father and mother. You and I could stand it."

"I would let you do it—if it were not for them," she said.

They looked at one another, both pale.

"Would you give up the whole moral show for me?" he demanded.

"Yes."

"You'd get a first-rate scoundrel."

"I wouldn't care if it were you."

"There's one thing," he said with a bluntness bordering on brutality, "all this is changing me into a man unfit to touch you. I warn you."

"What!"

"I tell you not to trust me!" he said almost savagely. "With heart and soul and body on fire for you—mad for you—I'm not to be trusted!"

"And I?" she faltered, deadly pale.

"You don't know what you're saying!" he said violently.

"I—I begin to think I do.... Garry—Garry—I am learning very fast!... How can I let you go!"

"The idea is," he said grimly, "for me to go before I go insane.... And never again to touch you—"

"Why?"

"Peril!" he said. "I'm just a plain blackguard, Shiela."

"Would it change you?"

"What do you mean?"

"Not to touch me, not to kiss me. Could you go on always just loving me?... Because if you could not—through the years that are coming—I—I had rather take the risk—with you—than lose you."

He stood, head bent, not trusting himself to speak or look at her.

"Good-night," she said timidly.

He straightened up, stared at her, and turned on his heel, saying good night in a low voice.

"Garry!"

"Good-night," he muttered, passing on.

Her heart was beating so violently that she pressed her hand to it, leaning against the door sill.

"Garry!" she faltered, stretching out the other hand to him in the darkness, "I—I do not care about the—risk—if you care to—kiss me—"

He swung round from the shadows to the dimly lighted sill; crossed it. For a moment they looked into one another's eyes; then, blinded, she swayed imperceptibly toward him, sighing as his arms tightened and her own crept up around his neck.

She yielded, resigning lips, and lids, and throat, and fragrant hair, and each slim finger in caress unending.

Conscious of nothing save that body and soul were safe in his beloved keeping, she turned to him in all the passion of a guiltless love, whispering her adoration, her faith, her trust, her worship of the man who held her; then, adrift once more, the breathless magic overwhelmed her; and she drew him to her, closer, desperately, hiding her head on his breast.

"Take me away, Garry," she stammered—"take me with you. There is no use—no use fighting it back. I shall die if you leave me.... Will you take me? I—will be—everything that—that you would have me—that you might wish for—in—in a—wife—"

She was crying now, crying her heart out, her face crushed against his shoulder, clinging to him convulsively.

"Will you take me, Garry? What am I without you? I cannot give you up! I will not.... Nobody can ask that of me—How can they ask that of me?—to give you up—to let you go out of my little world for ever—to turn from you, refuse you!... What a punishment for one instant's folly! If they knew they would not let me suffer this way!—They would want me to tell them—"

His dry lips unclosed. "Then *tell* them!" he tried to say, but the words were without sound; and, in the crisis of temptation, at the very instant of yielding, suddenly he knew, somehow, that he would not yield.

It came to him calmly, without surprise or shock, this stupid certainty of himself. And at the same moment the crisis was passing, leaving him stunned, impassive, half senseless as the resurgent passion battered at his will power, to wreck and undo it—deafening, imperative, wave on wave, in vain.

The thing to do was to hold on. One of them was adrift; the other dared not let go; he seemed to realise it, somehow. Odd bits of phrases, old-fashioned sayings, maxims long obsolete came to him without reason or sequence—"Greater love hath no man—no man—no man—" and "As ye do unto the least of these "—odd bits of phrases, old-fashioned sayings, maxims, alas! long obsolete, long buried with the wisdom of the dead.

He held her still locked in his arms. From time to time, unconsciously, as her hot grief spent itself, he bent his head, laying his face against hers, while his haggard, perplexed gaze wandered about the room.

In the dimness the snowy bed loomed beside them; pink roses patterned curtain and wall; the tiny night-light threw a roseate glow across her gown. In the fresh, sweet stillness of the room there was no sound or stir save their uneven breathing.

Very gently he lifted one of her hands and looked at it almost curiously— this small white hand so innocently smooth—as unblemished as a child's— this unsullied little hand that for an instant seemed to be slowly relaxing its grasp on the white simplicity around her—here in this dim, fresh, fragrant world of hers, called, intimately, her room.

And here where night and morning had so long held sacred all that he cared for upon earth—here in the white symbol of the world—her room— he gave himself again to her, without a word, without hope, knowing the end of all was near for them.

But it was she, not he, who must make the sign that ended all. And, after a long, long time, as she made no sign:

"Dearest," he breathed, "I know now that you will never go with me—for your father's sake."

That was premature, for she only clung the closer. He waited cautiously, every instinct alert, his head close to hers. And at last the hot fragrance of her tears announced the beginning of the end.

"Shiela?"

A stifled sound from his shoulder where her head lay buried.

"Choose now," he said.

No answer.

"Choose."

She cowered in his arms. He looked at the little hand once more, no longer limp but clenched against his breast. And he knew that the end was close at hand, and he spoke again, forcing her to her victory.

"Dearest, you must choose—"

"Garry!"

"Between those others—and me—"

She shrank out of his arms, turned with a sob, swayed, and sank on her knees beside the bed, burying her head in her crossed arms.

This was her answer; and with it he went away into the darkness, reeling, groping, while every pulse in him hammered ironic salutation to the victor who had loved too well to win. And in his whirling brain sounded the mocking repetition of his own words: "Nothing is lost through love! Nothing is lost—nothing—nothing!"—flouting, taunting him who had lost love itself there on the firing line, for a comrade's sake.

His room was palely luminous with the lustre of the night. On the mantel squatted a little wizened and gilded god peering and leering at him through the shadows—Malcourt's parting gift—the ugliest of the nineteen.

"For," said Malcourt—"there ought to be only eighteen by rights—unless further complications arise; and this really belongs to you, anyway."

So he left the thing on Hamil's mantel, although the latter had no idea what Malcourt meant, or why he made the parting offering.

Now he stood there staring at it like a man whose senses waver, and who fixes some object to steady nerve and brain.

Far in the night the voice of the ocean stirred the silence—the ocean which had given her to him that day in the golden age of fable when life and the world were young together, and love wore a laughing mask.

He listened; all the night was sighing with the sigh of the surf; and the breeze in the trees mourned; and the lustre died out in thickening darkness as he stood there, listening.

Then all around him through the hushed obscurity a vague murmur grew, accentless, sad, interminable; and through the monotone of the falling rain he heard the ocean very far away washing the body of a young world dead to him for ever.

Crouched low beside her bed, face quivering in her arms, she heard, in the stillness, the call of the sea—that enchanted sea which had given him to her that day, when Time and the World were young together in the blessed age of dreams.

And she heard the far complaint of the surf, breaking unsatisfied; and a strange wind flowing through the trees; then silence, suspense; and the world's dark void slowly filling with the dreadful monotone of the rain.

Storm after storm of agony and doubt swept her; she prayed convulsively, at random, reiterating incoherence in blind, frightened repetition till the stupefying sequence lost all meaning.

Exhausted, half-senseless, her hands still clung together, her tear-swollen lips still moved to form his name, asking God's mercy on them both. But the end had come.

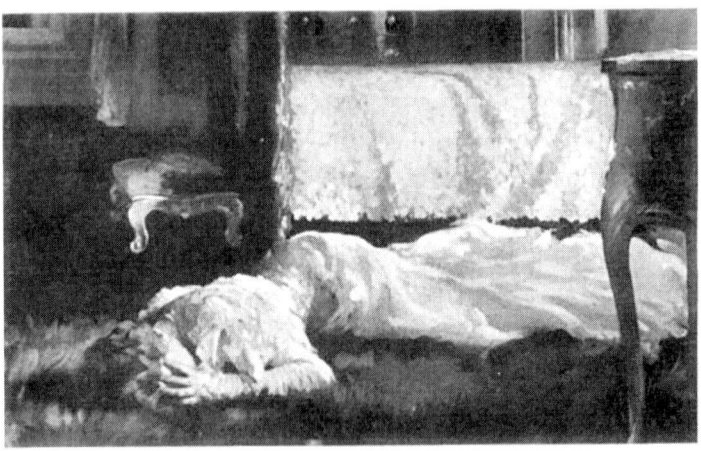

"Then fell prone, head buried in her tumbled hair."

Yes, the end; she knew it now—understood what had happened, what must be. And, knowing, she heard the sea-rain whispering their judgment, and the winds repeating it across the wastes.

She raised her head, dumb, rigid, listening, and stared through the shaking window into obscurity. Lightning flickered along the rim of the world—a pallid threat above the sea—the sea which had given them to one another and left them stranded in each other's arms there on the crumbling edges of destruction.

Her strained eyes divined, her straining senses comprehended; she cringed lower, aghast, swaying under the menace, then fell prone, head buried in her tumbled hair.

In the morning he left for the North and Portlaw's camp. Gray drove him to the station; Cecile, in distractingly pretty negligee waved him audacious adieu from her window.

"Shiela seems to be ill," explained Gray, as the motor car shot out into the haze of early morning. "She asked me to say good-bye for her.... I say, Hamil, you're looking rather ill yourself. This climate is sure to get a white man sooner or later, if he remains too long. But the North will put you into condition. You're going straight to Portlaw's camp on Luckless Lake?"

"Yes," said Hamil listlessly.

"Well, we'll be in New York in a week or two. You'll surely look us up when you're in town, won't you? And write me a line about Acton and father—won't you?"

"Surely," nodded Hamil absently.

And they sped on, the vast distorted shadow of the car racing beside them to the station.

CHAPTER XIX
THE LINE OF BATTLE

Portlaw's camp in the southern foot-hills of the Adirondacks was as much a real camp as the pretentious constructions at Newport are real cottages. A modesty, akin to smugness, designates them all with Heep-like humbleness under a nomenclature now tolerated through usage; and, from the photographs sent him, Hamil was very much disgusted to find a big, handsome two-story house, solidly constructed of timber and native stone, dominating a clearing in the woods, and distantly flanked by the superintendent's pretty cottage, the guides' quarters, stables, kennels, coach-houses, and hothouses with various auxiliary buildings still farther away within the sombre circle of the surrounding pines.

To this aggravation of elaborate structures Portlaw, in a spasm of modesty, had given the name of "Camp Chickadee"; and now he wanted to stultify the remainder of his domain with concrete terraces, bridges, lodges, and Gothic towers in various and pleasing stages of ruin.

So Hamil's problem presented itself as one of those annoyingly simple ones, entirely dependent upon Portlaw and good taste; and Portlaw had none.

He had, however, some thirty thousand acres of woods and streams and lakes fenced in with a twelve-foot barrier of cattle-proof wire—partly a noble virgin wilderness unmarred by man-trails; partly composed of lovely second growth scarcely scarred by that, vile spoor which is the price Nature pays for the white-hided invaders who walk erect, when not too drunk, and who foul and smear and stain and desolate water and earth and air around them.

Why Portlaw desired to cut his wilderness into a mincing replica of some emasculated British royal forest nobody seemed able to explain. While at Palm Beach he had made two sage observations to Hamil concerning the sacredness of trees; one was that there are no trees in a Scotch deer forest, which proved to his satisfaction that trees are unnecessary; the other embodied his memories of seeing a herd of calf-like fallow deer decorating the grass under the handsome oaks and beeches of some British nobleman's park.

Why Portlaw concerned himself at all with his wild, out-world domain was a mystery, too; for he admitted that he spent almost all day playing cards indoors or contriving with his cook some new and succulent experiment in the gastronomical field.

Sometimes he cast a leaden eye outdoors when his dogs were exercised from the kennel; rarely, and always unwillingly, he followed Malcourt to the hatchery to watch the stripping, or to the exotic pheasantry to inspect the breeding of birds entirely out of place in such a climate.

He did like to see a fat deer; the fatter the better; he was accustomed, too, to poke his thumb into the dead plumage of a plump grouse when Malcourt's men laid out the braces, on which he himself never drew trigger; and which interested him only when on the table.

He wanted plenty of game and fish on the place for that reason; he wanted his guests to shoot and fish for that reason, too. Otherwise he cared nothing for his deer, his grouse, and his trout. And why he suddenly had been bitten with a mania for "improving" the flawless wilderness about him, even Malcourt did not know.

Hamil, therefore, was prepared for a simple yet difficult problem—to do as little harm to the place as possible, and to appease Portlaw at the same time, and curb his meddlesome and iconoclastic proclivities.

Spring had begun early in the North; shallow snows were fading from the black forest soil along the streams' edges, and from the pebbled shores of every little lake; already the soft ice was afloat on pool and pond; muskrats swam; the eggs of the woodcock were beginning their chilly incubation; and in one sheltered spring-hole behind the greenhouse Malcourt discovered a solemn frog afloat. It takes only a single frog to make the spring-time.

That week the trailing fragrance of arbutus hung over wet hollows along the hills; and at night, high in the starlight, the thrilling clangour of wild geese rang out—the truest sky-music of the North among all the magic folk-songs of the wild.

The anchor-ice let go and went out early, and a few pioneer trout jumped that week; the cock-grouse, magnificent in his exquisite puffed ruff, paced the black-wet drumming log, and the hollow woodlands throbbed all day with his fairy drumming.

On hard-wood ridges every sugar-bush ran sap; the aroma from fire and kettle sweetened the air; a few battered, hibernating butterflies crawled out of cracks and crannies and sat on the sap-pans sunning their scarlet-banded wings.

And out of the hot South into the fading silver of this chill Northern forest-world came Hamil, sunburned, sombre-eyed, silent.

Malcourt met him at Pride's Fall with a buckboard and a pair of half-broken little Morgans; and away they tore into the woods, scrambling uphill, plunging downhill, running away most of the time to the secret satisfaction of Malcourt, who cared particularly for what was unsafe in life.

He looked sideways at Hamil once or twice, and, a trifle disappointed that the pace seemed to suit him, let the little horses out.

"Bad thing to meet a logging team," he observed.

"Yes," said Hamil absently. So Malcourt let the horses run away when they cared to; they needed it and he enjoyed it. Besides there were never any logging teams on that road.

Malcourt inquired politely concerning the Villa Cardross and its occupants; Hamil answered in generalities.

"You've finished there, then!"

"Practically. I may go down in the autumn to look it over once more."

"Is Cardross going to put in the Schwarzwald pigs?"

"Yes; they're ordered."

"Portlaw wants some here. I'd give ten dollars, poor as I am, if I could get Portlaw out in the snow and fully occupied with an irritated boar."

"Under such circumstances one goes up a tree?" inquired Hamil, smiling.

"One does if one is not too fat and can shed snowshoes fast enough. Otherwise one keeps on shooting one's 45-70. By the way, you were in New York for a day or two. How's the market?"

"Sagging."

"Money?"

"Scarce. I saw Mr. Cardross and Acton Carrick. Nobody seems enthusiastic over the prospect. While there are no loans being called there are few being made. I heard rumours of course; a number of banks and trust companies are getting themselves whispered about. Outside of that I don't know, Malcourt, because I haven't much money and what I have is on deposit with the Shoshone Securities Company pending a chance for some safe and attractive investment."

"That's Cardross, Carrick & Co."

"Yes." And as they whirled into the clearing and the big, handsome house came into view he smiled: "Is this Camp Chickadee?"

"Yes, and yonder's my cottage on Luckless Lake—a nice name," added Malcourt, "but Portlaw says it's safer to leave the name as it stands than to provoke the gods with boastful optimism by changing it to Lucky Lake. Oh, it's a gay region; Lake Desolation lies just beyond that spur; Lake Eternity east of us; Little Scalp Lake west—a fine bunch of names for a landscape in hell; but Portlaw won't change them. West and south the wet bones of the Sacandaga lie; and south-east you're up against the Great Vlaie and Frenchman's Creek and Sir William's remains from Guy Park on the Mohawk to the Fish House and all that bally Revolutionary tommy-rot." And as he blandly drew in his horses beside the porch: "Look who's here! Who but our rotund friend and lover of all things fat, lord of the manor of Chickadee-dee-dee which he has taught the neighbouring dicky-birds, who sit around the house, to repeat aloud in honour of—"

"For Heaven's sake, Louis! How are you, Hamil?" grunted Portlaw, extending a heavily cushioned, highly coloured hand of welcome.

Hamil and Malcourt descended; a groom blanketed the horses and took them to the stables; and Portlaw, with a large gesture of impatient hospitality, led the way into a great, warm living-room, snug, deeply and softly padded, and in which the fragrance of burning birch-logs and simmering toddy blended agreeably in the sunshine.

"For luncheon," began Portlaw with animation, "we're going to try a new sauce on that pair of black ducks they brought in—"

"In violation of the laws of game and decency," observed Malcourt, shedding his fur coat and unstrapping the mail-satchel from Pride's Fall.

"*Shut* up, Louis! Can't a man eat the things that come into his own property?" And he continued unfolding to Hamil his luncheon programme while, with a silver toddy-stick, heirloom from bibulous generations of Portlaws, he stirred the steaming concoction which, he explained, had been constructed after the great Sir William's own receipt.

"You've never tried a Molly Brant toddy? Man alive, you've wasted your youth," he insisted, genuinely grieved. "Well, wise men, chiefs, and sachems, here's more hair on your scalp-locks, and a fat buck to every bow!"

Malcourt picked up his glass. "*Choh*" he said maliciously; but Portlaw did not understand the irony in the Seminole salutation of The Black Drink; and the impudent toast was swallowed without suspicion.

Then Hamil's luggage arrived, and he went away to inspect his quarters, prepare for luncheon, and exchange his attire for forest dress. For he meant to lose no time in the waste corners of the earth when Gotham town might any day suddenly bloom like Eden with the one young blossom that he loved.

There was not much for him in Eden now—little enough except to be in her vicinity, near her at times, at intervals with her long enough to exchange a word or two under the smooth mask of convention which leaves even the eyes brightly expressionless.

Never again to touch her hand save under the formal laws sanctioned by usage; never again to wake with the intimate fragrance of her memory on his lips; never again to wait for the scented dusk to give them to each other—to hear her frail gown's rustle on the terrace, her footfall in the midnight corridor, her far, sweet hail to him from the surf, her soft laughter under the roses on the moon-lit balcony.

That—all of it—was forever ended. But he believed that the pallid northern phantom of the past was still left to him; supposed that now, at least, they might miserably consider themselves beyond peril.

But what man supposes of woman is vain imagining; and in that shadowy neutral ground which lies between martyrdom and sin no maid dwells for very long before she crosses one frontier or the other.

When he descended the stairs once more he found Portlaw, surrounded by the contents of the mail-sack, and in a very bad temper, while Malcourt stood warming his back at the blazing birch-logs, and gazing rather stupidly at a folded telegram in his hands.

"Well, Hamil—damn it all! What do you think of that!" demanded Portlaw, turning to Hamil as he entered the room; and unheeding Malcourt's instinctive gesture of caution which he gave, not comprehending why he gave it, Portlaw went on, fairly pouting out his irritation:

"In that bally mail-sack which Louis brought in from Pride's Fall there's a telegram from your friend, Neville Cardross; and why the devil he wants Louis to come to New York on the jump—"

"I have a small balance at the Shoshone Trust," said Malcourt. "Do you suppose there's anything queer about the company?"

Hamil shook his head, looking curiously at Malcourt.

"Well, what on earth do you think Cardross wants with you?" demanded Portlaw. "Read that telegram again."

Again Malcourt's instinct seemed to warn him to silence. All the same, with a glance at Hamil, he unfolded the bit of yellow paper and read:

"LOUIS MALCOURT,

"Superintendent Luckless Lake,

"Adirondacks.

"Your presence is required at my office in the Shoshone Securities Building on a matter of most serious and instant importance. Telegraph what train you can catch. Mr. Carrick will meet you on the train at Albany.

"NEVILLE CARDROSS.

"Answer Paid."

"Well, what the devil does it mean?" demanded Portlaw peevishly. "I can't spare you now. How can I? Here's Hamil all ready for you to take him about and show him what I want to have done—"

"I wonder what it means," mused Malcourt. "Maybe there's something wrong with the Tressilvain end of the family. The Shoshone Securities people manage her investments here—"

"The way to do is to wire and find out," grumbled Portlaw, leading the way to the luncheon table as a servant announced that function.

For it was certainly a function with Portlaw; all eating was more or less of a ceremony, and dinner rose to the dignity of a rite.

"I can't imagine what that telegram—"

"Forget it!" snapped Portlaw; "do you want to infect my luncheon? When a man lunches he ought to give his entire mind to it. Talk about your lost arts!—the art of eating scarcely survives at all. Find it again and you revive that other lost art of prandial conversation. Digestion's not possible without conversation. Hamil, you look at your claret in a funny way."

"I was admiring the colour where the sun strikes through," said the latter, amused.

"Oh! I thought you were remembering that claret is temporarily unfashionable. That's part of the degeneracy of the times. There never was and never will be any wine to equal it when it has the body of a Burgundy and the bouquet of wild-grape blossoms. Louis," cocking his heavy red face and considering a morsel of duck, "what is your opinion concerning the proper mélange for that plumcot salad dressing?"

"They say," said Malcourt gravely, "that when it's mixed, a current of electricity passed through it gives it a most astonishing flavour—"

"What!"

"So they say at the Stuyvesant Club."

Portlaw's eyes bulged; Hamil had to bend his head low over his plate, but Malcourt's bland impudence remained unperturbed.

"Good God!" muttered Portlaw; "Hamil, did you ever hear of passing electricity through a salad dressing composed of olive oil, astragon, Arequipa pepper, salt, Samara mustard, essence of anchovy, chives, distilled fresh mushrooms, truffles pickled in 1840 port—*did* you?"

"No," said Hamil, "I never did."

For a while silence settled upon the table while Portlaw struggled to digest mentally the gastronomic suggestion offered by Malcourt.

"I could send to town for a battery," he said hesitatingly; "or—there's my own electric plant—"

Malcourt yawned. There was not much fun in exploiting such a man. Besides, Hamil had turned uncomfortable, evidently considering it the worst of taste on Malcourt's part.

"What am I to do about that telegram?" he asked, lighting a cigarette.

Portlaw, immersed in sauce and the electrical problem, adjusted his mind with an effort to this other and less amusing question.

"Wire for particulars and sit tight," advised Portlaw. "We've just three now for 'Preference,' and if you go kiting off to town Hamil and I will be forced into double dummy, and that's a horrible mental strain on a man—isn't it, Hamil?"

"I *could* use the long-distance telephone," said Malcourt pensively.

"Well, for the love of Mike go and do it!" shouted Portlaw, "and let me try to enjoy this Andelys cheese."

So Malcourt sauntered out through the billiard-room, leaving an aromatic trail of cigarette smoke in his wake; and he closed all the intervening doors—why, he himself could not have explained.

He was absent a long time. Portlaw had terminated the table ceremony, and now, ensconced among a dozen fat cushions by the fire, a plump cigar burning fragrantly between his curiously clean-cut and sharply chiselled lips, he sat enthroned, majestically digesting; and his face of a Greek hero, marred by heavy flesh, had become almost somnolent in its expression of well-being and corporeal contentment.

"I don't know what I'd do without Louis," he said sleepily. "He keeps my men hustling, he answers for everything on the bally place, he's so infernally clever that he amuses me and my guests, he's on the job every minute. It would be devilishly unpleasant for me if I lost him.... And I'm always afraid of it.... There are usually a lot of receptive girls making large eyes at him.... My only safety is that they are so many—and so easy.... If Cardross hadn't signed that telegram I'd bet my *bottes-sauvage* it concerned some entanglement."

Hamil lay back in his chair and studied the forest through the leaded casement. Sometimes he thought of Portlaw's perverse determination to spoil the magnificent simplicity of the place with exotic effects lugged in by the ears; sometimes he wondered what Mr. Cardross could have to say to Malcourt—what matter of such urgent importance could possibly concern those two men.

And, thinking, he thought of Shiela—and of their last moments together; thought of her as he had left her, crouched there on her knees beside the bed, her face and head buried in her crossed arms.

Portlaw was nodding drowsily over his cigar; the April sunshine streamed into the room through every leaded pane, inlaying the floor with glowing diamonds; dogs barked from the distant kennels; cocks were crowing from the farm. Outside the window he saw how the lilac's dully varnished buds had swollen and where the prophecy of snow-drop and crocus under the buckthorn hedge might be fulfilled on the morrow. Already over the green-brown, soaking grass one or two pioneer grackle were walking busily about; and somewhere in a near tree the first robin chirked and chirped and fussed in its loud and familiar fashion, only partly pleased to find himself in the gray thaw of the scarcely comfortable North once more.

Portlaw looked up dully: "Those robins come up here and fatten on our fruit, and a fool law forbids us to shoot 'em. Robin pie," he added, "is not to be despised, but a sentimental legislature is the limit.... Sentiment always did bore me.... How do you feel after your luncheon?"

"All right," said Hamil, smiling. "I'd like to start out as soon as Malcourt comes back."

"Oh, don't begin that sort of thing the moment you get here!" protested Portlaw. "My heavens, man! there's no hurry. Can't you smoke a cigar and play a card or two—"

"You know I've other commissions—"

"Oh, of course; but I hoped you'd have time to take it easy. I've looked forward to having you here—so has Malcourt; he thinks you're about right, you know. And he makes damn few friends among men—"

The door opened and Malcourt entered slowly, almost noiselessly. There was not a vestige of colour in his face, nor of expression as he crossed the room for a match and relighted his cigarette.

"Well?" inquired Portlaw, "did you get Cardross on the wire?"

"Yes."

Malcourt stood motionless, hands in his pockets, the cigarette smoke curling up blue in the sunshine.

"I've got to go," he said.

"What for?" demanded Portlaw, then sulkily begged pardon and pouted his dissatisfaction in silence.

"When do you go, Malcourt?" asked Hamil, still wondering.

"Now." He lifted his head but looked across at Portlaw. "I've telephoned the stable, and called up Pride's Fall to flag the five-thirty express," he said.

Portlaw was growing madder and madder.

"Would you mind telling me when you expect to be back?" he inquired ill-temperedly.

"I don't know yet."

"Don't know!" burst out Portlaw; "hell's bells!"

Malcourt shook his head.

Portlaw profanely requested information as to how the place was to be kept going. Malcourt was patient with him to the verge of indifference.

"There's nothing to blow up about. Hastings is competent to manage things—"

"That conceited pup!"

"Hastings understands," repeated Malcourt, in a listless voice. "I've always counted on Alexander Hastings for any emergency. He knows things, and he's capable.... Only don't be brusque. He doesn't understand you as I do ... and he's fully your equal—fully—in every way—and then some—" The weariness in his tone was close to a sneer; he dropped his cigarette into the fire and began to roll another.

"Louis," said Portlaw, frightened.

"Well?"

"What the devil is the meaning of all this? You *are* coming back, aren't you?"

Malcourt continued to roll his cigarette, but after a while he spoiled it and began to construct another.

"*Are* you, Louis?"

"What?"

"Coming back here—soon?"

"If I—if it's the thing to do. I don't know yet. You mustn't press the matter now."

"You think there's a chance that you won't come back at *all*!" exclaimed Portlaw, aghast.

Malcourt's cigarette fell to pieces in his fingers.

"I'll come if I can, Billy. I tell you to let me alone.... I don't know where I am coming out—yet."

"If it's money you need, you know perfectly well—"

But Malcourt shook his head. From the moment of his entrance he had kept his face carefully averted from Hamil's view; had neither looked at him nor spoken except in monosyllabic answer to a single question.

The rattle of the buckboard on the wet gravel drive brought Portlaw to his feet. A servant appeared with Malcourt's suit-case and overcoat.

"There's a trunk to follow; Williams is to pack what I need.... Good-bye, Billy. I wouldn't go if I didn't have to."

Portlaw took his offered hand as though dazed.

"You'll come back, of course," he said, "in a couple of days—or a week if you like—but you'll be back, of course. You know if there's anything the matter with your salary just say so. I always meant you should feel perfectly free to fix your salary to suit yourself. Only be sure to come back in a week, won't you?"

"Good-bye," said Malcourt in a low voice. "I'd like to talk to Hamil—if he can give me a few moments."

Bareheaded, Hamil stepped out into the clear, crisp, April sunshine where the buckboard stood on the gravel.

The strong outdoor light emphasized Malcourt's excessive pallor, and the hand he offered Hamil was icy. Then his nervous grasp relaxed; he drew on his dog-pelt driving gloves and buttoned the fur coat to the throat.

"I want you—to—to remember—remember that I always liked you," he said with an effort, in curious contrast to his habitual fluency. "You won't believe it—some day. But it is true.... Perhaps I'll prove it, yet.... My father used to say that everything except death had been proven; and there remained, therefore, only one event of any sporting interest to the world....

He was a very interesting man—my father. He did not believe in death.... And I do not.... This sloughing off of the material integument seems to me purely a matter of the mechanical routine of evolution, a natural process in further and inevitable development, not a finality to individualism!... Fertilisation, gestation, the hatching, growth, the episodic deliverance from encasing matter which is called death, seem to me only the first few basic steps in the sequences of an endless metamorphosis.... My father thought so. His was a very fine mind—*is* a finer mind still.... Will you understand me if I say that we often communicate with each other—my father and I?"

"Communicate?" repeated Hamil.

"Often."

Hamil said slowly: "I don't think I understand."

Malcourt looked at him, the ever-latent mockery flickering in his eyes; then, by degrees, his head bent forward in the old half-cunning, half-wistful attitude as though listening. A vague smile touched the pallor of his face, and he presently looked up with something of his old debonair impudence.

"The truly good are always so interested in creating hell for the wicked," he said, "that sometimes the good get into the pit themselves just to see how hot it really is. And find the wicked have never been there.... Hamil, the hopelessly wicked—and there are few of them who are not mentally irresponsible—never go to hell because they wouldn't mind it if they did. It's the good who are hell's architects and often its tenants.... I'm speaking of all prisoners of conscience. The wicked have none."

He shrugged his shoulders.

"There's always an exit from one of these temporary little pits of torment," he said; "when one finds it too oppressive in the shade.... When one obtains a proper perspective, and retains one's sense of humour, and enough of conscience to understand the crime of losing time.... And when, in correct perspective, one realises the fictitious value of that temporary phase called the human unit, and when one cuts free from the absurd dogma concerning the dignity and the sanctity of that human unit.... I'm keeping you from your cigar and arm-chair and from Portlaw.... A good, kindly gossip, who fed my belly and filled my purse and loved me for the cards I played. I'm a yellow pup to mock him. I'm a pup anyhow.... But, Hamil, there is, in the worst pup, one streak not all yellow. And the very worst are capable of one friendship. You may not believe this some day. But it is true.... Good-bye."

"Is there anything, Malcourt—"

"Nothing you can do for me. Perhaps something I can do for you—" And, laughing, "I'll consult my father; he's not very definite on that point yet."

So Malcourt swung aboard the wagon, nodded again to Hamil, waved a pleasant adieu to Portlaw at the window, and was gone in a shower of wet gravel and mud.

And all that day Portlaw fussed and fumed and pouted about the house, tormenting Hamil with questions and speculations concerning the going of Malcourt, which for a while struck Hamil merely as selfish ebullitions; but later it came to him by degrees that this rich, selfish, over-fed, over-pampered, and revoltingly idle landowner, whose sole mental and physical resources were confined to the dinner and card tables, had been capable of a genuine friendship for Malcourt. Self-centred, cautious to the verge of meanness in everything which did not directly concern his own comfort and well-being, he, nevertheless, was totally dependent upon his friends for a full enjoyment of his two amusements; for he hated to dine alone and he loathed solitaire.

Therefore, in spending money to make his house and grounds attractive to his friends, he was ministering, as always, to himself; and when he first took Malcourt for his superintendent he did so from purely selfish motives and at a beggarly stipend.

And now, in the two years of his official tenure, Malcourt already completely dominated him, often bullied him, criticised him to his face, betrayed no illusions concerning the absolute self-interest which dictated Portlaw's policy in all things, coolly fixed and regulated all salaries, including his own, and, in short, matched Portlaw's undisguised selfishness with a cynicism so sparkling and so frankly ruthless that Portlaw gradually formed for him a real attachment.

There was no indiscriminate generosity in that attachment; he never voluntarily increased Malcourt's salary or decreased his responsibilities; he got out of his superintendent every bit of labour and every bit of amusement he could at the lowest price Malcourt would take; yet, in spite of that he really cared for Malcourt; he secretly admired his intellectual equipment; feared it, too; and the younger man's capacity for dissipation made him an invaluable companion when Portlaw emerged from his camp in November and waddled forth upon his annual hunt for happiness.

Something of this Hamil learned through the indiscriminate volubility of his host who, when his feelings had been injured, was amusingly naive for such a self-centred person.

"That damn Louis," he confided to Hamil over their after-dinner cigars, "has kept me guessing ever since he took command here. Half the time I don't understand what he's talking about even when I know he's making fun of me; but, Hamil, you have no idea how I miss him."

And on another occasion a week later, while laboriously poring over some rough plans laid out for him by Hamil:

"Louis agrees with you about this improvement business. He's dead against my building Rhine-castle ruins on the crags, and he had the impudence to inform me that I had a cheap mind. By God, Hamil, I can't see anything cheap in trying to spend a quarter of a million in decorating this infernal monotony of trees; can you?"

And Hamil, for the first time in many a day, lay back in his arm-chair and laughed with all his heart.

He had hard work in weaning Portlaw from his Rhine castles, for the other invariably met his objections by quoting in awful German:

"Hast du das Schloss gesehen—
Das hohe Schloss am Meer?"

—pronounced precisely as though the words were English. Which laudable effort toward intellectual and artistic uplift Hamil never laughed at; and there ensued always the most astonishing *causerie* concerning art that two men in a wilderness ever engaged in.

Young Hastings, a Yale academic and forestry graduate, did fairly well in Malcourt's place, and was doing better every day. For one thing he knew much more about practical forestry and the fish and game problems than did Malcourt, who was a better organiser than executive.

He began by dumping out into a worthless and landlocked bass-pond every brown trout in the hatchery. He then drew off the water in the brown-trout ponds, sent in men with seines and shotguns, and finally, with dynamite, purged the free waters of the brown danger for good and all.

"When Malcourt comes back," observed Portlaw, "you'll have to answer for all this."

"I won't be questioned," said Hastings, smiling.

"Oh! And what do you propose to do next?"

"If I had the money you think of spending on ruined castles "—very respectfully—"I'd build a wall in place of that mesh-wire fence."

"Why?" asked Portlaw.

"The wire deceives the grouse when they come driving headlong through the woods. My men pick up dozens of dead grouse and woodcock along the fence. If it were a wall they'd go over it. As it is, if I had my way, I'd restock with Western ruffed-grouse; cut out that pheasantry altogether, and try to breed our own native game-bird—"

"What! You can't breed ruffed-grouse in captivity!"

"I've done it, sir," said young Hastings modestly.

That night, over the plans, Portlaw voiced his distrust of Hastings and mourned aloud for Malcourt.

"That infernal Louis," he complained, waving his fat cigar, "hasn't written one line to me in a week! What the deuce is he doing down there in town? I won't stand it! The ice is out and Wayward and Cuyp and Vetchen are coming up for the fishing; and Mrs. Ascott, perhaps, is coming, and Miss Palliser, and, I hope, Miss Suydam; that makes our eight for Bridge, you see, with you and me. If Louis were here I'd have three others—but I can't ask anybody else until I know."

"Perhaps you'll get a telegram when the buckboard returns from Pride's Fall," said Hamil quietly. He, too, had been waiting for a letter that had not come. Days were lengthening into weeks since his departure from the South; and the letter he taught himself to expect had never come.

That she would write sooner or later he had dared believe at first; and then, as day after day passed, belief faded into hope; and now the colours of hope were fading into the gray tension of suspense.

He had written her every day, cheerful, amusing letters of current commonplaces which now made up his life. In them was not one hint of love—no echo of former intimacy, nothing of sadness, or regret, only a friendly sequence of messages, of inquiries, of details recounting the events of the days as they dawned and faded through the silvery promise of spring in the chill of the Northern hills.

Every morning and evening the fleet little Morgans came tearing in from Pride's Fall with the big leather mail-bag, which bore Portlaw's initials in metal, bulging with letters, newspapers, magazines for Portlaw; and now and then a slim envelope for him from his aunt, or letters, bearing the Palm Beach post-mark, from contractors on the Cardross estate, or from his own superintendent. But that was all.

His days were passed afoot in the forested hills, along lonely little lakes, following dashing trout-brooks or studying the United States Geological

Survey maps which were not always accurate in minor details of contour, and sometimes made a mockery of the lesser water-courses, involving him and his surveyors in endless complications.

Sometimes, toward evening, if the weather was mild, he and Portlaw took their rods for a cast on Painted Creek—a noble trout stream which took its name from the dropping autumn glory of the sugar-bush where the water passed close to the house. There lithe, wild trout struck tigerishly at the flies and fought like demons, boring Portlaw intensely, who preferred to haul in a prospective dinner without waste of energy, and be about the matter of a new sauce with his cook.

CHAPTER XX
A NEW ENEMY

One evening in April, returning with a few brace of trout, they found the mail-bag awaiting them on the hall table; and Portlaw distributed the contents, proclaiming, as usual, his expectation of a letter from Malcourt.

There was none. And, too peevish and disappointed to even open the heterogeneous mass of letters and newspapers, he slumped sulkily in his chair, feet on the fender, biting into his extinct cigar.

"That devilish Louis," he said, "has been away for several of the most accursedly lonely weeks I ever spent.... No reflection on you, Hamil—Oh, I beg your pardon; I didn't see you were busy—"

Hamil had not even heard him. He was busy—very busy with a letter—dozens of sheets of a single letter, closely written, smeared in places—the letter that had come at last!

In the fading light he bent low over the pages. Later a servant lighted the lamps; later still Portlaw went into the library, drew out a book bound in crushed levant, pushed an electric button, and sat down. The book bound so admirably in crushed levant was a cook-book; the bell he rang summoned his cook.

In the lamplit living-room the younger man bent over the letter that had come at last. It was dated early in April; had been written at Palm Beach, carried to New York, but had only been consigned to the mails within thirty-six hours:

"I have had all your letters—but no courage to answer. Now you will write no more.

"Dear—this, my first letter to you, is also my last. I know now what the condemned feel who write in the hour of death.

"When you went away on Thursday I could not leave my room to say good-bye to you. Gray came and knocked, but I was not fit to be seen. If I hadn't looked so dreadfully I wouldn't have minded being ill. You know that a little illness would not have kept me from coming to say good-bye to you.

"So you went away, all alone with Gray. I remained in bed that day with the room darkened. Mother and Cecile were troubled but could not bring themselves to believe that my collapse was due to your going. It was not logical, you know, as we all expected to see you in a week or two in New York.

"So they had Dr. Vernam, and I took what he prescribed, and nobody attached any undue importance to the matter. So I was left to myself, and I lay and thought out what I had to do.

"Dear—I knew there was only one thing to do; I knew whither my love—our love—was carrying me—faster and faster—spite of all I'd said. *Said!* What are words beside such love as ours? What would be my affection for dad and mother beside my love for you? Would your loyalty and your dear self-denial continue to help me when they only make me love you more intensely?

"There is only one thing clear in all this pitiful confusion; I—whom they took and made their child—cannot sacrifice them! And yet I *would!*—oh, Garry!—I would for you. There was no safety for me at all as long as there was the slightest chance to sacrifice everything—everybody—and give myself to you.

"Listen! On the second day after you left I was sitting with mother and Cecile on the terrace. We were quietly discussing the closing of the house and other harmless domestic matters. All at once there swept over me such a terrible sense of desolation that I think I lost my mind; for the next thing I knew I was standing in my own room, dressed for travelling—with a hand-bag in my hand.

"It was my maid knocking that brought me to my senses: I had been going away to find you; that was all I could realise. And I sank on my bed, trembling; and presently fell into the grief-stricken lethargy which is all I know now of sleep.

"But when I woke to face the dreadful day again, I knew the time had come. And I went to mother that evening and told her.

"But, Garry, there is never to be any escape from deception, it seems; I had to make her think I *wanted* to acknowledge and take up life with my husband. My life is to be a living lie!...

"As I expected, mother was shocked and grieved beyond words—and, dearest, they are bitterly disappointed; they all had hoped it would be *you.*

"She says there must positively be another ceremony. I don't know how dad will take it—but mother is so good, so certain of his forgiving me.

"It wrings my heart—the silent astonishment of Cecile and Gray—and their trying to make the best of it, and mother, smiling for my sake, tender, forgiving, solicitous, and deep under all bitterly disappointed. Oh, well—she can bear that better than disgrace.

"I've been crying over this letter; that's what all this blotting means.

"Now I can never see you again; never touch your hand, never look into those brown eyes again—Garry! Garry!—never while life lasts.

"I ask forgiveness for all the harm my love has done to you, for all the pain it has caused you, for the unhappiness that, please God, will not endure with you too long.

"I have tried to pray that the pain will not last too long for you; I will try to pray that you may love another woman and forget all this unhappiness.

"Think of me as one who died, loving you. I cling to this paper as though it were your hand. But—

"Dearest—dearest—Good-by.

"SHIELA CARDROSS."

When Portlaw came in from his culinary conference he found Hamil scattering the black ashes of a letter among the cinders.

"Well, we're going to try an old English receipt on those trout," he began cheerfully—and stopped short at sight of Hamil's face.

"What's the matter?" he asked bluntly.

"Nothing."

Hamil returned to his chair and picked up a book; Portlaw looked at him for a moment, then, perplexed, sorted his mail and began to open the envelopes.

"Bills, bills," he muttered, "appeals for some confounded foundlings' hospital—all the eternal junk my flesh is heir to—and a letter from a lawyer—let them sue!—and a—a—hey! what the devil—what the—"

Portlaw was on his feet, startled eyes fairly protruding as he scanned incredulously the engraved card between his pudgy fingers.

"O Lord!" he bellowed; "it's all up! The entire bally business has gone up! That pup of a Louis!—Oh, there's no use!—Look here, Hamil! I tell you I can't believe it, I can't, and I won't—*Look* what that fool card says!"

And Hamil's stunned gaze fell on the engraved card:

"Mr. and Mrs. Neville Cardross have the honour of announcing the marriage of their daughter Shiela to Mr. Louis Malcourt."

The date and place followed.

Portlaw was making considerable noise over the matter, running about distractedly with little, short, waddling steps. Occasionally he aimed a kick at a stuffed arm-chair, which did not hurt his foot too much.

It was some time before he calmed enough to pout and fume and protest in his usual manner, appealing alternately to Heaven as witness and to Hamil for corroboration that he had been outrageously used.

"Now, who the devil could suspect him of such intention!" wailed poor Portlaw. "God knows, he was casual with the sex. There have been dozens of them, Hamil, literally dozens in every port!—from Mamie and Stella up to Gladys and Ethelberta! Yes, he was Harry to some and Reginald to others—high, low—and the game, Hamil—the game amused him; but so help me kings and aces! I never looked for this—never so help me; and I thought him as safe with the Vere-de-Veres as he was with the Pudding Sisters, Farina and Tapioca! And now"—passionately displaying the engraved card—"look who's here!... O pip! What's the use."

Dinner modified his grief; hope bubbled in the Burgundy, simmered in the soup, grew out of gravy like the sturdy, eternal weed she is, parasitic in the human breast.

"He's probably married a million or so," suggested Portlaw, mollified under the seductive appeal of a fruit salad dressed with a mixture containing nearly a hundred different ingredients. "If he has I don't see why he shouldn't build a camp next to mine. I'll give him the land—if he doesn't care to pay for it," he added cautiously. "Don't say anything to him about it, Hamil. After all, why shouldn't he pay for the land?... But if he doesn't want to—between you and me—I'll come within appreciable distance of almost giving him what land he needs.... O gee! O fizz! That damn Louis!... And I'm wondering—about several matters—"

After dinner Portlaw settled down by the fire, cigar lighted, and began to compose a letter to Malcourt, embodying his vivid ideas concerning a new house near his own for the bridal pair.

Hamil went out into the fresh April night. The young grass was wet under the stars; a delicate fragrance of new buds filled the air.

He had been walking for a long time, when the first far hint of thunder broke the forest silence. Later lightning began to quiver through the darkness; a wind awaking overhead whispered prophecy, wailed it, foreboding; then slowly the woods filled with the roar of the rain.

He was moving on, blindly, at random, conscious only of the necessity of motion. Where the underbrush halted him he sheered off into the open timber, feeling his way, falling sometimes, lying where he fell for a while till the scourge of necessity lashed him into motion again.

About midnight the rain increased to a deluge, slackened fitfully, and died out in a light rattle of thunder; star after star broke out through the dainty vapours overhead; the trees sighed and grew quiet. For a while drumming drops from the branches filled the silence with a musical tattoo, then there remained no sound save, far away in the darkness, the muffled roar of some brook, brimming bank-high with the April rain. And Hamil, soaked, exhausted, and believing he could sleep, went back to the house. Toward morning sleep came.

He awoke restless and depressed; and the next morning he was not well; and not quite as well the next, remaining in his room with a headache, pestered by Portlaw and retinues of servants bearing delicacies on trays.

He had developed a cold, not a very bad one, and on the third day he resumed his duties in the woods with Phelps and Baker, the surveyors, and young Hastings.

The dull, stupid physical depression hung on to him; so did his cold; and he found breathing difficult at night. The weather had turned very raw and harsh, culminating in a flurry of snow.

Then one morning he appeared at breakfast looking so ghastly that Portlaw became alarmed. It seemed to be rather late for that; Hamil's face was already turning a dreadful bluish white under his host's astonished gaze, and as the first chill seized him he rose from the table, reeling.

"I—I am sorry, Portlaw," he tried to say.

"What on earth have you got?" asked Portlaw in a panic; but Hamil could not speak.

They got him to the gardener's cottage as a precautionary measure, and telephoned to Utica for trained nurses, and to Pride's Fall for a doctor. Meanwhile, Hamil, in bed, was fast becoming mentally irresponsible as the infection spread, involving both lungs, and the fever in his veins blazed into a conflagration. That is one way that pneumonia begins; but it ought not to have made such brutally quick work of a young, healthy, and care-free man. There was not much chance for him by the next morning, and less the following night when the oxygen tanks arrived.

Portlaw, profoundly shocked and still too stunned by the swiftness of the calamity to credit a tragic outcome, spent the day in a heavily bewildered condition, wandering, between meals, from his house to the cottage where Hamil lay, and back again to the telephone.

He had physicians in consultation from Utica and Albany; he had nurses and oxygen; he had Miss Palliser on the telephone, first in New York, then at Albany, and finally at Pride's Fall, to tell her that Hamil was alive.

She arrived after midnight with Wayward. Hamil was still breathing— if it could be called by that name.

Toward dawn a long-distance call summoned Portlaw: Malcourt was on the end of the wire.

"Is Hamil ill up at your place?"

"He is," said Portlaw curtly.

"Very ill?"

"Very."

"How ill?"

"Well, he's not dead."

"Portlaw, is he dying?"

"They don't know yet."

"What is the sickness?"

"Pneumonia. I wish to heaven you were here!" he burst out, unable to suppress his smouldering irritation any longer.

"I was going to ask you if you wanted me—"

"You needn't ask such a fool question. Your house is here for you and the servants are eating their heads off. I haven't had your resignation and I don't expect it while we're in trouble.... Mrs. Malcourt will come with you, of course."

"Hold the wire."

Portlaw held it for a few minutes, then:

"Mr. Portlaw?" — scarcely audible.

"Is that you, Mrs. Malcourt?"

"Yes.... Is Mr. Hamil going to die?"

"We don't know, Mrs. Malcourt. We are doing all we can. It came suddenly; we were caught unprepared—"

"Suddenly, you say?"

"Yes, it hit him like a bullet. He ought to have broken the journey northward; he was not well when he arrived, but I never for a moment thought—"

"Mr. Portlaw—please!"

"Yes?"

"Is there a chance for him?"

"The doctors refuse to say so."

"Do they say there is *no* chance?"

"They haven't said that, Mrs. Malcourt. I think—"

"Please, Mr. Portlaw!"

"Yes, madam!"

"Will you listen very carefully, please?"

"Certainly—"

"Mr. Malcourt and I are leaving on the 10.20. You will please consult your time-table and keep us informed at the following stations—have you a pencil to write them down?... Are you ready now? Ossining, Hudson, Albany, Fonda, and Pride's Fall.... Thank you.... Mr. Malcourt wishes you to send the Morgan horses.... If there is any change in Mr. Hamil's condition before the train leaves the Grand Central at 10.20, let me know. I will be at the telephone station until the last moment. Telegrams for the train should be directed to me aboard "The Seminole"—the private car of Mr. Cardross.... Is all this clear?... Thank you."

With a confused idea that he was being ordered about too frequently of late Portlaw waddled off bedward; but sleep eluded him; he lay there watching through his window the light in the window of the sick-room where Hamil lay fighting for breath; and sometimes he quivered all over in scared foreboding, and sometimes the thought that Malcourt was returning seemed to ease for a moment the dread load of responsibility that was already playing the mischief with his digestion.

A curry had started it; a midnight golden-buck superimposed upon a miniature mince pie had, to his grief and indignation, continued an outrageous conspiracy against his liver begun by the shock of Hamil's illness. But what completed his exasperation was the indifference of the physicians attending Hamil who did not seem to appreciate the gravity of an impaired digestive system, or comprehend that a man who couldn't enjoy eating might as well be in Hamil's condition; and Portlaw angrily swallowed the calomel so indifferently shoved toward him and hunted up Wayward, to whom he aired his deeply injured feelings.

"What you need are 'Drover's Remedies,'" observed Wayward, peering at him through his spectacles; and Portlaw unsuspiciously made a memorandum of the famous live-stock and kennel panacea for future personal emergencies.

The weather was unfavourable for Hamil; a raw, wet wind rattled the windows; the east lowered thick and gray with hurrying clouds; volleys of chilly rain swept across the clearing from time to time.

Portlaw and Wayward sat most of the time in the big living-room playing "Canfield." There was nothing else to do except to linger somewhere within call, and wait. Constance Palliser remained near whichever nurse happened to be off duty, and close enough to the sick-room to shudder at what she heard from within, all day, all night, ceaselessly ominous, pitiable, heart-breaking.

At length Wayward took her away without ceremony into the open air.

"Look here, Constance, your sitting there and hearing such things isn't helping Garry. Lansdale is doing everything that can be done; Miss Race and Miss Clay are competent. You're simply frightening yourself sick—"

She protested, but he put her into a hooded ulster, buckled on her feet a pair of heavy carriage boots, and drew her arm under his, saying: "If there's a chance Garry is having it, and you've got to keep your strength.... I wish this mist would clear; Hooper telephoned to Pride's for the weather bulletin, but it is not encouraging."

They walked about for an hour and finally returned from the wet woodland paths to the bridge, leaning on the stone parapet together.

A swollen brook roared under the arches, carrying on its amber wave-crests tufts of green grass and young leaves and buds which the promise of summer had tenderly unfolded to the mercy of a ruthless flood.

"Like those young lives that go out too early," murmured Constance. "See that little wind-flower, Jim, uprooted, drowning—and that dead thing tumbling about half under water—"

Wayward laid a firm hand across hers.

"I don't mean to be morbid," she said with a pathetic upward glance, "but, Jim, it is too awful to hear him fighting for just—just a chance to breathe a little—"

"I think he's going to get well," said Wayward.

"Jim! Why do you think it? Has any—"

"No.... I just think it."

"Is there any reason—"

"None—except you."

His voice within the last month or two had almost entirely lost its indistinct and husky undertone; the clear resonant quality, which had always thrilled her a little as a young girl, seemed to be returning; and now she felt, faintly, the old response awaking within her.

"It is very sweet of you to believe he'll live because I love him," she said gently.

Wayward drew his hand from hers and, folding his arms, leaned on the parapet inspecting the turbid water through his spectacles.

"There are no fights too desperate to be won," he said. "The thing to do is to finish—still fighting!"

"Jim?"

"Yes."

This time her hand sought his, drew it toward her, and covered it with both of hers.

"Jim," she said tremulously, "there is something—I am horribly afraid—that—perhaps Garry is not fighting."

"Why?" he asked bluntly.

"There was an—an attachment—"

"A what?"

"An unfortunate affair; he was very deeply in love—"

"Not ridiculously, I hope!"

"I don't know what you mean.... He cared more than I have believed possible; I saw him in New York on his way here and, Jim, he must have known then, for he looked like death—"

"You mean he was in love with that Cardross girl?"

"Oh, yes, yes!... I do not understand the affair; but I tell you, Jim, the strangest part was that the girl loved him! If ever a woman was in love with a man, Shiela Cardross was in love with Garry! I tell you I know it; I am not guessing, not hazarding an opinion; I *know* it.... And she married Louis Malcourt!... And, Jim, I have been so frightened—so terrified—for Garry— so afraid that he might not care to fight—"

Wayward leaned there heavily and in silence. He was going to say that men do not do such things for women any longer, but he thought of the awful battle not yet ended which he had endured for the sake of the woman beside him; and he said nothing; because he knew that, without hope of her to help him, the battle had long since gone against him. But Garry had nothing to fight for, if what Constance said was true. And within him his latent distrust and contempt for Malcourt blazed up, tightening the stern lines of his sun-burnt visage.

"Portlaw says that Louis is coming to-night, and that young Mrs. Malcourt is with him," he observed.

"I know it.... I was wondering if there was any way we could use her— make use of her—"

"To stir up Garry to fight?"

"Y-yes—something like that—I am vague about it myself—if it could be done without anybody suspecting the—O Jim!—I don't know; I am only a half-crazed woman willing to do anything for my boy—"

"Certainly. If there's anything that might benefit Garry you need not hesitate on account of that little beast Malcourt—"

She said in her gentle, earnest way: "Louis Malcourt is so very strange. He has treated Virginia dreadfully; they were engaged—they must have been or she could not have gone all to pieces the way she has.... I cannot understand it, Jim—"

"What's Louis coming here for?"

"Mr. Portlaw begged him to come—"

"What for? Oh, well, I guess I can answer that for myself; it's to save Portlaw some trouble or other—"

"You are very hard on people—very intolerant, sometimes—"

"I have no illusions concerning the unselfishness of Billy Portlaw. Look at him tagging after the doctors and bawling for pills!—with Garry lying there! He hustled him into a cottage, too—"

"He was quite right, Jim, Garry is better off—"

"So's William. Don't tell *me*, Constance; he's always been the same; he never really cared for anybody in all his life except Louis Malcourt. But it's a jolly, fat, good-humoured beast, and excellent company aboard the *Ariani!*" ... He was silent a moment, then his voice deepened to a clear, gentle tone, almost tender: "You've been rained on enough, now; come in by the fire and I'll bring you the latest news from Garry."

But when he returned to the fire where Constance and Portlaw sat in silence, the report he brought was only negative. A third doctor from Albany arrived at nightfall and left an hour later. He was non-committal and in a hurry, and very, very famous.

CHAPTER XXI
REINFORCEMENTS

All day Portlaw had been telephoning and telegraphing the various stations along the New York Central Railroad, following the schedule from his time-table and from the memoranda given him by young Mrs. Malcourt; and now the big, double, covered buckboard and the fast horses, which had been sent to meet them at Pride's, was expected at any moment.

"At least," Portlaw confided with a subdued animation to Wayward, "we're going to have a most excellent dinner for them when they arrive. My Frenchman is doing the capons in Louis XI style—"

"Somebody," said Wayward pleasantly, "will do you in the same style some day." And he retired to dress, laughing in an odd way. But Portlaw searched in vain for the humour which he had contrived somehow to miss. He also missed Malcourt on such occasions—Malcourt whose nimble intelligence never missed a trick!

"Thank the Lord he's coming!" he breathed devoutly. "It's bad enough to have a man dying on the premises without having an earthly thing to do while he's doing it.... I can see no disrespect to Hamil if we play a few cards now and then."

His valet was buttoning him up when Malcourt arrived and walked coolly into his room.

"Louis! Damnation!" ejaculated Portlaw, purple with emotion.

"Especially the latter," nodded Malcourt. "They tell me, below, that Hamil is very sick; wait a moment!—Mrs. Malcourt is in my house; she is to have it for herself. Do you understand?"

"Y-yes—"

"All right. I take my old rooms here for the present. Tell Williams. Mrs. Malcourt has brought a maid and another trained nurse for emergencies. She wanted to; and that's enough."

"Lord, but I'm glad you've come!" said Portlaw, forgetting all the reproaches and sarcasms he had been laboriously treasuring to discharge at his superintendent.

"Thanks," said Malcourt drily. "And I say; we didn't know anybody else was here—"

"Only his aunt and Wayward—"

Malcourt cast a troubled glance around the room, repeating: "I didn't understand that anybody was here."

"What difference does that make? You're coming back to stay, aren't you?"

Malcourt looked at him. "That's supposed to be the excuse for our coming.... Certainly; I'm your superintendent, back from a fortnight's leave to get married in.... That's understood." ... And, stepping nearer: "There's hell to pay in town. Have you seen the papers?"

"Not to-day's—"

"They're down-stairs. Wormly, Hunter & Blake have failed—liabilities over three million. There's probably going to be a run on the Shoshone Securities Company; Andreas Hogg and Gumble Brothers have laid down on their own brokers and the Exchange has—"

"What!"

"A nice outlook, isn't it? Be careful what you say before Mrs. Malcourt; she doesn't realise that Cardross, Carrick & Co. may be involved."

Portlaw said with that simple self-centred dignity which characterised him in really solemn moments: "Thank God, I'm in an old-line institution and own nothing that can ever pass a dividend!"

"Even your hens pay their daily dole," nodded Malcourt, eyeing him.

"Certainly. If they don't, it's a fricassee for theirs!" chuckled Portlaw, in excellent humour over his own financial security in time of stress.

So they descended to the living-room together where Constance and Wayward stood whispering by the fire. Malcourt greeted them; they exchanged a few words in faultless taste, then he picked an umbrella from the rack and went across the lawn to his house where his bride of a fortnight awaited him. Portlaw rubbed his pudgy hands together contentedly.

"Now that Louis is back," he said to Wayward, "this place will be run properly again."

"Is it likely," asked Wayward, "that a man who has just married several millions will do duty as your superintendent in the backwoods?"

"Well," said Portlaw, with his head on one side, "do you know, it is extremely likely. And I have a vague idea that he will draw his salary with great regularity and promptness."

"What are you talking about?" said Wayward bluntly.

"I'll tell you. But young Mrs. Malcourt does not know—and she is not to be told as long as it can be avoided: Cardross, Carrick & Co. are in a bad way."

"How bad?"

"The worst—unless the Clearing House does something—"

"What!"

"—And it won't! Mark my words. Wayward, the Clearing House won't lift a penny's weight from the load on their shoulders. *I* know. There's a string of banks due to blow up; the fuse has been lighted, and it's up to us to stand clear—"

"Oh, hush!" whispered Constance in a frightened voice; the door swung open; a gust of chilly air sent the ashes in the fireplace whirling upward among the leaping flames.

Young Mrs. Malcourt entered the room.

Her gown, which was dark—and may have been black—set off her dead-white face and hands in a contrast almost startling. Confused for a moment by the brilliancy of the lamplight she stood looking around her; then, as Portlaw waddled forward, she greeted him very quietly; recognised and greeted Wayward, and then slowly turned toward Constance.

There was a pause; the girl took a hesitating step forward; but Miss Palliser met her more than half-way, took both her hands, and, holding them, looked her through and through.

Malcourt's voice broke in gravely:

"It is most unfortunate that my return to duty should happen under such circumstances. I do not think there is any man in the world for whom I have the respect—and affection—that I have for Hamil."

Wayward was staring at him almost insolently; Portlaw, comfortably affected, shook his head in profound sympathy, glancing sideways at the door where his butler always announced dinner. Constance had heard, but she looked only at young Mrs. Malcourt. Shiela alone had been unconscious of the voice of her lord and master.

She looked bravely back into the golden-brown eyes of Miss Palliser; and, suddenly realising that, somehow, this woman knew the truth, flinched pitifully.

But Constance crushed the slender, colourless hands in her own, speaking tremulously low:

"Perhaps he'll have a chance now. I am so thankful that you've come."

"Yes." Her ashy lips formed the word, but there was no utterance.

Dinner was announced with a decorous modulation befitting the circumstances.

Malcourt bore himself faultlessly during the trying function; Wayward was moody; his cynical glance through his gold-rimmed glasses resting now on Malcourt, now on Shiela. The latter ate nothing, which grieved Portlaw beyond measure, for the salad was ambrosial and the capon was truly Louis XI.

Later the men played Preference, having nothing else to do after the ladies left, Constance insisting on taking Shiela back to her own house, and Malcourt acquiescing in the best of taste.

The stars were out; a warm, sweet, dry wind had set in from the southwest.

"It was what we've prayed for," breathed Constance, pausing on the lawn. "It was what the doctors wanted for him. How deliciously warm it is! Oh, I hope it will help him!"

"Is that *his* cottage?" whispered Shiela.

"Yes.... His room is there where the windows are open.... They keep them open, you know.... Do you want to go in?"

"Oh, *may* I see him!"

"No, dear.... Only I often sit in the corridor outside.... But perhaps you could not endure it—"

"Endure what?"

"To hear—to listen—to his—breathing—"

"Let me go with you!" she whispered, clasping her hands, "let me go with you, Miss Palliser. I will be very quiet, I will do whatever you tell me—only let me go with you!"

Miss Clay, just released from duty, met them at the door.

"There is nothing to say," she said; "of course every hour he holds out is an hour gained. The weather is more favourable. Miss Race will show you the chart."

As Shiela entered the house the ominous sounds from above struck her like a blow; she caught her breath and stood perfectly still, one hand pressing her breast.

"That is not as bad as it has been," whispered Constance, and noiselessly mounted the stairs.

Shiela crept after her and halted as though paralysed when the elder woman pointed at a door which hung just ajar. Inside the door stood a screen and a shaded electric jet. A woman's shadow moved across the wall within.

Without the slightest noise Constance sank down on the hallway sofa; Shiela crept up close beside her, closer, when the dreadful sounds broke out again, trembling in every limb, pressing her head convulsively against the elder woman's arm.

Young Dr. Lansdale came up-stairs an hour later, nodded to Constance, looked sharply at Shiela, then turned to the nurse who had forestalled him at the door. A glance akin to telepathy flashed between physician and nurse, and the doctor turned to Miss Palliser:

"Would you mind asking Miss Clay to come back?" he said quietly. "Oh!—has she gone to bed?"

Shiela was on her feet: "I—I have brought a trained nurse," she said; "the very best—from Johns Hopkins—"

"I should be very glad to have her for a few moments," said the doctor, looking at the chart by the light of the hall lamp.

Shiela sped down the stairs like a ghost; the nurse re-entered the room; the doctor turned to follow, and halted short as a hand touched his arm.

"Dr. Lansdale?"

He nodded pleasantly.

"Does it do any good—when one is very, very ill—to see—"

The doctor made a motion with his head. "Who is that young girl?" he asked coolly.

"Mrs. Malcourt—"

"Oh! I thought it might have been this Shiela he is always talking about in his delirium—"

"It *is*," whispered Constance.

For a moment they looked one another in the eyes; then a delicate colour stole over the woman's face.

"I'm afraid—I'm afraid that my boy is not making the fight he could make," she whispered.

"Why not?"

She was speechless.

"Why *not!*" ... And in a lower voice: "This corridor is a confessional. Miss Palliser—if that helps you any."

She said: "They were in love."

"Oh! Are they yet?"

"Yes."

"Oh! *She* married the other man?"

"Yes."

"Oh!"

Young Lansdale wheeled abruptly and entered the sick-room. Shiela returned in a few minutes with her nurse, a quick-stepping, cool-eyed young woman in spotless uniform. A few minutes afterward the sounds indicated that oxygen was being used.

An hour later Miss Race came into the hallway and looked at Shiela.

"Mr. Hamil is conscious," she said. "Would you care to see him for a second?"

A dreadful fear smote her as she crouched there speechless.

"The danger of infection is slight," said the nurse—and knew at the same instant that she had misunderstood. "Did you think I meant he is dying?" she added gently as Shiela straightened up to her slender height.

"Is he better?" whispered Constance.

"He is conscious," said the nurse patiently. "He knows"—turning to Shiela—"that you are here. You must not speak to him; you may let him see you for a moment. Come!"

In the shadowy half-light of the room Shiela halted at a sign from the nurse; the doctor glanced up, nodding almost imperceptibly as the girl's eyes fell upon the bed.

How she did it—what instinct moved her, what unsuspected reserve of courage prompted her, she never understood; but looking into the dreadful eyes of death itself there in the sombre shadows of the bed, she smiled with a little gesture of gay recognition, then, turning, passed from the room.

"Did he know you?" motioned Constance.

"I don't know—I don't know.... I think he was—dying—before he saw me—"

She was shuddering so violently that Constance could scarcely hold her, scarcely guide her down the stairs, across the lawn toward her own house. The doctor overtook and passed them on his way to his own quarters, but he only bowed very pleasantly, and would have gone on except for the soft appeal of Constance.

"Miss Palliser," he said, "I *don't* know—if you want the truth. You know all that I do; he is conscious—or was. I expect he will be, at intervals, now. This young lady behaved admirably—admirably! The thing to do is to wait."

He glanced at Shiela, hesitated, then:

"Would it be any comfort to learn that he knew you?"

"Yes.... Thank you."

The doctor nodded and said in a hearty voice: "Oh, we've got to pull him through somehow. That's what I'm here for." And he went away briskly across the lawn.

"What are you going to do?" asked Constance in a low voice.

"I don't know; write to my father, I think."

"You ought not to sit up after such a journey."

"Do you suppose I could sleep *to-night*?"

Constance drew her into her arms; the girl clung to her, head hidden on her breast.

"Shiela, Shiela," she murmured, "you can always come to me. Always, always!—for Garry's sake.... Listen, child: I do not understand your tragedy—his and yours—I only know you loved each other.... Love—and a boy's strange ways in love have always been to me a mystery—a sad one, Shiela.... For once upon a time—there was a boy—and never in all my life another. Dear, we women are all born mothers to men—and from birth to death our heritage is motherhood—grief for those of us who bear—sadness for us who shall never bear—mothers to sorrow everyone.... Do you love him?"

"Yes."

"That is forbidden you, now."

"It was forbidden me from the first; yet, when I saw him I loved him. What was I to do?"

Constance waited, but the girl had fallen silent.

"Is there more you wish to tell me?"

"No more."

She bent and kissed the cold cheek on her shoulder.

"Don't sit up, child. If there is any reason for waking you I will come myself."

"Thank you."

So they parted, Constance to seek her room and lie down partly dressed; Shiela to the new quarters still strange and abhorrent to her.

Her maid, half dead with fatigue, slept in a chair, and young Mrs. Malcourt aroused her and sent her off to bed. Then she roamed through the rooms, striving to occupy her mind with the negative details of the furnishing; but it was all drearily harmless, unaccented anywhere by personal taste, merely the unmeaning harmony executed by a famous New York decorator, at Portlaw's request—a faultless monotony from garret to basement.

There was a desk in one room; ink in the well, notepaper bearing the name of Portlaw's camp. She looked at it and passed on to her bedroom.

But after she had unlaced and, hair unbound, stood staring vacantly about her, she remembered the desk; and drawing on her silken chamber-robe, went into the writing-room.

At intervals, during her writing, she would rise and gaze from the window across the darkness where in the sick-room a faint, steady glow remained; and she could see the white curtains in his room stirring like ghosts in the soft night wind and the shadow of the nurse on wall and ceiling.

> "Dear, dear dad and mother," she wrote; "Mr. Portlaw was so anxious for Louis to begin his duties that we decided to come at once, particularly as we both were somewhat worried over the serious illness of Mr. Hamil.
>
> "He is very, very ill, poor fellow. The sudden change from the South brought on pneumonia. I know that you both and

Gray and Cecile and Jessie will feel as sorry as I do. His aunt, Miss Palliser, is here. To-night I was permitted to see him. Only his eyes were visible and they were wide open. It is very dreadful, very painful, and has cast a gloom over our gaiety.

"To-night Dr. Lansdale said that he would pull him through. I am afraid he said it to encourage Miss Palliser.

"This is a beautiful place—" She dropped her pen with a shudder, closed her eyes, groped for it again, and forced herself to continue—"Mr. Portlaw is very kind. The superintendent's house is large and comfortable. Louis begins his duties to-morrow. Everything promises to be most interesting and enjoyable—" She laid her head in her arms, remaining so, motionless until somewhere on the floor below a clock struck midnight."

At last she managed to go on:

"Dad, dear; what you said to Louis about my part of your estate was very sweet and generous of you; but I do not want it. Louis and I have talked it over in the last fortnight and we came to the conclusion that you must make no provision for me at present. We wish to begin very simply and make our own way. Besides I know from something I heard Acton say that even very wealthy people are hard pressed for ready money; and so Phil Gatewood acted as our attorney and Mr. Cuyp's firm as our brokers and now the Union Pacific and Government bonds have been transferred to Colonel Vetchen's bank subject to your order—is that the term?—and the two blocks on Lexington Avenue now stand in your name, and Cuyp, Van Dine, and Siclen sold all those queer things for me—the Industrials, I think you call them—and I endorsed a sheaf of certified checks, making them all payable to your order.

"Dad, dear—I cannot take anything of that kind from you.... I am very, very tired of the things that money buys. All I shall ever care for is the quiet of unsettled places, the silence of the hills, where I can study and read and live out the life I am fitted for. The rest is too complex, too tiresome to keep up with or even to watch from my windows.

"Dear dad and dear mother, I am a little anxious about what Acton said to Gray—about money troubles that threaten wealthy people. And so it makes me very happy to know that the rather overwhelming fortune which you so long ago set aside for me to accumulate until my marriage is at last at your disposal again. Because Gray told me that Acton was forced to borrow such frightful sums at such ruinous rates. And now you need borrow no more, need you?

"You have been *so* good to me—both of you. I am afraid you won't believe how dearly I love you. I don't very well see how you can believe it. But it is true.

"The light in Mr. Hamil's sick-room seems to be out. I am going to ask what it means.

"Good-night, my darling two—I will write you every day.

"SHIELA."

She was standing, looking out across the night at the darkened windows of the sick-room, her sealed letter in her hand, when she heard the lower door open and shut, steps on the stairs—and turned to face her husband.

"W-what is it?" she faltered.

"What is what?" he asked coolly.

"The reason there is no light in Mr. Hamil's windows?"

"He's asleep," said Malcourt in a dull voice.

"Louis! Are you telling me the truth?"

"Yes.... I'd tell you if he were dead. He isn't. Lansdale thinks there is a slight change for the better. So I came to tell you."

Every tense nerve and muscle in her body seemed to give way at the same instant as she dropped to the lounge. For a moment her mind was only a confused void, then the routine instinct of self-control asserted itself; she made the effort required of her, groping for composure and self-command.

"He is better, you say?"

"Lansdale said there was a change which might be slightly favourable.... I wish I could say more than that, Shiela."

"But—he *is* better, then?"—pitifully persistent.

Malcourt looked at her a moment. "Yes, he is better. I believe it."

For a few moments they sat there in silence.

"That is a pretty gown," he said pleasantly.

"What! Oh!" Young Mrs. Malcourt bent her head, gazing fixedly at the sealed letter in her hand. The faint red of annoyance touched her pallor—perhaps because her chamber-robe suggested an informality between them that was impossible.

"I have written to my father and mother," she said, "about the securities."

"Have you?" he said grimly.

"Yes. And, Louis, I forgot to tell you that Mr. Cuyp telephoned me yesterday assuring me that everything had been transferred and recorded and that my father could use everything in an emergency—if it comes as you thought possible.... And I—I wish to say"—she went on in a curiously constrained voice—"that I appreciate what you have done—what you so willingly gave up—"

An odd smile hovered on Malcourt's lips:

"Nonsense," he said. "One couldn't give up what one never had and never wanted.... And you say that it was all available yesterday?"

"Available!"

"At the order of Cardross, Carrick & Co.?"

"Mr. Cuyp said so."

"You made over all those checks to them?"

"Yes. Mr. Cuyp took them away."

"And that Lexington Avenue stuff?"

"Deeded and recorded."

"The bonds?"

"Everything is father's again."

"Was it yesterday?"

"Yes. Why?"

"You are absolutely certain?"

"Mr. Cuyp said so."

Malcourt slowly rolled a cigarette and held it, unlighted, in his nervous fingers. Young Mrs. Malcourt watched him, but her mind was on other things.

Presently he rose, and she looked up as though startled painfully from her abstraction.

"You ought to turn in," he said quietly. "Good night."

"Good night."

He went out and started to descend the stairs; but somebody was banging at the lower door, entering clumsily, and in haste.

"Louis!" panted Portlaw, "they say Hamil is dying—"

"Damn you," whispered Malcourt fiercely, "will you shut your cursed mouth!"

Then slowly he turned, leaden-footed, head hanging, and ascended the stairs once more to the room where his wife had been. She was standing there, pale as a corpse, struggling into a heavy coat.

"Did you—hear?"

"Yes."

He aided her with her coat.

"Do you think you had better go over?"

"Yes, I must go."

She was trembling so that he could scarcely get her into the coat.

"Probably," he said, "Portlaw doesn't know what he's talking about.... Shiela, do you want me to go with you—"

"No—no! Oh, hurry—"

She was crying now; he saw that she was breaking down.

"Wait till I find your shoes. You can't go that way. Wait a moment—"

"No—no!"

He followed her to the stairs, but:

"No—no!" she sobbed, pushing him back; "I want him to myself. Can't they let me have him even when he is dying?"

"You can't go!" he said.

She turned on him quivering, beside herself.

"Not in this condition—for your own sake," he repeated steadily. And again he said: "For the sake of your name in the years to come, Shiela, you cannot go to him like this. Control yourself."

She strove to pass him; all her strength was leaving her.

"You coward!" she gasped.

"I thought you would mistake me," he said quietly. "People usually do.... Sit down."

For a while she lay sobbing in her arm-chair, white hands clinched, biting at her lips to choke back the terror and grief.

As soon as your self-command returns my commands are void," he said coolly. "Nobody here shall see you as you are. If you can't protect yourself it's my duty to do it for you.... Do you want Portlaw to see you?— Wayward?—these doctors and nurses and servants? How long would it take for gossip to reach your family!... And what you've done for their sakes would be a crime instead of a sacrifice!"

She looked up; he continued his pacing to and fro but said no more.

After a while she rose; an immense lassitude weighted her limbs and body.

"I think I am fit to go now," she said in a low voice.

"Use a sponge and cold water and fix your hair and put on your shoes," he said. "By the time you are ready I'll be back with the truth."

She was blindly involved with her tangled hair when she heard him on the stairs again—a quick, active step that she mistook for haste; and hair and arms fell as she turned to confront him.

"It was a sinking crisis; they got him through—both doctors. I tell you, Shiela, things look better," he said cheerily.

CHAPTER XXII
THE ROLL CALL

As in similar cases of the same disease Hamil's progress toward recovery was scarcely appreciable for a fortnight or so, then, danger of reinfection practically over, convalescence began with the new moon of May.

Other things also began about that time, including a lawsuit against Portlaw, the lilacs, jonquils, and appleblossoms in Shiela's garden, and Malcourt's capricious journeys to New York on business concerning which he offered no explanation to anybody.

The summons bidding William Van Beuren Portlaw of Camp Chickadee, town of Pride's Fall, Horican County, New York, to defend a suit for damages arising from trespass, tree-felling, the malicious diversion of the waters of Painted Creek, the wilful and deliberate killing of game, the flooding of wild meadow lands in contemptuous disregard of riparian rights and the drowning of certain sheep thereby, had been impending since the return from Florida to her pretty residence at Pride's Fall of Mrs. Alida Ascott.

Trouble had begun the previous autumn with a lively exchange of notes between them concerning the shooting of woodcock on Mrs. Ascott's side of the boundary. Then Portlaw stupidly built a dam and diverted the waters of Painted Creek. Having been planned, designed, and constructed according to Portlaw's own calculations, the dam presently burst and the escaping flood drowned some of Mrs. Ascott's sheep. Then somebody cut some pine timber on her side of the line and Mrs. Ascott's smouldering indignation flamed.

Personally she and Portlaw had been rather fond of one another; and to avoid trouble incident on hot temper Alida Ascott decamped, intending to cool off in the Palm Beach surf and think it over; but she met Portlaw at Palm Beach that winter, and Portlaw dodged the olive branch and neglected her so selfishly that she determined then and there upon his punishment, now long overdue.

"My Lord!" said Portlaw plaintively to Malcourt, "I had no idea she'd do such a thing to me; had you?"

"Didn't I tell you she would?" said Malcourt. "I know women better than you do, though you don't believe it."

"But I thought she was rather fond of me!" protested Portlaw indignantly.

"That may be the reason she's going to chasten you, friend. Don't come bleating to me; I advised you to be attentive to her at Palm Beach, but you sulked and stood about like a baby-hippopotamus and pouted and shot your cuffs. I warned you to be agreeable to her, but you preferred the Beach Club and pigeon shooting. It's easy enough to amuse yourself and be decent to a nice woman too. Even I can combine those things."

"Didn't I go to that lawn party?"

"Yes, and scarcely spoke to her. And never went near her afterward. Now she's mad all through."

"Well, I can get mad, too—"

"No, you're too plump to ever become angry—"

"Do you think I'm going to submit to—"

"You'll submit all right when they've dragged you twenty-eight miles to the county court house once or twice."

"Louis! Are you against me too?"—in a voice vibrating with reproach and self-pity.

"Now, look here, William Van Beuren; your guests *did* shoot woodcock on Mrs. Ascott's land—"

"They're migratory birds, confound it!"

"—And," continued Malcourt, paying no attention to the interruption, "you did build that fool dam regardless of my advice; and you first left her cattle waterless, then drowned her sheep—"

"That was a cloud-burst—an act of God—"

"It was a dam-burst, and the act of an obstinate chump!"

"Louis, I won't let anybody talk to me like that!"

"But you've just *done* it, William."

Portlaw, in a miniature fury, began to run around in little circles, puffing threats which, however, he was cautious enough to make obscure; winding up with:

"And I might as well take this opportunity to ask you what you mean by calmly going off to town every ten days or so and absenting yourself without a word of—"

"Oh, bosh," said Malcourt; "if you don't want me here, Billy, say so and be done with it."

"I didn't say I didn't want you—"

"Well, then, let me alone. I don't neglect your business and I don't intend to neglect my own. If the time comes when I can't attend to both I'll let you know soon enough—perhaps sooner than you expect."

"You're perfectly welcome to go to town," insisted Portlaw, alarmed.

"I know it," nodded Malcourt coolly. "Now, if you'll take my advice you'll behave less like a pig in this Ascott matter."

"I'm going to fight that suit—"

"Certainly fight it. But not the way you're planning."

"Well—how, then?"

"Go and see the little lady."

"See *her*? She wouldn't receive me."

"Probably not. That's unimportant. For heaven's sake, Portlaw, you're becoming chuckle-headed with all your feeding and inertia and pampered self-indulgence. You're the limit!—with your thirty-eight-inch girth and your twin chins and baby wrists! You know, it's pitiable when I think what a clean-cut, decent-looking, decently set-up fellow you were only two years ago!—it's enough to make a cat sick!"

"Can I help what I look like!" bellowed Portlaw wrathfully.

"What an idiot question!" said Malcourt with weary patience. "All you've got to do is to cuddle yourself less, and go out into the fresh air on your ridiculous legs—"

"Ridiculous!" gasped the other. "Well, I'm damned if I stand *that*—!"

"You won't be able to stand at all if you continue eating and sitting in arm-chairs. You don't like what I say, do you?" with easy impudence. "Well, I said it to sting you—if there's any sensation left under your hide. And I'll say something else: if you'd care for somebody beside yourself for a change and give the overworked Ego a vacation, you'd get along with your pretty neighbour yonder. Oh, yes, you would; she was quite inclined to like you before you began to turn, physically, into a stall-fed prize winner. You're only thirty-seven or eight; you've a reasonable chance yet to exchange obesity for perspicacity before it smothers what intellect remains. And if you're anything except what you're beginning to resemble you'll stop sharp, behave yourself, go to see your neighbour, and"—with a shrug—"marry her. Marriage—as easy a way out of trouble as it is in."

He swung carelessly on his heel, supple, erect, graceful as always.

"But," he threw back over his shoulder, "you'd better acquire the rudiments of a figure before you go a-courting Alida Ascott." And left Portlaw sitting petrified in his wadded chair.

Malcourt strolled on, a humorously malicious smile hovering near his eyes, but his face grew serious as he glanced up at Hamil's window. He had not seen Hamil during his illness or his convalescence—had made no attempt to, evading lightly the casual suggestions of Portlaw that he and his young wife pay Hamil a visit; nor did he appear to take anything more than a politely perfunctory interest in the sick man's progress; yet Constance Palliser had often seen him pacing the lawn under Hamil's window long after midnight during those desperate hours when the life-flame scarcely flickered—those ominous moments when so many souls go out to meet the impending dawn.

But now, in the later stages of Hamil's rapid convalescence which is characteristic of a healthy recovery from that unpleasant malady, Malcourt avoided the cottage, even ceased to inquire; and Hamil had never asked to see him, although, for appearance' sake, he knew that he must do so very soon.

Wayward and Constance Palliser were visiting Mrs. Ascott at Pride's Fall; young Mrs. Malcourt had been there for a few days, but was returning to prepare for the series of house-parties arranged by Portlaw who had included Cecile Cardross and Philip Gatewood in the first relay.

As for Malcourt there was no counting on him; he was likely to remain for several days at any of the five distant gate-keepers' lodges across the mountains or to be mousing about the woods with wardens and foresters, camping where convenient; or to start for New York without explanation. All of which activity annoyed Portlaw, who missed his manager at table and at cards—missed his nimble humour, his impudence, his casual malice— missed even the paternal toleration which this younger man bestowed upon him—a sort of half-tolerant, half-contemptuous supervision.

And now that Malcourt was so often absent Portlaw was surprised to find how much he missed the veiled authority exercised—how dependent on it he had become, how secretly agreeable had been the half-mocking discipline which relieved him of any responsibility except as over-lord of the culinary régime.

Like a spoiled school-lad, badly brought up, he sometimes defied Malcourt's authority—as in the matter of the dam—enjoying his own perversity. But he always got into hot water and was glad enough to return to safety.

Even now, though his truancy had landed him in a very lively lawsuit, he was glad enough to slink back through the stinging comments to the security of authority; and his bellows of exasperation under reproof were half pretence. He expected Malcourt to get him out of it if he could not extract himself; he had no idea of defending the suit. Besides there was sufficient vanity in him to rely on a personal meeting with Mrs. Ascott. But he laughed in his sleeve at the idea of the necessity of making love to her.

And one day when Hamil was out for the third or fourth time, walking about the drives and lawns in the sunshine, and Malcourt was not in sight, Portlaw called for his riding-breeches and boots.

He had not been on a horse in years and it seemed as though only faith and a shoe-horn could get him into his riding-breeches; but with the aid of Heaven and a powerful valet he stood before his mirror arrayed at last; and presently went out across the lawn and through the grove to Malcourt's house.

Young Mrs. Malcourt in pink gingham apron and sun-bonnet was digging with a trowel in her garden when he appeared upon the landscape.

"I don't want you to tell Louis," he cautioned her with a very knowing and subtle smile, "but I'm just going to ride over to Pride's this morning and settle this lawsuit matter, and surprise him."

Shiela had straightened up, trowel in her gloved hand, and now stood looking at him in amused surprise.

"I didn't know you rode," she said. "I should think it would be very good for you."

"Well," he admitted, turning red, "I suppose I ought to ride now and then. Louis has been at me rather viciously. But you won't tell him, will you?"

"No," said Shiela.

"Because, you see, he doesn't think me capable of settling this thing; and so I'm just going to gallop over and have a little friendly chat with Mrs. Ascott—"

"Friendly?" very gravely.

"Yes," he said, alarmed; "why not?"

"Do you think Mrs. Ascott will receive you?"

"Well—now—Louis said something of that sort. And then he added that it didn't matter—but he didn't explain what I was to do when she refused to see me.... Ah—could—would you mind telling me what to do in that case, Mrs. Malcourt?"

"What *is* there to do, Mr. Portlaw, if a woman refuses to receive you?"

"Why—I don't know," he admitted vacantly. "What would *you* do?"

Young Mrs. Malcourt, frankly amused, shook her head:

"If Mrs. Ascott won't see you, she *won't!* You don't intend to carry Pride's Fall by assault, do you?"

"But Louis said—"

"Mr. Malcourt knows quite well that Mrs. Ascott won't see you."

"W-why?"

"Ask yourself. Besides, her lawyers have forbidden her."

But Portlaw's simple faith in Malcourt never wavered; he stood his ground and quoted him naïvely, adding: "You see Louis must have meant *something*. Couldn't you tell me what he meant? I'll promise to do it."

"I suppose," she answered, laughing, "that he meant me to write a note to Alida Ascott, making a personal appeal for your reception. He spoke of it; but, Mr. Portlaw, I am scarcely on such a footing with her."

Portlaw was so innocently delighted with the idea which bore Malcourt's stamp of authority, that young Mrs. Malcourt found it difficult to refuse; and a few moments later, armed with a friendly but cautious note, he climbed laboriously aboard a huge chestnut hack, sat there doubtfully while a groom made all fast and tight for heavy weather, then, with a groan, set spurs to his mount, and went pounding away through the forest, upon diplomacy intent.

Hamil, walking about the lawns in the sunshine, saw him come careering past, making heavy weather of it, and smiled in salute; Shiela on a rustic ladder, pruning-knife in hand, gazed over her garden wall until the woods swallowed rotund rider and steed. As she turned to descend, her glance fell upon Hamil who was crossing the lawn directly below. For a moment they looked at each other without sign of recognition; then scarcely aware of what she did she made him a carelessly gay salute with her pruning-knife, clinging to the ladder with the other hand in sheer fear of falling, so suddenly unsteady her limbs and body.

He went directly toward her; and she, her knees scarcely supporting her, mounted the last rung of the ladder and seated herself sidewise on the top of the wall, looking down at him, leaning on one arm.

"It is nice to see you out," she said, as he came to the foot of the sunny wall.... "Do you really feel as thin as you look?... I had a letter from your aunt to-day asking an outsider's opinion of your condition, and now I'll be able to give it.... You do look pathetically thin—but I shan't tell her that.... If you are tired standing up you may come into my garden where there are some very agreeable benches.... I would like to have you come if you care to."

She herself scarcely knew what she was saying; smile, voice, animation were forced; the havoc of his illness stared at her from his sharp cheek-bones, thin, bloodless hands, eyes still slow in turning, dull, heavy-lidded.

"I thought perhaps you would come to call," he said listlessly.

She flushed.

"You *did* come, once?"

"Yes."

"You did not come again while I was conscious, did you?"

"No."

He passed his thin hand across eyes and forehead.

She folded her arms under her breast and hung far over the shadow-dappled wall half-screened in young vine-leaves. Over her pink sun-bonnet and shoulders the hot spring sunshine fell; her face was in shadow; his, under the full glare of the unclouded sky, every ravage starkly revealed. And she could not turn her fascinated gaze or crush out the swelling tenderness that closed her throat to speech and set her eyes glimmering.

The lids closed, slowly; she leaned there without a word, living through in the space of a dozen pulse-beats, the agony and sweetness of the past; then laid her flushed cheek on her arms and opened her eyes, looking at him in silence.

But he dared not sustain her gaze and took refuge from it in a forced gaiety, comparing his reappearance to the return of Ulysses, where Dame Art, that respectable old Haus-Frau, awaited him in a rocking-chair, chastely preoccupied with her tatting, while rival architects squatted anxiously around her, urging their claims to a dead man's shoes.

She strove to smile at him and to speak coolly: "Will you come in? I have finished the vines and presently I'm going to dig. Wait a moment"—looking behind her and searching with one tentative foot for the ladder—"I will have to let you in—"

A moment later she met him at the grille and flung it wide, holding out her hand in welcome with a careless frankness not quite natural—nor was the nervously vigorous handshake, nor the laughter, light as a breeze, leaving her breathing fast and unevenly with the hue of excitement deepening on lip and cheek.

So, the handshaking safely over, and chatting together in a tone louder and more animated than usual, they walked down the moist gravel path together—the extreme width of the path apart.

"I think," she said, considering the question, with small head tipped sideways, "that you had better sit on this bench because the paint is dry and besides I can talk to you here and dig up these seedling larkspurs at the same time."

"Don't you want me to do some weeding?"

"With pleasure when you are a little stronger—"

"I'm all right now—"

He stood looking seriously at the bare flower-bed along the wall where amber shoots of peonies were feathering out into palmate grace, and older larkspurs had pushed up into fringed mounds of green foliage.

She had knelt down on the bed's edge, trowel in hand, pink sun-bonnet fallen back neglected; and with blade and gloved fingers she began transferring the irresponsible larkspur seedlings to the confines of their proper spheres, patting each frail little plant into place caressingly.

And he was thinking of her as he had last seen her—on her knees at the edge of another bed, her hair fallen unheeded as her sun-bonnet hung now, and the small hands clasping, twisting, very busy with their agony— as busy as her gloved fingers were now, restlessly in motion among the thickets of living green.

"Tell me," she said, not looking back over her shoulder, "it must be heavenly to be out of doors again."

"It *is* rather pleasant," he assented.

"Did you—they said you had dreadful visions. Did you?"

He laughed. "Some of them were absurd, Shiela; the most abominably grotesque creatures came swarming and crowding around the bed—faces without bodies—creatures that grew while I looked at them, swelling to gigantic proportions—Oh, it was a merry carnival—"

Neither spoke. Her back was toward him as she knelt there very much occupied with her straying seedlings in the cool shade of the wall.

Jonquils in heavy golden patches stretched away into sun-flecked perspective broken by the cool silver-green of iris thickets and the white star-clusters of narcissus nodding under sprays of bleeding-heart.

The air was sweet with the scent of late apple-bloom and lilac—and Hamil, brooding there on his bench in the sun, clasped his thin hands over his walking-stick and bent his head to the fragrant memories of Calypso's own perfume—the lilac-odour of China-berry in bloom, under the Southern stars.

He drew his breath sharply, raising his head—because this sort of thing would not do to begin life with again.

"How is Louis?" he asked in a pleasantly deliberate voice.

The thing had to be said sooner or later. They both knew that. It was over now, with no sign of effort, nothing in his voice or manner to betray him. Fortunately for him her face was turned away—fortunately for her, too.

There was a few moments' silence; the trowel, driven abruptly into the earth to the hilt, served as a prop for her clinched hand.

"I think—Louis—is very well," she said.

"He is remaining permanently with Mr. Portlaw?"

"I think so."

"I hope it will be agreeable for you—both."

"It is a very beautiful country." She rose to her slender, graceful height and surveyed her work: "A pretty country, a pretty house and garden," she said steadily. "After all, you know, that is the main thing in this world."

"What?"

"Why, an agreeable environment; isn't it?"

She turned smilingly, walked to the bench and seated herself.

"Your environment promises to be a little lonely at times," he ventured.

"Oh, yes. But I rather like it, when it's not over-populated. There will be a great deal for me to do in my garden—teaching young plants self-control."

"Gardens freeze up, Shiela."

"Yes, that is true."

"But you'll have good shooting—"

"I will never again draw trigger on any living thing!"

"What? The girl who—"

"No girl, now—a woman who can never again bring herself to inflict death."

"Why?"

"I know better now."

"You rather astonish me?" he said, pretending amusement.

She sat very still, thoughtful eyes roaming, then rested her chin on her hand, dropping one knee over the other to support her elbow. And he saw the sensitive mouth droop a little, and the white lids drooping too until the lashes rested on the bloom of the curved cheek. So he had seen her, often, silent, absent-minded, thoughts astray amid some blessed day-dream in that golden fable they had lived—and died in.

She said, as though to herself: "How can a woman slay?... I think those who have ever been victims of pain never desire to inflict it again on any living thing."

She looked up humbly, searching his face.

"You know it has become such a dreadful thing to me—the responsibility for pain and death.... It is horrible for humanity to usurp such a power—to dare interfere with life—to mar it, end it!... Children do not understand. I was nothing more a few months ago. To my intelligence the shallow arguments of those takers of life called sportsmen was sufficient. I supposed that because almost all the little children of the wild were doomed to die by violence, sooner or later, that the quicker death I offered was pardonable on the score of mercy." ... She shook her head. "Why death and pain exist, I do not know; He who deals them must know why."

He said, surprised at her seriousness: "Right or wrong, a matter of taste cannot be argued—"

"A matter of taste! Every fibre of me rebels at the thought of death—of inflicting it on anything. God knows how I could have done it when I had so much of happiness myself!" She swung around toward him:

"Sooner or later what remains to say between us must be said, Garry. I think the time is now—here in my garden—in the clear daylight of the young summer.... You have that last letter of my girlhood?"

"I burned it."

"I have every letter you ever wrote me. They are in my desk upstairs. The desk is not locked."

"Had you not better destroy them?"

"Why?"

"As you wish," he said, looking at the ground.

"One keeps the letters of the dead," she said; "your youth and mine"—she made a little gesture downward as though smoothing a grave—daintily.

They were very unwise, sitting there in the sunshine side by side, tremendously impressed with the catastrophe of life and with each other—still young enough to be in earnest, to take life and each other with that awesome finality which is the dread privilege of youth.

She spoke with conviction of the mockery of life, of wisdom and its sadness; he looked upon the world in all the serious disillusion of youth, and saw it strewn with the fragments of their wrecked happiness.

They were very emotional, very unhappy, very, very much in love; but the truly pathetic part of it all lay in her innocent conviction that a marriage witnessed by the world was a sanctuary within the circle of which neither she nor he had any reason to fear each other or themselves.

The thing was done; hope slain. They, the mourners, might now meet in safety to talk together over the dead—suffer together among the graves of common memories, sadly tracing, reverently marking with epitaphs appropriate the tombs which held the dead days of their youth.

Youth believes; Age is the sceptic. So they did not know that, as nature abhors a vacuum, youth cannot long tolerate the vacuity of grief. Rose vines, cut to the roots, climb the higher. No checking ever killed a passion. Just now her inexperience was driving her into platitudes.

"Dear Garry," she said gently, "it is such happiness to talk to you like this; to know that you understand."

There is a regulation forbidding prisoners to converse upon the subject of their misdemeanours, but neither he nor she seemed to be aware of it.

Moreover, she was truly convinced that no nun in cloister was as hopelessly certain of safety from world and flesh and devil as was her heart and its meditations, under the aegis of admitted wedlock.

She looked down at the ring she wore, and a faint shiver passed over her.

"You are going to Mrs. Ascott?"

"Yes, to make her a Trianon and a smirking little park. I can't quarrel with my bread and butter, but I wish people would let these woods alone."

She sat very still and thoughtful, hands clasped on her knee.

"So you are going to Mrs. Ascott," she repeated. And, still thoughtful: "I am so fond of Alida Ascott.... She is very pretty, isn't she?"

"Very," he said absently.

"Don't you think so?"—warmly.

"I never met her but once."

She was considering him, the knuckle of one forefinger resting against her chin in an almost childish attitude of thoughtful perplexity.

"How long are you to remain there, Garry?"

"Where?"—coming out of abstraction.

"There—at Mrs. Ascott's?"

"Oh, I don't know—a month, I suppose."

"Not longer?"

"I can't tell, Shiela."

Young Mrs. Malcourt fell silent, eyes on the ground, one knee loosely crossed over the other, and her small foot swinging gently above its blue shadow on the gravel.

Some details in the eternal scheme of things were troubling her already; for one, the liberty of this man to come and go at will; and the dawning perception of her own chaining.

It was curious, too, to be sitting here so idly beside him, and realise that she had belonged to him so absolutely—remembering the thousand thrilling intimacies that bound them immortally together—and now to be actually so isolated, so beyond his reach, so alone, so miserably certain of her soul's safety!... And now, for the first time, she missed the pleasures of fear—the exquisite trepidation that lay in unsafety—the blessed thrill of peril warning her to avoid his eyes, his touch, his—lips.

She glanced uneasily at him, a slow side gaze; and met his eyes.

Her heart had begun beating faster; a glow grew in her veins; she closed her eyes, sitting there surprised—not yet frightened.

Time throbbed on; rigid, motionless, she endured the pulsing silence while the blood quickened till body and limbs seemed burning; and suddenly, from heart to throat the tension tightened as though a cry, echoing within her, was being strangled.

"Perhaps you had better—go—" she managed to say.

"Why?"

She looked down at her restless fingers interlacing, too confused to be actually afraid of herself or him.

What was there to fear? What occult uneasiness was haunting them? Where might lie any peril, now? How could the battle begin again when all was quiet along the firing line—quiet with the quiet of death? Do dead memories surge up into furies? Can dead hopes burn again? Is there any resurrection for the insurgent passions of the past laid for ever under the ban of wedlock? The fear within her turned to impatience—to a proud incredulity.

And now she felt the calm reaction as though, unbidden, an ugly dream, passing, had shadowed her unawakened senses for a moment, and passed away.

As long as they lived there was nothing to be done. Endurance could cease only with death. What was there to fear? She asked herself, waiting half contemptuously for an answer. But her unknown self had now subsided into the obscurity from whence it rose. The Phantom of the Future was laid.

CHAPTER XXIII
A CAPITULATION

As Hamil left the garden Malcourt sauntered into view, halted, then came forward.

"I'm glad to see you," he said pleasantly.

"Thank you."

Neither offered to shake hands; Malcourt, lightly formal, spoke of Hamil's illness in a few words, using that excellent taste which was at his command when he chose to employ it. He expressed his pleasure in Hamil's recovery, and said that he was ready at any time to take up the unfinished details of Portlaw's business, agreeing with Hamil that there remained very little to talk over.

"The main thing, of course, is to squelch William's last hopes of any Rhine castles," continued Malcourt, laughing. "If you feel like it to-day I'll bring over the plans as you sketched them."

"In a day or two," nodded Hamil.

"Or perhaps you will lunch with m—with us, and you and I can go over the things comfortably."

But he saw by the scarcely perceptible change in Hamil's face that there were to be no such relations between them, informal or otherwise; and he went on quietly, closing his own suggestion:

"Or, if you like, we'll get Portlaw some morning after his breakfast, and end the whole matter by laying down the law to him."

"That would be perfectly agreeable to me," said Hamil. He spoke as though fatigued, and he looked it as he moved toward his house, using his walking-stick. Malcourt accompanied him to the road.

"Hamil," he said coolly, "may I suggest something?"

The other turned an expressionless face toward him: "What do you wish to suggest?"

"That, some day when you feel physically better, I'd like to go over one or two matters with you—privately—"

"What matters?"

"They concern you and myself."

"I know of no private matters which concern you and myself—or are ever likely to."

Malcourt's face darkened. "I think I warned you once that one day you would misunderstand my friendship for you."

Hamil straightened up, looking him coldly in the eye.

"Malcourt," he said, "there is no reason for the slightest pretence between us. I don't like you; I don't dislike you; I simply don't take you into consideration at all. The accident of your intrusion into a woman's life is not going to make any more difference to me than it has already made, nor can it affect my complete liberty and freedom to do and say what I choose."

"I am not sure that I understand you, Hamil."

"Well, you can certainly understand this: that my regard for—Mrs. Malcourt—does not extend to you; that it is neither modified nor hampered by the fact that you happen to exist, or that she now bears your name."

Malcourt's face had lost its colour. He began slowly:

"There is no reason, I think—"

"I don't care what you think!" said Hamil. "It is not of any consequence to me, nor will it govern me in any manner." He made a contemptuous gesture toward the garden. "Those flower-beds and gravel walks in there—I don't know whether they belong to you or to Mrs. Malcourt or to Portlaw; and I don't care. The accidental ownership of property will not prevent my entering it; but its ownership by you would prevent my accepting your personal invitation to use it or even enter it. And now, perhaps, you understand."

Malcourt, very white, nodded:

"It is so useless," he said—"all this bitterness. You don't know what you're saying.... But I suppose you can't help it.... It always has been that way; things go to smash if I try to do anything.... Well, Hamil, we'll go on in your own fashion, if we must—for a while. But"—and he laughed mirthlessly—"if it ends in a little shooting—you mustn't blame me!"

Hamil surveyed him in cold displeasure.

"I always expected you'd find your level," he observed.

"Yes, I'll find it," mused Malcourt, "as soon as I know what it ought to be. Under pressure it is difficult to ascertain such things; one's true level may be higher or lower. My father and I have often discussed this matter—and the ethics of straight shooting."

Hamil's eyes narrowed.

"If you mean that as a threat"—he began contemptuously; but Malcourt, who had suddenly assumed that curious listening attitude, raised his hand impatiently, as though silencing interruption.

And long after Hamil had turned on his heel and gone, he stood there, graceful head lowered a little and partly turned as though poetically appreciative of the soft twittering music which the bluebirds were making among the falling apple-bloom.

Then, slowly, not noticing Hamil's departure, he retraced his steps through the garden, head slightly inclined, as though to catch the murmur of some invisible companion accompanying him. Once or twice he nodded, a strange smile creeping over his face; once his lips moved as though asking a question; no sound came from them, but apparently he had his answer, for he nodded assent, halted, drew a deep breath, and looked upward.

"We can try that," he said aloud in his naturally pleasant voice; and, entering the house, went upstairs to his wife's apartments.

Shiela's maid answered his knock; a moment later, Shiela herself, gowned for the afternoon, came to the door, and her maid retired.

"Do you mind my stepping in a moment?" he asked.

She glanced back into her own bedroom, closed the door, and led the way to the small living-room at the other end of the house.

"Where's that maid of yours?" he asked.

"Sewing in my dressing-room. Shall I send her downstairs?"

"Yes; it's better."

So Shiela went away and returned shortly saying that her maid had gone; and then, with a questioning gesture to her husband, she seated herself by the open window and looked out into the sunshine, waiting for him to speak.

"Do you know," he said abruptly, "what saved Cardross, Carrick & Co. from going to the wall?"

"What?" The quick, crisp question sounded like the crack of a tiny whip.

He looked at her, languidly amused.

"You knew there was a panic?" he asked.

"Yes, of course."

"You knew that your father and Mr. Carrick were worried?"

"Yes."

"You didn't realise they were in bad shape?"

"Not—very. Were they?"

"That they needed money, and that they couldn't go out into the market and borrow it because nobody would lend any money to anybody?"

"I do not understand such details."

"Details? Ah—yes, quite so.... Then you were not aware that a run was threatened on the Shoshone Securities Company and certain affiliated banks?"

"Yes—but I did not suppose it meant anything alarming."

"And you didn't understand that your father and brother-in-law could not convert their securities into the ready cash they needed to meet their obligations—did you?"

"I do not understand details, Louis.... No."

"Or that they were desperate?"

Her face altered pitifully.

"On the edge of bankruptcy?" he went on.

"*What!*"

"Then," he said deliberately, "you don't know what helped them— what tided them over those two days—what pulled them through by the slimmest margin that ever saved the credit of anybody."

"Not—my money?"

"Yes; your money."

"Is it true, Louis?"

"Absolutely."

She leaned her head on her hand and sat gazing out of the open window. There were tears very near her eyes, but the lids closed and not one fell or even wet the thick lashes resting on her cheeks.

"I supposed it would please you to know what you have done."

The face she turned toward him was wonderful in its radiance.

She said: "I have never been as happy in all my life, I think. Thank you for telling me. I needed just—that."

He studied her for a moment, nimble wits at work. Then:

"Has your father—and the others—in their letters, said anything about it to you?"

"Yes, father has. He did not say matters had been desperate."

"I suppose he does not dare commit such a thing to paper—yet.... *You* do not burn your letters," he added blandly.

"I have no reason to."

"It might save servants' gossip."

"What gossip?"—in cold surprise.

"There's a desk full of Hamil's letters upstairs, judging from the writing on the envelopes." He added with a smile: "Although I don't pry, some servants do. And if there is anything in those letters you do not care to have discussed below stairs, you ought either to lock them up or destroy them."

Her face was burning hot; but she met his gaze with equanimity, slowly nodding serene assent to his suggestion.

"Shiela," he said pleasantly, "it looks to me as though what you have done for your family in that hour of need rather balances all accounts between you and them."

"What?"

"I say that you are square with them for what they have done in the past for you."

She shook her head. "I don't know what you mean, Louis."

He said patiently: "You had nothing to give but your fortune, and you gave it."

"Yes."

"Which settles your obligations toward them—puts them so deeply for ever in your debt that—" He hesitated, considering the chances, then, seriously persuasive:

"They are now in *your* debt, Shiela. They have sufficient proof of your unselfish affection for them to stand a temporary little shock. Why don't you administer it?"

"What shock?"—in an altered voice.

"Your divorce."

"I thought you were meaning that."

"I do mean it. You ought to have your freedom; you are ruining your own life and Hamil's, and—and—"

"Yours?"

"Let that go," he said almost savagely; "I can always get along. But I want you to have your freedom to marry that damned fool, Hamil."

The quick blood stung her face under his sudden blunt brutality.

"You think that because I returned a little money to my family, it entitles me to publicly disgrace them?"

Malcourt's patience was fast going.

"Oh, for Heaven's sake, Shiela, shed your swaddling clothes and act like something adult. Is there any reason why two people situated as we are cannot discuss sensibly some method of mitigating our misfortune? I'll do anything you say in the matter. Divorce is a good thing sometimes. This is one of the times, and I'll give you every reason for a successful suit against me—"

She rose, cheeks aflame, and in her eyes scorn ungovernable.

He rose too, exasperated.

"You won't consider it?" he asked harshly.

"No."

"Why not?"

"Because I'm not coward enough to ask others to bear the consequences of my own folly and yours!"

"You little fool," he said, "do you think your family would let you endure me for one second if they knew how you felt? Or what I am likely to do at any moment?"

She stood, without replying, plainly waiting for him to leave the room and her apartments. All her colour had fled.

"You know," he said, with an ugly glimmer in his eyes, "I need not continue this appeal to your common sense, if you haven't got any; I can force you to a choice."

"What choice?"—in leisurely contempt.

He hesitated; then, insolently: "Your choice between—honest wifehood and honest divorce."

For a moment she could not comprehend: suddenly her hands contracted and clinched as the crimson wave stained her from throat to brow. But in her eyes was terror unutterable.

"I—I beg—your pardon," he stammered. "I did not mean to frighten you—"

But at his first word she clapped both hands over her ears, staring at him in horror—backing away from him, shrinking flat against the wall.

"Confound it! I am not threatening you," he said, raising his voice; but she would not hear another word—he saw that now—and, with a shrug, he walked past her, patient once more, outwardly polite, inwardly bitterly amused, as he heard the key snap in the door behind him.

Standing in his own office on the floor below, he glanced vacantly around him. After a moment he said aloud, as though to somebody in the room: "Well, I tried it. But that is not the way."

Later, young Mrs. Malcourt, passing, saw him seated at his desk, head bent as though listening to something interesting. But there was nobody else in the office.

When at last he roused himself the afternoon sun was shining level in the west; long rosy beams struck through the woods turning the silver stems of the birches pink.

On the footbridge spanning the meadow brook he saw his wife and Hamil leaning over the hand-rail, shoulder almost touching shoulder; and he went to the window and stood intently observing them.

They seemed to be conversing very earnestly; once she threw back her pretty head and laughed unrestrainedly, and the clear sound of it floated up to him through the late sunshine; and once she shook her head emphatically, and once he saw her lay her hand on Hamil's arm—an impulsive gesture, as though to enforce her words, but it was more like a caress.

A tinge of malice altered Malcourt's smile as he watched them; the stiffening grin twitched at his cheeks.

"Now I wonder," he thought to himself, "whether it is the right way after all!... I don't think I'll threaten her again with—alternatives. There's no telling what a fool might do in a panic." Then, as though the spectacle bored him, he yawned, stretched his arms and back gracefully, turned and touched the button that summoned his servant.

"Order the horses and pack as usual, Simmons," he said with another yawn. "I'm going to New York. Isn't Mr. Portlaw here yet?"

"No, sir."

"Did you say he went away on horseback?"

"Yes, sir, this morning."

"And you don't know where?"

"No, sir. Mr. Portlaw took the South Road."

Malcourt grinned again, perfectly certain, now, of Portlaw's destination; and thinking to himself that unless his fatuous employer had been landed in a ditch somewhere, en route, he was by this time returning from Pride's Fall with considerable respect for Mrs. Ascott.

As a matter of fact, Portlaw had already started on his way back. Mrs. Ascott was not at Pride's Hall—her house—when he presented himself at the door. Her servant, evidently instructed, did not know where Mrs. Ascott and Miss Palliser had gone or when they might return.

So Portlaw betook himself heavily to the village inn, where he insulted his astonished stomach with a noonday dinner, and found the hard wooden chairs exceedingly unpleasant.

About five o'clock he got into his saddle with an unfeigned groan, and out of it again at Mrs. Ascott's door. They told him there that Mrs. Ascott was not at home.

Whether this might be the conventional manner of informing him that she declined to receive him, or whether she really was out, he had no means of knowing; so he left his cards for Mrs. Ascott and Miss Palliser, also the note which young Mrs. Malcourt had given him; clambered once more up the side of his horse, suppressing his groans until out of hearing and well on his way toward the fatal boundary.

In the late afternoon, sky and water had turned to a golden rose hue; clouds of gnats danced madly over meadow pools, calm mirrors of the sunset, save when a trout sprang quivering, a dark, slim crescent against the light, falling back with a mellow splash that set the pool rocking.

At gaze a deer looked at him from sedge, furry ears forward; stamped, winded him, and, not frightened very much, trotted into the dwarf willows, halting once or twice to look around.

As he advanced, his horse splashing through the flooded land fetlock-deep in water, green herons flapped upward, protesting harshly, circled overhead with leisurely wing-beats, and settled on some dead limb, thin, strange shapes against the deepening orange of the western heavens.

Portlaw, sitting his saddle gingerly, patronized nature askance; and he saw across the flooded meadow where the river sand had piled its smothering blanket—which phenomenon he was guiltily aware was due to him.

Everywhere were signs of the late overflow—raw new gravel channels for Painted Creek; river willows bent low where the flood had winnowed; piles of driftwood jammed here and there; a single stone pier stemming mid-stream, ancient floor and cover gone. More of his work—or the consequences of it—this desolation; from which, under his horse's feet, rose a hawk, flapping, furious, a half-drowned snake dangling from the talon-clutch.

"Ugh!" muttered Portlaw, bringing his startled horse under discipline; then forged forward across the drowned lands, sorry for his work, sorry for his obstinacy, sorrier for himself; for Portlaw, in some matters was illogically parsimonious; and it irked him dreadfully to realise how utterly indefensible were his actions and how much they promised to cost him.

"Unless," he thought cannily to himself, "I can fix it up with her—for old friendship's sake—bah!—doing the regretful sinner business—"

As the horse thrashed out of the drowned lands up into the flat plateau where acres of alders, their tops level as a trimmed hedge, stretched away in an even, green sea, a distant, rapping sound struck his ear, sharp, regular as the tree-tapping of a cock-o'-the-woods.

Indifferently convinced that the great, noisy woodpecker was the cause of the racket, he rode on toward the hard-wood ridge dominating this plateau where his guests, last season, had shot woodcock—one of the charges in the suit against him.

"The thing to do," he ruminated, "is to throw myself gracefully on her mercy. Women like to have a chance to forgive you; Louis says so, and he ought to know. What a devilishly noisy woodpecker!"

And, looking up, he drew bridle sharply.

For there, on the wood's edge, stood a familiar gray mare, and in the saddle, astride, sat Alida Ascott, busily hammering tacks into a trespass notice printed on white muslin, and attached to the trunk of a big maple-tree.

So absorbed was she in her hammering that at first she neither heard nor saw Portlaw when he finally ventured to advance; and when she did she dropped the tack hammer in her astonishment.

He dismounted, with pain, to pick it up, presented it, face wreathed in a series of appealing smiles, then, managing to scale the side of his horse again, settled himself as comfortably as possible for the impending conflict.

But Alida Ascott, in her boyish riding breeches and deep-skirted coat, merely nodded her thanks, took hold of the hammer firmly, and drove in more tacks, paying no further attention to William Van Beuren Portlaw and his heart-rending smiles.

It was very embarrassing; he sidled his horse around so that he might catch a glimpse of her profile. The view he obtained was not encouraging.

"Alida," he ventured plaintively.

"Mr. Portlaw!"—so suddenly swinging on him that he lost all countenance and blurted out:

"I—I only want to make amends and be friends."

"I expect you to make amends," she said in a significantly quiet voice, which chilled him with the menace of damages unlimited. And even in his perturbation he saw at once that it would never do to have a backwoods jury look upon the fascinating countenance of this young plaintiff.

"Alida," he said sorrowfully, "I am beginning to see things in a clearer light."

"I think that light will grow very much clearer, Mr. Portlaw."

He repressed a shudder, and tried to look reproachful, but she seemed to be very hard-hearted, for she turned once more to her hammering.

"Alida!"

"What?"—continuing to drive tacks.

"After all these years of friendship it—it is perfectly painful for me to contemplate a possible lawsuit—"

"It will be more painful to contemplate an actual one, Mr. Portlaw."

"Alida, do you really mean that you—my neighbour and friend—are going to press this unnatural complaint?"

"I certainly do."

Portlaw shook his head violently, and passed his gloved hand over his eyes as though to rouse himself from a distressing dream; all of which expressive pantomime was lost on Mrs. Ascott, who was busy driving tacks.

"I simply cannot credit my senses," he said mournfully.

"You ought to try; it will be still more difficult later," she observed, backing her horse so that she might inspect her handiwork from the proper point of view.

Portlaw looked askance at the sign. It warned people not to shoot, fish, cut trees, dam streams, or build fires under penalty of the law; and was signed, "Alida Ascott."

"You didn't have any up before, did you?" he asked innocently.

"By advice of counsel I think I had better not reply, Mr. Portlaw. But I believe that point will be brought out by my lawyers—unless"—with a brilliant smile—"your own counsel sees fit to discuss it."

Portlaw was convinced that his hair was stirring under his cap. He was horribly afraid of the law.

"See here, Alida," he said, assuming the bluff rough-diamond front which the alarm in his eyes made foolish, "I want to settle this little difference and be friends with you again. I was wrong; I admit it.... Of course I might very easily defend such a suit—"

"But, of course"—serenely undeceived—"as you admit you are in the wrong you will scarcely venture to defend such a suit. *Your* lawyers ought to forbid *you* to talk about this case, particularly"—with a demure smile—"to the plaintiff."

"Alida," he said, "I am determined to remain your friend. You may do what you will, say what you wish, yes, even use my own words against me, but"—and virtue fairly exuded from every perspiring pore—"I will not retaliate!"

"I'm afraid you can't, William," she said softly.

"Won't you—forgive?" he asked in a melting voice; but his eyes were round with apprehension.

"There are some things that no woman can overlook," she said.

"I'll send my men down to fix that bridge—"

"Bridges can be mended; I was not speaking of the bridge."

"You mean those sheep—"

"No, Mr. Portlaw."

"Well, there's a lot—I mean that some little sand has been washed over your meadow—"

"Good night," she said, turning her horse's head.

"Isn't it the sand, Alida?" he pleaded. "You surely will forgive that timber-cutting—and the shooting of a few migratory birds—"

"Good night," touching her gray mare forward to where he was awkwardly blocking the wood-path.... "Do you mind moving a trifle, Mr. Portlaw?"

"About—ah—the—down there, you know, at Palm Beach," he stammered, "at that accursed lawn-party—"

"Yes?" She smiled but her eyes harboured lightning.

"It was so hot in Florida—you know how infernally hot it was, don't you, Alida?" he asked beseechingly. "I scarcely dared leave the Beach Club."

"Well?"

"I—I thought I'd just m-m-mention it. That's why I didn't call on you—I was afraid of sunstroke—"

"What!" she exclaimed, astonished at his stuttering audacity.

He knew he was absurd, but it was all he could think of. She gave him time enough to realise the pitiable spectacle he was making of himself, sitting her horse motionless, pretty eyes bent on his—an almost faultless though slight figure, smooth as a girl's yet faintly instinct with that charm of ripened adolescence just short of maturity.

And, slowly, under her clear gaze, a confused comprehension began to stir in him—at first only a sort of chagrin, then something more—a consciousness of his own heaviness of intellect and grossness of figure—the fatness of mind and body which had developed so rapidly within the last two years.

There she sat, as slim and pretty and fresh as ever; and only two years ago he had been mentally and physically active enough to find vigorous amusement in her company. Malcourt's stinging words concerning his bodily unloveliness and self-centred inertia came into his mind; and a slow blush deepened the colour in his heavy face.

What vanity he had reckoned on had deserted him along with any hope of compromising a case only too palpably against him. And yet, through the rudiments of better feeling awakening within him, the instinct of thrift still coloured his ideas a little.

"I'm dead wrong, Alida. We might just as well save fees and costs and go over the damages together.... I'll pay them. I ought to, anyway. I suppose I don't usually do what I ought. Malcourt says I don't—said so very severely—very mortifyingly the other day. So—if you'll get him or your own men to decide on the amount—"

"Do you think the amount matters?"

"Oh, of course it's principle; very proper of you to stand on your dignity—"

"I am not standing on it now; I am listening to your utter misapprehension of me and my motives.... I don't care for any—damages."

"It is perfectly proper for you to claim them, if," he added cautiously, "they are within reason—"

"Mr. Portlaw!"

"What?" he asked, alarmed.

"I would not touch a penny! I meant to give it to the schools, here—whatever I recovered.... Your misunderstanding of me is abominable!"

He hung his head, heavy-witted, confused as a stupid schoolboy, feeling, helplessly, his clumsiness of mind and body.

Something of this may have been perceptible to her—may have softened her ideas concerning him—ideas which had accumulated bitterness during the year of his misbehaviour and selfish neglect. Her instinct divined in his apparently sullen attitude the slow intelligence and mental perturbation of a wilful, selfish boy made stupid through idleness and self-indulgence. Even what had been clean-cut, attractive, in his face and figure was being marred and coarsened by his slothful habits to an extent that secretly dismayed her; for she had always thought him very handsome; and, with that natural perversity of selection, finding in him a perfect foil to her own character, had been seriously inclined to like him.

Attractions begin in that way, sometimes, where the gentler is the stronger, the frailer, the dominant character; and the root is in the feminine instinct to care for, develop, and make the most of what palpably needs a protectorate.

Without comprehending her own instinct, Mrs. Ascott had found the preliminary moulding of Portlaw an agreeable diversion; had rather taken for granted that she was doing him good; and was correspondingly annoyed when he parted his moorings and started drifting aimlessly as a derelict scow awash, floundering seaward without further notice of the trim little tug standing by and amiably ready to act as convoy.

Now, sitting her saddle in silence she surveyed him, striving to understand him—his recent indifference, his deterioration, the present figure he was cutting. And it seemed to her a trifle sad that he had no one to tell him a few wholesome truths.

"Mr. Portlaw," she said, "do you know that you have been exceedingly rude to me?"

"Yes, I—do know it."

"Why?" she asked simply.

"I don't know."

"Didn't you care for our friendship? Didn't it amuse and interest you? How could you have done the things you did—in the way you did?... If you had asked my permission to build a dozen dams I'd have given it. Didn't you know it? But my self-respect protested when you so cynically ignored me—"

"I'm a beast all right," he muttered.

She gazed at him, softened, even faintly amused at his repentant bad-boy attitude.

"Do you want me to forgive you, Mr. Portlaw?"

"Yes—but you oughtn't."

"That is quite true.... Turn your horse and ride back with me. I'm going to find out exactly how repentant you really are.... If you pass a decent examination you may dine with Miss Palliser, Mr. Wayward, and me. It's too late anyway to return through the forest.... I'll send you over in the motor."

And as they wheeled and walked their horses forward through the dusk, she said impulsively:

"We have four for Bridge if you like."

"Alida," he said sincerely, "you *are* a corker."

She looked up demurely. What she could see to interest her in this lump of a man Heaven alone knew, but a hint of the old half-patient, half-amused liking for him and his slow wits began to flicker once more. De gustibus—alas!

CHAPTER XXIV
THE SCHOOL OF THE RECRUIT

When Portlaw arrived home late that evening there existed within his somewhat ordinary intellect a sense of triumph. The weak usually experience it at the beginning and through every step of their own subjugation.

Malcourt, having decided to take an express which stopped on signal at six in the morning, was reading as usual before the empty fireplace; and at the first glance he suspected what had begun to happen to Portlaw.

The latter bustled about the room with an air of more or less importance, sorted his letters, fussed with a newspaper; and every now and then Malcourt, glancing up, caught Portlaw's eyes peeping triumphantly around corners at him.

"You've been riding?" he said, much amused. "Are you stiff?"

"A trifle," replied the other carelessly. "I must keep it up. Really, you know, I've rather neglected the horses lately."

"Rather. So you're taking up riding again?"

Portlaw nodded: "I've come to the conclusion that I need exercise."

Malcourt, who had been urging him for years to exercise, nodded approval as though the suggestion were a brand-new one.

"Yes," said Portlaw, "I shall ride, I think, every day. I intend to do a good bit of tramping, too. It's excellent for the liver, Louis."

At this piece of inspired information Malcourt assumed an expression of deepest interest, but hoped Portlaw might not overdo it.

"I'm going to diet, too," observed Portlaw, watching the effect of this astounding statement on his superintendent. "My theory is that we all eat too much."

"Don't do anything Spartan," said Malcourt warningly; "a man at your time of life—"

"My—what! Confound it, Louis, I'm well this side of forty!"

"Yes, perhaps; but when a man reaches your age there is not much left for him but the happiness of overeating—"

"What d'y' mean?"

"Nothing; only as he's out of the race with younger men as far as a pretty woman is concerned—"

"Who's out!" demanded Portlaw, red in the face. "What sort of men do you suppose interest women? Broilers? I always thought your knowledge of women was superficial; now I know it. And you don't know everything about everything else, either—about summonses and lawsuits, for example." And he cast an exultant look at his superintendent.

But Malcourt let him tell the news in his own way; and he did, imparting it in bits with naive enjoyment, apparently utterly unconscious that he was doing exactly what his superintendent had told him to do.

"You *are* a diplomat, aren't you?" said Malcourt with a weary smile.

"A little, a little," admitted Portlaw modestly. "I merely mentioned these things—" He waved his hand to check any possible eulogy of himself from Malcourt. "I'll merely say this: that when I make up my mind to settle anything—" He waved his hand again, condescendingly.

"That man," thought Malcourt, "will be done for in a year. Any woman could have had him; the deuce of it was to find one who'd take him. I think she's found."

And looking up blandly:

"Porty, old fellow, you're really rather past the marrying age—"

"I'll do what I please!" shouted Portlaw, exasperated.

Malcourt had two ways of making Portlaw do a thing; one was to tell him not to, the other the reverse. He always ended by doing it anyway; but the quicker result was obtained by the first method.

So Malcourt went to New York next morning convinced that Portlaw's bachelor days were numbered; aware, also, that as soon as Mrs. Ascott took the helm his own tenure of office would promptly expire. He wished it to expire, easily, agreeably, naturally; and that is why he had chosen to shove Portlaw in the general direction of the hymeneal altar.

He did not care very much for Portlaw—scarcely enough to avoid hurting his feelings by abandoning him. But now he had arranged it so that to all appearances the abandoning would be done by Portlaw, inspired by the stronger mind of Mrs. Ascott. It had been easy and rather amusing to arrange; it saved wordy and endless disputes with Portlaw; it would give him a longed-for release from an occupation he had come to hate.

Malcourt was tired. He wanted a year of freedom from dependence, surcease of responsibility—a year to roam where he wished, foregather with whom he pleased, haunt the places congenial to him, come and go unhampered; a year of it—only one year. What remained for him to do after the year had expired he thought he understood; yes, he was practically certain—had always been.

But first must come that wonderful year he had planned—or, if he tired of the pleasure sooner, then, as the caprice stirred him, he would do what he had planned to do ever since his father died. The details only remained to be settled.

For Malcourt, with all the contradictions in his character, all his cynicism, effrontery, ruthlessness, preferred to do things in a manner calculated to spare the prejudices of others; and if there was a way to accomplish a thing without hurting people, he usually took the trouble to do it in that way. If not, he did it anyway.

And now, at last, he saw before him the beginning of that curious year for which he had so long waited; and, concerning the closing details of which, he had pondered so often with his dark, handsome head lowered and slightly turned, listening, always listening.

But nothing of this had he spoken of to his wife. It was not necessary. He had a year in which to live in a certain manner and do a certain thing; and it was going to amuse him to do it in a way which would harm nobody.

The year promised to be an interesting one, to judge from all signs. For one item his sister, Lady Tressilvain, was impending from Paris—also his brother-in-law—complicating the humour of the visitation. Malcourt's marriage to an heiress was the perfectly obvious incentive of the visit. And when they wrote that they were coming to New York, it amused Malcourt exceedingly to invite them to Luckless Lake. But he said nothing about it to Portlaw or his wife.

Then, for another thing, the regeneration and development, ethically and artistically, of Dolly Wilming amused him. He wanted to be near enough to watch it—without, however, any real faith in its continuation.

And, also, there was Miss Suydam. Her development would not be quite as agreeable to witness; process of disillusioning her, little by little, until he had undermined himself sufficiently to make the final break with her very easy—for her. Of course it interested him; all intrigue did where skill was required with women.

And, last of all, yet of supreme importance, he desired leisure, undisturbed, to study his own cumulative development, to humorously thwart it, or misunderstand it, or slyly aid it now and then—always aware of and attentive to that extraneous something which held him so motionless, at moments, listening attentively as though to a command.

For, from that morning four years ago when, crushed with fatigue, he strove to keep his vigil beside his father who, toward daybreak, had been feigning sleep—from that dreadful dawn when, waking with the crash of the shot in his ears, his blinded gaze beheld the passing of a soul—he understood that he was no longer his own master.

Not that the occult triad, Chance, Fate, and Destiny ruled; they only modified his orbit. But from the centre of things Something that ruled them was pulling him toward it, slowly, steadily, inexorably drawing him nearer, lessening the circumference of his path, attenuating it, circumscribing, limiting, controlling. And long since he had learned to name this thing, undismayed—this one thing remaining in the world in which his father's son might take a sporting interest.

He had been in New York two weeks, enjoying existence in his own fashion, untroubled by any demands, questions, or scruples concerning responsibility, when a passionate letter from Portlaw disturbed the placid interlude:

> "Confound it, Louis, haven't you the common decency to come back when you know I've had a bunch of people here to be entertained?
>
> "Nobody's heard a peep from you. What on earth do you mean by this?
>
> "Miss Palliser, Mrs. Ascott, Miss Cardross are here, also Wayward, and Gray Cardross—which with you and Mrs. Malcourt and myself solves the Bridge proposition—or would have solved it. But without warning, yesterday, your sister and brother-in-law arrived, bag and baggage, and Mrs. Malcourt has given them the west wing of your house. I believe she was as astonished as I, but she will not admit it.
>
> "I don't know whether this is some sorry jest of yours—not that Lady Tressilvain and her noble spouse are unwelcome—but for Heaven's sake consider Wayward's feelings—cooped up in camp with his ex-wife! It wasn't a very funny thing to do, Louis; but now that it's done you can come back and take care of the mess you've made.

"As for Mrs. Malcourt, she is not merely a trump, she is a hundred aces and a grand slam in a redoubled Without!—if that's possible. But Mrs. Ascott is my pillar of support in what might easily become a fool of a situation.

"And you, you amateur idiot!—are down there in town, humorously awaiting the shriek of anguish from me. Well, you've heard me. But it's not a senseless shriek; it's a dignified protest. I tell you I've learned to depend on myself, recently—at Mrs. Ascott's suggestion. And I'm doing it now by wiring Virginia Suydam to come and fill in the third table.

"Now I want you to come back at once. If you don't I'm going to have a serious talk with you, Louis. I've taken Mrs. Ascott into my confidence more or less and she agrees with me that I ought to lay down a strong, rigid policy and that it is your duty to execute it. In fact she also took me into her confidence and gave me, at my request, a very clear idea of how she would run this place; and to my surprise and gratification I find that her ideas of discipline, taste, and economy are exactly mine, although I thought of them first and perhaps have influenced her in this matter as I have in others. That is, of course, natural, she being a woman.

"I think I ought to be frank with you, Louis. It isn't good form for you to leave Mrs. Malcourt the way you do every week or two and disappear in New York and give no explanation. You haven't been married long enough to do that. It isn't square to me, either.

"And while I'm about it I want to add that, at Mrs. Ascott's suggestion—which really is my own idea—I have decided not to build all those Rhine castles, which useless notion, if I am not mistaken, originated with you. I don't want to disfigure my beautiful wilderness. Mrs. Ascott and I had a very plain talk with Hamil and we forced him to agree with us that the less he did to improve my place the better for the place. He seemed to take it good-humouredly. He left yesterday to look over Mrs. Ascott's place and plan for her a formal garden and Trianon at Pride's Hall. So he being out I wired also to Virginia and to Philip Gatewood, which will make it right—four at a table. Your brother-in-law plays a stiff game and your sister is a wonder!—five grand slams last night! But I played like a dub—I'd been riding and walking and canoeing all day with Mrs. Ascott and I was terribly sleepy.

"So come on up, Louis. I'll forgive you—but don't mind if I growl at you before Mrs. Ascott as she thinks I ought to discipline you. And, confound it, I ought to, and I will, too, if you don't look out. But I'll be devilish glad to see you.

"Yours,

"W. VAN BEUREN PORTLAW."

Malcourt, in his arm-chair by the open window, lay back full length, every fibre of him vibrating with laughter.

Dolly Wilming at the piano continued running over the pretty firework melodies of last season's metropolitan success—a success built entirely on a Viennese waltz, the air of which might have been taken from almost any popular Yankee hymn-book.

He folded Portlaw's letter and pocketed it; and lay for a while under the open window, enjoying his own noiseless mirth, gaily accompanied by Dolly Winning's fresh, clear singing or her capricious improvising.

Begonias bloomed in a riotous row on the sill, nodding gently in the river-wind which also fluttered the flags and sails on yacht, schooner, and sloop under the wall of the Palisades.

That day the North River was more green than blue—like the eyes of a girl he knew; summer, crowned and trimmed with green, brooded on the long rock rampart across the stream. Turquoise patches of sky and big clouds, leafy parapets, ships passing to the sea; and in mid-stream an anchored island of steel painted white and buff, bristling with long thin guns, the flower-like flag rippling astern; another battle-ship farther north; another, another; and farther still the white tomb—unlovely mansion of the dead—on outpost duty above the river, guarding with the warning of its dead glories the unlovely mansions of the living ranged along the most noble terrace in the world.

And everywhere to north, south, and east, the endless waste of city, stark, clean-cut, naked alike of tree and of art, unsoftened even by the haze of its own exudations—everywhere the window-riddled blocks of oblongs and cubes gridironed with steel rails—New York in all the painted squalor of its Pueblo splendour.

"You say you are doing well in everything except French and Italian?"

Dolly, still humming to her own accompaniment, looked over her shoulder and nodded.

"Well, how the dickens are you ever going to sing at either Opera or on the road or anywhere if you don't learn French and Italian?"

"I'm trying, Louis."

"Go ahead; let's hear something, then."

And she sang very intelligently and in excellent taste:

"Pendant que, plein d'amour, j'expire à votre porte,
Vous dormez d'un paisible sommeil—"

and turned questioningly to him.

"That's all right; try another."

So, serenely obedient, she sang:

"Chantons Margot, nos amours,
Margot leste et bien tournée—"

"Well, I don't see anything the matter with your French," he muttered.

The girl coloured with pleasure, resting pensively above the key-board; but he had no further requests to make and presently she swung around on the piano-stool, looking at him.

"You sing all right; you are doing your part—as far as I can discover."

"There is nothing for you to discover that I have not told you," she said gravely. In her manner there was a subdued dignity which he had noticed recently—something of the self-confidence of the very young and unspoiled—which, considering all things, he could not exactly account for.

"Does that doddering old dancing-master of yours behave himself?"

"Yes—since you spoke to him. Mr. Bulder came to the school again."

"What did you say to him?"

"I told him that you wouldn't let me sing in 'The Inca.'"

"And what did Bulder say?"

"He was persistent but perfectly respectful; asked if he might confer with you. He wrote to you I think, didn't he?"

Malcourt nodded and lighted a cigarette.

"Dolly," he said, "do you want to sing _Chaské_ in 'The Inca' next winter?"

"Yes, I do—if you think it is all right." She added in a low voice: "I want to do what will please you, Louis."

"I don't know whether it's the best thing to do, but—you may have to." He laid his cigarette in a saucer, watched the smoke curling ceilingward, and said as though to himself:

"I should like to be certain that you can support yourself—within a reasonable time from now—say a year. That is all, Dolly."

"I can do it now if you wish it—" The expression of his face checked her.

"I don't mean a variety career devoted to 'mother' songs," he said with a sneer. "There's a middle course between diamonds and 'sinkers.' You'll get there if you don't kick over the traces.... Have you made any more friends?"

"Yes."

"Are they respectable?"

"Yes," she said, colouring.

"Has anybody been impertinent?"

"Mr. Williams."

"I'll attend to him—the little squirt!... Who are your new friends?"

"There's a perfectly sweet girl in the French class, Marguerite Barret. I think she likes me.... Louis, I don't believe you understand how very happy I am beginning to be—"

"Do people come here?"

"Yes, on Sunday afternoons; I know nearly a dozen nice girls now, and those men I told you about—Mr. Snyder, Mr. Jim Anthony and his brother the artist, and Mr. Cass and Mr. Renwick."

"You can cut out Renwick," he said briefly.

She seemed surprised. "He has always been perfectly nice to me, Louis—"

"Cut him out, Dolly. I know the breed."

"Of course, if you wish."

He looked at her, convinced in spite of himself. "Always ask me about people. If I don't know I can find out."

"I always do," she said.

"Yes, I believe you do.... You're all right, Dolly—so far.... There, don't look at me in that distressed-dove fashion; I *know* you are all right and mean to be for your own sake—"

"For yours also," she said.

"Oh—that's all right, too—story-book fidelity; my preserver ever!— What?—Sure—and a slow curtain.... There, there, Dolly—where's your sense of humour! Good Lord, what's changing you into a bread-and-butter

The Firing Line | 301

boarding-school sentimentalist!—to feel hurt at nothing! Hello! look at that kitten of yours climbing your silk curtains! Spank the rascal!"

But the girl caught up the kitten and tucked it up under her chin, smiling across at Malcourt, who had picked up his hat, gloves, and stick.

"Will you come to-morrow?" she asked.

"I'm going away for a while."

Her face fell; she rose, placed the kitten on the lounge, and walked up to him, both hands clasped loosely behind her back, wistfully acquiescent.

"It's going to be lonely again for me," she said.

"Nonsense! You've just read me your visiting list—"

"I had rather have you here than anybody."

"Dolly, you'll get over that absurd sense of obligatory regard for me—"

"I had *rather* have you, Louis."

"I know. That's very sweet of you—and very proper.... You are all right.... I'll be back in a week or ten days, and," smilingly, "mind you have your report ready! If you've been a good girl we'll talk over 'The Inca' again and—perhaps—we'll have Mr. Bulder up to luncheon.... Good-bye."

She gave him her hand, looking up into his face.

"Smile!" he insisted.

She smiled.

So he went away, rather satiated with the pleasures of self-denial; but the lightly latent mockery soon broke out again in a smile as he reached the street.

"What a mess!" he grinned to himself. "The Tressilvains at Portlaw's! And Wayward! and Shiela and Virginia and that awful Louis Malcourt! It only wants Hamil to make the jolliest little hell of it. O my, O my, what an amusing mess!"

However, he knew what Portlaw didn't know, that Virginia would never accept that invitation, and that neither Wayward nor Constance Palliser would remain one day under the roof that harboured the sister of Louis Malcourt.

CHAPTER XXV
A CONFERENCE

When Malcourt arrived at Luckless Lake Sunday evening he found Portlaw hunched up in an arm-chair, all alone in the living-room, although the hour was still early.

"Where's your very agreeable house-party?" he inquired, looking about the empty room and hall with an air of troubled surprise.

"Gone to bed," replied Portlaw irritably,—"what's left of 'em." And he continued reading "The Pink 'Un."

"Really!" said Malcourt in polite concern.

"Yes, really!" snapped Portlaw. "Mrs. Ascott went to Pride's and took Wayward and Constance Palliser; that was Friday. And Gray and Cecile joined them yesterday. It's been a horrible house-party; nobody had any use for anybody else and it has rained every day and—and—to be plain with you, Louis, nobody is enchanted with your relatives and that's the unpleasant truth!"

"I don't blame anybody," returned Malcourt sincerely, removing his driving-gloves and shaking off his wet box-coat. "Why, I can scarcely stand them myself, William. Where are they?"

"In the west wing of your house—preparing to remain indefinitely."

"Dear, dear!" exclaimed Malcourt. "What on earth shall we do?" And he peered sideways at Portlaw with his tongue in his cheek.

"Do? I don't know. Why the devil did you suggest that they stop at your house?"

"Because, William, curious as it may seem, I had a sort of weak-minded curiosity to see my sister once more." He walked over to the table, took a cigarette and lighted it, then stood regarding the burning match in his fingers. "She's the last of the family; I'll probably never see her again—"

"She appears to be in excellent health," remarked Portlaw viciously.

"So am I; but—" He shrugged and tossed the embers of the match onto the hearth.

"But what?"

"Well, I'm going to take a vacation pretty soon—a sort of voyage, and a devilish long one, William. That's why I wanted to see her again."

"You mean to tell me you are going away?" demanded the other indignantly.

Malcourt laughed. "Oh, yes. I planned it long ago—one morning toward daybreak years ago.... A—a relative of mine started on the same voyage rather unexpectedly.... I've heard very often from him since; I'm curious to try it, too—when he makes up his mind to invite me—"

"When are you starting?" interrupted Portlaw, disgusted.

"Oh, not for a while, I think. I won't embarrass you; I'll leave everything in ship-shape—"

"*Where* are you going?—dammit!"

Malcourt looked at him humorously, head on one side. "I am not perfectly sure, dear friend. I hate to know all about a thing before I do it. Otherwise there's no sporting interest in it."

"You mean to tell me that you're going off a-gipsying without any definite plans?"

"Gipsying?" he laughed. "Well, that may perhaps describe it. I don't know; I have no plans. That's the charm of it. When one grows tired, that is the restful part of it—to simply start, having no plans; just to leave, and drift away haphazard. One is always bound to arrive somewhere, William."

He had been pacing backward and forward, the burning cigarette balanced between his fingers, turning his handsome head from time to time to answer Portlaw's ill-tempered questions. Now he halted, dark eyes roving about the room. They fell and lingered on a card-table where some empty glasses decorated the green baize top.

"Bridge?" he queried.

"Unfortunately," growled Portlaw.

"Who?"

"Mrs. Malcourt and I versus your—ah—talented family."

"Mrs. Malcourt doesn't gamble."

"Tressilvain and I did."

"Were you badly stung, dear friend?"

Portlaw muttered.

Malcourt lifted his expressive eyebrows.

"Why didn't you try my talented relative again to-night?"

"Mrs. Malcourt had enough," said Portlaw briefly; then mumbled something injuriously unintelligible.

"I think I'll go over to the house and see if my gifted brother-in-law has retired," said Malcourt, adding carelessly, "I suppose Mrs. Malcourt is asleep."

"It wouldn't surprise me," replied Portlaw. And Malcourt was free to interpret the remark as he chose.

He went away thoughtfully, crossing the lawn in the rainy darkness, and came to the garden where his own dogs barked at him—a small thing to depress a man, but it did; and it was safer for the dogs, perhaps, that they sniffed recognition before they came too near with their growls and barking. But he opened the gate, disdaining to speak to them, and when they knew him, it was a pack of very humble, wet, and penitent hounds that came wagging up alongside. He let them wag unnoticed.

Lights burned in his house, one in Shiela's apartments, several in the west wing where the Tressilvains were housed. A servant, locking up for the night, came across the dripping veranda to admit him; and he went upstairs and knocked at his wife's door.

Shiela's maid opened, hesitated; and a moment later Shiela appeared, fully dressed, a book in her hand. It was one of Hamil's architectural volumes.

"Well, Shiela," he said lightly; "I got in to-night and rather expected to see somebody; but nobody waited up to see me! I'm rather wet—it's raining—so I won't trouble you. I only wanted to say good night."

The quick displeasure in her face died out. She dismissed the maid, and came slowly forward. Beneath the light her face looked much thinner; he noticed dark shadows under the eyes; the eyes themselves seemed tired and expressionless.

"Aren't you well?" he asked bluntly.

"Perfectly.... Was it you the dogs were so noisy about just now?"

"Yes; it seems that even my own dogs resent my return. Well—good night. I'm glad you're all right."

Something in his voice, more than in the words, arrested her listless attention.

"Will you come in, Louis?"

"I'm afraid I'm keeping you awake. Besides I'm wet—"

"Come in and tell me where you've been—if you care to. Would you like some tea—or something?"

He shook his head, but followed her into the small receiving-room. There he declined an offered chair.

"I've been in New York.... No, I did not see your family.... As for what I've been doing—"

Her lifted eyes betrayed no curiosity; a growing sense of depression crept over him.

"Oh, well," he said, "it doesn't matter." And turned toward the door.

She looked into the empty fireplace with a sigh; then, gently, "I don't mean to make it any drearier for you than I can help."

He considered her a moment.

"Are you really well, Shiela?"

"Why, yes; only a little tired. I do not sleep well."

He nodded toward the west wing of the house.

"Do *they* bother you?"

She did not answer.

He said: "Thank you for putting them up. We'll get rid of them if they annoy you."

"They are quite welcome."

"That's very decent of you, Shiela. I dare say you have not found them congenial."

"We have nothing in common. I think they consider me a fool."

"Why?" He looked up, keenly humourous.

"Because I don't understand their inquiries. Besides, I don't gamble—"

"What kind of inquiries do they make?"

"Personal ones," she said quietly.

He laughed. "They're probably more offensively impertinent than the Chinese—that sort of Briton. I think I'll step into the west wing and greet my relations. I won't impose them on you for very long. Do you know when they are going?"

"I think they have made plans to remain here for a while."

"Really?" he sneered. "Well, leave that to me, Shiela."

So he crossed into the western wing and found the Tressilvains tête-à-tête over a card-table, deeply interested in something that resembled legerdemain; and he stood at the door and watched them with a smile that was not agreeable.

"Well, Helen!" he said at last; and Lady Tressilvain started, and her husband rose to the full height of his five feet nothing, dropping the pack which he had been so nimbly manipulating for his wife's amusement.

"Where the devil did you come from?" blurted his lordship; but his wife made a creditable appearance in her rôle of surprised sisterly affection; and when the two men had gone through the form of family greeting they all sat down for the conventional family confab.

Tressilvain said little but drank a great deal of whisky—his long, white, bony fingers were always spread around his glass—unusually long fingers for such a short man, and out of all proportion to the scant five-foot frame, topped with a little pointed head, in which the eyes were set exactly as glass eyes are screwed into the mask of a fox.

"Bertie and I have been practising leads from trick hands," observed Lady Tressilvain, removing the ice from her glass and filling it from a soda bottle which Malcourt uncorked for her.

"Well, Herby," said Malcourt genially, "I suppose you and Helen play a game well worth—ah—watching."

Tressilvain looked dully annoyed, although there was nothing in his brother-in-law's remark to ruffle anybody, except that his lordship did not like to be called Herby. He sat silent, caressing his glass; and presently his little black eyes stole around in Malcourt's direction, and remained there, waveringly, while brother and sister discussed the former's marriage, the situation at Luckless Lake, and future prospects.

That is to say, Lady Tressilvain did the discussing; Malcourt, bland, amiable, remained uncommunicatively polite, parrying everything so innocently that his sister, deceived, became plainer in her questions concerning the fortune he was supposed to have married, and more persistent in her suggestions of a winter in New York—a delightful and prolonged family reunion, in which the Tressilvains were to figure as distinguished guests and virtual pensioners of everybody connected with his wife's family.

"Do you think," drawled Malcourt, intercepting a furtive glance between his sister and brother-in-law, to that gentleman's slight confusion, "do you think it might prove interesting to you and Herby? Americans are so happy to have your countrymen to entertain—particularly when their credentials are as unquestionable as Herby's and yours."

For a full minute, in strained silence, the concentrated gaze of the Tressilvains was focused upon the guileless countenance of Malcourt; and discovered nothing except a fatuous cordiality.

Lady Tressilvain drew a deep, noiseless breath and glanced at her husband.

"I don't understand, Louis, exactly what settlement—what sort of arrangement you made when you married this—very interesting young girl—"

"Oh, I didn't have anything to endow her with," said Malcourt, so amiably stupid that his sister bit her lip.

Tressilvain essayed a jest.

"Rather good, that!" he said with his short, barking laugh; "but I da'say the glove was on the other hand, eh, Louis?"

"What?"

"Why the—ah—the lady did the endowing and all that, don't you see?"

"See what?" asked Malcourt so pleasantly that his sister shot a look at her husband which checked him.

Malcourt was now on maliciously humourous terms with himself; he began to speak impulsively, affectionately, with all the appearance of a garrulous younger brother impatient to unbosom himself to his family; and he talked and talked, confidingly, guilelessly, voluminously, yet managed to say absolutely nothing. And, strain their ears as they might, the Tressilvains in their perplexity and increasing impatience could make out nothing of all this voluntary information—understand nothing—pick out not one single fact to satisfy their desperately hungry curiosity.

There was no use interrupting him with questions; he answered them with others; he whispered ambiguities in a manner most portentous; hinted at bewildering paradoxes with an air; nodded mysterious nothings, and finally left them gaping at him, exasperated, unable to make any sense out of what most astonishingly resembled a candid revelation of the hopes, fears, ambitions, and worldly circumstances of Louis Malcourt.

"Good-night," he said, lingering at the door to look upon and enjoy the fruit of his perversity and malice. "When I start on that journey I mentioned to you I'll leave something for you and Herby—merely to show you how much I think of my own people—a little gift—a trifle! No—no!"—lifting his hand with smiling depreciation as Tressilvain began to thank him. "One must look out for one's own family. It's natural—only natural to make some provision. Good-night, Helen! Good-night, Herby. Portlaw and I will take you on at Bridge if it rains to-morrow. It will be a privilege for us to—ah—watch your game—closely. Good-night!"

And closed the door.

"What the devil does he mean?" demanded Tressilvain, peering sideways at his wife.

"I don't exactly know," she said thoughtfully, sorting the cards. She added: "If we play to-morrow you stick to signals; do you understand? And keep your ring and your fingers off the cards until I can make up my mind about my brother. You're a fool to drink American whisky the way you did yesterday. Mr. Portlaw noticed the roughness on the aces; you pricked them too deep. You'd better keep your wits about you, I can tell you. I'm a Yankee myself."

"Right—O! But I say, Helen, I'm damned if I make out that brother of yours. Doesn't he live in the same house as his wife?"

Lady Tressilvain sat listening to the uproar from the dogs as Malcourt left the garden. But this time the outbreak was only a noisy welcome; and Malcourt, on excellent terms with himself, patted every sleek, wet head thrust up for caresses and walked gaily on through the driving rain.

The rain continued the following day. Piloted by Malcourt, the Tressilvains, thickly shod and water-proofed, tramped about with rod and creel and returned for luncheon where their blunt criticisms on the fishing aroused Portlaw's implacable resentment. For they sneered at the trout, calling them "char," patronised the rather scanty pheasantry, commented on the kennels, stables, and gardens in a manner that brought the red into Portlaw's face and left him silent while luncheon lasted.

After luncheon Tressilvain tried the billiards, but found the game inferior to the English game. So he burrowed into a box of cigars, established himself before the fire with all the newspapers, deploring the fact that the papers were not worth reading.

Lady Tressilvain cornered Shiela and badgered her and stared at her until she dared not lift her hot face or open her lips lest the pent resentment escape; Portlaw smoked a pipe—a sure indication of smouldering wrath; Malcourt, at a desk, blew clouds of smoke from his cigarette and smilingly continued writing to his attorney:

"This is the general idea for the document, and it's up to you to fix it up and make it legal, and have it ready for me when I come to town.

"1st. I want to leave all my property to a Miss Dorothy or Dolly Wilming; and I want you to sell off everything after my death and invest the proceeds for her because it's all she'll have to live on except what she gets by her own endeavours. This, in case I suddenly snuff out.

"2d. I want to leave my English riding-crop, spurs, bridle, and saddle to a Miss Virginia Suydam. Fix it legally.

"3d. Here is a list of eighteen ladies. Each is to have one of my eighteen Chinese gods.

"4th. To my wife I leave the nineteenth god. Mr. Hamil has it in his possession. I have no right to dispose of it, but he will have some day.

"5th. To John Garret Hamil, 3d, I leave my volume of Jean DuMont, the same being an essay on Friendship.

"6th. To my friend, William Van Bueren Portlaw, I leave my dogs, rods, and guns with a recommendation that he use them and his legs.

"7th. To my sister, Lady Tressilvain, I leave my book of comic Bridge rules, and to her husband a volume of Methodist hymns.

"I'll be in town again, shortly, and expect you to have my will ready to be signed and witnessed. One ought always to be prepared, particularly when in excellent health.

"Yours sincerely,

"LOUIS MALCOURT."

"P.S. I enclose a check for the Greenlawn Cemetery people. I wish you'd see that they keep the hedge properly trimmed around my father's plot and renew the dead sod where needed. I noticed that one of the trees was also dead. Have them put in another and keep the flowers in good shape. I don't want anything dead around that lot.

"L.M."

When he had sealed and directed his letter he looked around the silent room. Shiela was sewing by the window. Portlaw, back to the fire, stood staring out at the rain; Lady Tressilvain, a cigarette between her thin lips, wandered through the work-shop and loading-room where, from hooks in the ceiling, a thicket of split-cane rod-joints hung, each suspended by a single strong thread.

The loading-room was lined with glass-faced cases containing fowling-pieces, rifles, reels, and the inevitable cutlery and ironmongery associated with utensils for the murder of wild creatures. Tressilvain sat at the loading-table to which he was screwing a delicate vise to hold hooks; for Malcourt had given him a lesson in fly-tying, and he meant to dress a dozen to try on Painted Creek.

So he sorted snell and hook and explored the tin trunk for hackles, silks, and feathers, up to his bony wrists in the fluffy heap of brilliant plumage, burrowing, busy as a burying beetle under a dead bird.

Malcourt dropped his letter into the post-box, glanced uncertainly in the direction of his wife, but as she did not lift her head from her sewing, turned with a shrug and crossed the floor to where Portlaw stood scowling and sucking at his empty pipe.

"Look at that horrid little brother-in-law of mine with his ferret eyes and fox face, fussing around those feathers—as though he had just caught and eaten the bird that wore them!"

Portlaw continued to scowl.

"Suppose we take them on at cards," suggested Malcourt.

"No, thanks."

"Why not?"

"They've taken a thousand out of me already."

Malcourt said quietly: "You've never before given such a reason for discontinuing card-playing. What's your real reason?"

Portlaw was silent.

"Did you quit a thousand to the bad, Billy?"

"Yes, I did."

"Then why not get it back?"

"I don't care to play," said Portlaw shortly.

The eyes of the two men met.

"Are you, by any chance, afraid of our fox-faced guest?" asked Malcourt suavely.

"I don't care to give any reason, I tell you."

"That's serious; as there could be only one reason. Did you think you noticed—anything?"

"I don't know what I think.... I've half a mind to stop payment on that check—if that enlightens you any."

"There's an easier way," said Malcourt coolly. "You know how it is in sparring? You forecast what your opponent is going to do and you stop him before he does it."

"I'm not *certain* that he—did it," muttered Portlaw. "I can't afford to make a mistake by kicking out your brother-in-law."

"Oh, don't mind me—"

"I wouldn't if I were sure.... I wish I had that thousand back; it drives me crazy to think of losing it—in that way—"

"Oh; then you feel reasonably sure—"

"No, confound it.... The backs of the aces were slightly rough—but I can scarcely believe—"

"Have you a magnifying glass?"

The pack has disappeared.... I meant to try that."

"My dear fellow," said Malcourt calmly, "it wouldn't surprise me in the slightest to learn that Tressilvain is a blackguard. It's easy enough to get your thousand back. Shall we?"

"How?"

Malcourt sauntered over to a card table, seated himself, motioned Portlaw to the chair opposite, and removed the cover from a new pack.

Then, to Portlaw's astonishment, he began to take aces and court cards from any part of the pack at his pleasure; any card that Portlaw called for was produced unerringly. Then Malcourt dealt him unbelievable hands—all of a colour, all of a suit, all the cards below the tens, all above; and Portlaw, fascinated, watched the dark, deft fingers nimbly dealing, shuffling, until his senses spun round; and when Malcourt finally tore up all the aces, and then, ripping the green baize cover from the table, disclosed the four aces underneath, intact, Portlaw, petrified, only stared at him out of distended eyes.

"Those are nice tricks, aren't they?" asked Malcourt, smiling.

"Y-yes. Lord! Louis, I never dreamed you could do such devilish things as—"

"I can. If I were not always behind you in my score I'd scarcely dare let you know what I might do if I chose.... How far ahead is that little mink, yonder?"

"Tressilvain?"

"Yes."

"He has taken about a thousand—wait!" Portlaw consulted his note-book, made a wry face, and gave Malcourt the exact total.

Malcourt turned carelessly in his chair.

"O Herbert!" he called across to his brother-in-law; "don't you and Helen want to take us on?"

"Rather!" replied Tressilvain briskly; and came trotting across the room, his close-set black eyes moving restlessly from Malcourt to Portlaw.

"Come on, Helen," said Malcourt, drawing up a chair for her; and his sister seated herself gracefully. A moment later the game began, Portlaw passing it over to Malcourt, who made it no trumps, and laid out all the materials for international trouble, including a hundred aces.

The games were brutally short, savage, decisive; Tressilvain lost countenance after the fastest four rubbers he had ever played, and shot an exasperated glance at his wife, who was staring thoughtfully at her brother.

But that young man appeared to be in an innocently merry mood; he gaily taunted Herby, as he chose to call him, with loss of nerve; he tormented his sister because she didn't seem to know what Portlaw's discards meant; and no wonder, because he discarded from an obscure system taught him by Malcourt. Also, with a malice which Tressilvain ignored, he forced formalities, holding everybody ruthlessly to iron-clad rule, taking penalties, enforcing the most rigid etiquette. For he was one of those rare players who knew the game so thoroughly that while he, and the man he had taught, often ignored the classics of adversary play, the slightest relaxing of etiquette, rule, precept, or precedent, in his opponents, brought him out with a protest exacting the last item of toll for indiscretion.

Portlaw was perhaps the sounder player, Malcourt certainly the more brilliant; and now, for the first time since the advent of the Tressilvains, the cards Portlaw held were good ones.

"What a nasty thing to do!" said Lady Tressilvain sharply, as her brother's finesse went through, and with it another rubber.

"It was horrid, wasn't it, Helen? I don't know what's got into you and Herby"; and to the latter's protest he added pleasantly: "You talk like a bucket of ashes. Go on and deal!"

"A—what!" demanded Tressilvain angrily.

"It's an Americanism," observed his wife, surveying her cards with masked displeasure and making it spades. "Louis, I never held such hands in all my life," she said, displaying the meagre dummy.

"Do you good, Helen. Mustn't be too proud and haughty. No, no! Good for you and Herby—"

"I wish you wouldn't call him Herby," snapped his sister.

"Not respectful?" inquired Malcourt, lifting his eyebrows. "Well, I'll call him anything you like, Helen; I don't care. But make it something I can say when ladies are present—"

Tressilvain's mink-like muzzle turned white with rage. He didn't like to be flouted, he didn't like his cards, he didn't like to lose money. And he had already lost a lot between luncheon and the impending dinner.

"Why the devil I continue to hold all these three-card suits I don't know," he said savagely. "Isn't there another pack in the house?"

"There *was*" said Malcourt; and ironically condoled with him as Portlaw accomplished a little slam in hearts.

Then Tressilvain dealt; and Malcourt's eyes never left his brother-in-law's hands as they distributed the cards with nervous rapidity.

"Misdeal," he said quietly.

"What?" demanded his sister in sharp protest.

"It's a misdeal," repeated Malcourt, smiling at her; and, as Tressilvain, half the pack suspended, gazed blankly at him, Malcourt turned and looked him squarely in the eye. The other reddened.

"Too bad," said Malcourt, with careless good-humour, "but one has to be so careful in dealing the top card, Herby. You stumble over your own fingers; they're too long; or perhaps it's that ring of yours."

A curious, almost ghastly glance passed involuntarily between the Tressilvains; Portlaw, who was busy lighting a cigar, did not notice it, but Malcourt laughed lightly and ran over the score, adding it up with a nimble accuracy that seemed to stun his relatives.

"Why, look what's here!" he exclaimed, genially displaying a total that, added, balanced all Portlaw's gains and losses to date. "Why, isn't that curious, Helen! Right off the bat like that!—cricket-bat," he explained affably to Tressilvain, who, as dinner was imminent, had begun fumbling for his check-book.

At Malcourt's suave suggestion, however, instead of drawing a new check he returned Portlaw's check. Malcourt took it, tore it carefully in two equal parts.

"Half for you, William, half for me," he said gaily. "My—my! What strange things do happen in cards—and in the British Isles!"

The dull flush deepened on Tressilvain's averted face, but Lady Tressilvain, unusually pale, watched her brother persistently during the general conversation that preceded dressing for dinner.

CHAPTER XXVI
SEALED INSTRUCTIONS

After the guests had gone away to dress Portlaw looked inquiringly at Malcourt and said: "That misdeal may have been a slip. I begin to believe I was mistaken after all. What do you think, Louis?"

Malcourt's eyes wandered toward his wife who still bent low over her sewing. "I don't think," he said absently, and sauntered over to Shiela, saying:

"It's rather dull for you, isn't it?"

She made no reply until Portlaw had gone upstairs; then looking around at him:

"Is there any necessity for me to sit here while you play cards this evening?"

"No, if it doesn't amuse you."

Amuse her! She rested her elbow on the window ledge, and, chin on hand, stared out into the gray world of rain—the world that had been so terribly altered for her for ever. In the room shadows were gathering; the dull light faded. Outside it rained over land and water, over the encircling forest which walled in this stretch of spectral world where the monotony of her days was spent.

To the sadness of it she was slowly becoming inured; but the strangeness of her life she could not yet comprehend—its meaningless days and nights, its dragging hours—and the strange people around her immersed in their sordid pleasures—this woman—her husband's sister, thin-lipped, hard-featured, drinking, smoking, gambling, shrill in disputes, merciless of speech, venomously curious concerning all that she held locked in the privacy of her wretchedness.

"Shiela," he said, "why don't you pay your family a visit?"

She shook her head.

"You're afraid they might suspect that you are not particularly happy?"

"Yes.... It was wrong to have Gray and Cecile here. It was fortunate you were away. But they saw the Tressilvains."

"What did they think of 'em?" inquired Malcourt.

"What do you suppose they would think?"

"Quite right. Well, don't worry. Hold out a little longer. This is a ghastly sort of pantomime for you, but there's always a grand transformation scene at the end. Who knows how soon the curtain will rise on fairyland and the happy lovers and all that bright and sparkling business? Children demand it—must have it.... And you are very young yet."

He laughed, seeing her perplexed expression.

"You don't know what I mean, do you? Listen, Shiela; stay here to dinner, if you can stand my relatives. We won't play cards. You'll really find it amusing I think."

"Do you wish me to stay?"

"Yes, I do. I want you to see something."

A few moments afterward she took her umbrella and waterproof and went away to dress, returning to a dinner-table remarkable for the silence of the diners. Something, too, had gone wrong with the electric plant, and after dinner candles were lighted in the living-room. Outside it rained heavily.

Malcourt sat beside his wife, smoking, and, unaided, sustaining what conversation there was; and after a while he rose, dragged a heavy, solid wooden table to the middle of the room, placed five chairs around it, and smilingly invited Shiela, the Tressilvains, and Portlaw to join him.

"A seance in table-tipping?" asked his sister coldly. "Really, Louis, I think we are rather past such things."

"I never saw a bally table tip," observed Tressilvain. "How do you do it, Louis?"

"I don't; it tips. Come, Shiela, if you don't mind. Come on, Billy."

Tressilvain seated himself and glanced furtively about him.

"I dare say you're all in this game," he said, with a rattling laugh.

"It's no game. If the table tips it tips, and our combined weight can't hold it down," said Malcourt. "If it won't tip it won't, and I'll bet you a hundred dollars that you can't tip it, Herby."

Tressilvain, pressing his hands hard on the polished edge, tried to move the table; then he stood up and tried. It was too heavy and solid, and he could do nothing except by actually lifting it or by seizing it in both hands and dragging it about.

One by one, reluctantly, the others took seats around the table and, as instructed by Malcourt, rested the points of their fingers on the dully polished surface.

"Does it really ever move?" asked Shiela of Malcourt.

"It sometimes does."

"What's the explanation?" demanded Portlaw, incredulously; "spirits?"

"I don't think anybody here would credit such an explanation," said Malcourt. "The table moves or it doesn't. If it does you'll see it. I'll leave the explanation to you, William."

"Have you ever seen it move?" asked Shiela, turning again to Malcourt.

"Yes; so has my sister. It's not a trick." Lady Tressilvain looked bored, but answered Shiela's inquiry:

"I've seen it often. Louis and I and my father used to do it. I don't know how it's done, and nobody else does. Personally I think it's rather a stupid way to spend an evening —"

"But," interrupted Portlaw, "there'll be nothing stupid about it if the table begins to tip up here under our very fingers. I'll bet you, Louis, that it doesn't. Do you care to bet?"

"Shouldn't the lights be put out?" asked Tressilvain.

Malcourt said it was not necessary, and cautioned everybody to sit absolutely clear of the table, and to rest only the tips of the fingers very lightly on the surface.

"Can we speak?" grinned Portlaw.

"Oh, yes, if you like." A bright colour glowed in Malcourt's face; he looked down dreamily at the top of the table where his hands touched. A sudden quiet fell over the company.

Shiela, sitting with her white fingers lightly brushing the smooth mahogany, bent her head, mind wandering; and her thoughts were very far away when, under her sensitive touch, a curious quiver seemed to run through the very grain of the wood.

"What's that!" exclaimed Portlaw.

Deep in the wood, wave after wave of motion seemed to spread until the fibres emitted a faint splintering sound. Then, suddenly, the heavy table rose slowly, the end on which Shiela's hands rested sinking; and fell back with a solid shock.

"That's—rather—odd!" muttered Tressilvain. Portlaw's distended eyes were fastened on the table, which was now heaving uneasily like a boat at anchor, creaking, cracking, rocking under their finger-tips. Tressilvain rose from his chair and tried to see, but as everybody was clear of the table, and their fingers barely touched the top, he could discover no visible reason for what was occurring so violently under his very pointed nose.

"It's like a bally earthquake," he said in amazement. "God bless my soul! the thing is walking off with us!"

Everybody had risen from necessity; chairs were pushed back, skirts drawn aside as the heavy table, staggering, lurching, moved out across the floor; and they all followed, striving to keep their finger-tips on the top.

Portlaw was speechless; Shiela pale, tremulous, bewildered; Tressilvain's beady eyes shone like the eyes of a surprised rat; but his wife and Malcourt took it calmly.

"The game is," said Malcourt, "to ask whether there is a spirit present, and then recite the alphabet. Shall I?... It isn't frightening you, is it, Shiela?"

"No.... But I don't understand why it moves."

"Neither does anybody. But you see it, feel it. Nor can anybody explain why an absurd question and reciting the alphabet sometimes results in a coherent message. Shall I try it, Helen?"

His sister nodded indifferently.

There was a silence, then Malcourt, still standing, said quietly:

"Is there a message?"

From the deep, woody centre of the table three loud knocks sounded—almost ripped out, and the table quivered in every fibre.

"Is there a message for anybody present?"

Three raps followed in a startling volley.

"Get the chairs," motioned Malcourt; and when all were seated clear of the table but touching lightly the surface with their finger-tips:

"A B C D E F"—began Malcourt, slowly reciting the alphabet; and, as the raps rang out, sig-nalling some letter, he began again in a monotonous voice: "A B C D E F G"—pausing as soon as the raps arrested him at a certain letter, only to begin again.

"Get a pad and pencil," whispered Lady Tressilvain to Shiela.

So Shiela left the table, found a pad and pencil, and seated herself near a candle by the window; and as each letter was rapped out by the table, she put it down in order.

The recitation seemed endless; Malcourt's voice grew hoarse with the repetition; letter after letter was added to the apparently meaningless sequence on Shiela's pad.

"Is there any sense in it so far?" asked Lady Tressilvain.

"I cannot find any," said Shiela, striving with her pencil point to divide the string of letters into intelligible words.

And still Malcourt's monotonous voice droned on, and still the raps sounded from the table. Portlaw hung over it as though hypnotized; Tressilvain had fallen to moistening his lips with the tip of his tongue, stealthy eyes always roaming about the candle-lit room as though searching for something uncanny lurking in the shadows.

Shiela shivered, wide-eyed, as she sat watching the table which was now snapping and cracking and heaving under her gaze. A slow fear of the thing crept over her—of this senseless, lifeless mass of wood, fashioned by human hands. The people around it, the room, the house were becoming horrible to her; she loathed them and what they were doing.

A ripping crash brought her to her feet; everybody sprang up. Under their hands the table was shuddering convulsively. Suddenly it split open as though rent by a bolt, and fell like a live thing in agony, a mass of twisted fibres protruding like viscera from its shattered core.

Stunned silence; and Malcourt turned to his sister and spoke in a low voice, but she only shook her head, shivering, and stared at the wreck of wood as though revolted.

"W-what happened?" faltered Portlaw, bewildered.

"I don't know," said Malcourt unsteadily.

"Don't know! Look at that table! Why, man, it's—it's *dying*!"

Tressilvain stood as though stupefied. Malcourt walked slowly over to where Shiela stood.

She shrank involuntarily away from him as he bent to pick up the pad which had fallen from her hands.

"There's nothing to be frightened about," he said, forcing a smile; and, holding the pad under the light, scanned it attentively. His sister came over to him, asking if the letters made any sense.

He shook his head.

They studied it together, Shiela's fascinated gaze riveted on them both. And she saw Lady Tressilvain's big eyes widen as she laid her pencil on a sequence; saw Malcourt's quick nod of surprised comprehension when she checked off a word, then another, another, another; and suddenly her face turned white to the lips, and she caught at her brother's arm, terrified.

"Will you keep quiet?" he whispered fiercely, snatching the sheet from the pad and crumpling it into his palm.

Sister and brother faced each other; in his eyes leaped a flame infernal which seemed to hold her paralyzed for a moment; then, with a gesture, she swept him aside, and covering her eyes with her hands, sank into a chair.

"What a fool you are!" he said furiously, bending down beside her. "It's in us both; you'll do it, too, when you are ready—if you have any sporting blood in you!"

And, straightening up impatiently, his eyes fell on Shiela, and he shrugged his shoulders and smiled resignedly.

"It's nothing. My sister's nerves are a bit upset.... After all, this parlour magic is a stupid mistake, because there's always somebody who takes it seriously. It's only humbug, anyway; you know that, don't you, Shiela?"

He untwisted the paper in his hand and held it in the candle flame until it burned to cinders.

"What was there on that paper?" asked Shiela, managing to control her voice.

"Why, merely a suggestion that I travel," he said coolly. "I can't see why my sister should make a fool of herself over the idea of my going on a journey. I've meant to, for years—to rest myself. I've told you that often, haven't I, Shiela?"

She nodded slowly, but her eyes reverted to the woman crouching in the chair, face buried in her brilliantly jewelled hands. Portlaw and Tressilvain were also staring at her.

"You'd better go to bed, Helen," said Malcourt coolly; and turned on his heel, lighting a cigarette.

A little later the Tressilvains and Shiela started across the lawn to their own apartments, and Malcourt went with them to hold an umbrella over his wife.

In the lower hall they separated with scarcely a word, but Malcourt detained his brother-in-law by a significant touch on the arm, and drew him into the library.

"So you're leaving to-morrow?" he asked.

"What?" said Tressilvain.

"I say that I understand you and Helen are leaving us to-morrow."

"I had not thought of leaving," said Tressilvain.

"Think again," suggested Malcourt.

"What do you mean?"

Malcourt walked up very close and looked him in the face.

"Must I explain?" he asked contemptuously. "I will if you like—you clumsy card-slipping, ace-pricking blackguard!... The station-wagon will be ready at seven. See that you are, too. Now go and tell my sister. It may reconcile her to various ideas of mine."

And he turned and, walking to a leather-covered chair drawn up beside the library table, seated himself and opened a heavy book.

Tressilvain stood absolutely still, his close-set eyes fairly starting from his face, in which not a vestige of colour now remained; and when at length he left the room he left so noiselessly that Malcourt did not hear him. However, Malcourt happened to be very intent upon his own train of thought, so absorbed, in fact, that it was a long while before he looked up and around, as though somebody had suddenly spoken his name.

But it was only the voice which had sounded so often and familiarly in his ears; and he smiled and inclined his graceful head to listen, folding his hands under his chin.

He seemed very young and boyish, there, leaning both elbows on the library table, head bent expectantly as he listened, or lifted when he, in turn, spoke aloud. And sometimes he spoke gravely, argumentatively, sometimes almost flippantly, and once or twice his laugh rang out through the empty room.

In the forest a heavy wind had risen; somewhere outside a door or shutter banged persistently. He did not hear it, but Shiela, sleepless in her room above, laid down Hamil's book; then, thinking it might be the outer door left carelessly unlocked, descended the stairs with lighted candle. Passing the library and hearing voices she halted, astonished to see her husband there alone; and as she stood, perplexed and disturbed, he spoke as though answering a question. But there was no one there who could have asked it; the room was empty save for that solitary figure. Something in his voice terrified her—in the uncanny monologue which meant nothing to her—in his curiously altered laugh—in his intent listening attitude. It was not the first time she had seen him this way.

"Louis!" she exclaimed; "what are you doing?"

He turned dreamily toward her, rose as in a trance.

"Oh, is it you?... Come in here."

"I cannot; I am tired."

"So am I, Shiela—tired to death. What time is it?"

"After ten, I think—if that clock is right."

She entered, reluctant, uncertain, peering up at the clock; then:

"I thought the front door had been left open and came down to lock it. What are you doing here at this hour? I—I thought I heard you talking."

"I was talking to my father."

"What!" she said, startled.

"Pretending to," he added wearily; "sit down."

"Do you wish me—"

"Yes; sit down."

"I—" she looked fearfully at him, hesitated, and slowly seated herself on the arm of a lounge. "W-what is it you—want, Louis?" she faltered, every nerve on edge.

"Nothing much; a kindly word or two."

"What do you mean? Have I ever been unkind? I—I am too unhappy to be unkind to anybody." Suddenly her eyes filled.

"Don't do that," he said; "you are always civil to me—never unkind. By the way, my relatives leave to-morrow. That will comfort you, won't it?"

She said nothing.

He leaned heavily on the table, dark face framed in both hands:

"Shiela, when a man is really tired, don't you think it reasonable for him to take a rest—and give others one?"

"I don't understand."

"A rather protracted rest is good for tired people, isn't it?"

"Yes, if—"

"In fact," with a whimsical smile, "a sort of endlessly eternal rest ought to cure anybody. Don't you think so?"

She stared at him.

"Do you happen to remember that my father, needing a good long rest, took a sudden vacation to enjoy it?"

"I—I—don't know what you mean!"—tremulously.

"You remember how he started on that restful vacation which he is still enjoying?"

A shudder ran over her. She strove to speak, but her voice died in her throat.

"My father," he said dreamily, "seems to want me to join him during his vacation—"

"Louis!"

"What are you frightened about? It's as good a vacation as any other—only one takes no luggage and pays no hotel bills.... Haven't you any sense of humour left in you, Shiela? I'm not serious."

She said, trembling, and very white: "I thought you meant it." Then she rose with a shiver, turned, and mounted the stairs to her room again. But in the stillness of the place something was already at work on her—fear—a slow dawning alarm at the silence, the loneliness, the forests, the rain—a growing horror of the place, of the people in it, of this man the world called her husband, of his listening silences, his solitary laughter, his words spoken to something unseen in empty rooms, his awful humour.

Her very knees were shaking under her now; she stared around her like a trapped thing, desperate, feeling that self-control was going in sudden, ungovernable panic.

Scarcely knowing what she was about she crept to the telephone and, leaning heavily against the wall, placed the receiver to her ear.

For a long while she waited, dreading lest the operator had gone. Then a far voice hailed her; she gave the name; waited interminable minutes until a servant's sleepy voice requested her to hold the wire. And, at last:

"Is it you?"

"Garry, could you come here to-night?"

"Danger? No, I am in no danger; I am just frightened."

"I don't know what is frightening me."

"No, not ill. It's only that I am so horribly alone here in the rain. I—I cannot seem to endure it." She was speaking almost incoherently, now, scarcely conscious of what she was saying. "There's a man downstairs who talks in empty rooms and listens to things I cannot hear—listens every day,

I tell you; I've seen him often, often—I mean Louis Malcourt! And I cannot endure it—the table that moves, and the—O Garry! Take me away with you. I cannot stand it any longer!"

"Will you come?"

"To-night, Garry?"

"How long will you be? I simply cannot stay alone in this house until you come. I'll go down and saddle my mare—"

"What?"

"Oh, yes—yes! I know what I'm doing—"

"Yes, I do remember, but—why won't you take me away from—"

"I know it—Oh, I know it! I am half-crazed, I think—"

"Yes—"

"I do care for them still! But—"

"O Garry! Garry! I will be true to them! I will do anything you wish, only come! Come! Come!"

"You promise?"

"At once?"

She hung up the receiver, turned, and flung open the window.

Over the wet woods a rain-washed moon glittered; the long storm had passed.

An hour later, as she kneeled by the open window, her chin on her arms, watching for him, out of the shadow and into the full moonlight galloped a rider who drew bridle on the distant lawn, waving her a gay gesture of reassurance.

It was too far for her to call; she dared not descend fearing the dogs might wake the house.

And in answer to his confident salute, she lighted a candle, and, against the darkness, drew the fiery outline of a heart; then extinguishing the light, she sank back in her big chair, watching him as he settled in his stirrups for the night-long vigil that she meant to share with him till dawn.

The whole night long once more together! She thrilled at the thought of it—at the memory of that other night and dawn under the Southern planets where a ghostly ocean thundered at their feet—where her awakened heart quickened with the fear of him—and all her body trembled with the blessed fear of him, and every breath was delicious with terror of the man who had come this night to guard her.

Partly undressed, head cradled in her tumbled hair, she lay there in the darkness watching him—her paladin on guard beneath the argent splendour of the moon. Under the loosened silken vest her heart was racing; under the unbound hair her cheeks were burning. The soft lake breeze rippled the woodbine leaves along the sill, stirring the lace and ribbon on her breast.

Hour after hour she lay there, watching him through the dreamy lustre of the moon, all the mystery of her love for him tremulous within her. Once, on the edge of sleep, yet still awake, she stretched her arms toward him in the darkness, unconsciously as she did in dreams.

Slowly the unreality of it all was enveloping her, possessed her as her lids grew heavy. In the dim silvery light she could scarcely see him now: a frail mist belted horse and rider, stretching fairy barriers across the lawn. Suddenly, within her, clear, distinct, a voice began calling to him imperiously; but her lips never moved. Yet she knew he would hear; surely he heard! Surely, surely!—for was he not already drifting toward her through the moonlight, nearer, here under the palms and orange-trees— here at her feet, holding her close, safe, strong, till, faint with the happiness of dreams come true, she slept, circled by his splendid arms.

And, while she lay there, lips scarce parted, sleeping quietly as a tired child, he sat his mud-splashed saddle, motionless under the moon, eyes never leaving her window for an instant, till at last the far dawn broke and the ghostly shadows fled away.

Then, in the pallid light, he slowly gathered bridle and rode back into the Southern forest, head heavy on his breast.

CHAPTER XXVII
MALCOURT LISTENS

Malcourt was up and ready before seven when his sister came to his door, dressed in her pretty blue travelling gown, hatted, veiled, gloved to perfection; but there was a bloom on cheek and mouth which mocked at the wearied eyes—a lassitude in every step as she slowly entered and seated herself.

For a moment neither spoke; her brother was looking at her narrowly; and after a while she raised her veil, turning her face to the merciless morning light.

"Paint," she said; "and I'm little older than you."

"You will be younger than I am, soon."

She paled a trifle under the red.

"Are you losing your reason, Louis?"

"No, but I've contrived to lose everything else. It was a losing game from the beginning—for both of us."

"Are you going to be coward enough to drop your cards and quit the game?"

"Call it that. But the cards are marked and the game crooked—as crooked as Herby's." He began to laugh. "The world's dice are loaded; I've got enough."

"Yet you beat Bertie in spite of—"

"For Portlaw's sake. I wouldn't fight with marked cards for my own sake. Faugh! the world plays a game too rotten to suit me. I'll drop my hand and—take a stroll for a little fresh air—out yonder—" He waved his arm toward the rising sun. "Just a step into the fresh air, Helen."

"Are you not afraid?" She managed to form the words with stiffened lips.

"Afraid?" He stared at her. "No; neither are you. You'll do it, too, some day. If you don't want to now, you will later; if you have any doubts left they won't last. We have no choice; it's in us. We don't belong here, Helen; we're different. We didn't know until we'd tried to live like other people, and everything went wrong." A glint of humour came into his eyes. "I've made up my mind that we're extra-terrestrial—something external and foreign to this particular star. I think it's time to ask for a transfer and take the star ahead."

Not a muscle moved in her expressionless face; he shrugged and drew out his watch.

"I'm sorry, Helen—"

"Is it time to go?"

"Yes.... Why do you stick to that little cockney pup?"

"I don't know."

"You ruined a decent man to pick him out of the gutter. Why don't you drop him back?"

"I don't know."

"Do you—ah—care for him?"

"No."

"Then why—"

She shook her head.

"Quite right," said Malcourt, rising; "you're in the wrong planet, too. And the sooner you realise it the sooner we'll meet again. Good-bye."

She turned horribly pale, stammering something about his coming with her, resisting a little as he drew her out, down the stairs, and aided her to enter the depot-wagon. There he kissed her; and she caught him around the neck, holding him convulsively.

"Nonsense," he whispered. "I've talked it all over with father; he and I'll talk it over some day with you. Then you'll understand." And backing away he called to the coachman: "Drive on!" ignoring his brother-in-law, who sat huddled in a corner, glassy eyes focused on him.

Portlaw almost capered with surprise and relief when at breakfast he learned that the Tressilvains had departed.

"Oh, everything is coming everybody's way," said Malcourt gaily—"like the last chapter of a bally novel—the old-fashioned kind, Billy, where Nemesis gets busy with a gun and kind Providence hitches 'em up in ever-after blocks of two. It takes a rotten novelist to use a gun on his villains! It's never done in decent literature—never done anywhere except in real life."

He swallowed his coffee and, lighting a cigarette, tipped back his chair, balancing himself with one hand on the table.

"The use of the gun," he said lazily, "is obsolete in the modern novel; the theme now is, how to be passionate though pure. Personally, being neither one nor the other, I remain uninterested in the modern novel."

"Real life," said Portlaw, spearing a fish-ball, "is damn monotonous. The only gun-play is in the morning papers."

"Sure," nodded Malcourt, "and there's too many shooting items in 'em every day to make gun-play available for a novel.... Once, when I thought I could write—just after I left college—they took me aboard a morning newspaper on the strength of a chance I had to discover a missing woman.

"She was in hiding; her name had been horribly spattered in a divorce, and the poor thing was in hiding—had changed her name, crept off to a little town in Delaware.

"Our enlightened press was hunting for her; to find her was termed a 'scoop,' I believe.... Well—boys pull legs off grasshoppers and do other damnable things without thinking.... I found *her*.... So as I knocked at her door—in the mean little farmhouse down there in Delaware—she opened it, smiling—she was quite pretty—and blew her brains out in my very face."

"Wh-what!" bawled Portlaw, dropping knife and fork.

"I—I want to see that girl again—some time," said Malcourt thoughtfully. "I would like to tell her that I didn't mean it—case of boy and grasshopper, you know.... Well, as you say, gun-play has no place in real novels. There wouldn't be room, anyway, with all the literature and illustrations and purpose and purple preciousness; as anachronismatically superfluous as sleigh-bells in hell."

Portlaw resumed his egg; Malcourt considered him ironically.

"Sporty Porty, are you going to wed the Pretty Lady of Pride's Hall at Pride's Fall some blooming day in June?"

"None of your infernal business!"

"Quite so. I only wanted to see how the novel was coming out before somebody takes the book away from me."

"You talk like a pint of shoe-strings," growled Portlaw; "you'd better find out whose horse has been denting the lawn all over and tearing off several yards of sod."

"I know already," said Malcourt.

"Well, who had the nerve to—"

"None of your bally business, dear friend. Are you riding over to Pride's to-day?"

"Yes, I am."

"I think I'll go, too."

"You're not expected."

"That's the charm of it, old fellow. I didn't expect to go; they don't expect me; they don't want me; I want to go! All the elements of a delightful surprise, do you notice?"

Portlaw said, irritably: "They asked Mrs. Malcourt and me. Nothing was said about you."

"Something will be said if I go," observed Malcourt cheerfully.

Portlaw was exasperated. "There's a girl there you behaved badly to. You'd better stay away."

Malcourt looked innocently surprised.

"Now, who could that be! I have, it is true, at times, misbehaved, but I can't ever remember behaving badly —"

Portlaw, too mad to speak, strode wrathfully away toward the stables.

Malcourt was interested to see that he could stride now without waddling.

"Marvellous, marvellous! — the power of love!" he mused sentimentally; "Porty is no longer rotund — only majestically portly. See where he hastens lightly to his Alida!

"Shepherd fair and maidens all —
Too-ri-looral!
Too-ri-looral!"

And, very gracefully, he sketched a step or two in contra-dance to his own shadow on the grass.

"Shepherd fair and maidens all —
Truly rural,
Too-ri-looral,
Man prefers his maidens plural;
One is none, he wants them all!
Too-ri-looral!
Too-ri-looral —"

And he sauntered off humming gaily, making playful passes at the trees with his riding-crop as he passed.

Later he aided his wife to mount and stood looking after her as she rode away, Portlaw pounding along heavily beside her.

"All alone with the daisies," he said, looking around him when they had disappeared.

Toward noon he ordered a horse, ate his luncheon in leisurely solitude, read yesterday's papers while he smoked, then went out, mounted, and took the road to Pride's Fall, letting his horse choose his own pace.

Moving along through the pretty forest road, he glanced casually right and left as he advanced, tapping his riding-boots in rhythm to the air he was humming in a careless undertone—something about a shepherd and the plural tastes of man.

His mood was inspired by that odd merriment which came from sheer perversity. When the depths and shallows of his contradictory character were disturbed a ripple of what passed for mirth covered all the surface; if there was any profundity to the man the ripple obscured it. No eye had ever penetrated the secrecy of what lay below; none ever would. Perhaps there was nothing there.

He journeyed on, his horse ambling or walking as it suited him, or sometimes veering to stretch a long glossy neck and nip at a bunch of leaves.

The cock-partridge stood on his drumming-log and defied the forest rider, all unseen; rabbit and squirrel sat bolt upright with palpitating flanks and moist bright eyes at gaze; overhead the slow hawks sailed, looking down at him as he rode.

Sometimes Malcourt whistled to himself, sometimes he sang in a variably agreeable voice, and now and then he quoted the poets, taking pleasure in the precision of his own diction.

> "C'est le jour des morts,
> Mirliton, Mirlitaine!
> Requiescant in pace!"

he chanted; and quoted more of the same bard with a grimace, adding, as he spurred his horse:

"*Poeta nascitur, non fit!*—the poet's nasty and not fit. Zut! Boum-boum! Get along, old fellow, or we'll never see the pretty ladies of Pride's this blooming day!"

There was a shorter cut by a spotted trail, and when he saw the first blaze glimmering through the leaves he steered his horse toward it. The sound of voices came distantly from the wooded heights above—far laughter, the faint aroma of a wood fire; no doubt some picnickers—trespassing as usual, but that was Mrs. Ascott's affair.

A little later, far below him, he caught a glimpse of a white gown among the trees. There was a spring down there somewhere in that thicket of silver birches; probably one of the trespassers was drinking. So, idly curious, he rode that way, his horse making no sound on the thick moss.

"If she's ornamental," he said to himself, "I'll linger to point out the sin of trespassing; that is if she is sufficiently ornamental—"

His horse stepped on a dead branch which cracked; the girl in white, who had been looking out through the birch-trees across the valley, turned her head.

They recognised each other even at that distance; he uttered a low exclamation of satisfaction, sprang from his saddle, and led his horse down among the mossy rocks of the water-course to the shelf of rock overhanging the ravine where she stood as motionless as one of the silver saplings.

"Virginia," he said, humorously abashed, "shall I say I am glad to see you, and how d'you do, and offer you my hand?—or had I better not?"

He thought she meant to answer; perhaps she meant to, but found no voice at her disposal.

He dropped his bridle over a branch and, drawing off his gloves, walked up to where she was standing.

"I knew you were at Pride's Hall," he said; "I'm aware, also, that nobody there either expected or wished to see me. But I wanted to see you; and little things of that sort couldn't keep me away. Where are the others?"

She strove twice to answer him, then turned abruptly, steadying herself against a birch-tree with one arm.

"Where are the others, Virginia?" he asked gently.

"On the rocks beyond."

"Picnicking?"

"Yes."

"How charming!" he said; "as though one couldn't see enough country out of one's windows every minute in the year. But you can't tell where sentiment will crop up; some people don't object to chasing ants off the dishes and fishing sticks out of the milk. I do.... It's rather fortunate I found you alone: saves a frigid reception and cruel comments after I'm gone.... After I'm gone, Virginia."

He seated himself where the sunlight fell agreeably and looked off over the valley. A shrunken river ran below—a mere thread of life through its own stony skeleton—a mockery of what it once had been before the white-hided things on two legs had cut the forests from the hills and killed its cool mossy sources in their channels. The crushers of pulp and the sawyers of logs had done their dirty work thoroughly; their acids and their sawdust poisoned and choked; their devastation turned the tree-clothed hill flanks to arid lumps of sand and rock.

He said aloud, "to think of these trees being turned into newspapers!"

He looked up at her whimsically.

"The least I can do is to help grow them again. As a phosphate I might amount to something—if I'm carefully spaded in." And in a lower voice just escaping mockery: "How are you, Virginia?"

"I am perfectly well."

"Are you well enough to sit down and talk to me for half an hour?"

She made no reply.

"Don't be dignified; there is nothing more inartistic, except a woman who is trying to be brave on an inadequate income."

She did not move or look at him.

"Virginia—dear?"

"What?"

"Do you remember that day we met in the surf; and you said something insolent to me, and bent over, laying your palms flat on the water, looking at me over your shoulder?"

"Yes."

"You knew what you were doing?"

"Yes."

"This is part of the consequences. That's what life is, nothing but a game of consequences. I knew what I was doing; you admit you were responsible for yourself; and nothing but consequences have resulted ever since. Sit down and be reasonable and friendly; won't you?"

"I cannot stay here."

"Try," he said, smiling, and made room for her on the sun-crisped moss. A little later she seated herself with an absent-minded air and gazed out across the valley. A leaf or two, prematurely yellow, drifted from the birches.

"It reminds me," he said thoughtfully, "of that exquisite poem on Autumn:

"'The autumn leaves are falling,
They're falling everywhere;
They're falling in the atmosphere,
They're falling in the air—'

—and I don't remember any more, dear."

"Did you wish to say anything to me besides nonsense?" she asked, flushing.

"Did you expect anything else from me?"

"I had no reason to."

"Oh; I thought you might have been prepared for a little wickedness."

She turned her eyes, more green than blue, on him.

"I was not unprepared."

"Nor I," he said gaily; "don't let's disappoint each other. You know our theory is that the old families are decadent; and I think we ought to try to prove any theory we advance—in the interests of psychology. Don't you?"

"I think we have proved it."

He laughed, and passing his arm around her drew her head so that it rested against his face.

"That is particularly dishonourable," she said in an odd voice.

"Because I'm married?"

"Yes; and because I know it."

"That's true; you didn't know it when we were at Palm Beach. That was tamer than this. I think now we can very easily prove our theory." And he kissed her, still laughing. But when he did it again, she turned her face against his shoulder.

"Courage," he said; "we ought to be able to prove this theory of ours—you and I together—"

She was crying.

"If you're feeling guilty on Shiela's account, you needn't," he said. "Didn't you know she can scarcely endure me?"

"Y-yes."

"Well, then—"

"No—no—no! Louis—I care too much—"

"For yourself?"

"N-no."

"For me? For Shiela? For public opinion?"

"No."

"For what?"

"I—I think it must be for—for—just for being—decent."

He inspected her with lively interest.

"Hello," he said coolly, "you're disproving our theory!"

She turned her face away from him, touching her eyes with her handkerchief.

"Or," he added ironically, "is there another man?"

"No," she said without resentment; and there was a certain quality in her voice new to him—a curious sweetness that he had never before perceived.

"Tell me," he said quietly, "have you really suffered?"

"Suffered? Yes."

"You really cared for me?"

"I do still."

A flicker of the old malice lighted his face.

"But you won't let me kiss you? Why?"

She looked up into his eyes. "I feel as powerless with you as I was before. You could always have had your will. Once I would not have blamed you. Now it would be cowardly—because—I have forgiven myself—"

"I won't disturb your vows," he said seriously.

"Then—I think you had better go."

"I am going.... I only wanted to see you again.... May I ask you something, dear?"

"Ask it," she said.

"Then—you are going to get over this, aren't you?"

"Not as long as you live, Louis."

"Oh!... And suppose I were not living?"

"I don't know."

"You'd recover, wouldn't you?"

"I don't know what you mean."

"Well, you'd never have any other temptation—"

She turned scarlet.

"That is wicked!"

"It certainly is," he said with great gravity; "and I must come to the scarcely flattering conclusion that there is in me a source of hideous depravity, the unseen emanations of which, like those of the classic upas-tree, are purest poison to a woman morally constituted as you are."

She looked up as he laughed; but there was no mirth in her bewildered eyes.

"There *is* something in you, Louis, which is fatal to the better side of me."

"The *other* Virginia couldn't endure me, I know."

"My other self learned to love your better self."

"I have none—"

"I have seen it revealed in—"

"Oh, yes," he laughed, "revealed in what you used to call one of my infernal flashes of chivalry."

"Yes," she said quietly, "in that."

He sat very still there in the afternoon sunshine, pondering; and sometimes his gaze searched the valley depths below, lost among the tree-tops; sometimes he studied the far horizon where the little blue hills stood up against the sky like little blue waves at sea. His hat was off; the cliff breeze played with his dark curly hair, lifting it at the temples, stirring the one obstinate strand that never lay quite flat on the crown of his head.

Twice she looked around as though to interrupt his preoccupation, but he neither responded nor even seemed to be aware of her; and she sighed imperceptibly and followed his errant eyes with her own.

At last:

"Is there no way out of it for you, Louis? I am not thinking of myself," she added simply.

He turned fully around.

"If there was a way out I'd take it and marry you."

"I did not ask for that; I was thinking of you."

He was silent.

"Besides," she said, "I know that you do not love me."

"That is true only because I *will* not. I could."

She looked at him.

"But," he said calmly, "I mustn't; because there is no way out for me—there's no way out of anything for me—while I live—down here."

"Down—where?"

"On this exotic planet called the earth, dear child," he said with mocking gravity. "I'm a sort of moon-calf—a seed blown clear from Saturn's surface, which fell here and sprouted into the thing you call Louis Malcourt." And, his perverse gaiety in full possession of him again, he laughed, and his mirth was tinctured with the bitter-sweet of that humorous malice which jeered unkindly only at himself.

"All to the bad, Virginia—all to the bow-wows—judging me from your narrow, earthly standard and the laws of your local divinity. That's why I want to see the real One and ask Him how bad I really am. They'd tell me down here that I'll never see Him. Zut! I'll take that chance—not such a long shot either. Why, if I am no good, the risk is all the better; He *is* because of such as I! No need for Him where all the ba-bas are white as the driven snow, and all the little white doves keep their feathers clean and coo-coo hymns from dawn to sunset.... By the way, I never gave you anything, did I?—a Chinese god, for example?"

She shook her head, bewildered at his inconsequences.

"No, I never did. You're not entitled to a gift of a Chinese god from me. But I've given eighteen of them to a number of—ah—friends. I had nineteen, but never had the—right to present that nineteenth god."

"What do you mean, Louis?"

"Oh, those gilded idols are the deities of secrecy. Their commandment is, 'Thou shalt not be found out.' So I distributed them among those who worship them—that is, I have so directed my executors.... By the way, I made a new will."

He looked at her cheerfully, evidently very much pleased with himself.

"And *what* do you think I've left to you?"

"Louis, I don't—"

"Why, the bridle, saddle, crop, and spurs I wore that day when we rode to the ocean! Don't you remember the day that you noticed me listening and asked me what I heard?"

"Y-yes—"

"And I told you I was listening to my father?"

Again that same chilly tremor passed over her as it had then.

The sun, over the Adirondack foot-hills, hung above bands of smouldering cloud. Presently it dipped into them, hanging triple-ringed, like Saturn on fire.

"It's time for you to go," he said in an altered voice; and she turned to find him standing and ready to aid her.

A little pale with the realisation that the end had come so soon, she rose and walked slowly back to where his horse stood munching leaves.

"Well, Virginia—good-bye, little girl. You'll be all right before long."

There was no humour left in his voice now; no mocking in his dark gaze.

She raised her eyes to his in vague distress.

"Where are the others?" he asked. "Oh, up on those rocks? Yes, I see the smoke of their fire.... Say good-bye to them for me—not *now*—some day."

She did not understand him; he hesitated, smiled, and took her in his arms.

"Good-bye, dear," he said.

"Good-bye."

They kissed.

After she was half-way to the top of the rocks he mounted his horse. She did not look back.

"She's a good little sport," he said, smiling; and, gathering bridle, turned back into the forest. This time he neither sang nor whistled as he rode through the red splendour of the western sun. But he was very busy listening.

There was plenty to hear, too; wood-thrushes were melodious in the late afternoon light; infant crows cawed from high nests unseen in the leafy tree-tops; the stream's thin, silvery song threaded the forest quiet, accompanying him as he rode home.

Home? Yes—if this silent house where he dismounted could be called that. The place was very still. Evidently the servants had taken advantage of their master's and mistress's absence to wander out into the woods. Some of the stablemen had the dogs out, too; there was nobody in sight to take his horse, so he led the animal to the stables and found there a lad to relieve him.

Then he retraced his steps to the house and entered the deserted garden where pearl-tinted spikes of iris perfumed the air and great masses of peonies nodded along borders banked deep under the long wall. A few butterflies still flitted in the golden radiance, but already that solemn harbinger of sunset, the garden toad, had emerged from leafy obscurity into the gravel path, and hopped heavily forward as Malcourt passed by.

The house—nothing can be as silent as an empty house—echoed his spurred tread from porch to stairway. He went up to the first landing, not knowing why, then roamed aimlessly through, wandering from room to room, idly, looking on familiar things as though they were strange—strange, but uninteresting.

Upstairs and down, in, around, and about he drifted, quiet as a cat, avoiding only his wife's bedroom. He had never entered it since their marriage; he did not care to do so now, though the door stood wide. And, indifferent, he turned without even a glance, and traversing the hall, descended the stairs to the library.

For a while he sat there, legs crossed, drumming thoughtfully on his boot with his riding-crop; and after a while he dragged the chair forward and picked up a pen.

"Why not?" he said aloud; "it will save railroad fare—and she'll need it all."

So, to his lawyer in New York he wrote:

"I won't come to town after all. You have my letter and you know what I want done. Nobody is likely to dispute the matter, and it won't require a will to make my wife carry out the essence of the thing."

And signed his name.

When he had sealed and directed the letter he could find no stamp; so he left it on the table.

"That's the usual way they find such letters," he said, smiling to himself as the thought struck him. "It certainly is hard to be original.... But then I'm not ambitious."

He found another sheet of paper and wrote to Hamil:

"All the same you are wrong; I have always been your friend. My father comes first, as always; you second. There is no third."

This note, signed, sealed, and addressed, he left with the other.

"Certainly I am not original in the least," he said, beginning another note.

"DOLLY DEAR:

"You have made good. *Continuez, chère énfant*—and if you don't know what that means your French lessons are in vain. Now the usual few words: don't let any man who is not married to you lay the weight of his little finger on you! Don't ignore convention unless there is a good reason—and then don't! When you're tired of behaving yourself go to sleep; and if you can't sleep, sleep some more; and then some. Men are exactly like women until they differ from them; there is no real mystery about either outside of popular novels.

"I am very, very glad that I have known you, Dolly. Don't tint yourself, except for the footlights. There are other things, but I can't think of them; and so,

"LOUIS MALCOURT"

This letter he sealed and laid with the others; it was the last. There was nothing more to do, except to open the table drawer and drop something into the side pocket of his coat.

Malcourt had no favourite spots in the woods and fields around him; one trail resembled another; he cared as much for one patch of woods, one wild meadow, one tumbling brook as he did for the next—which was not very much.

But there was one place where the sun-bronzed moss was deep and level; where, on the edge of a leafy ravine, the last rays of the sinking sun always lingered after all else lay in shadow.

Here he sat down, thoughtfully; and for a little while remained in his listening attitude. Then, smiling, he lay back, pillowing his head on his left arm; and drew something from the side pocket of his coat.

The world had grown silent; across the ravine a deer among the trees watched him, motionless.

Suddenly the deer leaped in an ecstasy of terror and went crashing away into obscurity. But Malcourt lay very, very still.

His hat was off; the cliff breeze played with his dark curly hair, lifting it at the temples, stirring the one obstinate strand that never lay quite flat on the crown of his head.

A moment later the sun set.

CHAPTER XXVIII
HAMIL IS SILENT

Late in the autumn his aunt wrote Hamil from Sapphire Springs:

"There seems to be a favourable change in Shiela. Her aversion to people is certainly modified. Yesterday on my way to the hot springs I met her with her trained nurse, Miss Lester, face to face, and of course meant to pass on as usual, apparently without seeing her; but to my surprise she turned and spoke my name very quietly; and I said, as though we had parted the day before—'I hope you are better'; and she said, 'I think I am'—very slowly and precisely like a person who strives to speak correctly in a foreign tongue. Garry, dear, it was too pathetic; she is so changed—beautiful, even more beautiful than before; but the last childish softness has fled from the delicate and almost undecided features you remember, and her face has settled into a nobler mould. Do you recollect in the Munich Museum an antique marble, by some unknown Greek sculptor, called 'Head of a Young Amazon'? You must recall it because you have spoken to me of its noble and almost immortal loveliness. Dear, it resembles Shiela as she is now—with that mysterious and almost imperceptible hint of sorrow in the tenderly youthful dignity of the features.

"We exchanged only the words I have written you; she passed her way leaning on Miss Lester's arm; I went for a mud bath as a precaution to our inherited enemy. If rheumatism gets me at last it will not be the fault of your aged and timorous aunt.

"So that was all, yesterday. But to-day as I was standing on the leafy path above the bath-houses, listening to the chattering of some excited birds recently arrived from the North in the first batch of migrants, Miss Lester came up to me and said that Shiela would like to see me, and that the doctors said there was no harm in her talking to anybody if she desired to do so.

"So I took my book to a rustic seat under the trees, and presently our little Shiela came by, leaning on Miss Lester's arm; and Miss Lester walked on, leaving her seated beside me.

"For quite five minutes she neither spoke nor even looked at me, and I was very careful to leave the quiet unbroken.

"The noise of the birds—they were not singing, only chattering to each other about their trip—seemed to attract her notice, and she laid her hand on mine to direct my attention. Her hand remained there—she has the same soft little hands, as dazzlingly white as ever, only thinner.

"She said, not looking at me: 'I have been ill. You understand that.'

"'Yes,' I said, 'but it is all over now, isn't it?'

"She nodded listlessly: 'I think so.'

"Again, but not looking at me she spoke of her illness as dating from a shock received long ago. She is a little confused about the lapse of time, vague as to dates. You see it is four months since Louis—did what he did. She said nothing more, and in a few minutes Miss Lester came back for her.

"Now as to her mental condition: I have had a thorough understanding with the physicians and one and all assure me that there is absolutely nothing the matter with her except the physical consequences of the shock; and those are wearing off.

"What she did, what she lived through with him—the dreadful tension, the endless insomnia—all this—and then, when the searching party was out all night long in the rain and all the next day—and *then*, Garry, to have her stumble on him at dusk—that young girl, all alone, nerves strung to the breaking point—and to find him, *that* way! Was it not enough to account for this nervous demoralisation? The wonder is that it has not permanently injured her.

"But it has not; she is certainly recovering. The dread of seeing a familiar face is less poignant; her father was here to-day with Gray and she saw them both.

"Now, dear, as for your coming here, it will not do. I can see that. She has not yet spoken of you, nor have I ventured to. What her attitude toward you may be I cannot guess from her speech or manner.

"Miss Lester told me that at first, in the complete nervous prostration, she seemed to have a morbid idea that you had been unkind to her, neglected and deserted her—left her to face some endless horror all alone. The shock to her mind had been terrible, Garry; everything was grotesquely twisted—she had some fever, you know—and Miss Lester told me that it was too pitiful to hear her talk of you and mix up everything with military jargon about outpost duty and the firing line, and some comrade who had deserted her under fire.

"All of which I mention, dear, so that you may, in a measure, comprehend how very ill she has been; and that she is not yet well by any means, and perhaps will not be for a long time to come.

"To-night I had a very straight talk with Mr. Cardross. One has to talk straight when one talks to him. There is not in my mind the slightest doubt that he knows exactly now what misguided impulse drove Shiela to that distressing sacrifice of herself and you. And at first I was afraid that what she had done from a mistaken sense of duty might have hastened poor Louis' end; but Mr. Cardross told me that from the day of his father's death he had determined to follow in the same fashion; and had told Mr. Cardross of his intention more than once.

"So you see it was in him—in the blood. See what his own sister did to herself within a month of Louis' death!

"A strange family; an utterly incomprehensible race. And Mr. Cardross says that it happened to his father's father; and *his* father before him died by his own hand!

"Now there is little more news to write you—little more that could interest you because you care only to hear about Shiela, and that is perfectly reasonable."

"However, what there is of news I will write you as faithfully as I have done ever since I came here on your service under pretence of fighting gout which, Heaven be praised, has never yet waylaid me!—*unberufen!*"

"So, to continue: the faithful three, Messieurs Classon, Cuyp, and Vetchen, do valiantly escort me on my mountain rides and drives. They are dears, all three, Garry, and it does not become you to shrug your shoulders. When I go to Palm Beach in January they, as usual, are going too. I don't know what I should do without them, Virginia having decided to remain in Europe this winter.

"Yes, to answer your question, Mr. Wayward expects to cruise as far South as Palm Beach in January. I happen to have a note from him here on my desk in which he asks me whether he may invite you to go with him. Isn't it a tactful way of finding out whether you would care to be at Palm Beach this winter?

"So I shall write him that I think you would like to be asked. Because, Garry, I do believe that it is all turning out naturally, inevitably, as it was meant to turn out from the first, and that, some time this winter, there can be no reason why you should not see Shiela again.

"I know this, that Mr. Cardross is very fond of you—that Mrs. Cardross is also—that every member of that most wholesome family cares a great deal about you.

"As for their not being very fashionable people, their amiable freedom from social pretension, their very simple origin—all that, in their case, affects me not at all—where any happiness of yours is concerned.

"I *do* like old-time folk, and lineage smacking of New Amsterdam; but even my harmless snobbishness is now so completely out of fashion that nobody cares. You are modern enough to laugh at it; I am not; and I still continue faithful to my Classons and Cuyps and Vetchens and Suydams; and to all that they stand for in Manhattan—the rusty vestiges of by-gone pomp and fussy circumstance—the memories that cling to the early lords of the manors, the old Patroons, and titled refugees—all this I still cling to—even to their shabbiness and stupidity and bad manners.

"Don't be too bitter in your amusement, for after all, you are kin to us; don't be too severe on us; for we are passing, Garry, the descendants of Patroon and refugee alike—the Cuyps, the Classons, the Van Diemans, the Vetchens, the Suydams—and James Wayward is the last of his race, and

I am the last of the French refugees, and the Malcourts are already ended. Pax!

"True it begins to look as if the gentleman adventurer stock which terminates in the Ascotts and Portlaws might be revived to struggle on for another generation; but, Garry, we all, who intermarry, are doomed.

"Louis Malcourt was right; we are destined to perish; Still we have left our marks on the nation I care for no other epitaph than the names of counties, cities, streets which we have named with our names.

"But you, dear, you are wise in your generation and fortunate to love as you love. For, God willing, your race will begin the welding of the old and new, the youngest and best of the nation. And at the feet of such a race the whole world lies."

These letters from Constance Palliser to her nephew continued during the autumn and early winter while he was at work on that series of public parks provided for by the metropolis on Long Island.

Once he was obliged to return to Pride's Hall to inspect the progress of work for Mrs. Ascott; and it happened during his brief stay there that her engagement was announced.

"I tell you what, Hamil," said Portlaw confidentailly over their cigars, "I never thought I could win her, never in the world. Besides poor Louis was opposed to it; but you know when I make up my mind—"

"I know," said Hamil.

"That's it! First, a man must have a mind to make up; then he must have enough intelligence to make it up."

"Certainly," nodded Hamil.

"I'm glad you understand me," said Portlaw, gratified. "Alida understands me; why, do you know that, somehow, everything I think of she seems to agree to; in fact, sometimes—on one or two unimportant matters, I actually believe that Mrs. Ascott thought of what I thought of, a few seconds before I thought of it," he ended generously; "but," and his expression became slyly portentous, "it would never do to have her suspect it. I intend to be Caesar in my own house!"

"Exactly," said Hamil solemnly; "and Caesar's wife must have no suspicions."

It was early November before he returned to town. His new suite of offices in Broad Street hummed with activity, although the lingering aftermath of the business depression prevented for the time being any hope of new commissions from private sources.

But fortunately he had enough public work to keep the office busy, and his dogged personal supervision of it during the racking suspense of Shiela's illness was his salvation.

Twice a week his aunt wrote him from Sapphire Springs; every day he went to his outdoor work on Long Island and forced himself to a minute personal supervision of every detail, never allowing himself a moment's brooding, never permitting himself to become panic-stricken at the outlook which varied from one letter to another. For as yet, according to these same letters, the woman he loved had never once mentioned his name.

He found little leisure for amusement, even had he been inclined that way. Night found him very tired; morning brought a hundred self-imposed and complicated tasks to be accomplished before the advent of another night.

He lived at his club and wrote to his aunt from there. Sundays were more difficult to negotiate; he went to St. George's in the morning, read in the club library until afternoon permitted him to maintain some semblance of those social duties which no man has a right to entirely neglect.

Now and then he dined out; once he went to the opera with the O'Haras; but it nearly did for him, for they sang "Madame Butterfly," and Farrar's matchless voice and acting tore him to shreds. Only the happy can endure such tragedy.

And one Sunday, having pondered long that afternoon over the last letter Malcourt had ever written him, he put on hat and overcoat and went to Greenlawn Cemetery—a tedious journey through strange avenues and unknown suburbs, under a wet sky from which occasionally a flake or two of snow fell through the fine-spun drizzle.

In the cemetery the oaks still bore leaves which were growing while Malcourt was alive; here and there a beech-tree remained in full autumn foliage and the grass on the graves was intensely green; but the few flowers that lifted their stalks were discoloured and shabby; bare branches interlaced overhead; dead leaves, wet and flattened, stuck to slab and headstone or left their stained imprints on the tarnished marble.

He had bought some flowers—violets and lilies—at a florist's near the cemetery gates. These he laid, awkwardly, at the base of the white slab from which Malcourt's newly cut name stared at him.

Louis Malcourt lay, as he had wished, next to his father. Also, as he had desired, a freshly planted tree, bereft now of foliage, rose, spindling, to balance an older one on the other corner of the plot. His sister's recently shaped grave lay just beyond. As yet, Bertie had provided no headstone for the late Lady Tressilvain.

Hamil stood inspecting Malcourt's name, finding it impossible to realise that he was dead—or for that matter, unable to comprehend death at all. The newly chiselled letters seemed vaguely instinct with something of Malcourt's own clean-cut irony; they appeared to challenge him with their mocking legend of death, daring him, with sly malice, to credit the inscription.

To look at them became almost an effort, so white and clear they stared back at him—as though the pallid face of the dead himself, set for ever in raillery, was on the watch to detect false sentiment and delight in it. And Hamil's eyes fell uneasily upon the flowers, then lifted. And he said aloud, unconsciously:

"You are right; it's too late, Malcourt."

There was a shabby, neglected grave in the adjoining plot; he bent over, gathered up his flowers, and laid them on the slab of somebody aged ninety-three whose name was blotted out by wet dead leaves. Then he slowly returned to face Malcourt, and stood musing, gloved hands deep in his overcoat pockets.

"If I could have understood you—" he began, under his breath, then fell silent. A few moments later he uncovered.

It was snowing heavily when he turned to leave; and he stood back and aside, hat in hand, to permit a young woman to pass the iron gateway—a slim figure in black, heavy veil drawn, arms piled high with lilies. He knew her at once and she knew him.

"I think you are Mr. Hamil," she said timidly.

"You are Miss Wilming?" he said in his naturally pleasant voice, which brought old memories crowding upon her and a pale flush to her cheeks.

There was a moment's silence; she dropped some flowers and he recovered them for her. Then she knelt down in the sleet, unconscious of it, and laid the flowers on the mound, arranging them with great care, while the thickening snow pelted her and began to veil the white blossoms on the grave.

Hamil hesitated after the girl had risen, and, presently, as she did not stir, he quietly asked if he might be of any use to her.

At first she made no reply, and her gaze remained remote; then, turning:

"Was he your friend?" she asked wistfully.

"I think he meant to be."

"You quarrelled—down there—in the South"—she made a vague gesture toward the gray horizon. "Do you remember that night, Mr. Hamil?"

"Yes."

"Did you ever become friends again?"

"No.... I think he meant to be.... The fault was probably mine. I misunderstood."

She said: "I know he cared a great deal for you."

The man was silent.

She turned directly toward him, pale, clear-eyed, and in the poise of her head a faint touch of pride.

"Please do not misunderstand his friendship for me, then. If you were his friend I would not need to say this. He was very kind to me, Mr. Hamil."

"I do not doubt it," said Hamil gravely.

"And you do not mistake, what I say?"

He looked her in the eyes, curious—and, in a moment, convinced.

"No," he said gently.... And, offering his hand: "Men are very ignorant concerning one another. Women are wiser, I think."

He took the slender black-gloved hand in his.

"Can I be of the least use to you?" he asked.

"You have been," she sighed, "if what I said has taught you to know him a little better."

A week later when the curtain fell on the second act of the new musical comedy, "The Inca," critics preparing to leave questioned each other with considerable curiosity concerning this newcomer, Dorothy Wilming, who had sung so intelligently and made so much out of a subordinate part.

Nobody seemed to know very much about her; several nice-looking young girls and exceedingly respectable young men sent her flowers. Afterward they gathered at the stage entrance, evidently expecting to meet and congratulate her; but she had slipped away. And while they hunted high and low, and the last figurante had trotted off under the lamp-lights, Dolly lay in her own dark room, face among the pillows, sobbing her heart out for a dead man who had been kind to her for nothing.

And, at the same hour, across an ocean, another woman awoke to take up the ravelled threadings of her life again and, through another day, remember Louis Malcourt and all that he had left undone for kindness' sake.

There were others, too, who were not likely to forget him, particularly those who had received, with some astonishment, a legacy apiece of one small Chinese gilded idol—images all of the *Pa-hsien* or of *Kwan-Yin*, who rescues souls from hell with the mystic lotus-prayer, "*Om mane padme hum.*"

But the true Catholicism, which perplexed the eighteen legatees lay in the paradox of the Mohammedan inscriptions across each lotus written in Malcourt's hand:

"I direct my face unto Him who hath created.

"Who maketh His messengers with two and three and four pairs of wings.

"And thou shall see them going in procession.

"This is what ye are promised: 'For the last hour will surely come; there is no doubt thereof; but the greater part of men believe it not.'

"Thus, facing the stars, I go out among them into darkness.

"Say not for me the Sobhat with the ninety-nine; for the hundredth pearl is the *Iman*—pearl beyond praise, pearl of the five-score names in one, more precious than mercy, more priceless than compassion—Iman! Iman! thy splendid name is Death!"

So lingered the living memory of Malcourt among men—a little while—longer among women—then faded as shadows die at dusk when the *mala* is told for the soul that waits the Rosary of a Thousand Beads.

In January the *Ariani* sailed with her owner aboard; but Hamil was not with him.

In February Constance Palliser wrote Hamil from Palm Beach:

"It is too beautiful here and you must come.

"As for Shiela, I do not even pretend to understand her. I see her every day; to-day I lunched with Mrs. Cardross, and Shiela was there, apparently perfectly well and entirely her former lovely self. Yet she has never yet spoken of you to me; and, I learn from Mrs. Cardross, never to anybody as far as she knows.

"She seems to be in splendid health; I have seen her swimming, galloping, playing tennis madly. The usual swarm of devoted youth and smitten middle-age is in attendance. She wears neither black nor colours; only white; nor does she go to any sort of functions. At times, to me, she resembles a scarcely grown girl just freed from school and playing hard every minute with every atom of heart and soul in her play.

"Gray has an apology for a polo field and a string of ponies, and Shiela plays with the men—a crazy, reckless, headlong game, in which every minute my heart is in my mouth for fear somebody will cannon into her, or some dreadful swing of a mallet will injure her for life.

"But everybody is so sweet to her—and it is delightful to see her with her own family—their pride and tenderness for her, and her devotion to them.

"Mrs. Cardross asked me to-day what I thought might be the effect on Shiela if you came. And, dear, I could not answer. Mr. Cardross joined us, divining the subject of our furtive confab in the *patio*, and he seemed to think that you ought to come.

"There is no reason to hesitate in saying that the family would be very glad to count you as one of them. Even a little snob like myself can see that there is, in this desire of theirs, no motive except affection for you and for Shiela; and, in a way, it's rather humiliating to recognise that they don't care a fig for the social advantage that must, automatically, accrue to the House of Cardross through such connections.

"I never thought that I should so earnestly hope for such an alliance for you; but I do, Garry. They are such simple folk with all their riches—simple as gentle folk—kind, sincere, utterly without self-consciousness, untainted by the sordid social ambitions which make so many of the wealthy abhorrent. There is no pretence about them, nothing of that uncertainty of self mingled with vanity which grows into arrogance or servility as the social weather-vane veers with the breeze of fashion. Rather flowery that, for an old-fashioned spinster.

"But, dear, there are other flowers than those of speech eloquent in the soft Southern air—flowers everywhere outside my open window where I sit writing you.

"I miss Virginia, but Shiela compensates when she can find time from her breathless pleasure chase to give me an hour or two at tea-time.

"And Cecile, too, is very charming, and I know she likes me. Such a coquette! She has her own court among the younger set; and from her very severe treatment of young Gatewood on all occasions I fancy she may be kinder to him one day.

"Mrs. Carrick is not here this winter, her new baby keeping her in town; and Acton, of course, is only too happy to remain with her.

"As for Gray, he is a nice boy—a little slow, a trifle shy and retiring and over-studious; but his devotion to Shiela makes me love him. And he, too, ventured to ask me whether you were not coming down this winter to hunt along the Everglades with him and Little Tiger.

"So, dear, I think perhaps you had better come. It really frightens me to give you this advice. I could not endure it if anything went wrong—if your coming proved premature.

"For it is true, Garry, that I love our little Shiela with all my aged, priggish, and prejudiced heart, and I should simply expire if your happiness, which is bound up in her, were threatened by any meddling of mine.

"Jim Wayward and I discuss the matter every day; I don't know what he thinks—he's so obstinate some days—and sometimes he is irritable when Gussie Vetchen and Cuyp talk *too* inanely—bless their hearts! I really don't know what I shall do with James Wayward. What would you suggest?"

On the heels of this letter went another.

"Garry, dear, read this and then make up your mind whether to come here or not.

"This morning I was sitting on the Cardrosses' terrace knitting a red four-in-hand for Mr. Wayward—he is *too* snuffy in his browns and grays!—and Mrs. Cardross was knitting one for Neville, and Cecile was knitting one for Heaven knows who, and Shiela, swinging her polo-mallet, sat waiting for her pony—the cunning little thing in her boots and breeches!—I mean the girl, not the pony, dear— Oh, my, I'm getting involved and you're hurrying through this scrawl perfectly furious, trying to find out what I'm talking about.

"Well, then; I forgot for a moment that Shiela was there within ear-shot; and eyes on my knitting, I began talking about you to Mrs. Cardross; and I had been gossiping away quite innocently for almost a minute when I chanced to look up and notice the peculiar expressions of Mrs. Cardross and Cecile. They weren't looking at me; they were watching Shiela, who had slipped down from the parapet where she had been perched and now stood beside my chair listening.

"I hesitated, faltered, but did not make the mistake of stopping or changing the subject, but went on gaily telling about your work on the new Long Island park system.

"And as long as I talked she remained motionless beside me. They brought around her pony—a new one—but she did not stir.

"Her mother and sister continued their knitting, asking questions about you now and then, apparently taking no notice of her. My monologue in praise of you became a triangular discussion; and all the while the pony was cutting up the marl drive with impatience, and Shiela never stirred.

"Then Cecile said to me quite naturally: 'I wish Garry were here.' And, looking up at Shiela, she added: 'Don't you?'

"For a second or two there was absolute silence; and then Shiela said to me:

"'Does he know I have been ill?'

"'Of course,' I said, 'and he knows that you are now perfectly well.'

"She turned slowly to her mother: 'Am I?' she asked.

"'What, dear?'

"'Perfectly well.'

"'Certainly,' replied her mother, laughing; 'well enough to break your neck on that horrid, jigging, little pony. If Garry wants to see you alive he'd better come pretty soon—'

"'Come *here?*'

"We all looked up at her. Oh, Garry! For a moment something came into her eyes that I never want to see there again—and, please God, never shall!—a momentary light like a pale afterglow of terror.

"It went as it came; and the colour returned to her face.

"'Is he coming here?' she asked calmly.

"'Yes,' I made bold to say.

"'When?'

"'In a few days, I hope.'

"She said nothing more about you, nor did I. A moment later she sent away her pony and went indoors.

"After luncheon I found her lying in the hammock in the *patio*, eyes closed as though asleep. She lay there all the afternoon—an unusual thing for her.

"Toward sundown, as I was entering my chair to go back to the hotel, she came out and stood beside the chair looking at me as though she was trying to say something. I don't know what it might have been, for she never said it, but she bent down and laid her cheek against mine for a moment, and drew my head around, searching my eyes.

"I don't know whether I was right or wrong, but I said: 'There is no one to compare with you, Shiela, in your new incarnation of health and youth. I never before knew you; I don't think you ever before knew yourself.'

"'Not entirely,' she said.

"'Do you now?'

"'I think so.... May I ask you something?'

"I nodded, smiling.

"'Then—there is only one thing I care for now—to'—she looked up toward the house—'to make them contented—to make up to them what I can for—for all that I failed in. Do you understand?'

"'Yes,' I said, 'you sweet thing.' And gave her a little hug, adding: 'And that's why I'm going to write a letter to-night—at your mother's desire—and my own.'

"She said nothing more; my chair rolled away; and here's the letter that I told her I meant to write.

"'Now, dear, come if you think best. I don't know of any reason why you should not come; if you know of any you must act on your own responsibility.'

"Last winter, believing that she cared for you, I did an extraordinary thing—in fact I intimated to her that it was agreeable for me to believe you cared for each other. And she told me very sweetly that I was in error.

"So I'm not going to place Constance Palliser in such a position again. If there's any chance of her caring for you you ought to know it and act accordingly. Personally I think there is and that you should take that chance and take it now. But for goodness' sake don't act on my advice. I'm a perfect fool to meddle this way; besides I'm having troubles of my own which you know nothing about.

"O Garry, dear, if you'll come down I may perhaps have something very, very foolish to tell you.

"Truly there is no idiot like an old one, but—I'm close, I think, to being happier than I ever was in all my life. God help us both, my dear, dear boy.

"Your faithful

"CONSTANCE."

CHAPTER XXIX
CALYPSO'S GIFT

Two days later as his pretty aunt stood in her chamber shaking out the chestnut masses of her hair before her mirror, an impatient rapping at the living-room door sent her maid flying.

"That's Garry," said Constance calmly, belting in her chamber-robe of silk and twisting up her hair into one heavy lustrous knot.

A moment later they had exchanged salutes and, holding both his hands in hers, she stood looking at him, golden brown eyes very tender, cheeks becomingly pink.

"That miserable train is early; it happens once in a century. I meant to meet you, dear."

"Wayward met me at the station," he said.

There was a silence; under his curious and significant gaze she flushed, then laughed.

"Wayward said that you had something to tell me," he added.... "Constance, is it—"

"Yes."

"You darling!" he whispered, taking her into his arms. And she laid her face on his shoulder, crying a little, laughing a little.

"After all these years, Garry—all these years! It is a long time to—to care for a man—a long, long time.... But there never was any other—not even through that dreadful period—"

"I know."

"Yes, you know.... I have cared for him since I was a little girl."

They stood a while talking tenderly, intimately of her new happiness and of the new man, Wayward.

Both knew that he must bear his scars for ever, that youth had died in him. But they were very confident and happy standing there together in the sunlight which poured into the room, transfiguring her. And she truly seemed as lovely, radiant, and youthful as her own young heart, unsullied, innocent, now, as when it yielded its first love so long ago amid the rosewood and brocades of the old-time parlour where the sun fell across the faded roses of the carpet.

"I knew it was so from the way he shook hands," said Hamil, smiling. "How well he looks, Constance! And as for you—you are a real beauty!"

"You *don't* think so! But say it, Garry.... And now I think I had better retire and complete this unceremonious toilet.... And you may stroll over to pay your respects to Mrs. Cardross in the meanwhile if you choose."

He looked at her gravely. She nodded. "They all know you are due to-day."

"Shiela?"

"Yes.... Be careful, Garry; she is very young after all.... I think—if I were you—I would not even seem conscious that she had been ill—that anything had happened to interrupt your friendship. She is very sensitive, very deeply sensible of the dreadful mistake she made, and, somehow, I think she is a little afraid of you, as though you might possibly think less of her—Heaven knows what ideas the young conjure to worry themselves and those they care for!"

She laughed, kissed him and bowed him out; and he went away to bathe and change into cool clothing of white serge.

Later as he passed through the gardens, a white oleander blossom fell, and he picked it up and drew it through his coat.

Shadows of palm and palmetto stretched westward across the white shell road, striping his path; early sunlight crinkled the lagoon; the little wild ducks steered fearlessly inshore, peering up at him with bright golden-irised eyes; mullet jumped heavily, tumbling back into the water with splashes that echoed through the morning stillness.

The stained bronze cannon still poked their ancient and flaring muzzles out over the lake; farther along crimson hibiscus blossoms blazed from every hedge; and above him the stately plumes of royal palms hung motionless, tufting the trunks, which rose with the shaft-like dignity of slender Egyptian pillars into a cloudless sky.

On he went, along endless hedges of azalea and oleander, past thickets of Spanish-bayonet, under leaning cocoanut-palms; and at last the huge banyan-tree rose sprawling across the sky-line, and he saw the white facades and red-tiled roofs beyond.

All around him now, as the air grew sweet with the breath of orange blossoms, a subtler scent, delicately persistent, came to him on the sea-wind; and he remembered it!—the lilac perfume of China-berry in bloom; Calypso's own immortal fragrance. And, in the brilliant sunshine, there under green trees with the dome of blue above, unbidden, the shadows of the past rose up; and once more lantern-lit faces crowded through the aromatic dark; once more the fountains' haze drifted across dim lawns; once more he caught the faint, uncertain rustle of her gown close to him as she passed like a fresh breath through the dusk.

Overhead a little breeze became entangled in the palmetto fronds, setting them softly clashing together as though a million unseen elfin hands were welcoming his return; the big black-and-gold butterflies, beating up against the sudden air current, flapped back to their honeyed haven in the orange grove; bold, yellow-eyed grackle stared at him from the grass; a bird like a winged streak of flame flashed through the jungle and was gone.

And now every breath he drew was quickening his pulses with the sense of home-coming; he saw the red-bellied woodpeckers sticking like shreds of checked gingham to the trees, turning their pointed heads incuriously as he passed; the welling notes of a wren bubbled upward through the sun-shot azure; high in the vault above an eagle was passing seaward, silver of tail and crest, winged with bronze; and everywhere on every side glittered the gold-and-saffron dragon-flies of the South like the play of sunbeams on a green lagoon.

Under the sapodilla-trees on the lawn two aged, white-clad negro servants were gathering fruit forbidden them; and at sight of him two wrinkled black hands furtively wiped two furrowed faces free from incriminating evidence; two solemn pairs of eyes rolled piously in his direction.

"Mohnin', suh, Mistuh Hamil."

"Good morning, Jonas; good morning, Archimedes. Mr. Cardross is in the orange grove, I see."

And, smiling, passed the guilty ones with a humorously threatening shake of his head.

A black boy, grinning, opened the gate; the quick-stepping figure in white flannels glanced around at the click of the latch.

"Hamil! Good work! I am glad to see you!"—his firm, sun-burnt hands closing over Hamil's—"glad all through!"

"Not as glad as I am, Mr. Cardross—"

"Yes, I am. Why didn't you come before? The weather has been heavenly; everybody wanted you—"

"*Everybody*?"

"Yes—yes, of course!... Well, look here, Hamil, I've no authority to discuss that matter; but her mother, I think, has made matters clear to her—concerning our personal wishes—ah—hum—is that what you're driving at?"

"Yes.... May I ask her? I came here to ask her."

"We all know that," said Cardross naïvely. "Your aunt is a very fine woman, Hamil.... I don't see why you shouldn't tell Shiela anything you want to. We all wish it."

"Thank you," said the younger man. Their hand grip tightened and parted; shoulder to shoulder they swung into step across the lawn, Cardross planting his white-shod feet with habitual precision.

His hair and moustache were very white in contrast to the ruddy sun-burnt skin; and he spoke of his altered appearance with one of his quick smiles.

"They nearly had me in the panic, Hamil. The Shoshone weathered the scare by grace of God and my little daughter's generosity. And it came fast when it came; we were under bare poles, too, and I didn't expect any cordiality from the Clearing House; but, Hamil, they classed us with the old-liners, and they acted most decently. As for my little daughter—well—"

And to his own and Hamil's embarrassment his clear eyes suddenly grew dim and he walked forward a step or two winking rapidly at the sky.

Gray, bare of arm to the shoulder, booted and bare-headed, loped across the grass on his polo-pony, mallet at salute. Then he leaned down from his saddle and greeted Hamil with unspoiled enthusiasm.

"Shiela is practising and wants you to come over when you can and see us knock the ball about. It's a rotten field, but you can't help that down here."

And clapping his spurless heels to his pony he saluted and wheeled away through the hammock.

On the terrace Mrs. Cardross took his hands in her tremulous and pudgy fingers.

"Are you sure you are perfectly well, Garry? Don't you think it safer to begin at once with a mild dose of quinine and follow it every three hours with a—"

"Amy, dear!" murmured her husband, "I am not dreaming of interfering, but I, personally, never saw a finer specimen of physical health than this boy you are preparing to—be good to—"

"Neville, you know absolutely nothing sometimes," observed his wife serenely. Then looking up at the tall young man bending over her chair:

"You won't need as much as you required when you rode into the swamps every day, but you don't mind my prescribing for you now and then, do you, Garry?"

"I was going to ask you to do it," he said, looking at Cardross unblushingly. And at such perfidy the older man turned away with an unfeigned groan just as Cecile, tennis-bat in hand, came out from the hall, saw him, dropped the bat, and walked straight into his arms.

"Cecile," observed her mother mildly.

"But I wish to hug him, mother, and he doesn't mind."

Her mother laughed; Hamil, a trifle red, received a straightforward salute square on the mouth.

"That," she said with calm conviction, "is the most proper and fitting thing you and I have ever done. Mother, you know it is." And passing her arm through Hamil's:

"Last night," she said under her breath, "I went into Shiela's room to say good-night, and—and we both began to cry a little. It was as though I were giving up my controlling ownership in a dear and familiar possession; we did not speak of you—I don't remember that we spoke at all from the time I entered her room to the time I left—which was fearfully late. But I knew that I was giving up some vague proprietary right in her—that, to-day, that right would pass to another.... And, if I kissed you, Garry, it was in recognition of the passing of that right to you—and happy acquiescence in it, dear—believe me! happy, confident renunciation and gratitude for what must be."

They had walked together to the southern end of the terrace; below stretched the splendid forest vista set with pool and fountain; under the parapet, in the new garden, red and white roses bloomed, and on the surface of spray-dimmed basins the jagged crimson reflections of goldfish dappled every unquiet pool.

"Where is the new polo field?" he asked.

She pointed out an unfamiliar path curving west from the tennis-courts, nodded, smiled, returning the pressure of his hand, and stood watching him from the parapet until he vanished in the shadow of the trees.

The path was a new one to him, cut during the summer. For a quarter of a mile it wound through the virgin hammock, suddenly emerging into a sunny clearing where an old orange grove grown up with tangles of brier and vine had partly given place to the advance of the jungle.

Something glimmered over there among the trees—a girl, coated and skirted in snowy white, sitting a pony, and leisurely picking and eating the great black mulberries that weighted the branches so that they bent almost to the breaking.

She saw him from a distance, turned in her saddle, lifting her polo-mallet in recognition; and as he came, pushing his way across the clearing, almost shoulder-deep through weeds, from which the silver-spotted butterflies rose in clouds, she stripped off one stained glove, and held out her hand to him.

"You were so long in coming," she managed to say, calmly, "I thought I'd ride part way back to meet you; and fell a victim to these mulberries. Tempted and fell, you see.... Are you well? It is nice to see you."

And as he still retained her slim white hand in both of his:

"What do you think of my new pony?" she asked, forcing a smile. "He's teaching me the real game.... I left the others when Gray came up; Cuyp, Phil Gatewood, and some other men are practising. You'll play to-morrow, won't you? It's such a splendid game." She was talking at random, now, as though the sound of her own voice were sustaining her with its nervous informality; and she chattered on in feverish animation, bridging every threatened silence with gay inconsequences.

"You play polo, of course? Tell me you do."

"You know perfectly well I don't—"

"But you'll try if I ask you?"

He still held her hand imprisoned—that fragrant, listless little hand, so lifeless, nerveless, unresponsive—as though it were no longer a part of her and she had forgotten it.

"I'll do anything you wish," he said slowly.

"Then *don't* eat any of these mulberries until you are acclimated. I'm sorry; they are so delicious. But I won't eat any more, either."

"Nonsense," he said, bending down a heavily laden bough for her. "Eat! daughter of Eve! This fruit is highly recommended."

"Oh, Garry! I'm not such a pig as that!... Well, then; if you make me do it—"

She lifted her face among the tender leaves, detached a luscious berry with her lips, absorbed it reflectively, and shook her head with decision.

The shadow of constraint was fast slipping from them both.

"You know you enjoy it," he insisted, laughing naturally.

"No, I don't enjoy it at all," she retorted indignantly. "I'll not taste another until you are ready to do your part.... I've forgotten, Garry; did the serpent eat the fruit he recommended?"

"He was too wise, not being acclimated in Eden."

She turned in her saddle, laughing, and sat looking down at him—then, more gravely, at her ungloved hand which he still retained in both of his.

Silence fell, and found them ready for it.

For a long while they said nothing; she slipped one leg over the pommel and sat sideways, elbow on knee, chin propped in her gloved hand. At times her eyes wandered over the sunny clearing, but always reverted to him where he stood leaning against her stirrup and looking up at her as though he never could look enough.

The faint, fresh perfume of China-berry was in the air, delicately persistent amid the heavy odours from tufts of orange flowers clinging to worn-out trees of the abandoned grove.

"Your own fragrance," he said.

She looked down at him, dreamily. He bent and touched with his face the hand he held imprisoned.

"There was once," he said, "among the immortals a maid, Calypso.... Do you remember?"

"Yes," she said slowly. "I have not forgotten my only title to immortality."

Their gaze met; then he stepped closer.

She raised both arms, crossing them to cover her eyes; his arms circled her, lifted her from the saddle, holding her a moment above the earth, free, glorious, superb in her vivid beauty; then he swung her to the ground, holding her embraced; and as she abandoned to him, one by one, her hands and mouth and throat, her gaze never left him—clear, unfaltering eyes of a child innocent enough to look on passion unafraid—fearless, confident eyes, wondering, worshipping in unison with the deepening adoration in his.

"I love you so," she said, "I love you so for making me what I am. I can be all that you could wish for if you only say it—"

She smiled, unconvinced at his tender protest, wise, sweet eyes on his.

"What a boy you are, sometimes!—as though I did not know myself! Dear, it is for you to say what I shall be. I am capable of being what you think I am. Don't you know it, Garry? It is only—"

"And locked in his embrace, she lifted her lips to his."

She felt a cool, thin pressure on her finger, and glanced down at the ring sparkling white fire. She lifted her hand, doubling it; looked at the gem for a moment, laid it against her mouth. Then, with dimmed eyes:

"Your love, your name, your ring for this nameless girl? And I—what can I give for a bridal gift?"

"What sweet nonsense—"

"What can I give, Garry? Don't laugh—"

"Calypso, dear—"

"Yes—Calypso's offer!—immortal love—endless, deathless. It is all I have to give you, Garry.... Will you take it?... Take it, then."

And, locked in his embrace, she lifted her lips to his.